Captive

Beautiful Monsters Volume I

Jex Lane

Captive: Beautiful Monsters Volume I © 2016 by Jex Lane.
All rights reserved.

Beautiful Monsters™ is a trademark of Jex Lane.

JexLane.com

Edited by Michelle Rascon

Cover Design by Jay Aheer

Library of Congress Control Number: 2016947874

ISBN 978-0-9977533-0-1

For Steve.

One

*T*hump.

Matthew grabbed his chest as a wave of ecstasy washed through him. Every part of him had been on edge since he had first felt the strange sensation a few moments ago. He ran his hands through his dark brown hair, then rubbed them across the stubble on his chin in a futile attempt to regain control.

It didn't work.

Thump.

Another wave of pleasure rippled through him. He had never felt anything like it; not even the moment just before he sunk his teeth into a soft neck—when the desire and anticipation coiled up in his stomach—could compare.

This time, it wasn't blood driving him. He had already fed tonight. His victim had been a young girl who he seduced away from a seedy downtown club, drunk and receptive to his suggestions. It had almost been too easy to lure her into a dark alleyway, even on a night as cold as this one.

A blanket of guilt wrapped around him. He always tried to go as long as he could without killing but no matter how much he resisted it, the hunger always won in the end. And she had been so sweet, too. Matthew's upper fangs descended, and he licked his lips with the memory of her blood filling his mouth and sliding down his throat.

He had just finished feeding when he felt it the first time, a deep 'thud' that vibrated within him, more a feeling than a sound. The sensation stirred his blood and bliss flooded through him. He had no choice but to seek out the source.

God, the feeling was irresistible, the pull of it stronger than anything he had ever felt before. It had been weak at first, hardly noticeable, but it grew stronger with each overwhelming *thump*.

He hadn't even bothered to hide the body of the girl; he just left her behind in the dirty alley. She deserved better than that, but he left her all the same.

Thump.

Fuck. It felt too good. He adjusted his jeans, resisting the urge to find a private place and take care of the uncomfortable bulge making them tighter. That thought had him laughing. He was being worse than a teenager, and he hadn't been one in a long time.

It had been seven long years since he was turned. The attack had happened only a few days after his thirty-second birthday, and on that night his entire life changed. His body stopped aging, he was stronger, faster, and his diet became a little more limited. His need for blood was ravenous.

And, god, did he feed.

A slave to his hunger, he was still unable to sate his thirst. The first year had been terrible for him and he'd taken a life nearly every night.

All it took was for a human to pass too close to him and his world would melt into the wonderful fragrance of blood…the flow of it pumping through their veins…the thud of their heartbeat…

Whenever he'd hunted, Matthew would silently beg for his prey to escape, but they never got away from him. By the time a human realized what he was—and understood the danger they were in—it was too late.

They fought.

They screamed.

They begged.

They died.

And he loved it.

And he hated himself for loving it.

Now that he was a little older, he could go as long as a week without feeding. He always fought to deny himself for as long as possible, but instinct always took over and a human would die so that he could continue to exist. He was a monster.

A terrible, rapacious monster.

Thump.

Matthew looked around. He was alone, surrounded by tall warehouse buildings and empty parking lots with dim streetlights, but he could smell trees and small animals nearby. He had to be approaching the outskirts of town.

It was a good-sized town with a busy nightlife that made feeding easy, but Matthew hadn't bothered to learn the name of it. He was just passing through on his way south. He couldn't even be sure what state he was in. Tennessee maybe?

He closed his eyes, stilled his breathing, and listened.

He was close now.

Around the other side of a warehouse, he could hear a lone human's heartbeat, fast but steady. He pushed his senses out farther to be sure whoever was on the other side of the building was truly alone.

A cat prowled a fenced-off alleyway between the warehouses. Rats scurried through the walls.

Only one human was around, perhaps even for miles.

Good.

If he had to kill, no one would hear the screams.

Thump.

Before he even knew what he was doing, Matthew jumped over the barbed wire fence and sprinted down the alleyway towards the back of the warehouse. He startled the cat, which hissed at him and darted away. The sound brought him back to his senses and he slid to a halt.

He balled his fists and his fingers turned into long, sharp claws. Blood droplets ran down them as the pointed tips pierced the soft flesh of his palms. He pressed deeper in a futile effort to regain command of his body. What the fuck was happening to him? And why did it feel so damn good?

Once he felt a bit more in control he slunk forward, keeping to the shadows, and cautiously glimpsed around the corner.

Mountains of junk littered the back of the warehouse. A chained fence topped with barbed wire enclosed the entire area, and beyond that was nothing but forest.

Matthew couldn't see the human from where he stood, but bright light streamed out from gaps in the piles of scrap metal heaped on the dirt ground. Why was the human working so late on such a cold night?

And none of what he saw explained what he was feeling. Or smelling. The scent coming from the human was divine, like night and earth. Heat welled up in Matthew's belly.

He took a few silent steps forward, snuck behind a tall pile, and looked through one of the gaps.

Once his eyes adjusted to the bright lights, he saw a man with dusty blond hair standing in the middle of the clearing, his back to Matthew.

The man shifted back and forth on his feet and pulled his phone out of the pocket of his black wool coat to check the time. Catching the numbers on the bright screen, Matthew saw it was a few hours after midnight. The man slipped his phone back into his pocket and let out a heavy sigh, his warm breath curling into the air above him.

Thump.

Lord almighty. Matthew fell to his knees and raked deep grooves into the hard dirt ground. He was so close to an orgasm that if someone touched him he might explode.

Matthew wanted to run over, pin the man against a wall, and take him forcefully. Even though he had no experience in how to please another man beyond his own self-gratification, he was fairly certain he could figure it out.

Both his upper and lower fangs itched with the erotic thought. Matthew closed his eyes and felt his irises burning red again.

For a long time he wasn't aware his eyes actually changed color. He assumed the burning he felt was simply tied to his hunger somehow…but a few months after his change, while he was in a bathroom waiting for his victim to finish taking a piss, Matthew caught himself in the mirror. His fangs were long and ready, and his fingers were claws—that much he was used to—but it shocked him to see the frightening crimson of his irises.

It was the first time he had truly seen the beast he had become.

While he had been distracted, his prey had seen Matthew studying himself and tried to escape, but he didn't get far. The memory of that messy kill brought a wave of shame down upon Matthew and pulled him back to his current situation.

Still kneeling on the ground, he felt a little more in control. He forced his fangs back up into his gums, focused on getting his claws to recede, and closed his eyes in an attempt to force them to return to their usual brown. He hoped, anyway. He didn't want to scare the man away before he got some answers.

At least he could pass as a human right now, his body was still warm from his earlier feeding. In a few hours, his skin would cool again and his heart would slow its beat to almost nothing. That was fine with him, he didn't enjoy the sound of it anymore; it was too loud. Especially now, as this man caused it to beat faster.

His attention shifted when the human stilled completely. He knew Matthew was here; the fall to the ground probably made a sound and alerted him.

Matthew rose back to his feet and looked through the gap once more.

The man, his back still to Matthew, turned his head to the side and cast a look over his shoulder. Intense blue eyes flashed in Matthew's direction, followed by a bright smile, revealing a set of perfect white teeth.

God, he was gorgeous.

Matthew had never seen anyone this good looking outside of a movie. And he had certainly never been this attracted to another man before. In college, spurred on by a group of women, he had drunkenly kissed another man. It hadn't bothered him, but it hadn't done anything for him either.

This was different. Just looking at this guy made his cock twitch.

The man shifted slightly. No fear came from him, his heart remained steady and his breathing continued unchanged. Instead, he smiled and stood up taller, as if happy something had come along to break his boredom.

This put Matthew on high alert. Humans were always alarmed when they heard unknown noises in the dark of night—they couldn't help it. But not this human. This one just stood in the light, smiling, not even bothering to turn all the way around.

Matthew's instincts told him to run away; there was danger here, even though the man he was staring at was smaller in stature and no doubt weaker. The man closed his eyes and breathed out heavily.

Th—

The fucking sensation began to swell within Matthew, but before it could finish, Matthew darted into the clearing and slipped his hand around the man's neck, pressing hard into the human's throat.

"Stop. Just…stop," Matthew said, his eyes turning red again, this time with desire.

The man took a step backwards and pressed against Matthew's erection.

Sucking in hard, Matthew responded by rubbing his throbbing cock against the man's ass. A deep purr rose up in Matthew's throat, and it surprised him…he didn't even know he could purr.

Matthew loosened his grip but didn't completely release his new victim. He began rubbing his fingers up the side of the man's neck and along his chiseled jaw.

He cursed the thick wool coat. The stiff upturned collar prevented Matthew's mouth from getting close to the man's neck. He was tempted to rip the coat off…but if he started removing articles of clothing he wouldn't be able to stop until the man was naked.

The thought made him shiver. Was the man enjoying this as much as he was? Matthew resisted the urge to slip his hands down the blond's body to find out if he was also hard. His fangs itched, wanting to elongate.

"What are you doing to me?" he whispered into the blond's ear.

The man grabbed Matthew's hand and gently tugged it away from his neck. Matthew froze as soft kisses brushed his wrist. It was unbearable. Growling, Matthew grabbed the man's hip with his free hand, his fingers digging in hard enough to leave bruises, and pressed himself forward. He needed more.

The man smiled against Matthew's wrist.

"I'm feeding. Then I will kill you, vampire."

Two

Matthew scoffed and took a step away from the man, who wasn't nearly powerful enough to kill him.

The man turned and flashed a devious smile at him, his blue eyes gleaming.

Matthew looked the man up and down for the first time. He could see now that he was wearing a perfectly pressed dark suit under his wool coat. Everything about the tempting man seemed flawless and refined. There wasn't a scuff on his black polished shoes, his dark blond hair was neatly cut and styled, and his strong jaw and face were shaven but there were hints of a five o'clock shadow that no amount of shaving could hide. All of him looked planned and perfected.

Matthew looked far different in his ragged jeans, tight black t-shirt, and worn boots. His stubble was hardly planned and his messy hair was long enough he could run his fingers through it. He pushed his hair back and settled his eyes on the man's bulging crotch. It seemed he was enjoying this, too. He looked delicious.

Matthew reached out to grab the man's burgundy tie and pull him in when he stopped himself, his hand hovering just inches away from the man's throat.

What was he doing? This man told him he was going to kill him and Matthew hadn't cared. All he wanted was to feel this man's touch on his bare skin. Heat swelled in him.

Again, his instincts screamed danger. Matthew dropped his hand and took another step away from the man. He needed to place some distance between them so he could think and try to break whatever hold this man had over him.

"How did you—?" The man seemed astonished Matthew managed to back away from him. He clearly had been expecting things to move further along than they had. His blue eyes began looking around, scanning the area for something. When it seemed he didn't find what he was looking for, he tilted his head forward slightly and gazed at Matthew. "Are you alone?"

Matthew didn't answer him and instead took another step away. Whatever influence the man had over him was waning. The man clenched his jaw, growing agitated.

"Where is your sire, fledgling?"

Fledgling? Matthew had never been called such a thing before. The way the word was speared at him, it was clearly meant to be an insult.

"You will answer me." The blond stepped forward and closed the distance.

Matthew trembled as he felt hot breath near his skin. The man leaned in and passionately kissed Matthew along his neck. A moan escaped his mouth and he tilted his head back, closing his eyes as the kisses forced him into submission.

For the millionth time tonight, Matthew lost all control and his vampire form was set loose; his fangs large and his claws long with desire. It didn't seem to bother the man, who pushed up Matthew's black shirt to expose his firm abs.

Still kissing his neck, the human ran his hand down Matthew, starting at his pecs, then tracing the valleys along his torso. In contrast to the rough kisses, his hands were going slow, seeming to savor the moans drifting from Matthew's mouth. The man's hand moved lower, massaging the flat area above the pelvic bone.

Matthew gasped when a warm index finger slid into his jeans and tugged at his belt, as if trying to sneak a peek. But as quickly as things seemed to be moving along, they stopped as the man pulled his lips away from Matthew's neck. Matthew opened his eyes and growled at him. The male didn't react to the growling, and instead kept his finger hooked on Matthew's waistband, silently promising to go on if he received an answer to his question.

Matthew desperately wanted the man to peel away his pants and grab his length, then rub it until he couldn't take it anymore. And that wouldn't take long. He hadn't had sex since before he was turned. It's not that he didn't want it; it's just he didn't think he could stop himself from losing control and killing his partner halfway through the act. That wasn't much of a turn on for him.

He flicked his eyes to the man's wicked lips and studied them. He imagined his length slipping into the human's hungry mouth, followed by a warm tongue teasing his head. The thought made his balls throb.

"I don't have a sire." He said the words carefully so as to not cut himself on his fangs.

The man didn't seem pleased by his answer. "Every vampire has a sire. You are too young to be this strong. I know you are borrowing power."

"You mean the bastard that turned me?"

Matthew had no idea what foul creature unceremoniously attacked him as he was returning home from the fire station, turned him, and then left him to fend for himself. He hadn't even seen the creature's face, nor did he have any idea what was happening to him, but right away he felt the need for blood and the need to kill. He knew he had to stay away from his family. He left them behind without saying goodbye.

Watching his wife and daughter one last time through the window, then leaving out of fear he might hurt them was the hardest thing he had ever done in his life. When he had finished the business of dying, he woke and killed three other families that night, but his family had been safe from him. A small comfort considering the pain he knew he had brought to others.

"I never even saw him. Please don't stop."

The man didn't move. He seemed to be considering what Matthew had told him. "You do not feel any connection to him?"

Matthew snarled in frustration and shook his head. Whoever—or whatever—this man was, he seemed to know more about vampires than him. The heat that had welled in him began to cool as questions filled his mind and the cloud of desire flooding his brain began to clear.

"What are you?" Matthew finally asked the question he should have a long while ago. He obviously wasn't a vampire and Matthew was reasonably certain no human could do something like this, and if vampires were real then maybe other creatures were, too. "How are you doing these things to me?"

The man's eyes flicked with surprise but he didn't release his grip on the waistband.

"You really have no idea what's going on here, do you?" he asked and moved his free hand to Matthew's face, but Matthew knocked it away. He didn't want this man's pity.

A noise from the trees beyond the fence drew Matthew's attention. He stilled and reached out with his senses. He heard a single heartbeat, but after a few moments of listening it was never followed by a second. A bird flew out from the branches, then off into the night.

There was nothing else out there. This man was getting to him.

Matthew had enough of being manipulated, but each time he looked at the man his desire grew again. The man slipped the rest of his fingers into Matthew's waistband, brushing his knuckles gently against skin, sending shivers down Matthew's spine.

"What are you?" Matthew asked again.

"I am an incubus," the creature answered this time.

"A sex demon?"

The incubus looked offended by the word 'demon' and, to punish Matthew, he tightened his grip on the jeans then slid his free hand along Matthew's stomach, setting his blood ablaze with desire.

"None of this is real," Matthew said, struggling to get each word out as his temperature rose.

"It is all real," the incubus said and pressed against Matthew's hard muscles. It seemed the incubus wanted more, too.

"This isn't right."

The man didn't stop.

"Enough!" Matthew yelled at him and grabbed the incubus' wrists—his claws digging in deep enough to draw blood—and shoved him away.

The incubus was stunned. "That is the second time you've broken from me tonight."

Matthew wasn't going to stick around to become this creature's dinner. He bolted back towards the alley he came in from…only to run head first into an invisible barrier. It felt as if he had run full force into a wall and he collapsed to the ground, dazed.

After a moment, Matthew roared and sprung to his feet, his body already healing the concussion he suffered. He reached out with his arm and moved forward. His hand met a hard surface but Matthew couldn't see anything.

"I take it you've never seen a vamp trap before," the incubus moved to the back of the clearing, near the chain link fence, closer to the forest, and swept his foot across the dirt revealing a concrete block hidden under it. Painted runic symbols covered the concrete.

Matthew stalked over to the incubus and reached out for him with a clawed hand only to hit another invisible barrier.

"You won't be able to cross it until the surrounding circle is broken," the incubus said and crossed his arms, making it clear he had no intention of setting Matthew free.

Matthew closed his eyes and took a few moments to process what happened to him. This incubus lured him in here to feed and then kill him, it was really not much different than what he had done to hundreds of humans. Perhaps this was divine karma, punishing him for his wickedness. But karma be damned, he wasn't going to die here.

Walking around his invisible circle cage, he reached out, trying to find any type of gap or hole he could escape through. He even tried jumping, but the wall seemed to rise up endlessly into the sky. He wondered what would happen if a vampire on a plane passed over one of these traps. Would they be crushed as the plane flew through the invisible wall? He chuckled at the thought and looked over at the incubus who seemed content watching him explore his cage.

When he found no way out, he kicked dirt aside and studied the runes below his feet. He had no tool to destroy them, and even if he could—assuming the incubus was telling the truth—only breaking the outer ring would let him free. And that was on the other side of the force-wall-thing that enclosed him. Defeated, Matthew flexed his claws and focused on returning to his human appearance.

He walked over to the incubus and stood before him. The incubus was calm, his face betraying none of his thoughts to Matthew.

"Am I going to be trapped here until sunrise or are you going to kill me some other way?" he asked, wondering just what abilities an incubus possessed.

Matthew wasn't sure what could actually kill a vampire. Drowning wouldn't work considering he didn't have to breathe, although his body still instinctively drew breath, and he needed air to speak. He guessed sunlight since every time the sun was about to rise panic forced him to go into hiding, and once it was up he couldn't move. He learned silver burned him when he brushed against a piece of jewelry. From what he read in fiction, stakes and decapitation might do the trick but he sure as hell wasn't going to test it out.

He wished he had snapped the man's neck when he had the chance.

"I have been fighting vampires for nearly a millennium. I have every possible means to kill a vampire at my disposal, but I have yet to decide which way your death would please me most." A sinful smile crossed the man's face and it was Matthew's turn to be stunned. Just how old was he? Had he been fighting vampires for his entire life? If so, that placed him at nearly a thousand.

Suddenly thirty-nine didn't seem so old. Matthew stopped aging the night he had been turned and wondered if other vampires counted their human years in their age. If not, he was seven. No wonder the man had been so shocked Matthew could break away from whatever he had been doing to him.

The incubus slipped his phone from his pocket and frowned as he checked the time. Matthew didn't need to see the time to know sunrise was well over four hours away.

"This only traps vampires? You can pass through freely?"

The incubus nodded.

"I have to say, whatever the hell you did to me has left me blue balled as fuck." Matthew adjusted his pants, trying to alleviate some of the pain.

The incubus laughed. "Finish if you want, I won't stop you." The incubus paused, then added, "Actually, I would enjoy watching you finish."

Matthew's cock stirred in response to the words and his eyes rolled back into his head. The idea of pulling his length out and finishing in front of the incubus was too much. "I get that I'm your prisoner and at your mercy, but I wish you would stop doing that," he said, opening his eyes again.

The incubus tilted his head and grinned. "That was all you."

Was it? It seemed unlikely. Maybe this incubus was playing with him. It was impossible for Matthew to separate his own desires from the ones this man forced upon him.

"Why do you kill vampires?" Matthew asked as he struggled to push the erotic thoughts away.

The incubus stood silent, watching him for so long Matthew didn't think he'd answer the question. Finally, he straightened out his sleeves and spoke. "Our two species have been at war for a long time."

"What are we fighting over?"

"All the classics: power, wealth, hunting grounds. The spark that set it in motion was love, I think. But the reason it began doesn't matter anymore, this war won't end until one side has eradicated the other."

The incubus dragged his eyes over Matthew's body, pausing at his crotch. It seemed the incubus was unfulfilled as well.

"It's a shame your sire abandoned you, you should have learned all this from him. At the very least, he should have warned you what territories to stay away from. You may have had a chance to see your hundredth birthday."

A sting of pain ran through Matthew. It hurt to learn that other vampires were taught by their sire while he had been abandoned.

God, he was lonely.

In the past seven years, the only conversations he had were with the humans he killed. Even the few other vampires he sensed wouldn't come near him; they ran when Matthew tried to approach them. Tonight had been the first time he felt alive in the seven years of being dead. Not even blood brought him this comfort.

His head bowed forward and his shoulders sagged as he struggled against the misery of his life.

His soon to be short life.

Three

The incubus seemed to sense the distress rising inside of Matthew. His expression softened to one of compassion. "Dying by the sun is extremely painful. If you would like, I will stake and kill you so you won't feel anything."

"Won't a stake kill me?" Matthew asked.

The incubus' eyes filled with pity again. Matthew hated it when he looked at him like that. It made him feel small.

"No, it'll shut you down and put you into a coma-like state. Then I'll decapitate you. You won't feel a thing."

The incubus walked over to one of the scrap piles and pushed aside a hidden panel. He pulled out a long, ornately scrolled wooden box and set it on a nearby table, flipping up two latches and pushing open the lid. Inside was a silver longsword, a sheathed dagger, three wooden stakes, a row of vials filled with different colored liquids, a syringe, a stick of green chalk, and a pair of dental pliers.

Looking over the items sent Matthew's instincts into overdrive and panic washed over him. He backed up, as far away from the incubus as he could get, and wondered how many other vampires had been caught in this trap. How many died in here? When he bumped into the invisible wall, he slid down to his knees and rubbed his temples.

"I don't want to die," Matthew whispered so low he wasn't sure the incubus would be able to hear it. "But if you are giving me the choice of my death, I'll wait for the sun. I wouldn't mind seeing it rise again."

The incubus nodded at him and closed the box.

It took every ounce of control Matthew had in him not to start begging the incubus to release him.

"What's your name?" Matthew asked just so he'd have something else to think about.

The incubus paced around the outside of the invisible cage. Was he hungry? He was eyeing Matthew like he was dinner. Maybe he liked seeing him on his knees.

"Tarrick."

Matthew had never heard a name like that before. "I'm Matthew. I'd say nice to meet you but...you know..."

Tarrick chuckled.

"Are you going to stay here until I'm dead?"

"I will."

Matthew was relieved he wouldn't be alone when it happened, even if the man staying with him was the one killing him.

"Could you stop that pacing?" Matthew asked. "Or maybe just come in here and feed off me."

Tarrick stopped and raised an eyebrow. "That's not going to happen."

"Why not? You obviously want to." Matthew wanted him to as well. If he was going to die anyway, he might as well have sex before it happened. He already knew the incubus could make him feel incredible. Wait. No. He wasn't thinking clearly right now. Or was he? This was maddening.

"Unless you were chained or drugged there's no way I'd step in there. I find it astonishing you're able to break my hold. You aren't even ten, are you?"

Ah, so they didn't include their human years. "Seven."

"Breaking my hold is something few vampires can do—even some vampire lords have trouble with me. I wonder who turned you." Tarrick's eyes studied him in a cool analytical manner, as if trying to work out a puzzle.

Matthew let out a heavy sigh. He wanted to know as well…if only so he could face the vampire who had discarded him.

"I give you my word I won't kill you if you come in here." Matthew wasn't sure he could keep his word but he had to try. His mind kept wondering what it would feel like to kiss him. What would his mouth taste like? Fuck. He was doing it again. This was ridiculous.

"I do not know you enough to trust your word. Feeding leaves me vulnerable and right now you are faster and stronger than I. Even at your age, vampires can be dangerous. I've lived a long time because I know my limits."

Matthew looked at the skyline, less than three and a half hours. "The sun doesn't bother you?"

"Not at all."

That made Matthew envious…he missed the sun. Matthew stood and walked over to Tarrick, who had stopped his pacing and stood near his box full of vampire slaying instruments. He still had hours left; maybe he could convince Tarrick to release him.

Tarrick raised an eyebrow. "If you are going to try to compel me, it won't work."

That grabbed Matthew's attention and he cocked his head. The idea he had an ability he didn't even know was there excited him, even if he'd never get the chance to use it. "Compel? What do you mean?"

"You've never compelled a human?"

"No, I didn't know it was something I could do. Do you know how it's done?"

"I know what I've seen. The vampire looks into the human's eyes, orders the human to do something, and the human does it. With weaker vampires it wears off in a few minutes and they can only command humans to do things that won't put their life at risk, but lords can turn humans into thralls indefinitely."

Hope swept through Matthew. If he was strong enough to break this powerful incubus' hold over him, maybe he could compel him. Matthew looked into Tarrick's eyes and focused. "Release me," he said.

Tarrick laughed. "It's not going to work on me. I promise you I'm immune. Even the oldest vampire could not compel the youngest incubus."

"Had to try," Matthew said with a sad smile.

His smile dropped when he realized he would be dead at sunrise. Hope faded and rage overwhelmed him. He didn't want to die trapped in this cage like an animal. He was a monster but he didn't deserve this. His vampire side came forward again. He could feel his eyes burning red and his fangs scraped his tongue, filling his mouth with blood. It was too much. The blood shattered what little control he had over himself and his instincts took over. In frantic desperation to escape, he began to scratch at the invisible wall that separated him from Tarrick.

Tarrick stood his ground. "Still yourself, young one."

"No!" How *dare* he give him orders. This man was his executioner—he had no right. Matthew didn't give a shit about his war and yet he was going to die because of it. A new surge of anger coiled in his belly and he looked into Tarrick's eyes once again. The anger sprung forward along with all the power he had within him. "RELEASE ME," Matthew roared.

Tarrick began to tremble. "...What?" but he wasn't asking Matthew, he was speaking to himself as he turned around and opened the vampire slaying kit against his will.

The compulsion had worked. Matthew couldn't believe it. He watched Tarrick take out the stick of green chalk. Tarrick paused, his hand shaking as he tried to fight what Matthew had done to him but it was no use. Matthew watched as his muscles tightened and he cried out as the pain grew more intense each moment he struggled against the command. Unable to resist any longer he leaned down and drew a single line across the outside circle of the trap, breaking the magic.

With the command finished and the compulsion broken, Tarrick dove for his sword. The box slammed shut before he could make it, nearly taking off his fingers. Matthew towered above Tarrick, his eyes red with anger. He dug his claws into the wooden box, leaving a long trail of marks on the lid. Tarrick straightened himself and faced Matthew. He showed no fear and Matthew couldn't smell any in him.

Tarrick backed away as Matthew stalked forward, trying to keep the distance between them. When the incubus hit the chain link fence and had nowhere else left to go, the fear came. He showed no outward signs of it but Matthew could smell a small amount welling up within him; just enough to keep his senses sharp and give him an edge. Tarrick had no weapon and stood no chance against Matthew.

Or maybe he did.

Matthew watched as ridged horns emerged from Tarrick's forehead. The horns jutted up then turned, heading towards the back of Tarrick's skull before finally scooping upwards again. They were black in color at the base but the tips of them were purple, a dark contrast to his blond hair. His ears grew pointed and Tarrick's fingertips turned into hardened claws. They weren't as long as Matthew's but they were still sharp and dangerous.

Tarrick repositioned into a defensive stance, his feet spread and firmly planted on the ground. He brought his claws up, ready to guard against an attack. He closed his eyes and breathed out. He was going to do that damned 'thumping' thing again.

Matthew sped forward and took a swing at Tarrick, who ducked under it then countered by taking a swipe at Matthew. Matthew brought his arm up to defend, and for his effort his skin was shredded; blood poured from the five long gashes.

He growled and caught Tarrick's second attack midair, gripping his wrist with such strength Tarrick had no hope of escape no matter how hard he struggled against the grasp. Matthew ignored the pain as Tarrick sank his other claw deep into his shoulder. Matthew slammed him into the fence, pressing his body against the incubus to trap him in place. With his free hand, Matthew grabbed Tarrick's horn and forced his head backwards, exposing his neck.

God, what would this man's mouth taste like? Unable to wait any longer Matthew pressed a kiss onto Tarrick's lips.

Tarrick froze.

Matthew didn't give him time to sort out what was happening. He thrust his tongue past the incubus' lips and greedily captured his mouth. Fire blazed inside Matthew as he laid claim to his prey.

The incubus began to respond. He brushed his tongue against Matthew's. Soft at first, then increasingly more aggressive. The kiss was intoxicating, addicting. Matthew moaned.

Tarrick removed his claws from out of Matthew's shoulder and melted into him. The incubus' hip rubbed against Matthew's hard erection, setting Matthew on fire. Still holding onto Tarrick's arm and horn, Matthew broke away from the incredible kiss.

Swallowing hard, Tarrick looked up at him.

Matthew let him go and bounded over the barbed wire fence, landing near some bushes on the other side. He stood and checked his wounds. They had stopped bleeding and the ones on his arm had already begun to heal. He'd have to feed sooner than normal to replace the blood his body was using to mend him.

"You aren't going to try to kill me?" Tarrick asked; surprise laced his words.

Matthew looked back at him and smiled. "Why would I do that? Tonight was the best night I've had in a long time."

"Because I was going to kill you."

Matthew flexed his claws. "I know. I wasn't a fan of that part of the night. I…" He swallowed as a mix of emotions pulsed through him. "I've learned more about vampires tonight than I have in the past seven years. And it was nice to talk to someone."

Matthew turned and headed into the tree line to leave. Then he froze.

They were not alone.

Four

Matthew reached out with his senses. There were humans nearby. Six of them. How had he not felt them before?

"I am sorry, but I cannot let you go," Tarrick said from the other side of the chain link fence. "If you surrender now, it'll be painless for you."

There was no way in hell Matthew was going to surrender now that he was free.

He sensed the humans moving closer. Was Tarrick expecting six humans to stop him when he could not? Six humans—hell, six dozen humans—would be no match for him.

A faint green glow floated in the empty air next to him and a petite human woman, with brown hair tied into a bun, materialized. She wore a long cloak that she swept aside to reveal a tight leather outfit that covered her from the top of her neck down to her boots. Across her chest was a sash with six silver throwing knives, and attached to her belt were various potions—much like the ones Matthew had seen in the box—and a folded crossbow. She had a silver chain coiled and attached to her hip.

She was holding a stake.

A vampire hunter? A *teleporting* vampire hunter? She smelled and looked human. But then again, so had the incubus.

Matthew focused and looked into her eyes. "Drop the stake," he commanded.

She laughed and launched herself at him with the stake in hand. His command was useless on her, not that he was sure how he had done it the first time.

Matthew brought up his arms to protect his chest but she didn't go for his heart like he thought she would. Instead, she drove the stake into his lower stomach and then pulled it out. Blood rushed from the wound.

Lots of blood.

It was bleeding far more than a wound like that should bleed.

He began to feel weaker, as if his energy was draining away. Matthew threw a punch at the woman and hit her square in her chest, sending her flying towards the chain link fence. A split second before crashing into it, she teleported to the other side and skidded across the dirt and concrete. She caught her breath and kipped up, grabbing her folding crossbow and flicking it to full size.

Tarrick slipped out of his wool coat and began to unbutton his shirt. "I want him alive, Silva."

"Yes, sir," she nodded.

Matthew bounded into the forest. This wasn't a fight he wanted. He'd never faced a vampire hunter before and he sure as fuck didn't want to face one now. Trees and small patches of snow blurred as he pushed himself to run as fast as possible. It wasn't working; he could sense the humans behind him. How on earth were they keeping up?

If he couldn't outrun them, he'd have to kill them.

Matthew slid and grabbed a tree trunk to bring himself to an abrupt stop. He honed in on one of the humans by scent and launched himself in that direction. There was no one there.

Bewildered, Matthew looked around.

A heartbeat later, he saw a cloaked man swinging twenty feet above him in a tree. He had one of his arms outstretched and a thin chain shot forward and hooked onto a tree branch. The hunter gave a tug and the chain began to reel into his sleeve, propelling the man forward at a wild speed. When he was nearly to the end of it, he whipped his arm and the chain unwrapped from the tree branch, leaving him soaring through the air. As the momentum slowed, he moved his other hand in front of him and another chain came out, repeating the process.

As the hunter soared above, he glanced down and caught sight of Matthew. Before he could pull out a weapon, Matthew jumped up and grabbed his feet, yanking the hunter down to the ground. The hunter fell hard, his bones cracking and he passed out cold. Matthew left the wounded hunter alive on the forest floor and sprinted away from the others.

Matthew needed more blood. The wound in his stomach hadn't begun to heal, though it should have by now. He sensed the five other hunters grouped nearby and if he stopped to feed, he'd be dead. Matthew ran for several minutes before he realized he was getting slower and that the hunters were keeping pace with him. They weren't bothering to attack. It seemed they were letting Matthew lose more blood and wear himself out. Matthew had no idea where he was now, he couldn't even tell if he was close to the town or not. With the sun rising in a few hours he had to shake them and find a safe place to stay for the day.

A faint green glow appeared directly in front of him. Matthew nearly crashed into a large man, only managing to dodge out of the way at the last moment.

Unlike the other vampire hunters, he wore no cloak and instead had on a fitted black leather doublet with a hood pulled over his head, buckled leather gloves, tall boots, and had a full-face mask on that was molded in the shape of a skull. Not an inch of his skin was exposed. He was armed with a sword, throwing knives, stakes, a large repeating crossbow, and various other tools that Matthew didn't have the time to identify.

Matthew darted away from him, not stopping to fight.

The green glow appeared again, this time slightly to his side and the small woman—'Silva' the incubus had called her—appeared. Matthew sped away from her. It was odd they weren't attacking, not even firing bolts from their crossbows at him. When it happened a third time it dawned on him they were corralling him. Matthew turned and went a different direction. It would bring him closer to the other hunters than he wanted but it was better than playing their game.

Thump.

Matthew cussed as he slid to a halt. He couldn't lose control again; if he did he'd end up right back in the hands of the creature who wanted to kill him. A bolt whistled in the air and Matthew knocked it away. Three more flew at him. He dodged the first, caught the second, then the third planted itself into Matthew's upper thigh. The silver coating burned like a bitch.

Matthew roared and pulled it out.

Damn these humans.

He turned to run only to find himself face to face with the masked hunter. The hunter raised his crossbow and squeezed the trigger. Three silver bolts sunk into Matthew's chest. Matthew lunged at the masked man, snatched his crossbow, and smashed it against a tree. A faint green aura surrounded the man. Oh no, this one wasn't going to get away from him. Before he could teleport away, Matthew pulled one of the bolts from his chest and drove it into the masked man's shoulder. He howled and disappeared.

Matthew smelled the man's blood a hundred feet to his left. He darted in that direction, and overheard a female hunter call out, "He's headed for you, Cullip." But Matthew was on the injured man—'Cullip'—before he could pull out another weapon.

He swiped his claws across his face, tearing off his mask. Under the mask was a man who looked to be in his late-forties. He had a short, greying goatee. Dozens of small thin scars littered his face.

Cullip's heart beat quicker causing more blood to ooze from the wound in his shoulder. Matthew's hunger was insatiable now. It didn't matter that he could sense four hunters in the trees nearby, he had to feed. He growled and lunged at Cullip.

The hunter grabbed a round metal ball that looked like a grenade from off his hip and threw it at Matthew. It hit his chest and exploded into a fine cloud of silver dust. Matthew inhaled before he had a chance to tell his body to stop breathing.

He screamed as the silver burned his lungs. It was a pain worse than any he had experienced before. The silver dust covered his face and chest as his skin turned red and boiled on contact. Matthew felt his last bit of strength draining from him. His body couldn't keep up with the injuries. Blood poured out of each of the wounds.

A silver chain wrapped around his chest and tightened. Matthew raised an arm to try to get free but another chain shot forward and wrapped around his wrist. The hunters wielding the chains yanked them hard, sending Matthew crashing face forward to the ground. The two bolts still lodged in his stomach sank deeper.

Pain racked him.

Before he could try to fight, Cullip's knees dug into his spine. The vampire hunter grabbed Matthew's arms and twisted them behind his back, like a police officer handcuffing a perpetrator, binding his wrists together with a thick silver chain.

"Lieutenant Silva, the collar," Cullip ordered.

The petite female approached, holding a metal collar. Matthew snarled and tried to bite her when she came close, but Cullip kneed him harder so he couldn't move. Matthew let out a gurgled cry as she snapped the collar around his neck. Mercifully, the collar wasn't made of silver, unlike the agonizing chains wrapped around his chest and binding his hands.

His body burned as the silver dug into him each time he tried to move.

Cullip grabbed the chains, pulling Matthew up into a kneeling position. The action sent a new wave of pain through him. Silva hooked a chain through a loop on Matthew's collar then left to tie the other end to a tree. A different hunter repeated the process with a second chain and a different tree.

They hadn't needed to. Matthew wasn't going anywhere. He couldn't move and his senses were shutting down. Hell, he could barely keep his eyes open. Every part of him was suffering. What they were doing to him was nothing short of torture.

Cullip came around and towered above Matthew. Matthew curled his lip up and flashed his fangs in defiance. The hunter reached down to Matthew's stomach and pulled the two silver bolts from it. Matthew opened his mouth with a silent scream and tears began to run down his face. God, he needed blood. He was certain he would die soon without it.

Cullip pulled the bolt out of his own shoulder. His face screwed up but he didn't make any sound as he did so.

"Here, Commander," Silva said as she tossed a glass vial to him. "He got you good."

Cullip—their commander, it seemed—snatched the vial from the air, flipped the top off with his thumb, and downed the contents. It was blood. Vampire blood. Matthew could smell it. He struggled against his chains, desperate for blood. The pain from the burning silver renewed and he stilled.

Matthew watched as the hunter's wounds stopped bleeding and the skin began to weave together.

"Yeah, this one's a strong son of a bitch. Ryans?" the commander asked.

Silva motioned at Matthew. "Vamp didn't kill him. Jake's healing him now."

Above them, the trees began to rustle violently. Matthew looked up to see Tarrick drop down and land gracefully in front of him.

Matthew's eyes widened.

Tarrick had no shirt on, and while his chest and abs rippled with beautifully honed muscles, it was his massive wings that drew Matthew's attention. They looked like dragon wings, mostly black but fading to purple along the edges. They matched his horns.

As if knowing Matthew was admiring them, Tarrick stretched them out; his wingspan nearly tripled that of his body.

They were extraordinary.

The hunters in the area all balled their right fist, pressed it against the opposite shoulder, and bowed to Tarrick.

"Lord General," Cullip said as he bowed.

Matthew wondered if he would be left chained to the trees until sunrise. He tried to ask but only a bloody gurgle escaped his lips. He swallowed and tried again but he couldn't speak. The silver had eaten away his vocal cords. His head fell forward against the collar and he didn't have the strength to lift it.

Tarrick walked to Matthew, gripped under his jaw, and tilted Matthew's limp head upwards. Tarrick looked down at him with concern.

"Any trouble with him?" Tarrick asked the commander, his gaze locked on to Matthew.

"Not much. He's strong but clearly not trained. A quick study. I find it strange he didn't kill Ryans. He had the chance to."

"He didn't try to kill me either when he had the opportunity."

A stunned look crossed the commander's face. "Did he actually compel you, sir? You weren't just playing with him back there?"

Had the hunters been there the entire time, watching? Matthew had been so sure they were alone. He hadn't heard their hearts beating or any breathing. Maybe they weren't human after all.

Tarrick lightly rubbed his thumb across Matthew's cheek. The gesture was comforting, tender. Matthew closed his eyes as more tears threatened to escape.

"He did."

Cullip stepped forward. "If I had known you were in danger..."

Tarrick waved his free hand in a dismissive gesture. "Don't worry, Commander, I won't punish you for something we had no idea was even possible. Dawn?"

Matthew opened his eyes again and strained against the chains.

Tarrick's grip on Matthew's jaw tightened. "Still yourself. I am not going to kill you tonight, young one."

"Three hours, sir," the female hunter answered.

Cullip looked Matthew up and down. "I don't know why he isn't out yet. Silva got him in the blood pouch."

"I suspect he has two pouches," Tarrick said.

Pouches? Matthew's thoughts turned groggy and dark spots pressed into his vision.

"Want me to stake him for transport?" Cullip asked.

Tarrick shook his head. He leaned down and kissed Matthew. Tarrick's lips brushed so gently against his, he almost didn't feel them as they stole away the last of his energy.

Darkness wrapped around him and he surrendered to it.

Five

The world returned to Matthew in pieces.

He was indoors. He could feel a firm mattress under his back and the air was warm. His body ached all over but it was healing; blood must have been given to him at some point. Four heartbeats filled his ears. He opened his eyes and white bright light flooded them. He winced in pain and closed them again.

"He's waking," a man said.

"Already? Get the hawthorn ready. Call the Lord General, let him know," a harsh sounding woman barked.

Matthew felt something warm within him flood his arm and spread across his chest. Blood.

He opened his eyes again, squinting against the light, and tried to sit up but was unable to move.

Affixed to sturdy bed rails, metal shackles bound his wrists and legs. He could feel the metal collar still around his neck, attached somehow to the bed, making it impossible to sit up. None of the metal was silver. Thank god.

Matthew turned his head to the side and saw an IV line with a bag of blood hanging from the stand, the life essence entering him one agonizingly slow drip at a time. Standing by the bag was a human male wearing green scrubs, holding a syringe, watching Matthew with apathetic eyes.

The room itself had several gurneys and beds, all empty. Cabinets filled with neatly organized medical supplies lined the walls. It looked like an infirmary.

A middle-aged human woman wearing a white lab coat sat at a desk, reviewing some charts. At the door stood two male hunters, one had his attention focused on Matthew while the other said something into his comm under his glove. "He'll be here in a moment, doctor."

The woman set aside the chart she was working on, stood up, and smoothed out her coat.

Matthew didn't want to see the incubus. *Tarrick*. He had let the man live and his kindness was repaid with pain and the loss of his freedom. If he ever got another chance to kill him, he would take it. He wouldn't make the same mistake twice.

"How long was I out?" Matthew's voice was hoarse and strained.

The two hunters shot a glance at each other but didn't answer. Their hands rested on the stakes on their belts. Neither the doctor nor the nurse answered either.

The lights in here were too bright for his eyes. He shut them again. What was Tarrick planning to do with him? Back in the forest, the hunter thought Tarrick was just playing with him. Was that the plan: play with the helpless vampire then kill him when he was done?

Now it was clear to Matthew that the war was very real, as was the hatred for vampires.

Footsteps approached. Matthew didn't bother to open his eyes as he resolved that he would do everything in his power to defy the incubus and try to escape.

Tarrick entered. The scent of night and earth filled Matthew's nostrils; it was fantastic.

"You told me a week," Tarrick said, his voice agitated.

"I am sorry, Lord General," the female doctor answered. "For a vampire his age it should have taken him a week or even more to heal the amount of silver he was exposed to. There is something else I need to show you."

Matthew heard someone flip open a chart and thumb through some papers. The room was silent as Tarrick read through the chart.

"Are you sure about this?" Tarrick asked, skeptical.

"I saw it first on the x-rays. Lord Tane verified it, though he had trouble believing what he felt. I cut him open to confirm visually. I'm sure."

"I should have been informed right away."

"This wasn't something I wanted to jump the gun on, Lord General, I had to be certain. The full report is going to be on your desk in the morning."

What the hell were they talking about? Was something wrong with him? Unable to resist his curiosity anymore, Matthew opened his eyes.

Tarrick looked up from the chart he was holding and flashed a dashing smile. He was in a tailored black tuxedo with a grey bow tie that went well with his sapphire eyes.

Damn it. He looked too good wearing a tux.

Matthew flushed with confusion. He had never crushed so hard on a man before. Part of him felt like maybe it should bother him, but it didn't—not even a little bit.

He closed his eyes again and pushed the thoughts away. He wasn't going to surrender to a self-indulgent infatuation. The incubus had to die for what he had done to him.

Tarrick set down the chart and crossed the room. Matthew heard him flick a light switch, then he felt him approach and lay a warm hand on his cheek.

"The lights are dim. They won't hurt your eyes anymore. Look at me," Tarrick said, his voice tender.

Matthew opened his eyes and narrowed them in an effort to show Tarrick how furious he was. Tarrick ignored the angry stare and instead moved his hand to Matthew's shoulder. He gently brushed his fingers over the wound he had inflicted, now only faint scars in the shape of his claw.

He didn't stop there. His hand moved down Matthew's chest then pushed the thin sheet covering him down to his hips.

Matthew came to the realization he was naked under the sheet and hoped Tarrick wouldn't expose him to everyone in the room, though none of the humans seemed the least bit phased or uncomfortable by what was happening. Perhaps this was business as usual when serving an incubus lord.

But for Matthew it was awkward, he didn't want to put on a show. Not that he had any choice in the matter. If Tarrick planned to molest him, there was nothing he could do about it. He was helpless. Maybe he could try to compel him again, but he wasn't sure how. When he tried with the hunter, she had laughed it off.

Tarrick ran his fingers over the three scars the crossbow bolts put on his chest. After circling them for a moment he moved his hand towards his lower stomach to the stake wound.

Matthew noticed a new scar across his abdomen, no doubt given to him by the doctor when she cut him open. In a few nights, all of these scars would be gone, healed by blood if he was given more of it. The slow dripping IV was driving him mad.

Tarrick's hand kept moving downwards, resting just above Matthew's pelvic bone. Matthew gritted his blunt teeth and moaned, his cock growing hard with anticipation, tenting the sheet. He hated himself for taking pleasure in anything Tarrick did to him.

"Gods, you respond so beautifully to me," Tarrick said, his eyes hungry.

Damn him.

Matthew's vampire side came forward. He growled and flashed his fangs at Tarrick. Then he growled at the others in the room for good measure. None of them reacted to him. Frustrating. He hoped to be rewarded with the sound of hearts beating quicker. Instead, he got nothing.

He struggled against his restraints to no avail; they were far stronger than him. At least his erection began to ease. The thin sheet on top of him did nothing to hide what was going on down there.

"Have his vocal cords healed?" Tarrick asked the doctor.

She took a step forward and smoothed her lab coat again. "Yes, Lord General, the vampire spoke just a few minutes ago."

"What did he say?"

"He asked how long he was unconscious."

"I see." Tarrick's hand tensed and his fingers massaged into Matthew's abdomen. If he slipped his hand just a few inches lower he'd be on his cock. Matthew gritted his teeth to hold back a moan. So much for that eased erection. "Give me the silent treatment if you wish but I can feel questions bubbling within you and I am the only one around here who will answer them for you."

Matthew glared at him with heated red eyes, defiant.

Tarrick leaned in so his face was just inches away. Matthew's gaze dropped to Tarrick's neck. He watched the vein pulse under the skin, calling to him. Would his blood taste like how he smelled? How exquisite would it feel running over his tongue and down his throat? His blood was no doubt strong and powerful. Matthew licked his lips.

"I know you enjoy talking to me."

Matthew wished he hadn't admitted that to Tarrick but, at the time, he thought he would never see the incubus again. Now Tarrick had even more power over him.

"You are only hurting yourself here." Tarrick reached over and grabbed Matthew's IV line. He thumbed the roller clamped to open up the line, letting more blood flow into Matthew's arm. It was a pleasing sensation but he wished for fresh blood from the vein. Tarrick's vein. His cock twitched at the thought of sinking his fangs into Tarrick's warm flesh.

The door behind them opened.

"What are you hiding in here? He smells wonderful," a sweet voice sang out.

Tarrick removed his hand from Matthew and turned to face the newcomer, bowing respectfully. "I am sorry for the delay, my dear."

The woman approached Matthew. He stopped breathing the moment he saw her.

She was stunning.

She smelled of rain and apple blossoms. Her eyes were the most intense green Matthew had ever seen. Surrounding her smooth, porcelain skin was a wild mane of red curly hair; the back pinned up with sparkling sapphires and emeralds. Her sultry lips were painted the same color as her fiery mane. She wore a plunging formal dress that matched the color of Tarrick's blue eyes. Her body curved in all the right ways. Matthew had never seen a woman like her in all his life.

A succubus. She had to be.

When she saw Matthew her face twisted up into a horrified expression.

The woman hissed at him and small claws came out. Instinctually, Matthew hissed back at her and bared his fangs.

He wished he hadn't.

She lunged at him, ready to swipe with her delicate claws. Matthew was helpless against the assault and he winced in anticipation of the pain. None came. Inches from his chest, Tarrick had grabbed the woman's hand and stopped the attack.

"He's no threat," Tarrick said, his voice reassuring and steady. The two hunters bared their stakes, ready to attack Matthew if either she or Tarrick ordered it. Even the doctor and nurse, who had been waiting on the far side of the room, seemed ready to fight if necessary. Tarrick released the woman's hand and motioned for the hunters to return to their post at the door.

The woman's gaze burned into Matthew. Only raw hatred filled her expression as she studied him. Once she seemed convinced Matthew couldn't hurt her, she straightened up and regained her composure. Her claws returned to normal fingers, nails painted with glossy red lacquer.

Matthew's skin began to crawl and her beauty faded away. He was certain she was doing this to him; turning him off the way Tarrick could turn him on.

"We're going to be late because you're playing with a vampire?" she asked, fire in her voice.

Tarrick seemed amused by her angry reactions. "Yes."

She scowled at him.

He grabbed her hand and pressed a kiss on it. "Do you have the ability to scan, Lady Rosaline?"

Matthew wished he knew more about incubi, or rather succubi in this case, and their abilities. He had no idea what the ability to 'scan' was but he had a feeling he was about to find out.

Rosaline cocked her head. "You know I do."

Tarrick stepped aside and motioned to Matthew.

"I am not going to touch it," she said, disgust in her voice.

It? That hurt. What had happened to her? He wanted to point out that he couldn't hurt her right now even if he wanted to, that there was no need for her to be so hateful, but he was unwilling to speak while Tarrick was in the room. Besides, he doubted she would listen.

"I won't make you, but trust me, you're going to wish you did when you had the chance," he said with a mischievous smile.

"Unlikely," she scoffed. She turned to leave. "Let's go. If we're any later, it'll be considered rude."

Tarrick didn't move to leave with her. "When others find out what he is, he'll be the talk at every party, every event for the next six months. And you'll have been one of the first to have seen what he is. It'll make you quite popular."

"I'm already popular. And it's just a vampire."

"A vampire who compelled me."

She stopped and turned to face Tarrick. "You're teasing me."

Tarrick shook his head. "I do enjoy teasing you. But right now I am serious. Scan him."

She stood still for several moments, as if struggling with the decision. Curiosity won. Rosaline reached towards his abdomen, then paused.

"If this is a joke or some sort of prank, I will have you severely punished, Lord General."

Tarrick nodded, accepting her threat.

She pressed her hand against Matthew's skin. His wounds ached below her touch. Rosaline closed her emerald eyes and Matthew felt something vibrate within him. It almost felt like an echo bouncing around in his belly.

Rosaline's eyes shot open and she stumbled away. What the hell did she see inside of him? Matthew tugged against his shackles, it was useless.

"How is this possible?" she gasped.

Tarrick laughed at her. "I told you."

"Kill it. It's too dangerous."

Tarrick shook his head. "The High King wants him alive."

"Why the hell would he want that?" she spat out, then looked as if she immediately regretted it.

Tarrick's voice lowered and his eyes grew dark. "Are you questioning his orders?"

Her eyes grew wide and she took a step away from Tarrick. "No, of course not. You know I would never." She gathered herself and whispered, "But I wouldn't mind knowing his reasoning."

Tarrick motioned for the nurse, who crossed the room and injected the contents of his syringe into Matthew's IV. Matthew felt drowsy as the liquid entered him. Tarrick rested his hand on Matthew's chest.

The last thing Matthew heard before being knocked out was: "We're going to use him to end the war."

Six

When Matthew next woke he could smell he was no longer in the infirmary, but he was still lying on a bed.

Vampires. There were five of them nearby.

He snapped his eyes open and his heart sank when he realized he was in a prison cell. He was no longer chained to anything but the metal collar was still secured around his neck.

With a stiff grunt, he sat up. His body was healed. How long had they kept him out?

He was still naked but folded on the end of the bed were a pair of jeans, underwear, and a black t-shirt, a similar outfit to the one he had worn the night they caught him. Except these were new and in the current style.

He looked around. His cell had nothing more than a bed with a blanket and, in the back, a showerhead hung from the ceiling. There was no obvious way to turn it on. The back wall was solid stone and the other three sides were silver-coated bars.

With no bathroom or toilet, it seemed these were designed for vampires. He wouldn't need to shave unless he willed his hairs to begin growing again and he previously only needed to use the toilet a few times since being turned. Each time he used it was after he drank a bottle of booze in an effort to get drunk. It tasted like shit and he didn't even get a buzz for his effort. Guess they weren't going to be giving him any alcohol.

The smell of fear drew his attention.

The two adjoining cells were occupied with a single vampire in each. Both kept their distance from Matthew. Across the sizable room another row of cells held three more vampires; two males, and a female. These ones each had an empty cell between them. All the vampires wore collars like his.

Cameras pointed at each of the cells. A heavy door framed the far end of the room, next to a mesh security window. Three hunters stood on the other side keeping guard in an observation room with monitors.

From a cell across the way, a male vampire bared his fangs and hissed at Matthew. He had long black hair, a goatee, and lots of scars.

It seemed the vampires were all scared of Matthew. Why? He was no threat to them.

He sighed and got dressed.

In the cell to his right, a petite female vampire whimpered. She sat on the floor as far away from Matthew as she could get; her arms hugged her knees. She barely looked eighteen. Her body was gaunt, her brown hair unkempt, and her eyes sunken. They hadn't been feeding her enough.

"Why are you so scared of me?" Matthew asked.

She winced and buried her head into her knees.

The outside door opened and Tarrick entered, wearing a tailored suit similar to the one he wore the night he and Matthew met. Only this time he was missing the wool coat and leather gloves covered his hands.

Following him was the older hunter, Commander Cullip, the petite hunter female who had staked him in the belly, Lieutenant Silva, and the four other hunters from their team—including the one Matthew had knocked out. He looked fine now.

Each of the vampires kneeled down on both knees and bowed their heads to Tarrick.

Weren't they at war? What had he done to them? They all looked broken. Except the male vampire who had hissed at him earlier. He was kneeling but his head was up in a small act of defiance. The vampire looked as if he disobeyed often, he had silver burns running up and down his arms and face.

Matthew squared up his shoulders and walked to the front of his cage. He certainly wasn't going to kneel.

Tarrick stood directly in front of him on the other side of the bars. "If you ask me, I'll tell you why they fear you."

Matthew narrowed his eyes and said nothing.

"I am happy to answer any of the questions you ask. I'm sure you'd like to know more about vampires. Or perhaps I could tell you about other supernatural creatures. Dragons, maybe? Witches? And I'm sure you've been wondering why you didn't sense the hunters the night I caught you in my trap."

Cullip grinned behind him. He looked amused at their success in tricking Matthew.

"And I know you are dying to ask what it is about you that makes you so different. So special."

He was, but he said nothing.

Tarrick smiled at Matthew. "This is a war of wills you will not win. I'm extremely patient and you are extremely young. But it will be fun seeing how long you last. In fact, I think the hunters have a pool going."

"We do, sir," Cullip said. "I give him six nights before he starts speaking to you."

A growl rose up in Matthew's chest. He sure as hell planned to last longer than six nights.

Tarrick chuckled. "Get the blood."

The two hunters in the back left the room and came back with bottles full of blood. Matthew wondered where they procured it; it smelled human.

Tarrick grabbed one and went to the cage to Matthew's left. The male vampire inside licked his lips. "May I have blood, Master?"

"You may." Tarrick held the bottle just outside the cage. "Rise."

The vampire stood but kept his head bowed. Making sure his arms did not hit the silver bars, the vampire took the bottle. His fangs came down and his irises turned dark red as he ripped the top off and began to drink. He downed the bottle in just a few gulps, set it outside his cage, and returned to kneeling.

Matthew watched as Tarrick moved on and repeated the process with each of the vampires. Even the defiant male called Tarrick 'Master' as he requested blood.

Jesus. This was cruel.

He would never call Tarrick 'Master.' He'd rather meet the sun.

Tarrick didn't feed the emaciated vampire in the cell next to him, though she clearly yearned with hunger. Her whole body was trembling and her fangs were out.

"I'll tell you why I'm not feeding her if you ask me," Tarrick said when he noticed Matthew watching her. "And if you'd like some blood, all you have to do is ask me for it."

Matthew kept his silence.

"No? Alright." Tarrick left the room, the hunters trailing behind him.

Matthew waited until he was sure none of the hunters would be coming back in and approached the hungry girl, who had slid back to sitting on the ground.

"You can feed on me if you'd like," Matthew told her. They had given him plenty of blood to heal.

The girl looked up, her eyes full of longing. With care, Matthew slid his wrist between the bars and motioned to her with it. She seemed to be struggling.

"Don't."

Matthew looked across the room over at the defiant vampire, whose expression flashed between one of anger towards him and one of concern for the girl.

"She'll be severely punished if she takes any blood that was not given to her by the incubus. As I will be for talking to you."

"Then why speak to me?"

"Because you are torturing her by offering your vein. I don't wish to see her hurt if she has a moment of weakness. I'm happy to be punished in her stead."

He cared for her. Matthew didn't want to see the girl starving but he didn't want to see her punished either. He withdrew his wrist back into his cage.

At least it seemed the male didn't fear Matthew anymore. Maybe he could press his luck. "Why are all these other vampires so scared of me?"

The vampire sat down on his bed and didn't answer the question. It seemed Matthew received all the information he was going to get.

The next night, Cullip, along with his team of hunters, took the long-haired, defiant vampire from his cell. For over an hour Matthew heard his screams coming from another room. Finally, they dragged the vampire back into his cell. Fresh whip marks burned across his skin. From that point on, the vampire growled at Matthew each time he looked at him.

Over the next five nights, none of the vampires spoke to him. Or each other. Matthew spent the nights looking for a weakness in the cage.

Many silver burns later he found none. He also tried to remove his collar without any luck.

Each night Tarrick would show up to feed the vampires bottled blood. He'd remind Matthew that he'd give him blood if he'd only ask for it. Matthew said nothing. Tarrick seemed amused by his silence.

Matthew did find out that the showers turned on one hour after sunset, stayed on for five minutes, then turned off. During this time, a hunter would bring clean clothes for each of the vampires. Matthew hadn't showered the first few nights because the showers were in the open and he didn't want to be nude in front of the others, though they showered without any inhibitions. Or maybe their dignity had been stripped from them and they had no choice in this place.

By the third night, he desperately wanted to be clean. He reluctantly stripped and stood under the lukewarm water. He sighed as the water washed over him, letting him forget this nightmare for a few brief moments.

When the water turned off he noticed the gaunt girl in the adjacent cell gazing at him, her mouth opened just enough to see her fangs. Her eyes were locked on Matthew's dick. He wasn't even hard and she looked impressed by it. She was wet and naked as well. Matthew couldn't help but notice that she would be attractive once she had some blood in her. She pulled her eyes away from his shaft and met his gaze.

Emilia.

The name appeared in his head as clearly as if she had spoken it. Was she telepathic?

She nodded at him.

An angry snarl from the cages across the room broke the moment. Emilia turned her attention to drying off. Matthew did as well. Not wanting to see her punished, he acted as if nothing out of the ordinary happened.

An hour later that same night three hunters entered. One held a formal dress. They forced the second female vampire to put it on.

"Who?" she dared ask, once changed, her voice hushed.

"Who do you think?" one of the hunters asked back.

"Lord Tane?"

The hunters laughed in response. One of them injected her with something and they dragged her from the room. Shortly before dawn she returned to her cell. She looked drained and bore cuts across her chest and back. Matthew wanted to rip the head off every hunter who had touched her, then track down this Lord Tane and rip his head off as well. God, he wanted to make them pay for torturing her.

On the sixth night, Cullip showed up with his team just after the sunset and stood in front of Matthew's cage. Refusing to give the hunter any satisfaction by showing fear, Matthew walked up to him and waited.

"You're being moved," Cullip said. "Since you are new to this, I'll tell you how this goes. We're not drugging you, so that means you need to behave. You can cooperate and there will be no pain. Or you try and fight and you'll be spending a week in the infirmary. Personally, I'm hoping you fight. I wouldn't mind taking you down again."

Studying the hunters, Matthew knew he couldn't take all six of them. Not when they were all armed with those silver grenades and chains…and swords…and crossbows. Damn, he wished he knew how to fight hunters.

"Turn around and give me your hands," Cullip ordered.

Matthew obeyed, slipping his hands through a rectangular slot in the bars. The commander pulled out iron shackles and cuffed his hands together behind his back. Cullip nodded to the hunters in the observation room and the cell door unlocked. He opened it and yanked Matthew out. Shackles were also placed on Matthew's legs, restricting his movement and forcing him to take small, quick steps as he was pushed forward.

Silva walked in front of him, Cullip was at his side while the other four took up the rear. They weren't messing around either; they were ready to take Matthew down if he showed the slightest sign of aggression. They led Matthew out into a hallway where six more hunters stood posted at different points in the hall, each saluting as Cullip passed.

Without exception, the hunters Matthew saw in this place wore a black leather outfit, each cut in a different fashion. One of the hunters standing in the hallway looked like a samurai, complete with a katana and all, while another looked like he belonged in the military with black combat boots, pants, and a long-sleeved shirt. No matter the design, every hunter was covered from neck to toe, and armed with stakes and silvered weapons.

The walls of the hallway were covered in a thick acrylic glass. Behind it, running the entire length of the hall, hung a mirror. Matthew had no reflection. Not even his clothes showed up.

Normally he could see his reflection just fine.

"You should ask the Lord General why you can't see your reflection."

Two of the hunter's behind him laughed. Matthew looked over his shoulder and scowled at them.

"Keep moving," Cullip said, shoving Matthew forward.

They stopped before an elevator at the end of the hall and waited in front of it for several moments until Cullip received what sounded like a text. He pressed the call button, the doors opened, and they entered a large elevator.

Matthew studied the numbers on the panel inside. There were two basement levels with four normal levels on top. Cullip put a key in the panel and pressed the button for the top floor. When the doors opened again, more hunters were standing guard in an opulently decorated hallway with a half dozen dark wooden doors.

Cullip marched forward, pulling Matthew along. They paused before thick double doors at the end of the hallway. The commander pulled out a key and opened them.

Inside, an immense suite sprawled before him. Expensive art and various weapons adorned the burgundy walls. In one corner of the room an open-air shower stood in front of a door which led to an expansive bathroom. Another door led to a huge walk-in closet. Sizable leather chairs and a desk sat before an impressive stone fireplace. Heavy curtains covered floor to ceiling windows. Opposite the windows, a large bed covered with dark silk sheets was flanked by heavy mahogany bookcases, displaying leather tomes. Everything in the room looked neat and orderly. Not even a pen was out of place. Tarrick's intoxicating scent touched everything.

Matthew trembled when he saw thick chains hanging from the back wall and ceiling.

Cullip dragged him over to the chains and pushed him down to his knees. The other hunters of his team joined them. They attached Matthew to the chains coming from the ceiling, replacing the shackles they used to transport him. At least his arms were no longer pinned behind his back.

Matthew started to bring his arms forward when the chains were pulled taut, raising his hands above his head. His abs flexed as he was stretched tight; forced to kneel but unable to rest on his boot heels. The position was uncomfortable; all of his weight was on his kneecaps or his wrists if he slumped too much.

Before he could stand, a hunter attached two more chains—coming out from the bottom of the wall—to his collar, making it impossible for him to move from the position.

Cullip double checked the chains and seemed satisfied.

"Let's go."

All of the hunters left the room, leaving Matthew alone to wonder just what Tarrick planned to do with him.

Seven

Just before two in the morning, nearly seven hours after the hunters chained him, Matthew was bored to death and trying to keep his mind off his hunger when Tarrick burst through the doors and stomped into his room.

And holy shit did he look different.

He was huge now, over seven feet tall, not including his massive wings. His ears pointed at the tips, his eyes glowed a bright purple, his feet were hooves—actual fucking hooves—and his legs bent backwards at the ankle. His horns made him look like a demon.

Tarrick's claws balled into fists and his wings scraped against the top of the doorframe as he entered.

Blood covered his body. It seeped out of the dozens of slashes he had on his chest and back. There were bite marks near his neck and on his arms—vampire bite marks, and he hadn't been a willing participant. One of his wings appeared ripped and his face bore purple bruises.

Matthew strained against his chains, the smell of the blood became too much. Having not fed in six nights, he felt famished. Starved. His skin tightened and his fangs itched, desperate to find a vein. He wanted to lick every one of Tarrick's wounds to taste his blood and speed along the healing process. He wanted to place his bite marks on Tarrick's neck.

Fuck. Matthew wanted to ravage the incubus in every way possible. He wanted to fuck him and destroy him all at once. He wasn't even sure why he felt this way…why every time the general showed up he was overwhelmed with lust and fear and…fuck, he wasn't even sure of his own emotions. Maybe loneliness plagued him for too long.

Tarrick let out a deafening roar and sent an accent table flying across the room. Matthew yelped as it splintered apart against the wall near him. Threatened, his vampire aspect came forward against his will.

Tarrick growled when he noticed Matthew. "Devil, I forgot the hunters moved you in here." His voice sounded much deeper than it had been before. His true form was formidable. "I'm in no mood for you tonight."

He picked up a landline phone.

"I need two feeders. Women," he said then hung up.

Matthew watched as Tarrick took off his pants—what was left of them anyway—and tossed them aside. His soft penis hung heavy against his legs. God, it would be massive when it was hard. Matthew always thought he was well-endowed, he certainly never got any complaints, but Tarrick's cock put his to shame. A trait of being a creature that fed off sex, he guessed.

Tarrick turned and Matthew saw his tail for the first time. Just like his horns and wings, the tail was black at the base and faded to purple. It ended in an arrowhead at its long length. It swayed as he walked over to the shower in the corner of the room and turned it on.

Multiple showerheads began to pour water down on him, and he sighed as water ran over his hard body, washing away the blood. As Tarrick relaxed he began to shrink back to his human height. His eyes returned to blue and his horns and claws melted back into his skin. He left his wings and tail out and his penis did indeed shrink, though it was still sizable for a human.

Tarrick's imposing incubus aspect made Matthew's vampire aspect feel somewhat inadequate. He didn't have horns, wings, or a tail, nor did he grow in size; just fangs and claws for him.

There was a knock at the door.

"Enter," Tarrick said.

Two attractive women walked in; one with short, bleach blonde hair, the other with long, silky brown. The thin robes covering their bodies hung open, revealing their skin as they both bowed. They were succubi. Matthew was learning to sense the subtle differences between a human and an incubus. They smelled sweeter, their hearts beat just a little faster, and their features were a little too perfect.

Tarrick shut off the water and grabbed a towel to dry off. Many of his wounds still bled.

The women removed their robes and stood naked in front of him. Their bodies' were perfection.

He didn't wait until he fully dried before grabbing the brunette and pulling her into him. She moaned as he captured her mouth in a hungry kiss.

The other woman kissed Tarrick's neck, careful to avoid his wounds. She worked her way across his shoulders while the blonde grabbed his thick length and began to stroke it. Matthew grew hard in his jeans as he watched Tarrick with the two women.

Tarrick growled when the brunette broke his kiss and began to work her way down his body, joining the blonde. She took his cock from the

blonde and wrapped her soft lips around it. Tarrick groaned and ran his
fingers through her long, brown hair. She took him completely into her
mouth, while she ran her fingers across his balls.

His wings stretched out as he bucked with pleasure. He placed his hand
on the back of her head, to hold her in place while he fucked her mouth.
She flashed a set of hazel eyes at him and grabbed his base in an effort to
slow him down. He moaned as he kept the pace he wanted.

Matthew noticed the smaller wounds on his skin began to close up and
heal, leaving only pink scars behind.

Tarrick pulled his length from her mouth and led the women over to
his bed. The blonde froze when she noticed Matthew.

"Ignore him," Tarrick whispered into her neck.

Matthew wished they wouldn't.

She responded to Tarrick by exposing more of her skin and moaning
as he kissed it. God her neck was lovely. Matthew wanted to sink his fangs
deep within her and pull her blood into his body. A desperate groan escaped him.

Tarrick glanced at Matthew, his sapphire eyes flared, and he returned
to worshiping the blonde's skin. He scooped her up in his arms and lay her
down below him on the bed, his hungry lips never leaving her. He grabbed
the base of his shaft and in one smooth motion sunk it into her sheath. She
bucked with pleasure as she stretched to fit him.

Tarrick impaled her a few times then grabbed the brunette's arm with
his tail and guided her down beside the blonde. He caressed the brunette's
pert nub with his thumb and slipped two fingers deep into her slick core.
She arched her back in response to his sensual touch. His tail wrapped
around her waist, as if to keep her in place.

God, what could he do with that tail? What would it feel like wrapped
around him? Matthew squirmed, his confined cock in pain with need.

Tarrick grunted as he continued stroking the brunette with his hand
while thrusting in and out of the blonde. Cries of pleasure escaped the lips
of both women.

Matthew watched in admiration of Tarrick's skill as the brunette began
to quake. She screamed out as Tarrick brought her to orgasm, her heat
pulsing around his fingers. Breathing hard, her body stilled and melted
into the bed, satisfied. Tarrick smiled at her then turned his focus to the
blonde.

Not leaving her, he sat up slightly and slipped a hand under her butt to
turn her hips and give himself better access. He reached down and played

with her clit as he drove into her, each plunge more aggressive than the last. She cried out with each push and flick of his fingers until she could take it no longer. Release began to crash over her.

Tarrick grunted as his balls tightened and his body tensed. His wings flapped excitedly as he thrust twice more and found his own release, chasing the woman's pleasure as she tightened around his length.

When his seed was expended, he carefully rolled off the blonde to avoid crushing his wings as he lay beside her on the silky sheets, enjoying the afterglow. Most of his wounds had healed, the bruising on his skin disappeared, the bite marks were nothing but pink scars that were slowly fading away. His wing was still ripped and a deep wound on his side threatened to begin bleeding again if too much pressure was applied.

"Do you need more, my lord? I can have another sent up," the brunette said when she noticed the wound.

Tarrick looked over at Matthew. Hungry.

"No need. Thank you, ladies," he said and stood up.

The girls got up with him and all three showered off. Watching the three beautiful wet bodies was agony to Matthew. They all had their release, and he couldn't even remember the last time he came. If one of his hands were free, he'd be taking care of himself right now. He didn't care anymore about having an audience.

Done showering, the woman put their robes back on and left with a bow.

With only a towel wrapped around his waist, Tarrick walked over to Matthew and towered above him. Matthew couldn't bring himself to look up and instead kept his gaze on the floor. Six nights without any blood pushed his limits and kneeling with his arms raised above him caused his muscles to ache. If he looked at Tarrick he wouldn't be able to resist talking to him, begging him even for some sort of relief.

"Still not speaking to me?" Tarrick asked.

Matthew said nothing.

Putting his hand under Matthew's chin, Tarrick forced him to look up. Matthew grimaced, turning his head to the side. The incubus growled and his claws came out. Matthew mentally prepared himself for the pain but none came. Instead, Tarrick kneeled in front of him and slashed open Matthew's shirt, peeling it away.

Matthew's abs tensed as claws ran down his torso, barely scraping the skin. The sensation felt incredible. He swallowed hard and tried to keep his composure.

Tarrick pressed one of his claws into his own thumb, a single drop of blood pooled on the pad. He grabbed Matthew's jaw and forced him to turn his head upwards. Tarrick held his thumb a few inches above Matthew's lips. The smell of blood was too much. Matthew opened his mouth and waited, silently begging for the blood like a baby bird.

A single drop fell into his mouth.

The drop of blood was pure ecstasy as it rolled down his tongue; the best thing Matthew had ever tasted. He felt high, as if plugged into every sound and every sensation that burst around him. Did all incubi taste this way? God, he needed more.

Tarrick didn't give him any. He put his claws away and ran his hands over Matthew's pecs, thumbing his nipples and squeezing them.

Matthew's chest vibrated with a deep purr. He wanted to touch Tarrick and wished he wasn't chained up. He flexed his arms against the shackles, raising his body up a few inches.

"Are you sure you don't want to talk to me? I can show you pleasures you've only ever dreamed of."

Matthew answered with a groan as Tarrick traced his hands down his chest and stomach. His body became rigid when the incubus unbuttoned his jeans and slowly dragged the zipper open.

Tarrick brushed his hand against Matthew's underwear and his painfully hard sex. Wanting more, he thrust his hips forward as the incubus pushed Matthew's jeans and underwear down, allowing his cock to spring free, jutting proudly from his hips.

Pleased at what he saw, Tarrick fluttered his wings.

"Mm. Beautiful." He grabbed the hard length and gently stroked. Jesus, his hand felt like it was made of wet silk as it slid with ease across Matthew's member.

His warm, firm hand worked up and down Matthew's shaft at an excruciatingly slow pace. Matthew jerked his hips. Even with the slow stroking, he was getting close.

Tarrick removed his hand from Matthew's cock. "If you want me to finish you, all you must do is ask for it."

Matthew roared and struggled against his chains. When that got no reaction from Tarrick, he focused and calmed himself. Fuck, he was ready to try to compel him to keep going but Tarrick stood and walked away.

"Suit yourself." Tarrick headed across the room, over to a closet door.

God damn it.

Chains rattled as Matthew snarled. He fucking hated the incubus who continued to ignore him, and yet the desire for release overwhelmed him. He hated that he felt this way but he needed Tarrick's hand back on him.

He had lost.

It shamed him, but he couldn't resist anymore. Matthew dropped his head and slumped against the chains.

"Tarrick," he whispered. The incubus stopped but didn't turn. Matthew swallowed hard as the words caught in his throat. He didn't want to say them and yet, eventually, he uttered, "Please finish me?"

Tarrick turned and smiled. He looked so powerful standing above his conquest, victorious.

He came back to Matthew and joined him down on his knees, off to the side. Matthew's thick length twitched eagerly. Tarrick grabbed Matthew's cock with both his hands. He gripped the base tight with one hand and with the other he stroked the shaft and head in a twisting motion.

It wasn't long before Matthew was to the point he couldn't hold back any longer; he howled, rose up, and pumped into Tarrick's grasp. His body throbbed as he shot long strings of semen onto the wood floor, narrowly missing Tarrick's thigh. It was a lot of cum, reminding him just how long it had been.

Matthew sighed and collapsed, his body held up by the shackles on his wrists.

He felt drained.

And hungry.

God, he needed to eat.

Matthew noticed all of Tarrick's wounds had healed. His wing was no longer ripped and the deep wound in his side only a light pink scar.

The incubus had been feeding on him; no wonder he felt so drained.

Tarrick went into his bathroom and came out with a wet hand towel. He seemed pleased as he gently ran it over Matthew's softening cock, and then wiped up the semen on the ground. He really did like things clean. Matthew appreciated it; he didn't want to be sticky all night.

The incubus pulled Matthew's pants back up and buttoned them before he grabbed the ripped black shirt and bundled it with the towel, tossing them into a nearby basket. He left through a side door and reemerged wearing dress trousers. He carried a shirt and tie on a hanger which he lay down on the bed. Was he going out again tonight?

He turned away from Matthew who watched as the incubus' wings began to fold into his back, and disappeared under his skin. His tail also receded into his body. It was amazing.

"Going back to the silent treatment?" Tarrick asked.

Matthew sighed. He had too many questions and he needed answers. And maybe he could learn enough to escape this place. "No."

There was a heavy knock at the door.

"Enter," Tarrick said.

Cullip entered the room alone holding his skull mask under one arm. He looked just as bad as Tarrick had earlier. His leather doublet bore many claw marks across it and silver specks on his clothes picked up the light as he moved.

He looked battle fatigued as if he had been fighting for hours, far different from earlier that night when he brought Matthew up here.

His doublet was open near the top. Matthew gasped when he saw silver colored runes tattooed all over his chest. As the hunter moved one of the runes turned bright green then faded away.

Cullip pressed a fist to his chest and bowed.

"Report," Tarrick commanded.

"We killed most of them. Two got away. I sent trackers after them but I'm not optimistic. We lost Lord Gram, and Hunter Evens, Rayn, and Ramirez. Lady Sulli is badly injured but the doc thinks she'll recover in time," Cullip said, his face as grim as the news.

"Is Karith with her?"

"He was. Lord Karith wasn't letting the doctors near her so I had to… escort him from the room."

"I'll go down in a few minutes to calm him. Tane?"

"Lord Tane is fine, he sustained fewer injuries than you. He's healing now."

Tarrick slipped on the shirt from the bed and began to button it up. "How the hell did they get past all of our alarms?"

Cullip ran a hand over his greying goatee. "I don't know yet, sir, but I aim to find out."

Tarrick shook his head. "They must have a witch," he said, mostly talking to himself. He finished with his shirt and tucked it in, then put on his tie.

"Then I'll find it and kill it."

"Yes. But for now, go get cleaned up, Commander. Maybe get a few hours of sleep. We'll do the full debrief in the morning."

"Yes, sir," Cullip bowed to Tarrick.

"Oh and Commander…"

"Yes, General?"

"You fought well tonight."

"With all due respect, I lost three of my men and Lord Gram. I did not fight well enough."

Tarrick didn't argue with him; instead, he dismissed his hunter from the room and sat down on the bed to put on his socks and shoes.

"Tonight's a bad night. We'll talk tomorrow," Tarrick said.

Matthew nodded.

Tomorrow night he was going to start getting some answers.

Eight

The moment the sun sunk behind the horizon, Matthew woke. He was pleasantly surprised to find he was no longer forced to kneel on the wooden floor, even if he was still chained. Instead, he was lying on a fold out cot.

The chains attached to his collar and shackles were longer now—secured to the wall instead of the ceiling—allowing him to move around just a bit. Someone even put a fresh shirt on him.

As he sat up and stretched his sore muscles, he noticed the smashed table had been cleared up, and Tarrick sat on his bed, leaning against a plush headboard. He wore only a pair of black pajama bottoms that hugged his hips just under the V. Matthew wanted to lick Tarrick there and maybe nip him. He pushed the thought away.

Surrounding Tarrick were dozens of folders full of paperwork. They looked like official reports and he was currently reading one of them.

Ever since meeting this man, Matthew had been imprisoned one way or another. He was tempted to return to silence, to see how much longer he could hold out, but he was so fucking hungry right now that wouldn't take much to provoke his vampire. Tarrick—who obviously knew how to control him—could prick his finger and Matthew would be completely at his mercy, willing to do anything for the blood.

The worst of it was that he knew the general hadn't even begun to unleash real tortures. He had seen the whip marks Cullip gave to the vampire back in the cells, and how the starving vampire, Emilia, ignored her instincts out of fear of what Tarrick would do to her. He saw how broken those vampires were. He was being treated differently for some reason. If he stayed silent, he'd never find out why.

Unsure of what to say, or where to begin, Matthew watched the general leaf through his papers. Tarrick sat up straighter and lowered the report. "If you'd like some blood, you only have to ask me for it."

It was eerie how well he could read Matthew. "Can I have some blood?"

"Yes," Tarrick smiled and picked up the landline phone from his side table. "Send him," he said and hung up. He watched Matthew for a moment. When Matthew said nothing, he went back to reading the report. "Why not start with a few easy questions and work your way up to the big ones?"

he suggested, without looking up.

Ah, the big questions…like, why they cut him open and what did the doctor find inside of him that made them all react in such an extreme way?

As much as Matthew wanted the answer, starting smaller seemed like a good idea, but he wasn't even sure which of those to pick. He feared that voicing some of his questions would make him seem too young and inexperienced. He shifted his weight around on the cot. Why did he even care what Tarrick thought about him?

"Are there really dragons?" Matthew finally asked.

Tarrick laughed and set down the report again. "I knew you wouldn't be able to resist that one. Yes, there are dragons. They've been forced to sleep, hidden away with their hordes. If any wake, we hunt them. Dragons are a threat to all of us. They seek to rule and have all bow before them. If you ever come across one, run."

The chains attached to his arms rattled as Matthew ran his hand through his hair and down his stubble. Dragons. "What about things like werewolves?"

"Weres exist but there's only a handful left. They, along with animal shifters, were once a third faction in this war but most of them were wiped out centuries ago. The few that are left stay out of our way or act as mercenaries. We don't actively hunt them down unless they start causing trouble."

"And fairies?" Matthew asked.

"Yes. I met a nymph once. That was a wild night." Tarrick chuckled, his abs contracting magnificently. "There are literally thousands of different types of supernatural beings. I'll give you a few books on it if you are interested in learning them all. Vampires and incubi are the most numerous."

Tarrick sorted his reports and folders into neat piles while he waited for Matthew to ask his next question.

"You keep saying 'incubi', what about 'succubi'?"

"Same species. We refer to ourselves as 'incubi' for ease. 'Incubus' refers to any gender, sort of how an 'actor' can be either male and female, while 'succubus''—much like 'actress''—is female only."

"What was that, er…thump…thing…you used on me?"

"I can send out a pulse that forces your body to release chemicals. It hits you like a 'thump'. I use it to draw prey to me from a distance."

"Can all incubi do it?"

Tarrick shook his head. "No, maybe one in a thousand. Most need to be physically close to affect prey that way."

"God, it was…" Matthew stopped himself. It had felt so good. So distracting. He didn't want Tarrick using it against him again.

Tarrick ran his fingers through his dusty blond hair to straighten it and smiled. "Perhaps you'd enjoy feeling it now?"

"I…it would be torture if you did it while I was chained up and couldn't touch you. You sitting there half-naked is bad enough." Matthew shifted on the cot, adjusting his tightening jeans. The action did not go unnoticed by Tarrick, whose eye's raked him with hunger.

"What about the mirror?" Matthew asked to take his mind off Tarrick's body. He was certain Tarrick would know he was asking why he couldn't see his reflection. Tarrick seemed to know everything that was happening in his…keep? Matthew wasn't actually sure where they were located. He had only seen an infirmary, a prison, and this room. He wished his chains were long enough to go to the windows so he could look outside.

"It's backed with real silver using a much older mirror-making technique. Most modern mirrors are aluminum or the silver is too diluted."

There was a knock at the door. Tarrick slipped off his bed and exited out into the hallway. When he came back in a human male followed.

The human looked as if he was lost in some sort of blissful haze. Was the human for him? Was he actually going to get to feed from a vein? He assumed he'd be getting some of that older bottled blood. Matthew's vampire aspect slipped forward.

"Hungry?" Tarrick asked with a playful smile.

Matthew huffed and didn't bother to answer. He walked forward, as far as his chains would let him. It wasn't far enough. He stopped several feet away from the human.

Tarrick held up his hand. "You can't have him yet."

Matthew couldn't believe it. Tarrick made him beg for this blood, told him he could have it, and now took it away. He hated these games. Matthew snarled, baring his large fangs. The human didn't react, his heartbeat steady, as if locked in some pleasant dream.

"This isn't a punishment, Matthew. I'm going to teach you how to compel correctly," Tarrick said.

"…What?" Matthew asked, confused.

"I thought you might try to compel me again at some point but when you didn't, I realized it's because you have no idea how you did it the first time."

"But…why would you teach me?"

"I'd rather have you in control of your abilities than not. It makes it easier for me to manage them. Besides, all vampires learn to compel, you should know how to do it."

If Tarrick wanted to teach him the tools that would help him escape he wasn't going to complain. "Aren't you afraid I'll use it on you?"

"No."

Matthew frowned. He would use it on Tarrick if he had the chance.

"Have you noticed everyone who has been around you wears contacts?" Tarrick asked.

Matthew hadn't noticed. He focused on Tarrick's eyes and sure enough, he had contacts in.

"We grew tired of losing our hunters to compulsions so our scientists found a way to prevent it. Years ago we used specially treated glasses and goggles—these days it's contacts. I can't say I'm a fan of wearing them, I've never had to before."

Matthew regarded Tarrick for a moment. Before him was a weaker creature—at least in his human form, from what he had seen—but carried himself with such confidence that Matthew felt his lesser. If he planned to escape he'd have to play a careful game, he'd have to learn.

"I'm going to release my hold on him and you're going to compel him to be calm."

"You have a hold over him? How?"

"Incubi are able to manipulate and direct emotions. And we can release pheromones to influence a person. Now, are you ready?"

Matthew nodded and focused.

Tarrick grabbed the human's shoulders. The human blinked several times and looked around, his eyes wide. He began to panic when he saw the red-eyed vampire in front of him.

"Relax," Matthew said to him, but it had no effect.

The man struggled in vain in Tarrick's arms. "Try again."

Matthew balled his fists and looked deeper into the human's eyes. "Relax," he told the human.

It didn't work. The human grew more frantic.

"Again," Tarrick encouraged.

"Relax," he said and still the human struggled. Matthew growled, frustrated.

"Don't get irate. Close your eyes. Feel the power deep inside you, push it forward into your command," Tarrick told him.

Matthew closed his eyes and focused within. For a moment, nothing happened. Then, he sensed them—small red strands of power swirling inside of him. They led deep into his belly, twisting and coiling power, waiting for him to direct it. He had never felt anything like it before.

He mentally grabbed a strand and pulled it up to his vocal cords. He opened his eyes again and pushed the powerful word forward, into the man's soul. "Relax."

The man stopped struggling in Tarrick's arms. Matthew smiled, his teeth parted slightly so his fangs wouldn't stab his gums.

"Well done. Command him to come to you," Tarrick said.

Matthew grabbed another strand of power. "Come to me."

Tarrick let the human leave his arms and walk into Matthew's. Matthew couldn't believe it. He looked up at Tarrick to make sure he wasn't going to take the man from him. Tarrick nodded, giving him permission to feed.

Matthew leaned in and smelled the man's neck. Controlling him made him feel so powerful. It was almost enough to make him forget he was a chained up prisoner.

His vampire side took over. Before he even knew what he was doing, he released the strands of power controlling the human and looked deep into the man's eyes. "I am terrifying."

The man began to scream and shriek as he struggled against Matthew. Matthew laughed and held him tighter. He plunged all four fangs into the soft flesh of the human's neck. Blood filled his mouth. The pumping adrenaline was divine.

The world faded away and only the blood flowing into his body mattered. He drank it with such greed that he wouldn't let a single drop spill. This was his kill. His blood.

The human's heartbeat began to slow. Matthew pulled harder on the blood, taking every drop he could. The man's heart stopped and Matthew stayed connected until no more blood came.

When it was done, he removed his fangs and let the body slump to the floor.

There was a knock at the door. "General?" a hunter's voice called out.

"Everything's fine," Tarrick called back.

"Yes, sir." Matthew could hear the hunter returning to his post.

The sight of the kill didn't seem to bother Tarrick. "I expected you to be kind to your prey. Let them slip from this world peacefully."

Matthew hung his head. "I wish it was that way. But..." He had trouble finding the words. He never wanted to hurt humans, and most of the time he was gentle with them, but sometimes he had to feed the beast lurking within.

"You can learn to pull away from prey without killing them then compel them to forget you," Tarrick offered as he watched Matthew struggle. "But given your age, and that you have no bonded sire, it'll be hard for you. And painful."

Over the years, he had tried to pull away from his prey while feeding but he never could. Once he started, there was no stopping.

"I can suffer the pain. Will you teach me?"

"I can try," Tarrick said.

Matthew raised his hand up and flexed his fingers while he studied his sharp claws. "I don't like losing control to the monster. No matter how good it feels." Matthew focused and forced his claws to recede into him.

"Control is important to you, isn't it?"

Matthew nodded once and he dropped his eyes to the human he had drained dry. "I've lost so much of it lately."

Tarrick took a step towards him. "Why don't you ask me the question you really want to?"

Matthew looked up at him. "What's wrong with me, Tarrick?"

Nine

Matthew stood, his soul exposed.

Tarrick always seemed to know what Matthew wanted. What he needed. He hated it. And hated that he was learning everything about vampires from a man who had been killing them for a millennium.

"Nothing is wrong with you," Tarrick assured. "But you are different."

"In what way?" Matthew took a step towards Tarrick, forgetting that he was at the end of his chain. His collar yanked him backwards. "Damn it."

Sympathy crossed Tarrick's eyes as if he felt bad Matthew was chained. Matthew didn't believe it, not even for a moment. If he truly felt bad about the collar, he could remove it.

"Do you know what a blood pouch is?" he asked.

Matthew absently ran his hand over his torso to the place where he had been stabbed with the stake. "I heard your hunter mention it. I assume it holds blood inside of me."

"Yes and no. The blood pouch holds condensed—for a lack of a better term—*blood energy*. It's where vampires draw their power. If you focus, you can direct the power to enhance your abilities. If, for example, you want to heal quicker, or push yourself to move faster, you'd tap into your blood pouch. It's what you draw from when you compel someone."

Matthew closed his eyes and felt strands of power inside of him. Focusing on them, they became visible in his mind's eye. Red and swirling, they clustered and twisted together in his belly, waiting on his command. This was new, and yet it felt natural, as if he had been able to see them all along but never gave it much thought. With this new knowledge, he wanted to try it out.

He grabbed many of the swirling bits of power and pulled it up to his ears. He listened.

There were people walking around the hallway outside, a dinner party two levels down, a human changing bed sheets, the idle chatter of hunters…he could hear everything. He counted the people. There were seventeen incubi in the building, not counting Tarrick, and sixty-three humans. Matthew wondered how many were hunters and how many served other roles, like the doctor or maybe cooks or maids.

He honed in on the five other vampires. He heard hearts beat only once every few minutes, except Emilia's, whose had stopped because she hadn't had blood in a long time. It was the absence of noise that helped him focus on them.

Expanding his hearing outwards, he discovered dozens of humans patrolling the grounds.

And a vampire. It was dodging each of the patrols, making its way closer. He listened as the vampire climbed up the outside wall, digging its claws into the stone.

"What are you doing?" Tarrick asked. Matthew had been standing still for many minutes with his eyes closed. The body at Matthew's feet was gone, it seemed Tarrick cleaned it up.

Matthew looked at the curtained window. "There's a vampire standing on your balcony."

Tarrick shook his head and crossed his arms over his bare chest. "No vampire could get that close to this place unnoticed. Even if it could, I'd be able to sense one standing on my balcony."

Matthew shrugged. He didn't care one way or the other if Tarrick believed him but he did wonder what the vampire was doing out there. Matthew continued to stare in that direction.

Irritated, Tarrick walked over to the curtains.

"There's no vampire, Matthew." He snapped the curtains apart.

He was right. There was no vampire out there. The balcony was empty.

The huge balcony outside of Tarrick's suite was made out of grey worked stone and ivy grew up the railing. Beyond, all he could see was the tops of winter trees with a single twisting road cut through it. There were no other buildings around.

Matthew could still hear nearly inaudible shifts of something moving around. It was up on the roof now.

"I swear I hear something out there."

"Oh," Tarrick smiled. "No heartbeat? And when it moves does it sound a little like gravel?"

Matthew listened. The gravel sound was so faint he almost didn't notice. "Yeah."

Tarrick retrieved his cell phone from his bedside. He entered a code into it that Matthew couldn't see. The doors to the balcony unlocked. Cold air filled the warm room as Tarrick opened both doors. Matthew wondered if the cold affected the incubus, it didn't seem to even though he had no shirt on and nothing on his feet.

Tarrick stepped out, walked to the end of the balcony, and shouted up to the roof. "Asper, would you like to come meet the new vampire?"

Tarrick didn't wait for an answer. He walked back into the room, leaving the door open behind him.

Matthew watched as a winged gargoyle dropped down from the roof and crawled into the room. It was the size of a large man, hunched over on all fours. It moved to Tarrick's side and froze, its face twisted into a permanent, horrifying sneer.

Matthew took a step back. It looked like it could rip him apart with its strength and he had no idea how to fight one. Tarrick dropped his hand down and stroked the head of the gargoyle. "Asper, this is Matthew. Matthew, Asper."

"Is he…your pet?" Matthew asked.

"*She* is most definitely not a pet. Gargoyles are intelligent and she chose me, not the other way around. Gargoyles do what they want. If she wanted to kill you now, there'd be little I could do to stop it."

"Uh, I'm sorry if I offended you," Matthew said to the gargoyle, who didn't move.

Tarrick nodded in approval. "I can see why you mistook her for a vampire. Most nights you won't hear any of them." Without any forewarning, the gargoyle walked out of the room. Tarrick closed the doors behind her and pressed a button on his phone to lock them. He slipped the phone into his pocket, then closed the curtains. "Were you trying to extend your hearing?"

"I…" Matthew stopped himself.

Tarrick made him feel at ease, as if he could tell him anything.

It wasn't real.

Matthew took a step back and fought against his influence. He narrowed his eyes. "You don't have to manipulate me. You already have me chained up. I'm answering your questions."

"It was just to keep you calm while Asper was in here. A gargoyle's power tends to be overwhelming for young vampires. Young incubi too. Tell me what you were doing."

Matthew felt the haze around him lift. "Yes, I was tapping into the power to enhance my hearing."

"And?" Tarrick raised an eyebrow.

"And I was counting the number of people in the building."

"How many?

"Right now? Excluding you and me, seventeen incubi, sixty-three humans, and five vampires. There's twelve hunters patrolling the grounds outside and another twelve standing guard."

"I didn't think you could tell the difference between an incubus and a human. You weren't able to the night I trapped you."

"No, I wasn't able to then. I can now."

Tarrick took out his phone again and pressed a button to call someone. "What's the current headcount?" He listened for a moment. "Thank you." Hanging up, Tarrick looked impressed. "Cullip said you were a quick study but, devil, I didn't expect you to be that quick."

"Is that why I'm different? Because I'm quick to learn?" Tarrick still hadn't actually answered the question he desperately wanted answered.

"Ah, no. But I do need to explain a bit more about blood pouches."

Tarrick grabbed one of the leather chairs from in front of the fireplace and dragged it over to Matthew, stopping just outside the limit of the chains. He sat down and spread his arms to rest over the back. Matthew wished Tarrick wasn't half-naked. He looked powerful in this position, masculine.

Like a king before his slave.

Matthew dragged his eyes across Tarrick's athletic arms, his bicep twitched when he motioned his hand forward, indicating to Matthew to take a seat on the cot. His muscles were perfection.

Matthew sat.

"Young vampires have one pouch, maybe two if they were turned by someone strong or old. Vampire lords have—"

"Lord? Like how everyone calls you lord?" Matthew interrupted.

"No. Incubi lords and ladies are a title only. With vampires, it is an actual physical change that happens centuries into life. They become stronger, resistant to silver, and they tend to gain new abilities like masking or a transformation. Most grow wings."

"Vampires can have wings?" Matthew couldn't hide how excited that news made him. He wanted to ask what it was like to fly but Tarrick looked annoyed by the interruption. He'd ask later.

"Yes. And as I was saying, vampire lords—the term used for either gender—sometimes gain an extra blood pouch during their change. Most end up with two. I've fought a handful that had three. Those lords were some of the most powerful vampires I've ever faced."

"I remember in the forest, you said you thought I had two. That means I had a powerful sire?"

"You don't have two pouches, Matthew." Tarrick leaned forward. "You have four."

Matthew placed his hand on his stomach. "Four? That means what? That I'm stronger than other vampires?"

"You have the potential to be. How often did you feed when you were on your own?"

"Uh," Matthew stuttered, caught off-guard by the question. He didn't like talking about the times he had killed. "It was every night at first. Sometimes whole families if I could convince them to invite me in. It was terrible the first few years so I started to fight the hunger, now I only need to eat once a week or so." Matthew was proud of the fact that he could ignore the hunger for so long. He hoped in the future he could go even longer.

Tarrick frowned. "And when you finally do feed, did you feel compelled to do so, as if you had no choice in your actions?"

Matthew nodded.

"You need to accept the fact you are a creature that feeds on blood. You are starving yourself and, as a result, your back two pouches have collapsed. It can be reversed but it'll take some time, and you'll need lots of blood to do it.

"You are incredibly lucky your hunger didn't send you into a blood rage. Killing a family or two doesn't compare to the amount of death and destruction a vampire lost in the rage can cause. The danger of exposure to the humans by a raging vampire is so extreme that it's one of the few things vampires and incubi work together to stop. The last thing either side wants is a war with humans, which is probably what would happen if they knew we existed."

"But what about Emilia? She's gone without blood for a long time. Why hasn't she raged?"

Tarrick raised his eyebrow. "Emilia? Has she talked to you much?"

Shit.

He forgot she hadn't actually spoken aloud.

"No. I swear she only gave me her name and that was it. Please don't hurt her because of me." Matthew stood and strained against his chains. He wouldn't forgive himself if the woman was punished for his mistake.

"Why do you care what happens to her?"

"I don't know. I just do. Please don't punish her, it really was just her name. Otherwise, she stayed away from me. She's afraid of me." Matthew wished there was something he could do to convince Tarrick not to hurt her.

Tarrick didn't say anything. If he came to a decision, he wasn't going to let Matthew in on it.

"Why haven't you been feeding her?" Matthew asked. Tarrick had said he'd answer the question if he asked it.

"She has the rare ability to give humans nightmares while they sleep. It drives them mad. She was using it on my hunters. As for your question about her raging, I know how long a vampire can go without food. I keep her near the edge but I won't let her fall over it. And she's not strong enough to be a threat anyway." Tarrick pressed his fingertips together and rested his chin on them. "I won't punish her, and I'll even start feeding her again if you swear that you will ask me for blood each night."

That meant Matthew would have to humble himself before Tarrick every night. He didn't want to. He ran his hand across the cold metal shackles and closed his eyes as more control slipped away.

"I swear it." He didn't have to open them to know that Tarrick was grinning at him. Matthew couldn't stand it.

"Matthew," Tarrick said.

Matthew opened his eyes but kept them focused on the ground. He heard Tarrick stand and approach. The incubus placed his warm hand on Matthew's cheek and gently tilted his head up. Matthew considered attacking him now that he stood close enough but decided against it. He'd only get one, maybe two punches in before Tarrick stepped out of his range. Then he'd be at his mercy. It was clear Tarrick had centuries of practice in torturing vampires. He didn't want his situation to get worse than it already was.

Matthew found the hand against his face irresistible. He hated Tarrick for being able to sway him by a touch or a look. He hated himself for not being strong enough to resist him.

"It might not seem like it now, but everything I do is to try and help you."

"Why? You kill vampires. You torture them." Matthew spat out the accusations harshly.

"The four blood pouches make you special but it's not the only thing."

"What else is wrong with me?" Matthew asked. He wanted to move his head away from Tarrick's hand but he couldn't. He was trapped by the light, tender touch.

"I told you, there's nothing wrong with you. You are beautiful. You are impossible." Tarrick's lips curled up as he stroked Matthew's face. "You are an incubus."

Ten

Matthew's brain raced through a rapid series of emotions: shock, confusion, anger, disbelief. He broke away from Tarrick's touch and took several steps back until he ran into the cot and dropped down to it.

"What did you say?"

"You are an incubus," Tarrick repeated.

Impossible. He is a vampire. He feeds on blood, not sex. Before he turned he had a healthy appetite for it. Before he met his wife, he played the field but nothing extreme; his partners numbered in the single digits. He had a good sex life with his wife, Alyssa, but it wasn't like what an incubus had. Or at least what he imagined an incubus' sex life was like.

"I can't be."

"You are. Incubi have something called a *soavik* that, just like a blood pouch, stores the energy we gather when we feed. In English, many incubi call it a 'seduction gland' but I hate the name. You have a soavik. It's located in the center of your four blood pouches."

Tarrick stepped forward and sat on the cot next to Matthew. Again, he considered attacking Tarrick but he wanted answers as to who and what he was, and sitting next to Tarrick felt nice.

"Tell me about your parents," Tarrick said.

Matthew shook his head. "I was an orphan, abandoned at a hospital when I was only a few days old." Whoever dropped him off left him with nothing but a first name, and no other hint as to where he belonged. Most of his childhood he spent feeling like a piece of trash blowing around from home to home. But that was before he met his wife; before he had a child of his own. A child he abandoned in order to keep safe. Guilt flowed through him.

"I see. How old were you when you were turned into a vampire? Your human age."

"Thirty-two." Matthew ran a hand through his brown hair, the chain rattled as he did so. "I don't feed off sex. I don't have wings or horns, and I can't seduce a person like you can.

"We have a theory about that."

We? Who else knew? That red-haired succubus was one, were there others? Someone had mentioned a king…

"Incubi undergo a few major transformations in their life. The first is when they come of age. It usually takes place during the later teen years. We gain our wings, horns, claws, and so on during this time. We also learn how to glamor our bodies as a way of making ourselves more attractive to whatever human we're hunting."

"So, it's an incubus puberty. How old were you?"

"I was a completely average seventeen when I went through the change. I gained most of my power during my second and third transformations." Tarrick grinned and rubbed his fingers down Matthew's temple, across his ear, then down the back of his neck.

Matthew trembled.

"You have such wonder in you. Everything is new and fresh. Everything amazes you. It's something I don't see much anymore. You are unlike anything I've ever seen."

Was he? Or maybe Tarrick was just playing with him. Maybe this is how he broke the other vampires.

"We think, and mind you this is just a theory, that you were born an incubus and just after your transformation began a vampire turned you, freezing the transformation in its early stages. It means you have the soavik but none of our physical traits, which come towards the end of the transformation. Now, none of this should be possible since vampires can only turn humans into vampires but here you are."

"But you said the transformation happens in late teens, I was thirty-two."

"I said it *usually* happens around late teens. There have been a few notable exceptions. All of whom ended up becoming powerful incubi."

Matthew pulled up his shirt a bit and ran his hand across the faded scar on his stomach, where the doctor had cut him open. "Is my, uh, gland… normal?"

Tarrick rested his hand over Matthew's. "We won't know until it's active but our best guess is that, yes, your soavik is normal."

"How come I've never felt it?"

"Have you had sex since becoming a vampire?"

Matthew's face turned red thanks to the fresh blood flowing through him. Because, no, he hadn't had sex in years and he was sitting next to a creature that fed on it. Thankfully, Tarrick didn't force an answer.

"You never got far enough along in your transformation to experience the first hunger. It'll be hard to ignore once it awakens. I will teach you how." Tarrick moved his hand up and rested it on Matthew's abs.

Matthew wasn't sure he wanted to learn to use it. It'd just be another hunger he'd have to fight. "If a vampire hadn't come along and turned me, what would have happened to me?"

"That depends on who found you first after you transformed. If it had been a vampire, you would have been killed. If it had been us, you'd be taken in and assigned to a household. They'd train you and in exchange you'd serve them."

And what happens to someone who was both? Matthew looked at his chains and found the answer. Slave. "Would my family have come with me?"

"You had a family?"

"Yeah. A wife and daughter. She was eleven when I was turned. She'd be eighteen now."

"It must have been hard for you to lose them."

Matthew thought of the last moment he saw them the night he was turned. Alyssa was cooking dinner while helping Lily with her homework. They were blissfully oblivious to him. Just a normal night. "I wish I could go see them. But I'm too afraid they'd see me and I don't want to scare them. Besides," Matthew tugged at one of the chains connected to his collar, "I don't think I'm going anywhere anytime soon."

Tarrick looked confused. "They're still alive? You didn't kill them?"

Matthew glared at him. "Why the shit would I kill my own family?"

"When vampires are turned, one of the first things they do is feed from their former family. It's an evolutionary imperative that breaks them from their old life and strengthens the bond with their sire. What are their names? I'll look in on them for you."

Matthew looked down at Tarrick's hand on his stomach. Tarrick was doing it again. He hadn't wanted to say anything about his family. He wanted to protect them. But Tarrick was touching him and manipulating him again, making his secrets fall loosely from his lips. Matthew pushed Tarrick's hand off him.

Sensing Matthew's growing agitation, Tarrick stood and stepped back far enough that Matthew could no longer reach him.

Matthew growled. "I don't want you near them."

"I have some of the best trackers in the world at my disposal—"

Matthew lunged against his chains, his vampire aspect ripping forward. "Then use them! I'm not going to make it easy for you to hurt my family."

Tarrick stood his ground, only a few inches from Matthew. "I won't hurt them," he promised, keeping his voice low.

"I don't believe you. You'd hurt them to hurt me."

"Quiet your temper, Matthew."

"I'm not wrong, am I?" he yelled, straining against his chains.

"I don't need them to hurt you." Tarrick's expression was hard as stone.

Matthew wasn't listening. "Stay away from them!"

Matthew found the red strands of power within him and pulled them up to his arm. He punched his right arm forward at Tarrick; cracks appeared in the wall where the chain was connected.

Tarrick took a step back when he saw the wall begin to buckle. "Calm yourself, Matthew."

"No! I won't let you near them." He would not be calm, not while his family was in danger. He pulled up even more power and punched forward again. A large section of concrete and plaster exploded out of the wall, his chain still connected to a chunk of it. Matthew grabbed the chain and swung his arm forward, sending the block of concrete flying at Tarrick.

Tarrick tried to dodge out of the way but it caught him in the shoulder and sent him sliding across the room into the far wall.

With a snarl, Matthew tried to pry the collar off his neck. It wouldn't budge.

Already transforming into his incubus form, Tarrick stood slowly. His horns came forward and his eyes turned purple. He didn't bring his wings out, but even without them he looked downright terrifying.

"Attacking me was a mistake," he said as he grabbed a kanabō—a spiked metal club nearly five feet long—from off the wall, then strode towards Matthew. With each step he took, he grew taller and wider, his massive hooves pounding against the ground.

Desperate, Matthew pulled every strand of power he could find into making himself stronger and ripped the collar in two, tossing it aside. Then, he pulled against the second chain running from his other arm to the wall to try and break away from it, but he wasn't fast enough.

Tarrick swung his weapon.

Matthew sped out of the way, the kanabō missing him by a hair's breadth. He yanked his right hand in to pull the makeshift concrete flail back to him. He whipped his hand forward as quick as he could and sent it flying at Tarrick.

With exceptional grace, Tarrick dove forward and rolled at Matthew as the block soared over his head. He came to his feet and swung the kanabō into Matthew's ribs, the bone snapped under the impact of the blow. The sharp spikes, coated in silver, pierced his skin and he went flying backwards. He was airborne until the chain attached to his left hand ran out of slack and his shoulder was pulled from the socket as he yanked to a stop by the shackle. He hit the ground hard, belly down.

Agony.

Matthew cried out as he crawled to his knees. His body began to heal the ribs but he didn't have time to pop his shoulder back in before Tarrick was on him. Tarrick's heavy weapon cracked against Matthew's face, fracturing his skull and breaking his jaw. His head whipped to the side and he spat blood. The silver spikes melted off half the skin on his face.

Reaching within to find the strands of power, Matthew forced his body to heal the broken bones. Before Tarrick could hit him once more, he sprung to his feet, ignoring the pain, and he clawed at Tarrick's face, leaving behind five gushing wounds.

Tarrick grabbed Matthew's hanging arm and yanked it down. Matthew howled. He pushed away, but that proved to be a mistake as it gave Tarrick the room to swing at him again. He smashed the kanabō against his good arm, shattering the bone.

Then he kicked Matthew square in the chest with a hoof, sending him flying backwards and back down to the floor. With controlled movements, Tarrick raised the weapon over his head and drove it down into Matthew's stomach. Blood filled his mouth and sprayed the air as he coughed it up.

Matthew needed to heal. He reached down to find the power in him but he had nothing left.

Behind Tarrick, hunters teleported into the room. They watched as Tarrick brought his weapon down again and again, breaking Matthew's body.

Mercy. He tried to say it but nothing came out.

Tarrick had none.

He kept hitting Matthew with deliberate, calculated strikes until finally he brought the weapon down on Matthew's skull and darkness took him.

Eleven

Pain.

Every inch of him suffered. Matthew's body was shattered. It took him hours to even open his eyes the first night. He looked up and saw the ceiling of a jail cell. He couldn't move, not even enough to tilt his head up to look around. His senses were limited, he couldn't smell, and his vision remained blurry. He could hear, but not well; he suspected one of his eardrums had burst.

He felt a new collar around his neck, this one tight and heavy. He wore no shirt or shoes and uncompromising metal pinched his wrist and legs. At one point he heard screams. It took him a while to realize they were coming from him.

Blood.

He needed blood. He couldn't heal without any. Forced to lay in agony, trapped in his own body, he didn't even have the energy to slip out of his vampire aspect.

Time ticked by, but he had no idea how much. He wanted to keep count, but his mind was fuzzy and caused him to forget. Was it weeks? The only release he got was when he passed out, or when the sun rose and forced him to sleep.

He couldn't bear this.

****

Pain. Each night Matthew woke as soon as the sun set, and each night he desperately wanted to stay asleep. Being awake meant misery.

Tonight, when Matthew opened his eyes, Tarrick stood over him. He wore a suit and bore none of the injuries Matthew had inflicted.

Fear flooded Matthew and he struggled to get away from Tarrick, but he couldn't move.

Tarrick watched him for a while before he finally placed his hand on Matthew's chest. "Still yourself, young one."

A wave of calm flooded him and he didn't fight it. It was the first pleasurable feeling he had felt in weeks. Tears fell from the edges of Matthew's eyes.

Mercy.

Blood.

He would ask Tarrick for it, beg even. He would submit to any humiliation, if only he could get blood. He had no idea it could be like this. He had no idea the hunger could get this bad or that his body could be so broken and hurt.

He tried to speak but his words were garbled as if his brain couldn't put them in the correct order.

"I didn't want to hurt you this way. I shouldn't have let it get this far. Sometimes I forget what it's like to be young: rash, untrained, and out of control." Tarrick leaned into Matthew's good ear. "If you ever attack me again, you better make sure you kill me because this punishment is just a small taste of the pain I will unleash upon you. Blink if you understand."

Matthew slowly closed his eyes and reopened them.

"Good." Tarrick straightened back up, his hand still on Matthew's chest. "There are those who think I should keep you like this for a year or two. They think it'll make you pliable, but I don't want you broken. I want your fealty. And I think you've learned your lesson. Am I correct?"

Matthew tried to say 'yes' but only jumbled syllables escaped. He gave up trying to speak and blinked once.

Tarrick removed his hand from Matthew and disappeared from his view only to reappear a moment later with a bottle of blood. Matthew licked his lips and silently prayed Tarrick wasn't going to tease him with it.

Tarrick unscrewed the lid and slipped his hand under Matthew's neck to tilt his head up. With his other hand, he brought the bottle to Matthew's lips and tipped it, slow and careful.

Blood filled Matthew's mouth and a moan escaped. The thick liquid overwhelmed him as he swallowed and his body began to warm. His skin itched as the life essence began to heal him. One bottle wasn't enough. Matthew would need gallons to fully heal from such massive damage, but it might be enough to take away some of the pain and maybe even heal the head injuries making him unable to speak.

When he emptied the bottle, he looked up at Tarrick.

"Rest."

Matthew drifted to sleep as his body repaired itself.

The next night, Matthew could sit up with tremendous effort. Many of his bones were still cracked or broken, though his arm had been popped back into the socket. The skin that had been ripped off him began to grow back, red and tender. His senses were still dull.

He was in the cell at the end of the prison. He wore the same jeans as during the fight. They were ripped and sticky with putrid blood, with leg shackles clamped over them. The metal bracers on his forearms were long and tight, different than the shackles he wore previously.

Matthew couldn't do much more than sit up. At least his vampire aspect receded at some point. Claws made it hard to do anything with his hands.

The other vampires watched him from their cells. Had he been here the whole time? Had they heard him screaming? They didn't seem afraid of him anymore. Or, at least, they weren't cowering away.

He was sad to see that Emilia still looked thin and hungry. At least it didn't seem like Tarrick punished her beyond denying her blood. Would Tarrick keep his word and feed her if he asked for blood? He hoped he hadn't ruined that for her by attacking him.

Her defiant protector paced around his cell with new scars across his body. The second female had a long cut across her face that was healing. She watched from her bed but she looked blank, hollow. The other two males appeared just as empty as they watched Matthew.

Cullip entered the jail, accompanied by his team of five other hunters. The door to Matthew's cell unlocked and Cullip walked in. He unlocked the shackles around Matthew's ankles and tossed them out of the cage.

The shower turned on for his cell but none of the others.

"Undress," Cullip ordered.

Matthew wasn't sure he could manage it with his cracked left femur and shattered kneecap. He groaned as he pushed himself off the bed and to his feet, putting his weight on his right side. His hands ached as he struggled to push his jeans and underwear down.

"Shower," Cullip said once Matthew finally took his clothes off.

Matthew took a step for the shower and collapsed to the ground. He grabbed the edge of the bed and tried to pull himself up, but he wasn't strong enough and collapsed down again.

Cullip frowned as he picked Matthew up and set him down on the bed, then left the cell. He didn't bother to close the door behind him as he rejoined the group of hunters.

They seemed to be waiting for something, Tarrick most likely. The silence made Matthew conscious of just how naked he was. He teetered between not giving a shit because of the amount of pain he felt, and wishing something covered him. He rested his hands in his lap.

The hunters looked bored.

"Are you human?" Matthew asked Cullip, his voice strained. He wanted to know the answer, but he also wanted to see if he could speak again. He was pleased he could, but it took a lot of energy and left him feeling exhausted.

Some of the hunters chuckled.

"Yes," Cullip answered. Matthew was surprised he had. He assumed everyone in this damned place had orders not to talk to him or answer any of his questions.

"You're stronger than a human," Matthew said with some effort.

Cullip nodded but didn't offer any explanation. Matthew wanted to ask more but he began to tire. He closed his eyes and listened to the water falling from the showerhead. It relaxed him and made him drowsy.

When he opened his eyes again, Tarrick was standing in front of him. Did he fall asleep? He hadn't even heard him enter.

"It's good to see you up," Tarrick said with a smile, his blue eyes scanning up and down Matthew's body.

Matthew knew he looked terrible, bruised and raw with scars littering his skin. He didn't want to look this bad. Not when Tarrick looked so good right now, wearing wool grey pants and a white button-up shirt with his sleeves rolled up.

He chuckled when he realized that Tarrick was influencing him and didn't have the strength to fight it.

Tarrick raised an eyebrow. "What has you amused?"

"You. Me." Matthew sighed and his amusement turned into a crippling sadness. He didn't want to fight anymore. He was playing a game he didn't know the rules to. Each time he tried to resist, he ended up beaten and broken. He hung his head.

"He's enhanced by magic," Tarrick said, drawing Matthew's attention away from his thoughts.

He was confused until Tarrick motioned to Cullip, who was standing at the entrance of the cell.

"Show him," Tarrick said to the commander.

Cullip removed his bandolier of silver throwing knives and handed it to another hunter, then he unbuttoned his doublet and held it apart, exposing his chest. There were plenty of scars, but more prominent were the hundreds of runic tattoos that covered every inch of his skin.

They looked like they continued down his arms and to his back. Every now and then, one would grow green and fade away, just like he saw before in Tarrick's room.

A symbol that looked like two swirling lines encased within a circle inscribed just below his left shoulder began to glow and caught Matthew's eye. It flashed. Cullip teleported a few feet forward into the cage, next to Tarrick.

"Magic…" Matthew said under his breath.

"Each one holds a different spell. Unfortunately, vampires and incubi have a hard time using magic," Tarrick said, answering Matthew's next couple of questions before he had the chance to ask them. "Thank you, Commander."

Cullip nodded then began to button up his doublet as he went to get his weapons back.

"Do they all have them?" Matthew asked, looking at the other hunters. No wonder their outfits covered most of their skin. The green glow would stand out in the darkness of night.

"Yes, though not as many. It takes time to find the witches who can create and empower them. The commander has had over five hundred years to gather his."

Five hundred years? He didn't even look fifty. "But he's human…"

Tarrick smiled and began to unbutton his shirt. Matthew watched as his fingers worked their way down, revealing more and more of his tantalizing skin. "He is. I can extend his lifespan, and I do so because he is exceptional at his job."

Which was killing vampires. Matthew wondered just how he extended his life. Did he have to sleep with him? He thought about asking but became too embarrassed by the question, especially in a room full of hunters and vampires all watching him.

He forgot his question when Tarrick sat next to him, his arms rubbing against his. Matthew swallowed.

Jesus his skin felt good. Warm.

Tarrick took his shoes and socks off and carefully set them aside. What was he doing? Tarrick stood again, unbuckled his belt and took his pants off revealing tight boxer briefs that showcased his wonderful package.

If he wasn't in so much pain or so tired, Matthew would have been hard right now, but as it was, he doubted he could get it up even if Tarrick began licking his cock.

Mm. He wondered just how good head would be from an incubus.

Tarrick folded his pants and set them on the end of the bed with his shirt and belt. He put his hands under Matthew's armpits and gently pulled up. "Come."

With Tarrick's help, Matthew limped over to the shower. Each time he stumbled, Tarrick's strong arms tensed and kept him standing. Tarrick, who normally stood shorter than Matthew, was now a few inches taller. Could he shrink and grow at will?

The moment he entered the water, it began to run red as it washed the blood from Matthew's body. It felt good as the water warmed his cold skin. Closing his eyes, his worries seemed to melt away.

Tarrick left him for a moment, then returned with a bar of soap and stood behind him, wrapping an arm around his waist to make sure he wouldn't fall.

Matthew whimpered as the incubus worked up and down his back with the soap. Each pass over a cut or bruise stung, no matter how delicate the touch. Circling around, Tarrick cleaned every inch, making his way across the skin with precise, gentle strokes.

Matthew stood upright for as long as he could but he began to fade fast. His knees buckled and he collapsed forward into strong arms that gripped him tight enough to keep him from falling but not so tight as to crush his broken bones.

His head found the dip in Tarrick's shoulder and he sobbed into it.

"Shhh, young one, it will be okay," Tarrick said and planted a kiss on Matthew's forehead. Matthew could hear Tarrick's blood rushing under his skin and the quick, rhythmic beat of his heart. It was too enticing; both his upper and lower set of fangs came out. "I think these hunters will take issue if you try to bite me."

Here in Tarrick's arms, Matthew had forgotten about the hunters. He wished they were gone. "Can I have some blood?"

"'May I'." Tarrick corrected him.

He was such a damned perfectionist. Who the hell says 'may I' anymore?

Matthew tilted his head up and looked into Tarrick's blue eyes. "May I have some blood?"

Tarrick shifted Matthew's body so that he could hold him up with just one arm. He ran his free hand down Matthew's face in an affectionate gesture. "Master."

God no. He didn't want to call him 'Master'. He had sworn to himself he'd never do it, that he'd rather die than submit. But he didn't want to die. Matthew closed his eyes tight and his face twisted with pain.

Tarrick didn't rush him. They stood with the water running down them, their bodies close, as if he knew the internal struggle that Matthew was fighting.

Matthew's body began to tremble as every last bit of hope shattered inside of him. "May I…" Matthew lost his voice and it took him a few moments to find it again. "May I have some blood…Master?"

Tarrick had won. The last remaining shred of control Matthew held over his life slipped away.

Victorious, Tarrick leaned in and claimed his prize by kissing Matthew deep. His tongue slipped past his fangs and dominated his mouth with aggressive fervor.

The desire for blood began to overwhelm Matthew as the kiss ignited him. He tried to fight the inevitable attack but his vampire side took over. His claws came out and he slipped his arms around Tarrick to hold him in place…only to be yanked away and thrown into the silver bars of the cage, falling to the ground against them.

Pain blazed through his body and he growled in anger when he saw Cullip standing over him. The growl became a cry, too weak to move away from the bars burning into him.

Tarrick snarled at Cullip, upset that his prize was pulled from his arms.

"Sir, he isn't Matthew right now," he said and held his ground to his lord.

Tarrick scowled at his commander then looked down at Matthew who was struggling to move away from the silver. After a moment, Tarrick nodded to Cullip who, in turn, motioned an order to his hunters.

Matthew hissed at Tarrick when he slipped his arms under him and picked him up, cradling him. He brought Matthew over to the bed and set him down. He rolled him onto his side and pushed him over, leaving some empty room on the bed.

The next thing Matthew knew, a complacent human woman was lying with him. He wrapped an arm around her and licked her neck idly a few times before he bit into her soft flesh. It took him a long time to drain her of blood, and when he was finished he fell asleep with his fangs embedded in her flesh.

Twelve

The next night, Matthew woke to an empty prison. All the other vampires were absent from their cells, and the observation room was deserted.

Matthew felt better—still covered with cuts and burns, and sore all over, but his bones mended. As his senses returned to him, Matthew heard the heartbeats of hunters out in the hall, standing guard.

He got dressed in the clothes that were laid out for him.

Now that he wasn't crippled with pain, he could see that the metal bracers on his forearms had runic symbols etched into them. They didn't glow, but they reminded him of the ones he saw on Cullip's chest. The bracers were strong with no visible seams on them.

He played with the collar on his neck, it was thin, no more than a quarter of an inch thick and only a few inches tall, but it showed no signs of budging. It had a single loop in the back to attach a chain. He felt runes etched on it as well. He couldn't find a seam on this one either…did they weld the damn thing to him?

With nothing else to do, he lay down and rested.

Six hours after sunset Tarrick entered the room, wearing tan slacks and a light blue Oxford button-down. Other than when he was naked or in sleepwear, it was the most casual Matthew had ever seen him. On his belt rested a wooden stake and a silver bomb.

Tarrick looked somber. In his hand was a folder, thick with paper.

Matthew stood, hesitant to approach. Why was he armed? Why were his hunters waiting outside in the hall?

"Kneel," Tarrick commanded as he stood in front of the cage.

Matthew balled his fists and looked at the ground. For a brief moment, he considered rebelling but he wouldn't gain anything by it and he'd just end up back in pain. He lowered himself to both knees and bowed his head forward as he had seen the other vampires do whenever Tarrick entered.

"Kneel down on your left knee only. Rest your right arm on your right leg, your left fist should be on the floor. Keep your head bowed."

Matthew adjusted.

"Good. When I enter a room, you will kneel. You stay down until I, or someone who outranks me, tells you to rise. If you ever see me kneel, you do the same. Right now I only have one guest in this house that outranks me, but I will tell you when others show up. Do you remember the red-haired woman when you were in the infirmary?"

He could never forget her, she was the most alluring and repulsive creature he had ever seen. How is it she outranked Tarrick? He was a general, a warrior. She was no fighter. "Rosaline," he answered.

"*Lady* Rosaline. If you see her, you are to kneel to her. She is to be addressed as 'my lady'. Do you understand?"

"Yes." Matthew nodded.

"Yes, what?"

Matthew closed his eyes and clenched his jaw. "Yes, *Master*."

"I know you are still healing, but don't ask for blood. I'm not giving you any today. Raise your head, but stay on your knees."

He wondered why he would get no blood today when Tarrick had been so adamant about him feeding each night. Matthew looked up. "Why am I on one knee and not two like the other vampires?"

"Slaves and servants kneel on both knees. I don't want you to be a slave. Warriors kneel on their left knee and everyone else kneels down on their right knee."

Tarrick might call him a warrior, but the collar on his neck and the bracers on his arms showed what he really was. Then again, the bracers weren't shackles; they looked and felt more like armor. The collar, however, spoke volumes.

"So, I am to be your warrior? To kill vampires for you?" Matthew asked. Vampires had done nothing for him, but they hadn't hurt him either. He didn't want to kill his own kind.

"To kill anyone I order you to. Yes." Tarrick sighed. "But that might not come to pass, your ultimate fate is not in my hands, but rather those who outrank me in our society. I wield a great deal of influence but it has limits. You saw how Lady Rosaline reacted to you when she found out what you were, and her mind can't be changed. There are others like her, and right now the incubi are divided on what should be done with you. They are scared of the power you will one day wield. We need to win them over or you'll be executed."

Matthew didn't expect Tarrick to be so open, but maybe he should have considering Tarrick had always been straightforward every time Matthew asked a question.

"I wish you could see that I'm trying to save you," Tarrick said.

"Why? No one sees me as anything but a vampire."

"That's not true." Tarrick looked offended. He clutched the folder he was holding tighter.

Matthew felt a twinge of regret. Tarrick hadn't been kind to him, but he did see him as something more than just a vampire. He had recognized him as different that first night and told him what he was instead of keeping it from him. At the very least, he hadn't killed him yet.

"Yes you are a vampire, an impossible vampire, but you are also one of us. Incubi have always taken care of our own. We stand as one—that is one of the cornerstones of our culture. Or at least it used to be. It still means something to me, even if others have forgotten it."

Tarrick paced around the room as if deciding to admit something to Matthew. "I've spent most of my life locked in an endless war against vampires. We have truces from time to time, but they never last. I don't think you are some random happenstance. I think you exist to be a bridge between our two species.

"Maybe that means you can bring about lasting peace or maybe it means you'll force one side to submit through carnage, I don't know. But before we can find out, we need to make sure you survive. That does mean you'll be killing vampires—many vampires—to prove your worth to the incubi. Do you think you'll be able to do that?"

It was a lot to process. He noticed Tarrick wasn't pushing any influence on him and was thankful for it. It would just muddle his thoughts and make him resentful later. After the beating he took from Tarrick, he knew he couldn't afford to lose control again, but he had no idea how to command the beast within him—Tarrick did. He could teach him to tame his beast…and how to use *all* of his powers.

Matthew didn't have many choices in front of him. Resist and die or play this game and maybe live. It wasn't a hard decision. He had to be smarter this time. He would wait and learn to master all of his abilities. He would win over every damned incubus there was. He would kill any vampire that threatened him. He would become powerful…unstoppable. Then he would kill any who stood against him.

Matthew shot a devious smile at Tarrick. "Not if you keep me locked up…Master."

Tarrick looked thrilled. He smiled for a moment, then his face fell back to the somber look he wore when he walked in, as if he was trying to keep the mood as serious as possible. "We have little time. The High King wants you alive for now but the opinion of his court can sway his decision and the ones who want you dead are powerful."

"The High King?" Matthew asked.

"High King Malarath. He has ruled longer than I've been alive. There are other kings and queens all over the world but they all kneel to him. We'll start your training next week."

"Why wait?"

Tarrick ignored his question and instead asked one of his own. "You may rise. Have you examined your new collar and bracers?"

Matthew stood and rubbed his fingers across the runes on the bracer. "They're magical, aren't they?"

"Yes, and I need to warn you about them so that you don't inadvertently kill yourself. We had a witch weave several spells into them. If you compel anyone without my permission, you'll be punished. But, if you compel me, Commander Cullip, the High King, or his hunter commander, Imperator Prescott, the collar and bracers will explode."

Matthew stopped rubbing the bracer.

"The four of us are the only ones who can remove them. If you or anyone else attempts to remove them, they'll trigger the spells. You'll survive a bracer explosion, but your arms will be gone and those will take a while to grow back. You won't survive the collar explosion—it will take your head off."

Matthew liked his head right where it was.

"You shouldn't have to worry about them exploding during a battle, they are designed to take a great deal of punishment. Only the most powerful creatures could even attempt to take them off."

"'Shouldn't have to'?"

"Well, if the collar explodes, you won't be worrying about anything anymore," Tarrick teased. "There's also a tracking spell in it. If you try to run you won't get far."

Matthew was not amused. "Why not make these for all your prisoners?"

"Magic doesn't come cheap. The cost to have these made was tremendous and witches don't have an unlimited font of power. It's why we don't have vamp traps everywhere." Tarrick sighed and slapped the folder he was holding against his leg.

"Where are the other vampires?" Matthew looked around at the empty cages.

"I had them removed. I wanted to give you some privacy but didn't want you destroying my room again. I know you'll be angry at me for not leading with this, but I needed you to have a clear head on those other matters before we addressed this one."

White rage flashed through Matthew and his vampire aspect forced itself forward. He balled his claws into his hands, blood began to drop on the floor. "You found my family."

"Yes. I punished you for thirty-seven days. My trackers found them two days after you told me about them."

"Did you hurt them?" Matthew asked in an angry whisper. The desire to break out of this cage and strangle Tarrick flushed through him. It took every ounce of control he had to stand in place, his fists clenched and muscles trembled; strained.

"I told you that I would not, and I did not, but I do have some bad news." His eyes softened and he sighed. "Your wife died two years ago of cancer."

Matthew blinked. "What?"

"Alyssa Callahan had glioblastoma multiforme, a rare brain cancer. She fought it for a year before it took her."

"No," he couldn't accept this. She couldn't be gone. Not after everything he sacrificed to save her.

"Your wife is dead, Matthew," Tarrick said. He was firm. "I have her full medical report here if you'd like to read it."

"NO!" Matthew let out a heartbreaking wail and punched the cage doors. The silver burned him. He didn't care. He punched them again and again. They didn't budge; he wasn't throwing his strength into it. It wasn't satisfying. He reached deep and drew power to his fist and punched the bars one more time. The cage gave a few inches, leaving a dent, and it made him feel a little better.

Cullip and Silva teleported into the room, from out of the hallway. She had a crossbow ready while Cullip's hand rested on his silver longsword. Tarrick held up his hand as a command for them not to take action just yet.

Matthew took a few steps back and looked at his bleeding knuckles. "I should have been there."

"You couldn't have been. Leaving your family gave her five more years than she would have had if you stayed. Even if you didn't feel the need to kill her right after you were turned, your hunger would have put her in danger."

He was right. Humans were so fragile. All it would take was a split second of losing control and she'd be dead. Bloody tears began to fall from his eyes. He touched his face and looked at the blood on his claws. He had never bled from his eyes before. They didn't seem to want to stop.

Tarrick took a step towards the cage. "I've lost many mates and children over the years. I know this pain you feel. It is a pain with no equal."

Matthew didn't want to think about it. He didn't want to talk about it. If he did he'd go back to attacking the cage. "My daughter?"

"She went to live with her aunt in Oregon. She would have been starting Purdue next year."

"What do you mean 'would have been'?" Matthew snarled, flashing his large fangs.

Tarrick rubbed the back of his neck. "You're an incubus."

"So you've told me," he snapped. He wasn't in the mood for games.

"You are an incubus, Matthew," Tarrick said again.

Matthew growled and stepped up to the cage door. "I know, why the fuck do you keep saying—" He stopped. It dawned on him, "She's a succubus?"

"Which proves to us beyond a shadow of a doubt that you were born incubus. I removed her from Oregon—it's vampire territory. She's about to undergo her first transformation soon. If it happened while she was there, she would have been killed. Young, untrained succubi aren't exactly subtle."

God, if Tarrick hadn't found out about her, he might have lost his daughter as well. He couldn't have handled that. He was barely holding it together now. Every now and then an overpowering wave of grief rolled through him. He pushed it away and focused on getting information about his daughter. "Where is she now?"

"I've sent her to live with a friend of mine named Lord Teleclus, he lives in a safe territory on the east coast that rarely sees vampires. He's older than I am. A retired Spartan warrior actually, but he'll fight if he has to. He's powerful and can protect her."

Matthew would kill anyone that dare lay a hand on her. Teleclus, the Spartan…he committed the name to memory. He couldn't believe Lily was turning into a succubus. "He'll sleep with her?" he asked.

Tarrick smiled. "You are thinking like a human. Being with him is one of the best things that can happen to a young succubus. She can learn how to navigate our society without being thrown to the lions. And yes, he will teach her how to use her abilities. Your daughter is becoming a creature that feeds on sex, I hope you can come to terms with that."

Matthew raised his claws to his hair and scratched at his skull. "She's my baby girl. She's too young. And he's what? Jesus. Twenty-something hundred years old?"

"Twenty-five hundred."

He always thought he'd be chasing off teenage boys, not men that were over two thousand years old. All of it was out of his hands now, anyway. He didn't know what the transformation was really like for a succubus. He couldn't guide her even if he wanted to.

"Does she know about me?"

"No. I decided she shouldn't know because we do not yet know your fate. I think it would be cruel to give her father back only to take him away. She would resent us and she needs us right now."

Matthew nodded in agreement. "But don't a lot of incubi know about me? Is it possible she'll hear about me from them?"

"Only the most elite incubi and a few select hunters—" Tarrick motioned over to Cullip and Silva, "—know about you, all of which are under orders right now to not speak of you outside of certain circles. Breaking an order from our High King is a death sentence. No one will breathe a word until we decide the time is right."

That gave him hope. He wanted to see her again. He wanted to apologize for leaving, for missing so much of her growing up, and for not being there when her mother passed. He wanted to ask her for forgiveness.

"If you want to keep her safe, don't let the vampires know she exists."

"I won't. Is she…her mother was human…will she be a half incubus?"

"Ah, no," Tarrick said. "As long as one parent is incubus the child will become one too. My own father was human."

Matthew sat down on the bed and buried his face in his hand. Alyssa was dead. He'd rather Tarrick smash him apart than face this. He always hoped he'd find the courage to go back to her one day and try to turn her into a vampire so they could be together forever. "How is Lily handling it?" he asked, rubbing his eyes with his palms.

"She was a little shocked at first but she's handling it well, considering. She has your temper, thankfully not your strength."

"Did you personally go out and get her?"

Tarrick nodded.

He had saved his daughter. Matthew owed Tarrick more than he could know. "Thank you."

"You're welcome." Tarrick slipped the folder he was holding onto the floor of the cell. "There are photos of Lillian in the file. You start training next week. Be ready for it."

Thirteen

Matthew spent the remainder of the week alone in the prison tormented by grief. It came and went in waves. He'd be fine for hours, then he'd remember what his wife's laugh sounded like or her smile, and he'd be crippled by emotions. He'd cry until he had nothing left, then rage would fill him.

The first few nights he put four more dents in the silver bars surrounding his cage. Each time Cullip or Silva would enter, looking ready to knock him out in case he somehow managed to break the door down. He couldn't though; the bars were strong and he didn't have blood in him to draw upon. No wonder Tarrick stopped feeding him.

All of the attacking left him drained to the point where his knuckles no longer resealed the wounds after each outburst. They oozed what little blood he had left in him.

As the week went on, it got a little easier and he was able to keep his anger under control.

The photos of his daughter calmed him. They were recent and she looked so happy in each one. She had his brown hair, but her mother's big hazel eyes. One of the photos was of her with a swim team, another featured her at a baseball game with a boy, and the last showed her holding a fat orange cat. He studied them for hours, burning the images into his memory so he could never forget them.

When he woke the seventh night, his hunger was overwhelming. Going so long without blood, especially since he hadn't fully healed, proved to be hard on him.

He reached for the folder with the photos and his wife's medical file in it, but it was missing. He growled as he looked around for it, only to see the other vampires were back in their cells.

An hour after showers, Tarrick entered, wearing a suit again, accompanied by Silva and four other hunters. With them was a drugged-out looking human.

The vampires all kneeled. Matthew kneeled. The smell of the human caused each of them to lick their lips, their fangs down.

Tarrick walked to Matthew's cell.

"Ask," Tarrick said to Matthew.

"May I have blood, Master?" It didn't stick as hard in his throat this time. He wished it had.

"Yes, but in a moment. You may rise."

Matthew still had cuts and bruises covering his body and his knuckles were still seeping blood. He looked like shit but he didn't miss the flicker of hunger that crossed Tarrick's face as Matthew stood and rolled his shoulders back. Tarrick's eyes lingered on Matthew's shirtless chest. Guess he wasn't the only one who was hungry tonight.

Tarrick motioned to Emilia. "Get her out."

The hunters pulled her from her cage. She dropped to her knees in front of Tarrick, hunched over, head bent down. Matthew's heart broke, she looked so small.

A low growl came from the cage of her defiant protector vampire. "Be quiet, Stolus," Silva said to the vampire. His whole body tensed up and he stopped growling.

"I know that you gave Matthew your name, Emilia," Tarrick said. Matthew looked away from her in shame. He shouldn't have been so careless. Stolus narrowed his eyes at Matthew and curled up his lips in a silent threat.

Emilia trembled.

"Do not worry, vampire. Matthew persuaded me not to punish you, and you might even get blood again soon."

On hearing that she dared a glance up at Tarrick, longing for blood, and almost as quickly, she bowed her head again.

Silva came forward and grabbed Emilia by her arm.

"Go to the back of the cage," Silva ordered Matthew.

Matthew looked at Tarrick. "Do as she says."

He moved to the back of his cage. The door unlocked and Emilia was put in the cell with him. Then, the human was ushered into the cell.

Locked in together, Emilia looked terrified. Her claws were out, ready to strike at him if he came too close. Matthew stayed where he was.

Tarrick motioned to Emilia. "She is going to share a cell with you for a while and I will give you a human each night. You have to feed on it first and she can have whatever blood you leave behind." No...he couldn't feed on a human without draining it dry. "Do not give her any blood from your vein. Do not let her eat first."

Matthew took a step forward towards Tarrick, which earned him a growl from Emilia. "There will be nothing left for her, Master." He wasn't sure how often Tarrick wanted him to call him 'master' but it seemed to please him each time. And right now seemed like a good time to please him.

"You wanted to learn how to pull away from a human mid-feed. I told you it would not be easy."

"Is there no other way to learn this?"

"There are, but I've chosen this way," Tarrick said, his face serious enough that Matthew dared not fight him. Tarrick motioned to the human. "Eat."

Matthew didn't have to be told twice; he was far too hungry to resist. He ignored Emilia's growl as he raced up to the human and sunk his teeth into his neck. He heard Emilia move away, then everything around him faded as he pulled on the blood. He got lost in the sweet, irresistible taste. Power began to return to him and he pulled the blood into him faster.

As the man's heart began to slow, Matthew heard Emilia whimper and take a step closer to him. She wasn't going to get any of this. This blood belonged to him. A deep growl formed in his chest as a warning. He pulled the man a step away from her and kept drinking until he was done.

When he had taken it all, he let the man's body fall to the ground.

He forced claws and fangs away as he regained control of himself. Damn it. He hadn't even tried to stop during feeding. Smelling her distress, he couldn't bring himself to look at her.

"I'm sorry," he said.

Stolus snarled at him again, but fell silent when a hunter banged against his cell bars.

"We'll try again tomorrow," Tarrick said. The hunters removed the body from the cell while Tarrick gave blood to the other vampires. Then he left.

Disappointed with himself, Matthew thought maybe breaking a feed would be easier if he wasn't so hungry already.

After an hour, he was finally brave enough to look at his new cellmate. She was huddled in the corner, her knees to her chest and her head down.

Matthew spent the night sitting in the other corner of the cell, not wanting to panic her. He wished he knew exactly why she feared him. Could she sense his blood pouches? Or that he was an incubus? Or maybe she just knew he was different and that scared her.

"You can have the bed, I'll sleep on the ground," Matthew told her as day approached. She didn't acknowledge him. It didn't matter if she took the bed or not, Matthew would stay where he was. For some reason, he wanted her to like him, or at least not fear him. And he wanted her to forgive him for being weak.

He fell asleep first, back flat on the hard ground, and when he woke the next night he found she had moved to the bed. He was happy she had done so. Once she was up, she went back to the far side of the cell.

When the showers turned on it was a little awkward for him. She stripped and got under the water. Now that most of his wounds healed, he desperately needed to wash the dried blood from his skin, but he wasn't going to join her. Instead, he stayed put and averted his eyes.

She rinsed off and was out of the shower after only a minute. She wrapped a towel around herself and when Matthew looked at her, she motioned to the shower.

Since the shower would shut off soon, he was out of his clothes and washing in moments. She didn't avert her eyes. Matthew wasn't sure if she was watching him out of fear or longing. Maybe it was his blood she wanted, but he had a feeling it was something else. He hoped not. He wasn't going to sleep with a woman he couldn't even talk to.

During the feeding that night, Matthew was once again unable to resist his instinct to keep his prey to himself. He felt terrible, pathetic.

The next five nights were no better either. Emilia kept to her side of the cage and he tried to break feeding but was never able to. Stolus growled at him each time he failed to do so. He deserved it.

After another failed attempt to stop feeding on the sixth night, Cullip and his hunters stayed in the prison after Tarrick had left.

"We're moving you," Cullip said.

The hunters shackled him as usual, placing them right over the bracers. The chains were cold against his back without a shirt on. With all the feeding, his body actually felt warm for once, and his heart beat against his chest.

He had assumed he'd be going up to Tarrick's room again, but was surprised when they exited the ground floor. They passed human servants and other hunters as Cullip, along with his team of five, took him out a side door.

Dark and cold, the night called to him, and he took in a deep breath, letting the air fill his dead lungs. He wanted to run through the forest and hunt. Instead, he was pushed into a heavy black van waiting for them. Once seated, a hunter chained his collar to the reinforced siding. The hunters piled in and took the other seats.

"Where are you taking me?" Matthew asked.

Cullip knocked on the cage that separated the back from the driver. "You'll see."

Matthew looked out the back windows as they drove off, the gravel driveway crunching beneath the wheels. He could finally see where he was being held captive.

It was an impressive stone keep that rose four stories high with immaculately groomed and cared for grounds. It looked like it belonged in Europe, not the United States. Dozens of gargoyles sat frozen on the roof, covered by a light dusting of snow.

They passed through large iron gates connected to a stone wall that encompassed the entire estate. Matthew could sense hunters on patrol.

The drive was quiet; the dark road cut through an ominous forest. Ten minutes later they turned off the main road. For a brief moment he thought the car would crash into some trees, but they passed right through them. He was in awe.

"Magic?" he asked.

Cullip nodded.

Guess that's one way to keep people from accidently driving down your road.

A few moments later they arrived at another guarded gate. There was a large sign just inside that read 'Welcome to Ashwood VHA Pennsylvania. Est 1753.'

Beyond were five buildings. A main building in the center echoed Tarrick's stone keep, but with a story shorter and it looked more like a school than a home. Flanking it were two square buildings, appearing to be dorms. Another building also looked like nicer living quarters. The fifth building was a massive enclosed dome in the back.

As they drove in, Matthew saw training dummies, stables, an obstacle course...and he sensed hundreds, maybe a thousand, heartbeats nearby.

"Holy shit," Matthew said. "This is where you train hunters, isn't it?"

Cullip shifted forward. "One of the locations."

He frowned. He had no idea there were so many vampire hunters...

The van came to a stop outside the dome building. Two young hunters stood guard at the door. They saluted when Cullip exited and their hearts sped when they saw Matthew. They must be students.

Matthew was led inside and he could hardly believe what he saw: an arena. The large dirt area in the middle had maybe a hundred hunters training. They were broken apart into smaller groups; mostly empty seating surrounded it.

Cullip ushered Matthew up the stairs and to a platform with a good view of the arena below. Matthew saw his destination—a silver cage, only a few feet wide but at least ten feet tall. Chains hung inside of it.

"If you feel the need to try and escape tonight, please do so. I'll give the kid who drags your ass back here a pass on their finals," he said as he removed the shackles and pushed him in.

What a dick. Matthew didn't respond, but he wanted to punch the magically enhanced human in the throat and collapse his windpipe.

"Hands up."

Matthew raised his hands and Cullip chained them. They were loose enough that Matthew's feet touched the ground but tight enough that he wasn't going anywhere.

Cullip and his team left Matthew hanging with nothing to do besides watch the hunters training below. There were seven groups of twelve and each had an instructor leading them in different tasks. One group practiced hand to hand combat while another completed pushups.

Matthew received curious glances from the group looking the greenest. Had they never seen a vampire this close before?

A few hours passed and no one came for him. Matthew closed his eyes and reached out with his senses. He extended his hearing and was surprised to find there were many levels below the arena. He listened and could hear slow heartbeats.

Vampires.

Nearly a hundred of them.

He guessed that made sense, hunters had to be trained somehow, but it also made him a little sad knowing so many vampires were imprisoned here. He spent the night watching the hunters train. He was happy for it; it gave him something to think about other than his wife. As the night went on, teams left and new ones filled the space. Matthew mused that they must spend most of their time awake at night and sleep in the day to mirror vampires.

Two hours before sunrise, Cullip and his team returned and brought Matthew back to Tarrick's keep. Matthew had no idea what the hell any of this was about and he didn't really feel like asking Cullip about it; his answers always left him wanting more.

Walking down the mirrored hallway, Cullip and his hunters led Matthew past the door to the prison cells and into one at the end of the hall. Matthew gasped when he entered the room.

It was a torture chamber for vampires.

Chains hung from the ceiling, stakes and silvered weapons lined the wall, there was a table with restraints on it, and a cabinet full of alchemical items. Laying out on a rolling tray were dental pliers, silver cutting instruments, clamps, and saws.

It looked clean, but Matthew could smell old blood under the scent of bleach. Cullip pulled his arm forward but he didn't budge. He didn't want to enter this room.

"Did I do something wrong?" Matthew asked, his eyes creased with worry.

"Move or I'll force you to move," Cullip said and pulled on Matthew's arm again.

Matthew reluctantly moved to the center of the room. Panic spread as Cullip chained him and used a crank to reel him up. Once Matthew was hanging a few inches off the ground Cullip locked the crank in place and ordered his hunters to wait outside. After the door closed, he removed a bullwhip from the wall, along with a bucket, which he poured a brown liquid into. He dipped the whip into the bucket.

"I'm going to ask you a series of questions," Cullip finally said. "For every one you get wrong, you'll be whipped. Understand?"

He understood the concept, but not why this was happening.

"How many hunters were in the arena when I first put you in there?"

There were seven groups of twelve hunters, plus their instructors. Also Cullip and his team. "Ninety-seven," Matthew answered.

Cullip walked around to Matthew's backside and the whip came down on him with a *crack*.

Matthew screamed. The brown liquid felt terrible. The wound burned worse than silver and it seemed to slow his healing.

"A hundred-and-three," Cullip corrected him. "There were two hunters watching in the stands along with four guards stationed inside the ring. One of the cadets was cut, what was his name?"

Matthew remembered the kid getting cut, the blood smelled wonderful. He got stares when his fangs came down but put them away as quickly as he could once the cadet had been dismissed to go to the infirmary.

"I don't know," he said and braced himself as the whip cracked against his back. He cried out again.

"Williams, it was said many times. How many above ground stories did the main building have?"

"Three." Matthew winced.

"Correct. What is the name of my team of hunters?"

Matthew had no clue. The name had been said over the comms the hunters wore but there was so much chatter out of those things Matthew tuned it out. He started to replay the night in his head, hoping to come up with the name. Moments later he was roaring as the whip split his skin.

"My team is called the Wardens. We're Tarrick's personal bodyguards and the highest-ranking hunters currently at Ashwood. 'Ashwood' is both the estate and academy."

Cullip asked Matthew twenty questions total. By the end of the session, Matthew had received eighteen lashes. When he was let down from the chains, he slumped to the ground and the hunters dragged him back to his cell.

They threw him in, belly down.

He didn't bother moving and instead went to sleep right where they left him.

Fourteen

Each night Matthew was dragged to Ashwood VHA and placed in the small cage. Near sunrise, Cullip asked his questions. At first, Matthew only got a few answers correct each session. Then, as he focused on the details of the evening, he got better. And the questions got harder.

Cullip asked him things like, 'What was the hair color of the driver?' or 'List the weapons the guards had on them.' There were hundreds of hunters he studied each night. He memorized them and their actions; he even started to learn their names. It wasn't just hunters either, he had to memorize each person he passed on his way to the training facility and back. He was whipped for failing to notice how many flowers were in the vase a maid was carrying.

A week later, Matthew could answer most of the questions.

His observational skills were improving, but each night he still had four or five lashes on his back he had to focus on and heal. The brown liquid coating the whip slowed his natural healing, making him even hungrier than normal and greedy for the human he was given.

Fifteen nights. It took fifteen nights before Matthew successfully broke away from a human while feeding. It wasn't easy for him, but he was sick of the vampire ruling him and not the other way around. And he was tired of seeing Emilia so hungry and scared.

Finally, Matthew removed his fangs from the human male's neck. It was painful and he wanted to sink them back in right away. All of his nature told him to finish the feed.

But he resisted. The human in his arm was weak, his heartbeat slow, and there wasn't as much blood left in him as Matthew would have liked. He held the human forward to Emilia. She wouldn't come close to him while he was holding prey, so he set the man on the bed.

She was on him the moment Matthew took a step away. Her fangs dug into the human's neck and she drank deeply.

"Well done, Matthew," Tarrick applauded, watching from just outside the cage, as he did each night.

Matthew smiled. "Thank you, Master." He hoped he could do it again tomorrow, and earlier, too; she needed a lot more blood.

"Cullip tells me that you were able to answer the majority of his questions last night," Tarrick said. "I think it's time we started to teach you how to actually fight."

Cullip, who was standing at his usual spot behind Tarrick, nodded in agreement.

Matthew wondered when Tarrick would be teaching him how to use his incubus abilities but he wasn't going to ask here, not with so many around who didn't know about him.

Tarrick paced back and forth, his hands behind his back. "Tomorrow we're going to assess what you can do."

Matthew flashed a playful smile. "Getting my ass handed to me by you and the commander is not enough of an assessment?"

Tarrick chuckled.

Over the nights, he wished he'd been placed back into Tarrick's room, if only to be closer to the incubus. He'd sometimes catch the general's eyes wandering to his abs...and lower. Matthew wished it was Tarrick's hands and not his eyes tracing his abs...and lower.

His feelings might just be Tarrick's influence on him, but he stopped caring. The more Tarrick liked him the more he'd trust him and teach him what he wanted to know.

Matthew's plan was still firm in his mind. He'd learn everything he could from the incubi then he'd defeat anyone who threatened his freedom. It would take him years, maybe even decades, but he had time. He was immortal after all.

"We have something else in mind. Something a little more on par for your skill level," Tarrick said but didn't go into details.

Matthew laughed and put his hand to his heart. "Ouch."

An incubus entered the room. Matthew hadn't seen many incubi, though he could feel them in the building. The house usually had fifteen of them at any given time, and there were more at the academy.

He was flawless, expected for an incubus. He shared the same features as Tarrick: dusty blond hair, dark blue eyes, and a strong jaw, but he was thinner and maybe a few years younger—they looked like brothers, except he wore stylish jeans and a t-shirt with a jacket over. Matthew couldn't imagine Tarrick in jeans.

The other female vampire in the room let out a whimper when he entered. A cruel smile formed on the incubus' lips and she cowered back. He must be Lord Tane. He was the only incubus that called the female vampire to him, and she always returned cut up. Matthew suppressed a growl.

"Did you need something, father?" the incubus asked.

Tarrick's son? That was shocking. Matthew had planned to kill him at some point for what he was doing to the vampire woman but he needed Tarrick to be on his side. Not to mention, Tarrick saved his daughter's life. Killing the general's son in return was no longer an option. He'd have to find some other way to punish Tane.

Tarrick motioned to Matthew. "I need you to scan him and tell me the status of his blood pouches."

Tane frowned. "He can't just feel them and tell you?"

Tarrick looked annoyed. "Do as I order, Tane."

"Yes, sir," Tane said, with the slightest hint of mockery in his voice. He motioned to the hunters. "Get him out of there."

Matthew turned and stuck his hands through the gap in the bar and the hunter cuffed his hands behind his back. The door opened and he stepped out.

Tane walked up to him and put his hands on Matthew's abdomen. He looked so much like Tarrick, but he didn't feel anything like him. His hands were colder and the movements against his skin were rough. Even his smell was wrong. Matthew didn't enjoy his touch even a little.

A deep growl began to rise up in his chest.

"Your plaything is making it hard for me to scan him," Tane said as he pressed his hands harder against Matthew's flesh.

"Stop it, Matthew," Tarrick said, his voice thick with warning.

With some effort, Matthew stopped.

Tane closed his eyes and Matthew felt the same echoing sensation that happened when Rosaline had scanned him. He opened his eyes and removed his hands. "They're healing but it'll be a month before he can actually start using them. His healthy ones are full right now. Is that it? I have a party to get to."

"Yes. Have fun tonight," Tarrick said, but Tane was already walking out the door.

Cocky bastard. It appeared Cullip shared the opinion by the frown that shot across his face.

Matthew went back into his cage. The hunters took time to clean up the dead body lying on the bed. Emilia was back in her corner.

"You won't be going to the academy tonight so get some rest," Tarrick said and left with the hunters.

Matthew sat down in his corner, his head bowed down between his knees. The past few weeks had been rough on him. Learning about his wife had been devastating, and while he managed to hide his grief from the other vampires, it hadn't been easy.

He hated these cages. He hated that the other vampires got punished for talking. It made the nights so boring. He sometimes reached out and listened to others in the building. He'd catch snippets of conversation, but it was hard to listen in if the person talking was moving around.

He suspected that some of the rooms had some sort of magical ward on them. He'd be following the sound of a person's heartbeat then abruptly he couldn't hear any noise from them as they entered a room. Tarrick's room was one of those.

Tonight Matthew was listening in on the hunters in the hallway. They were usually quiet while on guard duty but sometimes they'd idly chatter. There was some big blockbuster movie that had just hit the theaters and they were talking about it. Matthew had only been to one movie since he turned. The screen hurt his eyes and sitting close to so many humans for two hours was nearly impossible for him to manage at the time.

His eyes snapped open when he felt a hand brush across his face. Emilia was standing in front of him. She cupped her hand to his cheek. Matthew looked up into her brown eyes. She was looking better already.

"I'm sorry it took me so long," Matthew said. "I hope you know that I was trying."

She nodded.

Her hand felt good on his face. He leaned into it. Her touch reminded him of Alyssa and the way she could comfort him with just a brush of her hand.

Matthew fought back tears.

Emilia grabbed Matthew's arm and tugged on it. He stood. She led him over to the bed and made him lay down on his side. She slipped down into his arms and spooned against him. He put his arm around her stomach and pulled her closer.

He didn't know why she was doing this now after weeks of fearing him, but he didn't care. It was nice to hold someone in his arms. They stayed like that all night and slept that way during the day.

The next night's feeding went better; he pulled his fangs from the human woman when he had only taken about a quarter of her blood. Phantom pain rolled through his body, burning his muscles, encouraging him to continue drinking. He pushed it away and set the human down on the bed.

Emilia was drinking from the woman before he even let her go.

Tarrick looked pleased. He was wearing a knee-length embroidered grey jacket with big, shiny black buttons. Underneath, he wore a white button-up shirt and tight black trousers that were tucked into tall, polished riding boots. It looked like a uniform.

"It's good to see yesterday wasn't a fluke. Normally a vampire your age can't do that without their sire present. You really are remarkable."

Pride swelled within Matthew. He couldn't help it.

"Tonight you're going to fight some vampires," Tarrick said and motioned for the hunters to prep Matthew for travel. "It's not going to be a sparring match either. They've been promised their freedom if they kill you. Do not leave them alive."

Matthew had never fought a vampire before, let alone killed one. He didn't want to, but he knew this was coming when he submitted to Tarrick.

Tonight he was in black tactical pants, a white tank top, and black boots. It was the first time he was given something other than jeans. The hunters shackled his arms behind his back and put his legs in irons. Once he was out of the cage, Tarrick put a hand on his shoulder. It felt good.

"I have confidence that you will perform admirably tonight, but there will be a few watching that do not believe in your abilities. You need to prove them wrong."

Just who was going to be there? He assumed he would be fighting in front of Tarrick, Cullip, and maybe a handful of hunters. He hoped it wasn't Tane or Rosaline—both made his skin crawl.

"I won't let you down, Master."

Outside, Matthew was placed into the van and joined by the Wardens while Tarrick entered a limo; Matthew could sense three other incubi in there with him. There were two other cars, both full of hunters, forming their caravan. Ten minutes later they arrived at Ashwood Academy, and Matthew couldn't believe what he sensed. Every building was nearly empty, except for the arena...because everyone was there.

More than everyone.

He sensed thousands of heartbeats, easily double of what was normally around.

This wasn't some assessment, this was an exhibition and he was the one on display.

"You have got to be kidding me," he said under his breath.

The limo went around to the front of the building while the van pulled up to a side entrance. Cullip ordered the other hunters and the driver to clear out. He waited to speak until they were alone.

"The Lord General didn't want to do this yet but he has less time than he initially thought. Your goal tonight isn't just to kill the vampires, but to put on a show." He unhooked the chain connecting Matthew's collar to the van. The commander giving him advice surprised Matthew.

"I'm not sure how I'm going to be able to do that. I haven't exactly won my last few fights."

"That's because you lost control in those fights. You are going to be outnumbered and out armed. If you lose control this time, you will lose the one advantage you have—your ability to adapt. But, I wasn't talking about the fight."

"Then what the hell do you mean?"

The commander didn't answer. Instead, he smirked as he pulled Matthew from the car. "Keep your head, vampire."

That was the plan. His only plan actually.

Cullip escorted him into the building and through the passageway leading to the arena. The smell of so many humans in the auditorium overpowered him. The air buzzed with excited energy. With everyone talking, the loud noises would make it near impossible to rely on sound during the fight. Cullip pulled Matthew to a stop just outside of the door leading into the fighting area. Runes lined the frame.

"Don't try to jump out of the arena. There's a vamp trap separating it from the audience," Cullip warned while a guard removed Matthew's leg shackles. Cullip raised the back of his gloved hand to his mouth and spoke into it, "He's ready to come out."

"Go ahead, Commander," Tarrick's voice replied.

Cullip opened the doors and light flooded them. Matthew swallowed hard and stepped out into the show.

Fifteen

A sea of hunters filled the oval arena. Most wore black leather uniforms, each one uniquely designed to fit an individual hunter's fighting style, while the rest were in cadet outfits or street clothes.

At one end of the arena stood two platforms. One had an empty throne with ornate chairs flanking it, also empty. The other platform, situated closer to the arena, sat Tarrick in the center of it, surrounded by incubi. Lady Rosaline was to his left, and a large, dark-skinned man sat to his right. There were ten others sitting on the platform, including Lord Tane who had a human on his lap.

Matthew sensed at least forty more incubi scattered in the stands. Non-lords and ladies, maybe.

The audience hushed.

Matthew felt self-conscious as all eyes landed on him. Jesus, what were they expecting? He didn't know how to fight, not really.

Cullip removed the shackles from his arms and teleported up to the platform, standing behind Tarrick. Matthew rubbed his bracers. He really hoped Tarrick was right and they wouldn't explode during a fight.

Closing his eyes, he reached out with his senses, but all the humans so close made it hard for him to pinpoint anything. His nerves weren't helping.

The hairs on the back of his neck began to tingle. He snapped his eyes open and surged forward as a sword swept the air behind him. The crowd went wild with excitement.

Matthew stumbled around to face his attacker: a male vampire, with long ashen hair and sunken eyes. In his hand was a silvered longsword. He darted to the left then right, moving so fast he blurred. He slashed twice; the first shallow stroke sliced Matthew across the chest. The second cut deep into his shoulder.

Matthew tried to back away before a third hit, only to have a bolt sink into his thigh. That's when he saw what he was facing: four vampires total, three males, and one female. They all looked hungry with long fangs and claws and irises burning red.

What the fuck was Tarrick thinking? He had never fought even a single vampire, let alone four. This was hardly 'on par' with his skill level.

Threatened, Matthew's fangs and claws came forward. He growled and pulled the silver bolt from his leg while trying to dodge more sword swings.

One of the vampires—a hulk of a beast that looked like he belonged in pro wrestling—let loose another bolt from the crossbow he held. Matthew sidestepped it only to get sliced in the arm again.

The third male vampire, moving fast, flanked Matthew. The vamp clawed him across the back. Matthew let out a howl as the wounds stung with sharp pain. He whipped around to see the vampire retreating. This one was wearing gloves with clawed metal tips at the end, coated in the shit that slowed his healing.

Fuck.

The poison would be a problem. He needed to be able to heal. Matthew avoided another bolt and a thrust of the sword, only to come face to face with the female vamp.

Her thin lips twisted into a grin as she flicked her long fingers at Matthew. Some sort of kinetic blast hit him hard and he went flying into the invisible vamp trap, hitting it with a painful *thwack*. Some of the audience members flinched away as he slammed into the force wall and slid to the ground.

What the hell? Vampires could do that?

As Matthew made it to his feet, he watched all four vampires stalk towards him. Pinned against the wall and outmatched, he felt lost. All four had hurt him in some way and he hadn't even touched one.

The metal-clawed vampire launched himself forward and ran his claws across Matthew's chest. Deep, red ribbons of blood bloomed across his white tank top, joining the sword wounds. He swiped at the vamp but he was already gone.

The vamp came at him again, clawing him as he rushed by, and retreating before Matthew could react.

A desperate idea came to Matthew. He pushed power into his arm, strengthening it, and when the metal-clawed vampire came at him a third time, Matthew readied. He punched the vamp in the chest as hard as he could.

His fist met flesh and bone and blood.

The audience gasped.

Matthew smiled as he looked down to see the vampire impaled on his arm, still alive but not moving. He pulled his arm out of the vampire and before it could hit the ground, Matthew grabbed the vamp's chest and jaw and pulled them apart, separating the head from the body. The body began to decay right in front of his eyes.

His roar of victory cut short when another bolt hit him, this time on the side of his neck. Matthew wailed and pulled it out.

Before he could come up with any sort of plan to stop the vamp with the crossbow, another blast from the female hit him. This time he went flying down the length of the arena, slammed into the dirt and tumbled across it until he slid to a stop.

He stood and looked at what he was facing. The woman stayed in the back, behind the two remaining males. The vampire with the sword advanced, and the big vampire with the crossbow reloaded and fired again.

This time, Matthew snatched the bolt from the air and the next as well. The silver burned into his palms and he dropped the bolts at his feet. Frustrated, the big vampire tossed the crossbow aside and joined the advance. He looked like he was better with his fists anyway.

Matthew had two bolt wounds, burned palms, bruises, claw marks across his chest, arms, and back that he couldn't heal right now, and he was covered in dirt. This wasn't much of a show so much as a beating. He got lucky with the vampire he killed, but there were three more and none had a scratch on them. He needed to even this up *and* he needed to find a way to impress these incubi.

He saw the woman bring up her hand again for another attack.

Fuck that.

Matthew pushed the red strands of power into his speed and he began to move so quickly that it seemed as if the entire world froze around him. Even the other vampires looked as if they were moving in slow motion compared to him.

He couldn't keep this up long, it was burning away a lot of blood… blood he needed for the rest of the fight.

Not wasting any time, he weaved through the two males, who were nearly on him, and grabbed the woman, pressing her against the wall of the arena. He stopped using up blood energy and the world resumed to normal. To a human, and even to these vampires, it looked as if Matthew teleported from one end of the arena to the other.

The vampire gasped and struggled to get away from him, clawing at his arms. He ignored it and looked into her eyes.

"Stop fighting me. Kill the big one instead," he said as he compelled her.

He could feel his will overtaking hers and knew she was under his command. He let her go and she marched towards the large male. That evened up the odds a little, two on two. He noticed the audience quieted...not a good sign.

No one had told him he couldn't compel tonight; they should have if they didn't want him to use the ability.

He watched as the woman tossed the large man across the arena with a flick of her wrist. Matthew turned his attention to the vampire with the sword, who leered and rushed forward. He was fast. Matthew ducked under his blade and shifted back as another strike came at him.

He wasn't sure how to counter a sword without a weapon of his own. All he could do was twist and dodge the attacks, but he couldn't keep this up. His wounds were bleeding profusely, refusing to heal. Sooner or later, the vampire would get a hit in.

It was sooner.

The sword made contact with his forearm, burning him. He reeled back, leaving himself open for attack. The vampire lunged forward with lightning quick speed and sliced the inside of Matthew's upper arm then followed it with a large, burning gash across his hip.

The vampire swung again and Matthew blocked it with his bracer, a resounding *clang* filled the air. No explosion. He was thankful for that, at least.

He rushed at the vampire and tried to punch him in the jaw but the vampire clawed him across the face and drove the silver longsword into Matthew's gut. He looked down to his abdomen and saw copious amounts of blood pouring out from around the sword.

Damn it. The fucker pierced one of his blood pouches.

Matthew was out of time. He wouldn't last much longer. Not with this blood loss. He needed to take this guy down—*now.*

The vampire tried to yank the sword out of Matthew, but Matthew grabbed the hilt to keep it in place, then dodged a punch from the vamp. He stepped into him, grabbed his arm, and snapped the vampire's wrist.

As the vampire recoiled, Matthew pulled the sword out of his own belly and swung. He sliced the vampire across his neck, spraying blood in the air, and before the vampire could heal, Matthew finished the job with another swing. The body fell away from him.

He let out a thunderous roar and the crowd went wild.

At the other end of the arena, his compelled female tossed the big vampire around but Matthew's control of her waned as he lost blood. Even worse, he was losing control of himself. His mind clouded and the desire to revel in blood overwhelmed him.

No.

He couldn't let himself fall to it. He'd become a wild thing, and he'd lose the fight. God. How can he control himself when he was this hungry and the scent of blood was everywhere? He froze in place as he struggled, pushing away the haze—it worked…for now. But he was having trouble keeping the female under his command and she stopped attacking the other vampire.

No longer pinned, the big-ass vampire rushed at Matthew, who tried to react but was too slow—the vampire slammed into him. Matthew lost hold of the sword and fell to the ground, rolling across the dirt.

Before he stopped sliding, the massive vampire was on his ass—moving far faster than anything that large should have been capable of moving. The vampire grabbed Matthew, lifted him above his head, and threw him back on the ground so damned hard that Matthew bounced.

The vamp raised his foot to stomp down into Matthew's midsection, but he rolled out of the way.

Using the last strands of power he could find, Matthew channeled them into his leg and slammed his heel into the vampire's knee. The knee bent backwards and the vampire howled.

Matthew got to his feet and dug his claws into the vampire's neck, pushing past ligaments, muscles, and veins. He grabbed hold of the spine. Yanking as hard as he could, he pulled the spine out of the vamp's body. The creature collapsed and began to decay.

Cheers erupted from the stands.

Bloody and dirty, Matthew limped over to the woman, who stood in place, still trying to fight the compulsion. He grabbed her shoulders and put his lips on her throat, his fangs scraping her soft skin.

"Matthew," Tarrick's voice rose above the noise. Everyone fell silent. Even with the thousands of people here, a pin could be heard dropping. Matthew halted, but he couldn't take his eyes off her neck.

"Did I give you permission to take her blood?" Tarrick asked, his voice severe.

He lowered his head. The shame of being reprimanded in front of such a large audience humiliated him.

"May I have her blood, Master?" Matthew asked. He was so hungry.

"No." Tarrick's harsh answer echoed across the arena.

Matthew glared over his shoulder at Tarrick who stood on the edge of the platform. He was torn between taking her blood or following Tarrick's command. Then, he heard Cullip whisper 'submit' under his breath, so quiet that he was the only one in this entire arena who could have possibly heard it.

What Cullip told him back in the van made sense now—*this* was the show, not the killing or the fighting. It was the submission after, to demonstrate he could be controlled; that he wasn't a threat to the incubi.

He set the woman down on her knees and in one smooth motion, kicked up the sword he lost earlier into his hand and beheaded her.

Matthew threw the sword onto the ground in front of him so it stuck upright in the dirt, and he kneeled down facing towards Tarrick's platform, clutching the wound on his belly.

"You fought well, Matthew."

"Thank you, Master," he said, keeping his head bowed.

"You managed to surprise me tonight."

"How so, Master?"

"Did you know vampires are unable to compel other vampires?"

Matthew glanced back at the woman, her body sinking in on itself. He smiled. Another power he possessed others did not. "I can't say I agree with that statement, Master."

A few chuckles rose up from the crowd.

Then he heard it. Screams. He stood and took a few steps to his right.

"Did I tell you to rise?" Tarrick asked, annoyed.

"Forgive me, but your hunters are dying."

In an outline of green light, Cullip appeared beside him. "What do you mean?"

"The group of six on patrol in the forest to the west only has four now. Their hearts are racing."

Cullip raised his hand to his mouth. "Walla, report." There was no answer. "Dispatch open Ashwood Yellow's comms." Screams and panicked commands came through Cullip's communication device. He pressed the top of his glove and the sounds were cut off. He pointed at two veteran hunters in the audience. "Sine. Price. Go." Two teams of six hunters stood and teleported out.

"It's three now," Matthew said.

"How many vampires?" Cullip asked.

Matthew didn't get a chance to answer as alarms began to sound. Loud and piercing. He put his hands over his ears from the pain.

Around him the whole audience was moving. Instructors were ushering newer students to safety, while some hunters were teleporting from the building, and others took up defensive positions around the incubi. The warrior incubi were taking off their shirts and arming themselves.

Matthew fell to the ground and rolled onto his back, still clutching his ears. The shrill of the alarms became too much. He didn't know how to block it out. His body shut down from hunger and pain. He doubted he could move anymore.

He watched as a section of the roof exploded, leaving behind a massive hole. Concrete and dust rained down around him. A body dropped down into the arena, its face shredded beyond recognition, but the black leather outfit told him it was a hunter. Then a vampire appeared, hovering above the roof with massive grey bat-like wings.

A lord.

She was beautiful.

Her hair silk black, her skin pale as snow, her lips stained red with blood.

She looked down at Matthew. No, she looked *into* him, as if she could see every part of him. As if she could see his soul, assuming he had one anymore. The strangest sensation spread within him.

Soon. The word appeared in his head. She was a telepath, like Emilia.

The lord smiled and she flew away as hunters teleported up to the roof. They shot silver chains at her but she avoided them, all as if they were a minor nuisance at best. Matthew saw Tarrick and three other incubi unfold their wings and fly after her.

Cullip, who had been calling out orders the entire time, stood above him. "Sorry, Matthew," he said as he drove a wooden stake into his heart.

Sixteen

Matthew was real tired of getting knocked out. Waking up disorient-ed and unaware of his surroundings felt terrible. He opened his eyes and panicked for a split second, then realized he was on the foldout cot in Tarrick's room.

Once again, chains ran from the wall to his shackles and collar, but with plenty of slack. The wall had been repaired, and—if he were to guess—re-inforced. The room remained spotless, as always.

He had no shirt on, and wore jeans, but no socks or shoes.

Tarrick slept on top of his bed sheets, surrounded by reports. A tablet lay face down on his chest as if he fell asleep reading it. He wore suit pants and a button-down shirt, wrinkled from sleeping in them. He was going to hate that when he woke up.

Matthew sat up silently and ran his hand down his chest, checking where the stake had plunged into him. There was no wound. All his other injuries healed as well, and he wasn't hungry. He must have had a trip to the infirmary. A few days, at least, must have passed since the attack.

He let his eyes wander around the room, memorizing its contents in case Cullip asked him about it. He studied the bookcases and read the titles and authors of each book. He noted which weapons hung where on the wall, and what each piece of art looked like, along with the statues and trinkets throughout the room.

One statue, in particular, drew his eye: a white marble bust of a striking woman. When his eyes fell upon her, he felt at peace.

After a few minutes, he had committed to memory the entire room. He didn't want to spend his time watching Tarrick sleep and risk becoming uncomfortably hard, so instead he closed his eyes and reached out with his senses. The magic preventing him from listening in didn't seem to prevent him from listening out. Once he counted all the people in the keep—un-surprised that the number of hunters on patrol had doubled—he settled on listening to music while he waited.

"How long have you been up?" a silky, masculine voice inquired.

Matthew opened his eyes and smiled as Tarrick stretched awake.

"Not long, Master, maybe fifteen minutes."

Tarrick began to tidy up the reports on his bed. "What were you doing just now?"

"A few rooms away, someone is playing Tchaikovsky's Violin Concerto. I was listening to it."

Tarrick seemed surprised. Matthew knew he didn't look like the type who would listen to concertos. It always threw people when they found out. "Do you enjoy Tchaikovsky?"

"My wife did. She was a violinist and could play it perfectly. How long have I been out?" he asked, changing the subject out of fear that grief might overtake him.

Tarrick smoothed out his bed sheets. "Five days."

"So long? I should have healed quicker than that," Matthew stood and stretched, he didn't fail to notice Tarrick eyeing him.

"You did. I kept you out a few extra days."

"Why?"

Tarrick went into his closet for a few moments then came back out holding a fresh suit on a hanger; he laid it down on his bed and began to unbutton his shirt. "There were some new discussions about you and if the order came down to kill you, I thought it kinder not to wake you first."

"Oh. Was I that bad?"

"No. You did exactly what I needed you to do—better actually—it's why you're alive and awake now." He slipped his shirt off then started to take off his pants.

Matthew's other questions floated away as he watched Tarrick remove the rest of his clothes. He could feel Tarrick's influence wrapping around him like a warm blanket, heating him at his core. Tarrick hadn't needed to, Matthew would have been turned on either way, but it made him feel incredible so he didn't fight it.

Tarrick entered his shower and Matthew watched as he washed off. God, he wanted to join him, to feel their bodies pressed against each other as the water dripped down them. He walked forward and strained against the chains.

"Do you enjoy watching me shower?" Tarrick teased as he lathered up his chest, his muscles flexing under his flawless skin. When Tarrick turned away from him, Matthew's eyes roamed down the curve of his back, leading to two perfect dimples.

Matthew wanted to tell him that he enjoyed every part of it, but all he could manage was, "Yes."

"Yes, what?"

Matthew watched in awe as Tarrick's cock got rock hard, nearly hitting his belly.

"Yes, Master," he almost liked saying 'master' this time because of the pleasing reaction it evoked from Tarrick. Almost.

"Would you like me to touch myself?" He palmed his soapy length and it twitched under his touch.

Matthew moaned. It was too much. His own steel hard cock pressed painfully against his jeans. "I'd enjoy it more if I was touching you. Or you were touching me."

Tarrick didn't say anything. Instead, he continued to stroke himself with hungry eyes locked on Matthew.

Matthew couldn't take it anymore. He tore himself away from Tarrick's influence and backed up—nearly reaching the wall. He wanted to snarl at Tarrick; his fangs itched to come down. "Why do you tease me so?"

Tarrick smiled and released his cock; it began to grow soft almost right away. "I was just seeing how much you could take before you broke my hold."

Matthew's face winced with pain. Did Tarrick not desire him as well? The way he'd look or touch him sometimes made him think Tarrick wanted him. Maybe he was wrong. Maybe Tarrick saw him as nothing more than a meal, the same way Matthew saw humans. He vowed to break away from his hold sooner if he did it again. He couldn't take this teasing. He wanted to get closer to Tarrick so he could continue to learn how to use his abilities, but this was too tortuous for him. There had to be another way to get what he wanted.

Unlike Tarrick, his cock didn't get soft right away. He had wanted to fuck Tarrick and had ever since he first saw him, and that desire was growing stronger. Half the time he wasn't sure if it was something the incubus was doing to him, or if it was his own feelings.

He adjusted himself and sat down on his cot.

"Well, you have your answer, *Master*." He didn't bother to hide his frustration.

"Watch your tone with me, *vampire*," Tarrick sneered. His eyes grew dark and his shoulders squared. Anger and steam rose around him making him look frightening. Matthew's eyes flicked to the kanabō on the wall, the memory of it smashing his body to bits sent a chill through him. God, he didn't want to piss Tarrick off again.

He hung his head, still feeling the sting of rejection. "Forgive me, Master."

That seemed to placate Tarrick, who went back to showering. Matthew kept his eyes averted this time. The minutes passed in silence and questions swelled up inside of Matthew until he couldn't resist asking one. "Can you get erect and flaccid at will?"

"Yes," Tarrick said, turning off the shower to dry off.

"That must be nice."

"It is. Sometimes getting hard at will is a necessity, like when I'm injured. We can also secrete a lubricant out of our skin if we need it," Tarrick said, no longer sounding angry.

Matthew scrunched his nose.

"That sounds…uh." It sounded gross but Matthew didn't want to insult Tarrick.

"It's convenient. Sometimes we need to feed quickly and foreplay isn't an option. And you weren't complaining when I was running my hand down your dick."

Ah, that's why his hand had felt so silky. Wonderfully silky. Still, it sounded gross.

"Do you think I'll be able to do that?"

Tarrick shrugged and began to dress. "Most likely, but we won't know for sure until we force your soavik to start working."

"When will that be?" Matthew wanted to start learning about his incubus side. What could he do? Would he be able to influence emotions like other incubi? Hold a human still without the need to compel them? He was also worried. Turning on that side of him might bring disadvantages, like the need to feed on sex. Matthew didn't want to have to feed on both sex and blood each night.

"We'll consider triggering it to activate once you master your vampire abilities. And when I trust you. Teaching you these things will be intimate. I need to know you won't snap my neck if you get frustrated."

Intimate? Matthew wondered how Tarrick would be teaching him and smiled as his imagination ran away from him. He then cursed himself for being so weak around Tarrick. He had just resolved to stop thinking of him that way and his will was already breaking.

Tarrick finished dressing then stacked his reports into a single neat pile. "Cullip will be here soon to take you to the academy."

"I can't say I'm enjoying those whippings." Matthew rotated his shoulder blade. He hated the sting on his back, but he was getting used to it. It didn't hurt as much anymore, though it still pained him.

"But they are effective, are they not?"

"Yeah, I guess. When I enter a room I see details I never noticed before."

"Tell me about this room." Tarrick gestured his hand around him.

Matthew motioned his head at the stack of reports on Tarrick's desk. "One of those was open on your bed. It was a requisition request for additional resources to accommodate the extra hunters that you ordered into the area. Are they here because of the attack on the academy?"

"Yes and no. They are here because the vampires have been aggressively attacking the incubi estates in this area. The attack on the academy was just one of many we've had to fight off these past few months. The one leading these attacks has a personal vendetta against me so she's brought the war to my territory."

"Their leader was the lord I saw flying?"

Tarrick nodded. "Ascelina."

"Why the vendetta?"

Tarrick came around his bed and sat down on it facing Matthew. "We've been fighting for centuries but this latest aggression is because I took her son and daughter prisoner."

Her daughter? "Emilia...and Stolus is her son?"

"Yes, how did you know?" Tarrick asked.

"She and Emilia felt the same. It's hard to explain. For Stolus, I just guessed because of how he tries to protect Emilia."

"Did Ascelina say anything to you?"

Yes. '*Soon.*' Whatever that meant. "No," he lied. "Is she a telepath like Emilia is?" He knew the answer, but the question would help sell the lie. Matthew listened to Tarrick's heartbeat for any sign he might see through Matthew's deception. He was relieved when there was no change to his heart rate or breathing.

"Yes, she is."

"Is telepathy common for vampires?"

"No, not at their skill level. Some lords can read surface thoughts. What other details do you see in this room?"

Matthew looked over to the bookshelf. "All of your books look like first editions. You have a lot on war strategies and tactics, plus a huge section on Norse Sagas. Were you a Viking?"

"You know a lot about history," Tarrick said not answering the question.

"It was my minor in college. But you knew that. If you found my family in two days, there's no way you didn't run some sort of background check on me."

Tarrick smiled. "You're right, I did know. I was never a seafarer, but I was born near Oslo in Norway during the rule of Sveinn Tjúguskegg, or Sweyn Forkbeard as his name is in English."

Ah, so he was born in that era. At six-two, Matthew was taller than Tarrick by at least four inches. "I thought Norse were tall."

"I'm seven-eight, I'd hardly call that short." Tarrick sat up straight as if to show he was taller, but his size didn't change. He was just bragging. He didn't need to brag; Matthew knew full well how big Tarrick could get.

"You know what I mean, Master."

"Humans love to rewrite history. Back then the average male was a few inches shorter than how I choose to appear now."

Matthew shook his head and continued his observations. "There's a woman's earring that's fallen behind your side table."

Tarrick retrieved it and Matthew smiled, knowing he wouldn't be able to leave it there once he knew of it. "She's been looking for this for days."

"You've changed three of the paintings on the wall since I was last here. A human was in this room about two hours before I woke—a maid, based on the smell of cleaning products. There's a gargoyle moving to a new spot on the roof. You had a fire going in the fireplace a few days ago. The small figurine of the bear facing me on your bookshelf has a camera in it."

Tarrick raised an eyebrow.

"I can hear the electricity buzzing."

"After our little bout, Cullip refused to let you back in here unless he had a hunter watching you at all times."

The thought of Cullip refusing to let Tarrick do something amused Matthew...although the general was probably just humoring his commander.

"That statue wasn't here last time," Matthew motioned to the marble bust of the woman. "Who is she? She's beautiful."

Tarrick walked over to the bust and ran his hand along her face, then dipped his head to the statue. "Ilertha. She is the incubus goddess."

That was not what Matthew was expecting. "You don't worship...you know, God?"

"I assume you mean the Jewish and Christian god. No. But I do love feeding on his servants. I enjoy the sin. The conflict inside of them is delicious," Tarrick said, still watching the statue.

"You seduce priests?"

Tarrick flashed a devious smile at him.

Matthew wasn't sure how he felt about that. He was never big into religion, but he tried to be respectful towards others who were into it. Then again, he killed humans now. He even loved it when they feared him, so it made sense incubi had their own monstrous preferences.

"Is there a vampire god?"

"Yes, they call him the Blood God, but not much is known about him, even to the vampires. He's never walked this planet."

"…Your god has?"

Tarrick nodded. "Unlike the god humans worship, our gods are tangible—real—and can come down from their realms to walk among us. Though it has been thousands of years since it last happened." Tarrick walked back over to the bed and leaned against it, watching Matthew.

"That doesn't sound very god-like."

"Our gods can bless and curse us, and when we die our souls go to them. What do you think a god should be?"

He wasn't sure. He wasn't even sure he had a soul anymore. Matthew studied the statue and felt a wave of serenity wash over him. The room around him faded away. Then the statue blinked.

"Holy shit!" Startled, Matthew jerked backwards.

"What is it?" Tarrick asked, standing and in a defensive posture.

"You didn't see that? She moved!"

Tarrick relaxed his body. "I did not. It's a statue, Matthew. They don't move."

Matthew was tempted to point out that he had a roof full of gargoyles that moved, but decided against it when he heard Cullip exiting the elevator down the hall. Matthew knew what he saw, but he wasn't going to argue with Tarrick.

Seventeen

When Cullip brought Matthew back to Ashwood Academy, he assumed he'd be chained in the silver cage and left alone the rest of the night. Instead, he was brought down into the dirt arena, where he had fought the vampires.

There were four groups of twelve hunters practicing. The trainees were nervous. They didn't show it, but Matthew smelled the fear around him. Each time one would shoot Matthew a glance, an instructor would yell at them and force them to do exercises for not focusing on their own task.

Cullip removed Matthew's shackles. "Do I need to threaten you or do you know by now what we'll do to you if you don't behave?"

Matthew didn't answer; the commander landed on his shit list when he staked him.

"General Tarrick might put up with your bullshit, but I won't. You'll answer my questions when I ask them, vampire."

"I'll behave," Matthew growled. With tons of hunters around him, it wasn't as if he had much of a choice. He could kill maybe four or five before they took him down.

"Good. Let's teach you to fight."

****

The remainder of the week fell into routine. Matthew shared the bed with Emilia and he'd wake with her in his arms. He never assumed she'd want him there; he waited until she gave him permission to join. Stolus didn't seem to mind. He only growled if Matthew did something that would result in her being hurt. Matthew did his best to avoid that.

An hour after waking, he'd shower, splitting the time in half with Emilia. Shortly after the water cut out, Tarrick would show up with the Wardens. His bodyguards often had minor wounds on their faces as if they had been out fighting vampires, but the general was always unblemished. Matthew would kneel before him and ask for blood. He'd feed on half the human and give the other half to Emilia.

Out of curiosity, he asked where all the humans were coming from.

Tarrick told him they were unwanted souls that no one would miss: vagrants, bums, transients. Or they were humans that had once served the incubi and were sentenced to death for some betrayal. He learned that he was the only vampire they had that was getting humans to feed on, the rest were getting blood from blood banks or humans they didn't kill.

None of the hunters acted like they cared that he was killing humans in front of them. They seemed to have more loyalty to incubi than to humans. Matthew wondered if it was that way for all hunters or just this team.

After feeding, Cullip would bring him over to Ashwood Academy and teach him basic fighting, such as stances, how to correctly throw a punch (Matthew learned his previous technique was terrible), and how to block an attack.

The hunters that trained around him began to get used to him being there and their nerves settled by the end of the week. He'd hear an occasional nasty comment directed at him, but for the most part, they just focused on their own training.

At the end of each night, Cullip would bring him back and ask his twenty questions. Matthew ended up with many red stripes the first night of training because it was hard to focus on Cullip's teachings while keeping his senses open to what was happening around him. But he adapted, and a few nights later he could answer nearly each question, suffering only two or three lashes.

Matthew was a fast study and Cullip a skilled trainer. By the end of the week he was told they'd be moving to basic weapons the next night.

Matthew found himself looking forward to it.

****

He woke that next night to Emilia squirming in his arms. Normally he roused before her by a few minutes and he would lie still until she also woke.

Blood. The smell of blood was everywhere.

He shot out of bed and pulled Emilia defensively behind him.

All of the cages were open, including his. The six hunter guards on this level had been dragged into the jail and were dead on the ground. Each was brutally clawed, their bodies shredded. The cameras and the observation room were smashed to pieces.

Ascelina, the vampire lord, stood in front of him. Her black claws were long and covered with blood. Her grey wings were out but folded against her back. Her red eyes matched the color of her corset. She didn't look older than mid-twenties, but Matthew could feel she was centuries old; maybe even older than Tarrick.

Overwhelming power rolled off her and pressed into him. In response, his vampire side came forward and he took a step away from her. Emilia pushed past him as she dove into her mother's arms.

"You're here," she cried. It was the first time Matthew heard Emilia speak, her voice sounded soft and gentle.

"I told you I was coming," Ascelina said as she embraced her daughter and planted a kiss on her head.

Stolus stood behind her, claws out and ready for a fight. The other three vampires joined him. Ascelina released Emilia into Stolus' arms and approached Matthew. He hissed at her. He couldn't help it…her power was terrifying.

He heard Ascelina's voice in his head: *Matthew. You do not have to fear me.*

She pressed her hand hard onto his abdomen and scanned him. It felt different than when Rosaline had done it. Rather than an echo, it felt as if she was stirring the blood within him and using it to 'see' his insides. When she finished, she watched him for a moment, as if she didn't believe what she felt even though the proof was in front of her.

He swallowed and fought to keep control of himself. He didn't want to start attacking her because he felt threatened by her strength. He wasn't sure it was a fight he could win. Actually, he knew for certain he'd lose.

Ascelina ran her hand up his body then across his collar and down his arms to his bracers. She frowned as she held the bracer up and studied it. She dropped his arm and looked over to Emilia who had broken from her brother's hold and rejoined her mother.

Emilia reached up and touched Matthew's collar. "You cannot come with us."

His shoulders sank and he leaned his head forward. As long as the incubi could track him, he couldn't leave.

Forgive me. Emilia's voice said in his mind as she moved her hand up to cup his face.

"Forgive you for what?" he asked, leaning into the touch.

I have been reading your thoughts. I know what you are. My mother does too. We don't care that you were an incubus—you are a vampire now. One of us. And we want to help you.

Matthew looked to the lord. Help him? All other vampires ran from him…feared him…would she really help him?

Ascelina nodded.

No one else knows. Emilia continued telepathically. *Not even my brother. It will stay that way until you choose otherwise.*

"Can't you remove the collar? I don't want to stay here as a slave."

Not yet. We will find a way but we need time. You must stay. Learn what you can from them, as you planned.

Matthew frowned.

My mother brought you a gift. Her attack on the academy the other week was a distraction. She compelled a handful of hunters before she began killing their patrols.

How had she compelled them when they all wore those contacts preventing it?

Neither Emilia nor Ascelina answered his question, though they likely heard him think it. Emilia continued.

In a few moments, vampires will be attacking this keep. They are common mercenaries—unimportant. She sent them here for you. Kill them so the incubi will trust you. The hunters she compelled at the academy will be releasing the imprisoned vampires. Reinforcements will be too busy there and won't be arriving at the estate.

"I don't enjoy killing."

Both Emilia and Ascelina smiled as if he had said something funny. Matthew growled and Emilia's smile dropped. *You must. Killing the vampires will earn the incubi's trust. You will be closer to your goal. She disabled all the vampire wards here. The incubi will need your help.*

"And when the time is right—when you are ready—I will come for you," Ascelina said from behind her daughter.

Matthew didn't know what to say. This was the first time since becoming a vampire someone helped him without first hurting him.

Matthew cupped Emilia's face in his hand, mirroring how she held him. He leaned down and tenderly brushed his lips against hers as a thank you. She pressed her soft lips into his, then broke away.

You should know we don't fear you because you are powerful—like the incubus general thinks—it's because you have a powerful aura around you. It reeks of death and destruction. I have never felt the like. It wasn't until I had blood I was strong enough to overcome it. It makes you too easy for vampires to track. Learn to suppress it. Hide it.

Aura of death? That didn't sound like something he wanted. Matthew had no idea how he'd learn to suppress an aura, but he would try.

"Vend, come in," Cullip's voice came over one of the dead hunter's intercom.

"It's about to begin. Are you ready, young one?" Ascelina asked Matthew.

Right now? Jeez. Matthew, who had been wearing only jeans, tossed on a grey shirt and boots in record time.

"Vend, I swear if you are slacking again—" Cullip's voice started.

Green light traced the air and Cullip appeared in the middle of the vampires.

"—I will beat the living sh—" Adrenaline flooded him as he realized he had made a terrible mistake by teleporting to his guard. He went for his sword.

Ascelina was on him before his hand even touched the hilt. Moving even faster than Matthew could see, she drew his weapon and tossed it aside. Then she reached up to his eyeballs and plucked both of his contacts out.

Before Cullip registered what Ascelina had done, she grabbed the back of his neck and held him in place. He began to glow green but she dug her claw into his shoulder, right where the teleportation rune was located, preventing the spell from triggering.

Cullip squeezed his hand into a fist and alarms began to sound throughout the keep. Matthew grabbed his ears and bent over, as did the other vampires.

The sound didn't seem to affect Ascelina who looked into the commander's eyes. "You are to kill Lord General Tarrick for daring to touch my children."

"You bitch," Cullip said as he struggled against the command.

His will was strong but in the end, it was no match against Ascelina. Matthew felt terrible as he watched Cullip surrender to the command. Ascelina withdrew her claws from his rune.

Cullip retrieved his sword and teleported away.

Ascelina retrieved a stick from a small bag on her belt. She snapped it. The alarms stopped. Matthew's ears were thankful.

Ascelina appeared before Matthew and swiped him across his face with her claws. What the fuck? Matthew growled and lunged at her but she hit him in his chest and he went flying to the back of his cell.

Two hunter guards teleported into the smashed up observation room just in time to see Ascelina throwing Matthew around.

Ascelina grabbed her daughter and grouped up with the other vampires. She glanced back at Matthew one last time. *Don't trust a word that comes from Tarrick's mouth. Good luck, Matthew.*

She pulled out five small stones from her bag and tossed them around the group in one rapid motion. When the last one landed on the ground, a bright green light flashed and all the vampires were gone.

Matthew stood and walked out of his cell.

"Get back in there," one of the hunters ordered, his crossbow raised.

"Listen to me. The vampire lord just compelled Cullip to kill Tarrick, you need to warn him."

"Get back in your cage," another hunter said.

Damn it. He could go kill every single vampire attacking this place but it would mean shit if Tarrick died. Ascelina hadn't made this easy for him.

Calls for help began to come in over the hunter's comm. They were reports that over forty vampires were scaling the walls and had taken out the patrols and front guards.

"I can help. Please let me," Matthew said to the two hunters. This would all be for nothing if he couldn't even get into the fight.

"I won't say it again," the first hunter warned.

Matthew spotted a key ring on one of the dead hunters that looked just like the one Cullip had. He was out of time and done dealing with these two. He pulled on his strands of swirling power, dumped it into his speed, then ran out from the jail, swooping down to snatch the keys as he left. He was out of the room and down the hall before the hunter could even pull the trigger on his crossbow.

Above him, he heard doors and windows breaking. Weapons clashed as hunters attacked the vampires. The scent of death was everywhere.

Matthew reached the door to the stairwell and unlocked it. He wasn't sure where he should go first. He had no idea where Tarrick would be, the battle above him made it impossible to pin down the location of anyone. If he ran right into the fray the other hunters would attack him, and he'd need to defend himself on two fronts.

He heard a woman scream on the fourth floor—the resident wing—and his decision was made easy. He ascended the stairs at a lightning pace and exited the hallway that led to Tarrick's room. All the doors in this wing were closed.

He heard the scream again. Second door on his left. He broke it down and burst into the room. No lights were on but he could see just fine. Two vampires had come through the window and dragged the woman from her bed. One was about to sink his fangs into her.

Matthew ripped the vampire away from her and tossed him back out the window, he went flying off into the dark. He then grabbed the other vampire and tore him in half, roaring in satisfaction as blood and viscera sprayed across the room.

Emilia and Ascelina were probably right to laugh at him…his vampire side did enjoy killing, even if he had trouble admitting it.

The woman cried and cowered away into a corner. Matthew dropped the body then flipped on a light so she could see him.

"I'm not going to hurt you, Lady Rosaline," he said. She stood in her succubus form, claws out, as were her red wings and small horns; her ears small and pointed. She wasn't like Tarrick, who grew huge and bulky in his incubus form, she had grown a few inches but that was it. Matthew had a feeling that was as large as she could get. She hissed at him when he took a step towards her. "I swear to you, I'm on your side here."

Fear pumped through her, too panicked to respond to him.

"I really hope you forgive me for this." Matthew sighed as he scooped her up and looked into her eyes. "Relax."

Her tense body melted into his arms as the command took hold. He made sure the command would only last a few hours before it released her.

"Are you injured?"

"No," she shook her head.

Cries came from other rooms. He carried her into her bathroom and set her down inside. "Lock the door and don't open it until this is over. Do you understand?"

She nodded. He shut the door and heard it lock behind him.

Matthew walked out into the hall as a young, stout hunter ran in from the stairwell. Matthew recognized him as a trainee from the academy, Ruck. He attempted to hide his fear but the poor kid had probably never been in a real fight before.

Matthew laughed to himself. Neither had he until recently. This kid was even better trained. That put things into an odd perspective.

The third door on the right opened and three vampires poured out. Matthew could smell blood on them; they had just killed the occupant of that room.

Ruck's heart was beating a million miles an hour as he fumbled to pull out one of the silver grenades from his belt. The vampires ran at him. Matthew was faster. He plucked three grenades from the hunter's belt and poured power into his arm as he tossed them at the vampires' chests as hard as possible. Two hit the mark with a *crunch* as the grenades went through the vampires' ribs and blasted open within their chests.

The vampires howled as they melted away from the inside out. The third grenade exploded just behind the last vampire standing. The silver dust coated the vampire's head and back. The vampire screamed and surged at Matthew. Ruck pulled out silver throwing spikes and tossed them. One landed in the vampire's eye and the other two in his torso. The vampire stumbled and Matthew used the opening to rip off his head.

When the vampire fell away he felt a silver sword press against his neck.

He turned and faced the boy. "Hunter Ruck, Commander Cullip has been compelled by Ascelina to kill my master. You need to warn the hunters that he's not fighting on their side right now."

Ruck studied Matthew for a moment then glanced at the dead vampires. He lowered his sword and began speaking into his comm.

Matthew ignored him and focused on the rooms in this wing. Most rooms were empty or the occupants dead. Rosaline was still alive, and to his right there was another incubus alive and alone, locked in his room. Matthew couldn't sense Tarrick anywhere nearby.

"Lady Rosaline is locked in her bathroom. Stay here and protect these two," Matthew ordered Ruck. He didn't wait for a response before he dashed off to find more vampires to kill.

Eighteen

Matthew entered the stairwell again and went down two levels.
He exited into a hallway and, from what he could tell, one way
led to a dining hall—he could smell the food—and the other led to what
looked like sitting rooms and maybe offices.

He heard a crash in the dining hall and smelled Lieutenant Silva. She
was bleeding.

Matthew entered the room to see a vampire standing on the table,
armed with an axe, bringing it down on Silva. She teleported behind the
vampire and pushed a stake through his back, penetrating his heart. He
slumped over and rolled off the table.

Matthew looked her over. There was a long, bleeding slash on her arm
but it wasn't deep and she ignored it. It looked as if she had been eating
alone when the attacks started. A second vampire already lay decaying on
the ground.

A female vampire crawled through the window. Matthew poured power into his speed and yanked her into the room. She struggled uselessly
against him as he sank his fangs into her, drinking deep to replace the
energy he lost.

Silva pulled out another stake and walked towards him. He growled at
her and kept drinking. She studied the vampire writhing in his arms, put
her stake back on her belt, and picked up the axe the vampire used against
her. She didn't attack him, though.

"The general isn't going to be happy you are taking blood without his
permission."

Matthew scowled at the tiny woman and cut his feeding short. He
pushed the vampire at Silva and she cut off his head.

"Hopefully the general shows some mercy considering the circum-
stances," he said.

Silva raised an eyebrow as if she wasn't convinced Tarrick would show
any mercy. Matthew didn't think he would either, but that was tomorrow's
problem.

"Is it true Cullip is compelled?" she asked.

"Yes." Then he added a small lie, "I tried to stop it for all the good it did me." He pointed at the claw marks on his face. They were just pink scars now but Silva knew he received them recently. "Where's my master? I should go to him."

"We don't know. I need to get to the command center. If Cullip has been compromised then I'm the ranking hunter here right now."

"I'll take you, where is it?"

"I can teleport. You meet me there. Third floor. Exit the stairs to the left, go to the back, double doors in the center of all the wi—"

Matthew picked her up and they were in the command center before she finished the word 'wings'. The seven hunters in the room brought up weapons when he appeared. One shot him in the neck with a silver tipped bolt. At least the whole thing wasn't silver this time.

"God damn it," he said as he set Silva down, pulled the bolt from his neck, and tossed it aside.

"Put your weapons down. He's fighting with us," Silva ordered. "I'm taking over."

"Lieutenant," one of the men acknowledged. The hunters saluted. This might have been a surprise attack but Matthew could see they were trained to handle situations like these. Everyone here had a role and, even without their general or commander, the machine ran smoothly.

Matthew looked around. In the back of the huge room were three chairs set up almost like thrones. All were empty. Most hunters stood around a large round table in the center of the room, cluttered with papers, including maps of each level of the keep. There were even little figurines to represent hunter teams.

One wall was covered in monitors displaying images of the battle. Three human dispatchers sat in front of it, communicating the locations of vampires to hunters and coordinating attacks. Matthew heard one of them talking to someone at the academy; it sounded as if the battle wasn't going well there. A large screen in the middle displayed the fighting going on in the grand foyer of the estate.

Matthew pointed at the screen. "I should go there but I can't fight vampires and hunters at the same time."

"Dispatch," Silva yelled across the room at the humans working in front of the monitors. "Let the front ranks know Matthew is heading out and he is not to be attacked."

"Yes, sir," one acknowledged and Matthew heard the order repeated through all the open comms in the area.

"You need that axe?" Matthew asked.

She held it out to him but didn't release it when he grabbed it. She didn't say anything. Instead, she just stared at him through her dark brown eyes.

"I won't betray you. If I do, it's horrible pain followed by a terrible death for me. I know my place, Lieutenant." He tapped the collar around his neck.

Satisfied, she relinquished the axe and began barking orders at the hunters in the room.

Matthew sped to the foyer and came to a stop on the balcony above the marble double staircases. Most of the hunters were pinned up there.

He looked over the iron railing—bodies littered the grand foyer. At least thirteen hunters were dead, two incubi, and Matthew counted the decaying remains of ten or twelve vampires. What was once a grand piano, was now nothing more than a pile of splintered wood with the body of a hunter lying on top of the pile.

More vampires were poured in, trapping hunters. One wildly fired an AK-47, riddling the area with bullets. Hunters raised their hands up and bullets slammed into invisible force walls. More of that rune magic.

Matthew wondered what bullets would do to him. He guessed it wasn't much, considering hunters didn't use guns. Or at least he hadn't seen a hunter use a gun yet.

The knight-looking hunter, with a full-face helmet, shiny metal armor, and a tall shield, was making his way down the stairs to the hunters trapped below. Bullets bounced off his metal shield. Matthew wondered if it was magic as well.

A vampire rushed up to the knight. The knight moved the shield to his side with startling speed and kicked the vampire square in the chest with a heavy boot, sending it tumbling back down the stairs.

The vampire with the assault rifle fired at the chandelier, killing the lights. It was dark for a moment and Matthew could hear a hunter die with a scream. He noticed some hunters' eyes began to glow green. Then flares lit up the room.

Matthew had to take out the one with the gun if the rest of the hunters were going to get into this fight. He jumped off the balcony, aiming for another vampire. Matthew crushed it and the vampire's body folded in on itself, still alive but out of the fight for a while. Some hunter would probably kill him before he managed to heal.

Matthew leaped at the vampire with the gun. Before he landed, a large silver blade lopped the vampire's head off and it dropped to the ground.

Lord Tane stood before Matthew holding a huge claymore, shirtless with minor cuts across his body. His horns looked just like Tarrick's, except his were a brighter purple at the tips. His eyes were a brighter purple as well.

Matthew growled at the loss of his kill. Tane grinned and ducked as a vampire took a swipe at him. He surged around and cleaved the vampire in two.

"I've killed fourteen of your kind today. Are you even at half that?" Tane asked and parried a sword swing from another vampire.

God, he wanted to rip this little shit's head off every time he saw him. The fact he was right didn't help. Matthew sped forward with his axe and chopped the head off the vampire attacking Tane. Then he turned and ripped the heart out of another.

A wild female vampire jumped on Matthew's back and sunk her fangs deep into his neck. Matthew tried to grab her off but she was slippery and dodged his claws.

Tane drove his claymore through the back of the vampire's neck, killing her instantly. The blade drove deep into Matthew's shoulder. The silver burned through his muscles. Matthew pulled away from the huge sword, grabbed Tane by his neck, and pressed him against the wall.

"You son of a bitch," Matthew roared at him.

Tane brought his sword up to Matthew's chin. "You want to be number sixteen? I saved your life."

Three silver bolts hit Matthew in his upper shoulder. Warnings. Matthew growled and released Tarrick's son. Tane peeled away and swung at another vampire while Matthew ripped the bolts out of his shoulder.

He was getting hungry again. Tane pissed him off. Also, pushing himself to use his speed and enhance his strength had used up a lot of his energy. Unless he fed again—which would leave him vulnerable—he'd have to rely on his normal vampire speed. He'd still be faster than a human, just not faster-than-a-speeding-bullet fast.

He didn't want to burn out like he had back at the arena.

But…Tane was beating him in kills. His pride couldn't allow that. Matthew brought up just a small bit of red energy and put it into his speed, testing to see if using less still achieved what he needed. He surged past three vampires and took off their heads with his axe.

So, he *could* use less energy and it still achieved the desired effect.

An injured hunter lay on the ground near a damaged vase. Matthew scooped him up and dropped him off with the group up on the second floor. The rest of the hunters were advancing down the foyer and were handling the remaining vamps. Matthew wasn't needed here anymore.

He ran outside.

It was cold with snow on the ground.

Far more than forty vampires were attacking tonight, contradictory to the initial call over the comm. Matthew counted eighteen decomposing bodies out front and nearly double that in dead hunters. Three incubi were lying dead as well, their wings and necks snapped with bite marks all over their bodies.

Matthew looked up into the night sky to see the moon in its first quarter.

Against the stars, a vampire lord—a male with dark bat wings—gave chase to the black incubus Matthew had seen sitting next to Tarrick during the arena fight. The incubus was huge, easily bigger than Tarrick in full form. His wings were dark at the base but faded down to white tips. His horns had the same coloring. He fought with a double bladed weapon and wielded it with great skill. The vampire lord used his claws and fly-by attacks. He was quicker than the incubus but the fight looked equally matched.

The body of a second vampire lord dropped from the sky and bounced on the ground, nearly crushing Matthew. A succubus landed on the lord and drove a stake into his heart. Watching the succubus fight was breathtaking. She wasn't delicate like Rosaline. She was fierce, with big wings and ram-like horns that faded from black to blue, curling to the sides of her short, dark hair.

She caught Matthew staring at her and snarled at him. Matthew bowed his head to her and lowered his shoulders, submissive. She took off back into the air to help fight the other vampire lord.

Matthew had to ignore their fight for now. There was nothing he could do against flying opponents.

He turned his attention to a group of five vamps that jumped over the stone wall surrounding the keep. They looked older and faster than the ones Matthew had been taking down inside. He wasn't sure he could take them alone.

The vampires reached the keep walls and began to scale the side, climbing vines or using their claws to jump higher. Matthew tucked his axe into the back of his pants and followed them up the wall. He seemed to be the only one to have noticed this group. They were headed right for Tarrick's balcony.

Matthew had an idea, one he wasn't sure would work.

He jumped over the railing and appeared behind all five. They were trying to break through the glass into the room but weren't having any luck. Why wasn't this impenetrable glass everywhere in the keep? Tarrick probably thought that with nearly a thousand hunters so close by at the academy, his estate was not in any danger. Or maybe he relied on those vampire wards Ascelina disabled.

Matthew looked up and was surprised to see that the gargoyles hadn't moved from their perches. But then he noticed pieces of decaying vampires spread around the roof and some of the gargoyles had blood on their arms. Jeez, those things were scary.

"Hey boys and girls," Matthew said to the vampires, ignoring the gargoyles.

They turned and hissed at him. Matthew pointed to his eyes. They all looked. Matthew dug deep and brought up power into his command.

"Fight for me," he said as he tried to compel all five at once.

He felt their will's wrestling against his. They were strong but he was stronger and one by one they submitted to his command.

"Come," he told his five compelled vampires.

He drew out his axe then jumped off the balcony, dropping four stories to the ground. He landed with an 'oof' and it felt like he sprained an ankle. He pushed some threads of energy into healing so it wouldn't slow him down.

The other five were far more graceful, but in Matthew's defense, this was the first time he had ever jumped off something so high.

There were dozens of vampires outside, fighting their way to the foyer to reclaim it.

The blood in the air, the moon above him, the death, the thrill of killing...Matthew's vampire side was set loose and he gave into it, tearing down all who stood in his path. Behind him, his compelled vampires ripped apart any left standing.

Together, they were like a battering ram and his foes fell before him in an exsanguinated mess. He reveled in it.

His brutal flank attack proved to be the needed distraction and it broke the vampires apart, scattering them, allowing hunters in.

Matthew wasn't happy to see the hunters joining the fray...these were his kills. He pulled red coils into every part of his body and charged over a vampire, sending him to the ground and stomping its head in. He sliced a different vampire across the chest with his axe while he ripped the throat out of another one with his claw.

He didn't stop. Killing one after another.

Within a span of less than a minute, fifteen vampires lay dead at his feet. Matthew didn't even notice he was covered head to toe with deep wounds and blood. He couldn't even feel his injuries right now.

Fuck, he felt amazing.

Powerful.

Invincible.

Emilia had told him he had an aura of death. He hoped everyone here, not just the vampires, could feel it now. Matthew brought up power to his lungs, leaned his head back, and let out a bellowing roar that could be heard for miles.

Matthew watched as all of the vampires cowered away from him and began to retreat. He released his compelled vampires—let them run if they wanted. Let them tell all other vampires what he was capable of. It was over.

Almost.

There was one creature Matthew desired to conquer.

The vampire lord above him broke away from his battle with the two incubi and fled.

Matthew pushed power into his arm then launched his axe at the lord. The weapon tumbled end over end through the air and sliced off one of the lord's wings at the base.

The lord plummeted to the ground. Matthew was on him before it could stand, pinning the lord under him and sinking his fangs into its neck. The lord struggled and hissed but Matthew gave him no quarter as he drank his powerful blood with an unquenchable need.

It was thrilling.

With a surge of power, the vampire lord managed to push Matthew away from him. He was on his feet and running before Matthew could shake off his blood haze. The vampire lord vanished into the snowy forest and got away.

Matthew howled. His prey lost.

Everything behind him had gone quiet.

He turned. At least twenty hunters stood with their weapons aimed at Matthew.

As did Tane, the huge black incubus, the warrior succubus with horns that faded to blue, and two other incubi Matthew didn't know. One, a female with maroon horns, and the other, a male with charcoal wings. All of them stood ready to attack.

Matthew smiled.

Killing the incubi would give him such a sweet release. They had abused him, mistreated him. He owed them death and he would start by killing Tane.

Nineteen

Matthew licked his lips and took a step towards Tane, who stood his ground.

A green outline appeared on the grassy area between Tane and Matthew. Silva teleported in.

She didn't have a weapon in her hand. Her mistake. He would kill her too if she wished for death that badly.

"Stand down, Matthew," she ordered.

He would not. He would fight them all. With the vampire lord's blood in him, he was powerful enough to take them all on. Matthew stalked towards her.

"Control yourself."

Matthew's chest rumbled with a deep growl. He closed his eyes and balled up his fists. His claws dug into his palms as he struggled to command his body.

His mind began to clear. There was no way he could fight five warrior incubi, he hadn't even been able to take on Tarrick and some of these incubi looked similar in skill level, if not better. Hell, even Tane alone could probably handle him. Not to mention he couldn't take on six hunters before, and even if he had learned to fight a little, there was no way he could take on twenty.

This was not a battle he could win. He killed plenty of vampires tonight—that would have to sate him for now. But Matthew was having a hard time getting his vampire side to recede. He needed to put some distance between him and the battle. Between him and all this blood.

"I give you my word I will return before sunrise," he said and poured power into running from the keep.

Bolts and silver chains flew at Matthew, but he was long gone by the time they reached their destination.

He wasn't sure where he was headed as he ran deep into the surrounding forest. He knew the hunters could track him but they would probably be busy with their wounded, and there was Ashwood Academy to deal with. Matthew wasn't sure if that battle was still going on, but he couldn't risk going there. With his control paper-thin as it was, more killing would shatter it.

Wherever Matthew ended up going, he needed to be sure he could retrace his steps. He planned to keep his word and return before sunrise. He slowed and leaned against a tree, closed his eyes, and reached out with his senses.

He let out a sigh, relieved no one followed him. Maybe Silva was going to give him some time before sending someone to come get him. He hoped that was the case.

This was the first time he had been alone outside since Tarrick captured him. Relaxing, he let his mind drift. Even in winter, the entire forest felt alive around him. He could sense sleeping deer, coyotes, foxes, and birds, along with other smaller animals.

He loved the glowing sensation emanating from the trees...but part of him felt unwelcome here. He was a dead thing after all, disconnected from nature. The frozen ground below his feet tugged at him—almost as if it called him to sleep beneath it.

He shook the feeling away and concentrated on trying to find a destination. With the exception of the Ashwood Estate and the Academy, there was nothing for miles and miles. Matthew pulled up more threads of power and extended his senses out farther. The faint scent of blood floated across his nose.

Tarrick's blood.

It was maybe seven or eight miles away.

Matthew pushed off the tree and rushed towards the smell. He slowed when he drew close to a clearing. Moonlight streamed down on the area, giving him more than enough light to see. Many of the smaller trees were splintered apart, there were deep bloody grooves in the ground, blood on rocks, and weapons stuck in branches.

Jesus, this had been one hell of a fight.

Matthew held back a gasp when he entered the clearing.

Cullip was lying face down in the center of a grove. His uniform was thrashed and there were deep cuts and bruises all over him. His left arm was gone, ripped from his body, but he wasn't bleeding from his shoulder. It looked as if he managed to drink some vampire blood to seal the wound, and then continued attacking Tarrick—as if losing his arm was a trivial matter.

The compulsion Ascelina had on him must have forced him to keep going and going until he was dead or unconscious. Right now it was the latter—he was alive but only just. His heartbeat sounded faint and fading. The snow around him stained red with blood pouring from his other wounds.

Tarrick sat against a tree in his full incubus form, mostly naked except for the remnants of his shredded suit pants that clung to his hips. Holding his insides, Tarrick's belly was wide open and his wings were smashed, twisted in the wrong directions. Half of his right horn was snapped off and his tail lay limp at his side. There was a silver dagger embedded in his shoulder.

Tarrick swallowed when he saw Matthew and tried to speak but blood coated his vocal cords and the only sound he made was a gurgle. He coughed and tried again.

"Going to kill me? You could…wait a few minutes…" he struggled to say.

Matthew rushed over to him and reached out to run his hand down his face only to realize he was still in his vampire form, claws and all. Tarrick must have thought he escaped and was here to kill him.

"No, Master, the keep was under attack. I stayed and fought the vampires. I tried to find you during the battle but couldn't. What can I do here? I think you'll bleed out if I try to carry you back to the keep. Cullip is worse off. Do you want me to go get a doctor?"

Tarrick looked up at Matthew with his bright purple eyes, pleased. Then he nodded at Cullip. "Give him your blood…tie him…"

"But if he dies, won't he become a vampire?"

Tarrick tried to smile but it fell from his face. "No…he won't die."

Matthew sat down by Cullip. He gently rolled the commander's body over and pulled him into his lap. He sank his fangs into his wrist, just below the bracers, and brought his wrist to Cullip's mouth. Nothing happened at first as blood seeped from his mouth and down his greying goatee.

Matthew adjusted him, sitting him up a bit more. Then Cullip swallowed. And again. He began suckling on the wound. Matthew heard his heart grow stronger as blood healed him. The small wounds on his body began to stitch together.

When he was sure Cullip was stable, he pulled away and licked the puncture marks on his wrist to seal them. The only thing he could find to tie Cullip up with was a silver chain. Matthew dragged Cullip to a tree and tied him sitting upright to it. He worked fast, the chain burning his hands.

Matthew returned to Tarrick, whose own heartbeat was getting weaker.

"Can I use my blood to heal you?"

"A little…it's not…as…"

'A little' was better than nothing. Matthew bit his wrist again and placed it against Tarrick's lips, who drank a few mouthfuls. Matthew could feel his heart improving, but not by much.

"Bleed on my…" Tarrick struggled with the words then looked down to his stomach and the deep gash across it.

"Don't talk, I understand." Matthew cursed his bracers—this would be easier without them. He cut deep into an artery in his wrist and blood came pouring out. He held it over Tarrick's gash and watched as the skin began to stitch together. He wasn't sure it was doing anything internally but at least his guts wouldn't be trying to fall out of him anymore.

He didn't dare remove the dagger while Tarrick was so fragile.

Matthew forced his body to stop the bleeding, licking the skin to help the healing along.

He kneeled next to Tarrick, who was much bigger than him right now. He began licking the minor cuts on his skin. Matthew moaned as he collected a few drops of Tarrick's blood with each caress of his tongue. It tasted better than the vampire lord's. *Much* better.

Tarrick tried to put his arm around Matthew's waist to pull him in but he was unable to lift his limb. Then Matthew felt Tarrick try to take hold of his mind with weak, delicate threads.

Running his tongue up Tarrick's neck, Matthew whispered into his ear. "You don't have to use your hold over me. I'll do whatever you need. But, uh, try to remember I've never been with an incubus before. Or a man."

Matthew had hoped his first time with Tarrick would have been in his room, on those black silk sheets. Or in the shower. Or bent over that wooden desk of his. But they didn't have the luxury right now.

Tarrick managed a smile this time. "Undress…"

Matthew stood up and, with tremendous effort, forced his claws away. There was no way he could stop his eyes from burning red or retract his fangs right now. The blood, the desire, the high from battle…his vampire side refused to relinquish any more control.

He reached behind him, pulled his soiled shirt over his head, and tossed it away. He yanked off his boots and socks, unbuckled his jeans (which were in no better shape than the shirt), slipped them off along with his underwear, and stood naked in front of Tarrick.

Neither man grew hard yet but Matthew did see the end of Tarrick's tail twitch as he eyed Matthew up and down, that seemed like a good sign.

Tarrick tried to motion for Matthew to kneel beside him but all he managed was to curl his clawed fingers. Matthew got the idea and kneeled down on the cold mud next to him.

He wasn't sure what to do so he resumed licking Tarrick's cuts across his broad chest. Once the cuts were sealed, Matthew began lightly kissing Tarrick's chest and worked his way up to his neck. Tarrick responded with a grunt of pleasure.

Matthew enjoyed the sound and kissed him with greater fervor. Being so close to his neck made his fangs itch. He wanted to sink them into Tarrick's flesh badly. Even if he only got a drop.

His cock grew hard at the thought of his fangs slipping in. Tarrick was so weak right now, he wouldn't be able to stop him and Matthew was certain Tarrick wouldn't let him bite him in the future. He fought against the idea—he'd be punished later if he acted on it—but it kept gnawing at him. His fangs grew longer as he licked Tarrick's neck in the area above his jugular.

Tarrick moaned in response.

That was too much. All restraint was lost. Matthew needed this, punishment be damned.

He pressed his body against Tarrick's, pinning his cock between them, and gently sunk his upper fangs into Tarrick's neck. They slid in so easily. He let them sit in his soft flesh. He wanted to suck hard and let blood fill his mouth but Tarrick couldn't survive losing any more than he already had.

Even without taking the blood, this felt wonderful.

Matthew started rubbing his trapped length against Tarrick's side and moaned.

Tarrick, who seemed just a little stronger, wrapped one arm around Matthew's waist and with his other, gripped Matthew's hair. He gently pulled.

Matthew removed his fangs and licked up the two delicious drops of blood they brought up with them. His saliva sealed the puncture marks and they began to disappear.

Using the arm wrapped around Matthew's waist, Tarrick guided him down into his lap then tugged again on Matthew's hair to lean him back. Matthew didn't resist; he arched his back and exposed his proud length, torso, and collared neck to Tarrick.

All of his stomach muscles flexed and tightened as he strained to keep his body in a position that was not quite sitting up, nor lying down.

Tarrick raked his violet eyes up and down Matthew and seemed pleased by what he saw. He didn't release Matthew's hair as he brought up his other hand and rubbed his palm along Matthew's sex, taking great care not to harm him with his claws.

Matthew moaned as heat welled deep within him. Tarrick's hand moved up his length and when fingers brushed against his sensitive head, Matthew bucked with fiery need, his abs contracting tight and hard.

The incubus ran the pad of his finger along Matthew's slit, smearing the drop of pre-cum that had collected there. He brought his finger to his mouth and licked it. Having never seen another male do that before, Matthew's jaw went slack and he let out a quiet groan. It was taboo to him and yet one of the sexiest things he had ever witnessed.

"Exquisite," Tarrick whispered as he brought his hand down and scraped the tips of his sharp claws over Matthew's tight abs.

Matthew whimpered and his abs danced under the light touch of the fine points.

Tarrick traced his claws along the grooves, giving attention to each individual muscle. Matthew knew he was a meal—one that Tarrick was enjoying unhurried. The incubus savored every moment and Matthew couldn't take much more. It was too slow and his cock needed attention.

He brought his hand up and stroked his length.

Tarrick dug his claw into Matthew's scalp and forced him to arch his head back even farther, leaving Matthew's neck open and vulnerable. The hard collar dug painfully into the skin. Tarrick leaned in.

"Did I give you permission to touch yourself?" he whispered, his warm lips brushing against Matthew's neck, just above the metal.

"Master…" Matthew moaned but didn't release his cock. He wanted to beg for more but lost the thought when Tarrick pressed his claws harder into Matthew's abdomen, drawing forth five small pinpricks of blood. Matthew hissed through his fangs. It was a perfect balance of pain and pleasure.

"Did I give you permission?" Tarrick asked again, his heated breath curled around Matthew's neck, warming him against the freezing night air.

"No, Master," Matthew managed to breathe out.

"Then why is your hand still grabbing your dick?" Tarrick scraped his teeth along the area just below his chin.

Matthew wished he'd bite his neck. Just the thought of Tarrick sinking his teeth into him, even if they were blunt, had his cock twitching against his palm.

"Please. I need more." He squeezed the base of his shaft.

Matthew, who had no illusions he'd be topping Tarrick—ever—wondered what it would feel like to be impaled on Tarrick's cock, to have the incubus inside of him. Would it hurt or feel amazing? He couldn't imagine it being anything but pure pleasure. The idea of trying something new both excited him and made him a little nervous.

Tarrick smiled against his skin and licked him on his neck. Matthew's abs began to burn as he strained to stay in this position.

"I'll have to punish…" Tarrick began, but before he could finish he slumped back against the tree trunk that had been propping him up. He struggled to stay conscious for a few brief moments. His eyes fluttered, then slid closed. His body went limp.

Tarrick was dying.

Twenty

Matthew pushed himself out of Tarrick's lap, put his hand on the general's chest, and listened.

He didn't understand, it had felt like Tarrick was getting stronger but now his skin felt cold and his heart weakened. Matthew wasn't sure what to do. He knew incubi fed on sexual energy, but beyond that he was at a loss. Maybe his internal injuries were just too severe, maybe there was no coming back from this amount of damage.

Incubi were strong, no doubt, but they didn't possess vampire healing abilities or constitution. Matthew had his head smashed in and came back from it, but if the same thing happened to Tarrick, he'd be dead.

Matthew growled. If Tarrick died, his future would be too uncertain. His fate would be in the hands of other incubi and none seemed as receptive to the idea of a vampire incubus.

He moved in front of Tarrick and pushed his legs apart so he could kneel between them. He wasn't sure if anything would work at this point but he had to try something. Anything. Matthew leaned in and brushed his lips against Tarrick's. Nothing happened. He turned his kiss aggressive, to see if there would be any response. There wasn't.

Pulling away, he looked at the broken body before him. Tarrick's breathing was too labored.

Matthew brought out his claws and ripped off what was left of Tarrick's clothing, and then he forced his claws away.

He spat in his hand and touched Tarrick's limp cock. Carefully he began to rub it. The large member responded with a twitch. Matthew had never jerked off another man but he was plenty familiar with what he enjoyed himself. Keeping with long, steady strokes he brought down his other hand and grabbed the base of Tarrick's cock. He twisted his hand around the base, gripping hard enough to add pressure and friction, but not so hard that it'd hurt.

Tarrick's sex stiffened beneath his hands.

He gasped at it. He had seen Tarrick's cock before while he was in his incubus form, but that was from across the room and it had been flaccid. Holding his hard cock in his hands made him appreciate just how impressive this thing was. The head itself was nearly the size of Matthew's fist and the fat rod was as long as his forearm.

It was a thing of beauty, but Matthew prayed Tarrick would never try to fuck him at this size. There was just no way he could fit something this large inside of him.

Matthew traced his finger down one of the veins that ran to the underside, then gently cupped Tarrick's smooth balls. They were so large they spilled around his hand as he played with them.

This wasn't enough. He needed to give Tarrick more. Matthew leaned down and flicked his tongue across the head. A strained gasp escaped Tarrick's lips. Encouraged, Matthew ran his tongue around the head and dipped it across his slit. He savored the salty taste, it was like ecstasy on his tongue.

Tarrick stirred but it wasn't working fast enough, his heart still slowed.

Matthew had an idea. If both incubi and vampires used life energy, he wondered if they could share it between them. He closed his eyes but didn't stop licking. He felt the red swirls of energy stored in his blood pouches. They were bright and strong right now, coiled, waiting for his command.

Grabbing a thread, he pulled it up to his tongue, but didn't use it to enhance anything; instead, he let it flow out of him and into Tarrick.

Tarrick's breathing began to pick up.

It was working.

Matthew wanted to give him more. He sat up, caressing Tarrick's cock with one hand and grabbing the back of Tarrick's neck with the other, pulling them together into a kiss. Tarrick didn't respond, but Matthew didn't stop. He reached inside of him and grabbed more coils of power. He pushed them into Tarrick through the kiss.

As if begging for more, Tarrick's lips began to move.

Matthew, happy to oblige, gripped tighter onto Tarrick's sex and pumped his hand up and down, sending a thread of energy into Tarrick with each stroke. Unable to help himself, he parted Tarrick's teeth with his tongue and explored his mouth.

Tarrick's heartbeat began to strengthen and he stirred.

Matthew didn't let up, he kept going until Tarrick's hands came up around his back and yanked Matthew into him.

Startled by his sudden strength, Matthew stopped stroking and tried to pull away but Tarrick wouldn't let him move. A low growl came from deep within Tarrick's chest and he gripped Matthew's hair hard, pinning him into the kiss.

Tarrick took control of the feeding and began draining energy from Matthew at a frightening pace. Matthew tried to slow him but it was as if the floodgates opened and could not be forced closed.

He panicked.

If Tarrick took everything from him, it would leave him helpless out here in the forest. And if this didn't work—if Tarrick didn't heal—that meant a painful, deadly sunrise for him in the morning.

Matthew grabbed onto a few of the strands that were being sucked away from him and redirected them into making himself stronger.

"Stop!" he yelled and pushed away from Tarrick using one short burst of power. Matthew's claws came forward as he broke free and tumbled backwards onto the cold ground. He looked up at Tarrick and paused in awe. Most of the general's injuries were healing before his eyes. The bones in his wings were twisting and snapping back into place accompanied by a terrible crunching sound. His cuts began to stitch together and bruises began to fade away from his skin.

Tarrick reached up, pulled the dagger out of his shoulder, and tossed it away. The wound sealed almost instantly.

After a few moments, Matthew could hardly tell that Tarrick had even been wounded tonight…if it wasn't for the snapped horn—which hadn't repaired itself—and the condition of his clothes.

Matthew felt so drained he could sleep for a month. He stayed on the ground as Tarrick pushed himself up to his feet and loomed above him. His rigid cock jutting out from his hips. Matthew smiled, happy to see that Tarrick would be alright. But his smile faded when he realized Tarrick was studying him with hungry eyes.

A continuous low growl came from the general. He wasn't done feeding.

Matthew propped himself up on his elbows and began to scoot away but Tarrick took a step forward, closing the gap between them.

"Master…?" Matthew asked.

He had no idea what Tarrick was doing.

Tarrick growled again. No. This wasn't Tarrick.

This was Tarrick's monster.

So the great general could lose control after all. Matthew wasn't too thrilled to find that out. He flipped over, pushed himself onto his feet, and dashed out of the grove. He pulled up one of the last threads of power he had left, but before he could use it to enhance his speed he was hit from behind and he slammed belly first into a tree.

Snow fell off the branches and crashed to the ground around them.

Ribs cracked. Matthew redirected the energy into healing them.

Tarrick's body pressed into Matthew's back, pinning him between the incubus and the rough tree trunk. Matthew struggled to get away but it was useless, he was too weak and Tarrick too strong now.

Tarrick reached down to Matthew's hip and dug his claws into it, piercing the skin. The scent of his blood filled the air. Matthew ignored the pain as Tarrick took a few steps away from the tree, pulling Matthew with him.

He pushed his hand against the base of Matthew's neck, just under the collar, and bent him over, forcing his ass up.

Dear god, Tarrick was going to take Matthew right here while he was in his full incubus form.

"Please, don't do this," Matthew said as he thrashed about, trying to get away.

Tarrick answered him by digging his claws deeper into Matthew's hip and neck. His tail came up and wrapped around Matthew's legs. It was useless, he couldn't escape no matter how hard he fought. The incubus had total control of him.

Tarrick nestled his huge cock on Matthew's crack and slid up and down with the promise that penetration would be soon. It would be impossible, though. Besides this being his first time, Matthew had no idea how he could physically accommodate him. There was no way his hole could stretch that large.

Matthew twisted his head back to see Tarrick looming above him in the dark night.

"I beg you. Please. It will be too painful for me...please."

Tarrick responded by thrusting harder against his crack. His cock became wet as lubricant oozed from it.

"Master..." Matthew cried, "Tarrick..."

Tarrick stopped. Matthew felt claws flex at the base of his neck as control returned to Tarrick. Relief washed through him when he felt Tarrick's entire body shrink down to his usual size.

He didn't let go of Matthew though. His claws still tightly grasped his neck and bore into his hips.

"On your knees," Tarrick commanded.

Matthew steadied himself on the tree trunk and dropped to both of his knees.

Tarrick pulled Matthew's hips up while shoving his shoulders down to the ground, keeping Matthew's hole exposed.

He leaned over Matthew's back and whispered close to his ear. "I'm sorry your first time is going to be this way but I have to take you right now. I have to finish. I'm not sure I can hold my control if you try to escape or run. Do you understand?"

Vampire or incubi, it didn't matter—when it came down to it, they were both predators. Only in this case, Matthew was his prey and if he tried to run, the monster would chase. And then the monster would have his way with him.

That was the last thing Matthew wanted. Tarrick would destroy him.

"I understand."

Tarrick's tail uncoiled from Matthew's leg and he released Matthew's neck, but not his hip. He ran a claw down his back, leaving behind small lines of blood—along with that fucking ooze stuff—and ended by grabbing Matthew's firm butt cheek and squeezing hard.

A low growl came from Matthew's chest. It was bad enough he didn't get to participate, he didn't want to have to spend his time fighting for control over his vampire instincts, which told him to attack the man dominating him.

Tarrick ignored Matthew's growl. He grabbed the base of his cock and guided it to Matthew's hole then teased the head against it, wetting it with his lube.

Matthew grew hard and trembled as anticipation built in him. He was nervous. His insides were at war with both his desire for Tarrick and his fear of him. In the past, no matter how often Matthew resisted, Tarrick was always the victor.

Even now that Matthew had a plan, deep down he feared that, in the end, Tarrick would see through him and Matthew would forever be his prisoner. His slave. Matthew couldn't bear that thought. He was made to be a conqueror, he could feel it in his bones, and one day they would all see it when he forced them all to their knees before him.

Right now, though, his desire was winning the battle within him.

Tarrick didn't wait any longer, he pushed his length forward and grunted as he entered Matthew's hole. Matthew groaned as Tarrick worked his way in, inch by inch. He was ill prepared for the size of it and it burned. He reached back and pressed on Tarrick's hip as a silent request for him to stop.

Snarling, Tarrick flexed his claws into Matthew's flesh but still stopped, allowing Matthew to adjust to the feeling.

Matthew dropped his hand back to the frozen ground once the burning eased. Tarrick continued into him, stretching him and filling him completely. The incubus paused for a moment before withdrawing and thrusting back in hard. Heavy breaths accompanied each push.

Matthew groaned. The feeling of Tarrick's cock inside of him was better than he expected, or even imaged. He had no idea it could feel so good.

He desperately wanted to grab his own length and stroke it each time Tarrick drove into him, but he didn't have permission. He wasn't sure if he really needed it or if Tarrick had just been playing with him, but he sure as hell wasn't going to risk doing anything that would piss Tarrick off right now.

Tarrick's thrusts became frantic, a slave to the hunger driving him. His balls slapped aggressively against Matthew's skin with each plunge.

Matthew pushed his hips back, sending Tarrick deeper inside of him. They both moaned with pleasure.

Tarrick snaked his tail up Matthew's leg and wrapped it around his cock. The tail squeezed and rubbed his sex, it was like a dozen fingers coiling around him, each moving on their own.

It felt incredible. Matthew was in heaven.

Working his tail with exceptional skill, Tarrick continued to pound away, and Matthew couldn't take it anymore, he dug his claws into the hard ground as his balls tightened and he exploded with heat. His body jerked hard as he came on the forest floor.

Tarrick tightened his grip and plunged into Matthew three more times before his own body began to quake with release. He cried out as he filled Matthew's tight tunnel with his hot seed.

He didn't release Matthew right away. Instead, he held him still while he enjoyed the afterglow of his climax, running his hands gently down Matthew's back.

Matthew sighed when Tarrick finally withdrew from him and uncoiled his tail from his cock. He was surprised when Tarrick planted a tender kiss between his shoulder blades before he stood.

Drained, Matthew rolled over. He needed to rest and heal. Looking up at Tarrick, he watched as he forced the rest of his incubus side away.

"Come." Tarrick offered his hand.

Taking it, Matthew got to his feet, his legs shaky. Tarrick led Matthew back into the grove.

Tarrick kneeled next to the still unconscious commander and cupped his hand on Cullip's cheek. "I am sorry my old friend."

Matthew put his pants and shoes back on then looked at the horizon. The sky began to lighten.

"The sun'll be up soon," Matthew said.

"Can you make it to the keep in time?" Tarrick asked, his attention still on Cullip.

Matthew nodded. "I think so."

"Go."

Matthew darted away. He was tired. And it wasn't because the sun was about to rise. It was meeting a vampire lord who promised to help him, the battle, the sex, the deep emotional drain he felt within his soul. It all wore on him.

But he pushed past it and focused on crossing the miles back to the keep.

By the time he arrived, dawn was upon him and the sky had turned a beautiful purple hue. The sun would break over the horizon in a few minutes. The lure of sleep pulled at Matthew but he pushed it away, he still had a little time and he had a promise to honor.

Matthew didn't pause outside the estate, though he did take in everything he saw as he passed by. The grounds were in shambles. Statues had crumbled, the main gate was broken down, blood covered the grass and walls, trees and bushes uprooted, windows shattered, cars overturned.

The dead hunters and incubi had been removed and the decayed vampire bodies were piled on the grass. What was left of them would burn when the sun rose. There were over twenty hunters on patrol around the area, with many others rushing about to carry out their tasks. Matthew ran past all of it so quickly that by the time the hunters knew he was there, he was already inside heading up to the command center.

The inside wasn't any better than the outside. The bodies were gone but the place was a mess. Blood painted everything, the marble pillars were cracked and crumbled, art on the walls had been destroyed, weapons strewn about, urns were smashed, wood splinters and glass littered the floors. Servants and hunters both were cleaning up the mess.

Screams came from the infirmary. He sensed it was full of injured hunters and incubi. He passed a hunter sleeping in a chair and another hunter who was consoling a crying friend.

Matthew opened the doors to the command center and came to a stop in front of Silva. She was standing by the round table in the center, looking down at a large screen displaying casualty reports and current deployment of hunters at both the estate and the academy. Tane and the warrior succubus were standing on the other side of the table, busy reading reports and giving orders.

Before Silva even registered who Matthew was, she had her folding crossbow out and aimed at him. Damn, her reactions were quick. The other hunters in the room drew their weapons a fraction of a second later. Tane and the female warrior brought out their claws.

Matthew stood still, relieved he hadn't been shot this time.

A voice came over Silva's comm: "Lieutenant, Matthew just ran by. Heading inside."

"Thank you, Pine," she said into her gloved hand. Silva lowered her crossbow. "I'm surprised to see you."

"I gave you my word, didn't I?" Matthew could feel the sun near the horizon. "Tarrick and the commander are eight miles west of here. Bring a doctor with you."

"Who is in need of the doctor?" Tane asked.

"Cullip. Your father is fine now."

Then Matthew felt the sun break the horizon. He couldn't resist the pull of sleep anymore. His eyes rolled back and he dropped to the ground, dead to the world.

Twenty-One

When Matthew next woke, he realized three things were wrong right away. The first was that he could feel the sun still high in the sky. Never before had he woken while the sun was still up. As far as he knew, vampires couldn't wake during the day, not even to save their own lives. And yet, he was awake now.

The second thing he noticed was that his abdomen was aching. It was a minor throbbing deep within him but he couldn't ignore it no matter how much he tried.

The third thing was that he was horny. And not just a little turned on either, no, he needed relief and he needed it now. It was a thirst he needed to find a way to quench.

Matthew was laying naked on the cot with a sheet over him. He hadn't bothered to open his eyes since the sun was putting him back to sleep. He almost surrendered to it when he heard two hunters enter the room.

Tarrick's room. He'd been here often enough to know the smell of it. The mahogany bookcases, the fireplace, the wood polish on the floor, the scent of night and earth. But Tarrick wasn't in the room right now.

The hunters—one male, one female—came and stood over him.

Matthew wasn't shackled. That seemed careless…or maybe not since vampires couldn't move during the day. They didn't have to keep him shackled, just so long as he was tied up before nightfall. Or perhaps Tarrick was trusting him enough to not have him chained.

Matthew laughed to himself. Tarrick wouldn't do that, even if he had saved Tarrick's life.

He didn't want the hunters to know he was awake so he didn't move or open his eyes.

"You want to prop him up while I get the shirt on?" the female hunter asked the male. The male must have nodded because there was no other response. They were here to dress him. Made sense; each time he had woken in Tarrick's room he had fresh clothes on.

"Damn, he's a big one," the female said as she pulled back the sheet covering his erect cock.

He could feel heat rising in her as she looked at it. It pleased Matthew that she seemed to enjoy it.

"For a vampire I guess," the male said.

The woman giggled. "Whatever, Vin, you're just jealous."

"Hardly." The male, Vin, place his gloved hands under Matthew's shoulders and pulled him up. Once the hunters got a shirt onto Matthew, they set him back down. He felt the woman move to the end of the bed and slip underwear around his feet and up his legs. She stopped before they were pulled up all the way. God, he wished she'd keep going. Maybe brush her hand along his cock.

"How the hell are we going to get his pants zipped up over that?"

"We'll manage."

"He must be having one hell of a dream." She paused, her heart sped just a bit. "Have you ever wondered what they feel like?"

Vin laughed. "A vampire dick? Hell no, get your mind out of the gutter, Flores."

Matthew rarely heard hunters like this. It was nice to hear them being...normal. More than just cruel jailers and killers of his kind.

"Touch it if you'd like," Matthew said and opened his eyes. He tried to sit up but he could only move enough to turn his head—the sun keeping him weak.

Both hunters jumped back.

Flores, wearing tactical pants and a leather turtleneck that hugged her curves, grabbed a stake from her belt of weapons.

Vin, who was tall and fit, flicked his wrist and a silver blade sprung out from under his sleeve. Matthew couldn't see any other weapons on him. He guessed they were all hiding under his long coat. They both looked to be in their early twenties, younger hunters.

Matthew desperately wanted Flores to touch him. Or even Vin. He needed to feel their hands on him.

Vin was stunned. "How is he awake?"

"He wasn't given a ring, right?" Flores asked.

"Not that I've heard of."

A ring? What the hell did they mean by that?

"Call dispatch and tell them," Flores said.

Vin raised his comm. If he called dispatch, Matthew wouldn't get the release he so desperately needed right now. This would all be over. He couldn't let that happen.

He couldn't do anything to them with his vampire powers since they both wore contacts, making it impossible to compel them. But maybe he could stop them some other way. He could feel other abilities waking in-side of him—incubus abilities. Maybe he could hold them the same way Tarrick could hold him.

His desire for them was overwhelming.

"Don't do that. Come here and touch me," he said.

Vin paused.

"What is it?" Flores asked after she noticed he stopped moving.

"I think he's...holding me..." Vin struggled to get the words out.

"He's a vamp, not an incubus, he can't do that."

Vin flicked his arm and his blade disappeared up the sleeve. He walked over to Matthew and put his hands on his chest, exploring his pecs and nipples.

"Take off your gloves," Matthew commanded. He wanted to feel skin on skin.

Vin removed his gloves, set them down on the bed, and resumed his journey across Matthew's chest. Flores cussed as she lifted her comm up.

"Come join," he said to stop her from warning other hunters.

Flores froze, fighting against him, but after a moment she approached the bed and took off her gloves. She reached down and tentatively touched Matthew's hard length while Vin pinched his nipple.

Matthew moaned and rolled his eyes back into his head. God, they felt so good.

"That's enough, Matthew," a harsh female voice said.

Matthew opened his eyes to see Silva standing behind the two hunters. Green light filled the air and six other hunters teleported in. How the hell did they get here so fast? Matthew had stopped the hunters from using their comms. Then he remembered about the damn camera hidden on the bookshelf.

"Let them go," she said.

Matthew whined. He wished he could move. Silva walked over to Mat-thew and put her hand on his shoulder.

"Let them go," she repeated.

Matthew huffed. He wasn't sure how to let the hunters go. He wasn't even sure what he was doing to them. He closed his eyes and focused. He could feel golden threads leaving him and wrapping their way around the two hunters. He pulled the threads back into him.

When Vin and Flores were free of his hold, they looked around, con-fused.

"Commander, I don't know how—" Flores started.

She was cut off when Silva held up her hand. "Not now, Flores. You two go wait for me outside."

The two young hunters grabbed their gloves and left the room. Silva pulled the sheet up over Matthew's waist so he was no longer exposed.

Flores had called Silva 'Commander'. Matthew wondered just how much time had passed since the attack on the keep. And what had happened to Cullip? Was he dead? Or was he still compelled? It was clear Silva was in charge now.

"Go back to sleep," Silva ordered. Her orders always held an edge of respect to them. She didn't threaten, she didn't try to be an alpha, she just gave the order with authority and expected it to be followed. Matthew liked that. He liked her. The little commander. He vowed he wouldn't kill her if he could avoid it.

Matthew was still horny but the appeal of sleep was too tempting. He closed his eyes.

Before he slipped away he heard Silva telling the other hunters that he was to be shackled even during the day now and only 'class three' and above were allowed to interact with him. Matthew wasn't quite sure what that meant, but he guessed it was hunters that could fight against incubi influence.

He surrendered to the light.

When he next woke, it was nighttime.

The pain in his abdomen was still there, stronger now, and he was still horny. And worse, he was hungry for blood. It felt like forever since he last had any.

He gritted his teeth as he sat up on the cot, pressing his hands into his stomach where the pain emanated. He was dressed and his arms were shackled and chained to the wall. There was a chain attached to the back of his collar as well.

Tarrick, wearing a suit as always, was working at the desk in the corner of the room. He had a laptop open in front of him but was leaning back in his chair, reading a report.

Matthew wanted him.

Tarrick's blue eyes looked over the report at Matthew. "From now on, when you wake in here, you'll kneel. You won't speak or stand until I, or someone who outranks me, gives you permission to," he said then went back to the report.

Uh, well Matthew hadn't expected that to be the first thing Tarrick told him. He had hoped that Tarrick would answer some questions that were on his mind, or maybe talk about what had happened back in the forest.

Matthew slid off the cot and down to his left knee. He bowed his head forward and waited.

And waited.

Tarrick continued working all night, ignoring Matthew.

Matthew listened as Tarrick made phone calls, often ordering hunter's to new locations or asking for updates on situations involving vampires. Sometimes he'd give a report to someone who outranked him. Every now and then, a hunter would enter to drop off more reports or answer some questions for Tarrick.

At one point Silva entered. Tarrick ordered her to graduate the latest class of hunters a month early. It sounded as if the attack had left them shorthanded in the area.

One of the more interesting events of the night, at least to Matthew, was when a human servant brought Tarrick a plate of cheese and cut meats for him. Tarrick ate the food while he worked. Matthew had assumed incubi survived solely off sex, just as he could only have blood, and had no idea they could eat other things.

Matthew missed food sometimes. It didn't compare to blood, but once in a while he'd get a craving for barbecue. The craving would pass as soon as the food neared him, and the idea of even trying it repulsed him.

The sun was near rising and Tarrick still hadn't talked to him. The pain in Matthew's abdomen gradually began to worsen. Near dawn he was shifting around on his knees trying to find a position that would satisfy Tarrick and lessen the pain. He couldn't find any.

His hard manhood ached inside of his pants for a good part of the night as well. It would ease, but then he'd remember the sex with Tarrick or the hunters touching him and his erection would be back.

Matthew's eyelids grew heavy as dawn approached. He struggled to stay awake.

"You may go to the cot and sleep," Tarrick said.

Matthew wanted to ask him one of the million questions bouncing around his head. What happened to Cullip? Was Tarrick mad at him for his actions during the battle? He had taken blood without his permission and lost control at the end but surely he had some praise too. Matthew had, after all, saved his life.

He even wanted to know more about the other incubi he saw during the battle. Or how much time had passed since that night. Or even if he could have some blood, just a little, to take the edge off.

But he said nothing as he lay down. Sleep claimed him right away.

The next night, and the one after, he woke, kneeled, and waited. Again Tarrick ignored him each night and continued working.

The pain inside of him was beginning to become unbearable and erotic thoughts filled his mind…thoughts of sucking Tarrick's cock…riding it… it had to be his gland, the soavik, causing this, the pain was in the same place the doctor had cut into him and where Rosaline had scanned him.

On top of the pain in his stomach, his vampire scratched at him, hungry. He stayed on his knees but every now and then a low growl would rumble across his chest. Once he realized he was doing it he'd stop but it would happen each time Tarrick made too much noise or moved around the room.

Tarrick ignored the growling and at the end of each night, he'd dismiss Matthew back to his cot.

The following day Matthew woke while the sun was still up. He could hear and smell Tarrick having sex with another man.

God, he was so hungry. He'd give anything to join them. He tried to move but nothing happened, he couldn't even open his eyes. He was pinned inside his own body and forced to listen to Tarrick screwing someone else. It was torture.

Eventually, sleep took him again.

When he woke that night he sat on the cot for a few minutes, struggling against the pain and hunger. The smell of Tarrick overpowered his senses and Matthew stared at him, shooting daggers his way. Tarrick, in a grey suit with a fitted vest and no jacket, was typing something on his laptop.

When Matthew didn't kneel Tarrick looked up from his work.

Matthew narrowed his eyes at him but said nothing.

Tarrick glanced over at the kanabō hanging on the wall. It was the only warning Matthew needed. He groaned in pain as he got down on his knee.

He was kneeling for a few hours when a new wave of pain hit him. His whole body contracted and shivered. He needed to feed, blood or sex, he didn't care, he needed something.

"Master…please…" he begged, unable to stay quiet anymore.

"If you speak again without my permission you'll be punished," Tarrick said and went back to his task.

Matthew fell forward, down on both of his knees and wrapped his arms around his stomach. His head bowed forward so low it was nearly on the ground. He might be punished for not kneeling correctly but the pain was too great to care.

Tarrick's doors burst opened.

"What are you doing to him?" a furious voice asked.

He heard Tarrick stand. "Lady Rosaline, I'm not sure what you mean."

"He's obviously suffering through his transformation—I can smell the pheromones from down the hall."

Matthew looked up. Rosaline looked just as beautiful as she had the first time he saw her, but dangerous too. Like her namesake: a rose, so alluring but covered in thorns. She wore a white flowing empire dress with green flowers printed on it. It flattered her curvy body and her curly red hair.

Matthew desired her. But then again, he desired anything that walked on two legs right now. He was so hungry.

Tarrick shrugged. "How could he be? He's just a vampire. A wretched creature that cares for nothing except inflicting pain."

That wasn't true. Matthew cared for many things; inflicting pain was not among them. At least it wasn't when he was in control of himself. Tarrick knew that.

"Tarrick, don't you dare..." Rosaline warned him.

"'He's a fluke of nature. He might have a soavik but that doesn't make him an incubus. He's not part of a family or a house. At his core, he'll always be just a vampire. He could never be one of us.' That is what you told the High King right before you recommended that we kill him, correct?"

Rosaline slapped him across the face. The *smack* echoed in the room.

Tarrick stood stunned for a moment but didn't retaliate. "I apologize, my lady. I did not mean to upset you."

"Yes, you did. You are letting him suffer to prove a point to me."

"Why do you care if he suffers? You've advocated for his death since the moment you found out about him."

"I..." She looked over to Matthew.

Tears formed in Matthew's eyes. The words—her words—Tarrick quoted stung him deeply. He didn't want to be a fluke and he wanted a family again, people to care for, people to love. He hated all his years of being alone. He couldn't dispute the fact that he was a vampire, but that didn't mean he wasn't also an incubus. His own daughter was an incubus now and he'd do anything to protect her.

Matthew bowed his head so he didn't have to look at Rosaline.

"I didn't expect him to save my life," she said, her voice low.

"Did you read the report?" Tarrick asked.

"I did."

"Then you know you were the first one he saved that night."

"Yes," she sighed. "You've made your point. You can stop punishing him."

"No, he's earned this punishment."

"What could he have possibly done to earn this?"

Matthew wanted to know as well. Tarrick grabbed one of the leather chairs from in front of the fireplace and set it so that it was facing Matthew, just outside the range of his chains.

"Return to kneeling correctly, Matthew," Tarrick ordered.

Matthew struggled back to his one knee. He kept his head and shoulders down.

"I'll let him tell you. Care to take a seat?" Tarrick asked.

There was a pause, then Lady Rosaline sat down in the chair in front of Matthew.

"Look up," Tarrick ordered.

Matthew did so. Rosaline's beauty stunned him.

Tarrick stood behind the chair, towering over the both of them. "Matthew, please tell us everything you did wrong during the assault."

Twenty-Two

Matthew swallowed hard. He knew Tarrick had the reports and was aware of what he had done. He didn't want to list every fuck up he made. This only served to humiliate him in front of Rosaline. Magnificent Rosaline.

"Master I, uh…" He sighed and gathered the strength he'd need to get through this. "I drank blood without your permission. Twice."

Both were silent, waiting for him to continue.

"I compelled Lady Rosaline." Matthew hung his head in shame. "Please forgive me."

Rosaline said nothing.

"What else?" Tarrick asked.

"I lost my temper at Lord Tane and threatened him. I disobeyed the hunters when they ordered me back to my cell. I lost control at the end of the battle and couldn't stand down when Lieuten…Commander Silva ordered me to."

That was everything, he hoped. He couldn't think of anything else but then again, he lost control so maybe there was more.

"And after the battle, when you were with me, what did you do wrong there?"

Matthew racked his brain. He had done everything he could to save Tarrick. Then it came to him. "I bit you. I was weak. Please forgive me, Master."

"He bit you?" Rosaline asked. She looked disturbed.

Tarrick nodded. "He didn't take any blood, he just put his fangs in me."

"Yeah, they like to do that during sex." She absentmindedly rubbed the area above her collarbone.

"Anything else?" Tarrick asked him.

Matthew shook his head.

"You should not have released those vampires you had compelled. Now the vampires know of your ability before we wanted them to and those were five extra vampires that could be dead."

"It won't happen again, Master," he said and kept his head down.

Tarrick came around the chair and stopped in front of Matthew. He reached under Matthew's chin and forced him to look up. "And Ascelina?"

What did Tarrick know? Did he know Ascelina had sent these vampires for Matthew to kill? Or that she would one day help him get his freedom?

"I wasn't able to stop her from compelling Cullip."

"Nor would I expect you to be able to. Tell me what happened down in the prison that night."

"She was there when we woke, the hunters were already dead. Cullip teleported and when I tried to stop her from compelling him, she threw me around like I was nothing, then used some stones to teleport out."

Tarrick's claws came out and dug into Matthew's neck where he held him. Matthew whimpered and tried to pull away but the claws only dug deeper as he struggled.

"You are lying to me. I'll give you one chance to correct that."

What did he know? Matthew couldn't risk him knowing what Emilia and Ascelina had talked to him about. He would just have to accept the punishment.

"It is the truth," Matthew lied. He could feel his blood dripping down his neck, coming from the points where Tarrick's claws pierced his skin.

"The hunter's wear a device that records the time their heart stop beating. She appeared two minutes before you woke, killed the hunters, and didn't leave until ten minutes later. That means she was there talking to you. I want to know what it was you two spoke of."

Matthew's eyes rolled back as he closed them. God, what could he tell him? Not the truth, but it had to be something he'd believe.

"I...I begged her to take me away from here. But she didn't know how to get the collar off. I'm sorry, Master. It's just...I don't want to spend the rest of my life in a cage or chained up." At least the last part was true. Matthew wanted to look away but Tarrick held his head firmly in place. Tarrick's face was stone, emotionless and unreadable.

"Why did you join the fight? You could have sat in your cell. No one would have blamed you for following the orders of the hunters."

"I watched her compel the commander. I didn't want him to kill you. And I heard Lady Rosaline scream. I might not want to be a slave, but that doesn't mean I could just let everyone die."

Tarrick released Matthew. "Those are the reasons I'm punishing him, my lady."

Matthew looked at the ground again.

Rosaline shifted in her chair. "And what about everything he did right that night? He saved me. He saved you, Cullip, dozens of hunters. He killed—what?—nearly thirty vampires on his own."

Tarrick waved his hand dismissively. "So what? He's just a tool, a weapon for us to use. That's what he should be doing. It's what is expected of him."

A low growl came up from Matthew's chest. Is that all Tarrick saw him as? A tool? Deep within him more pain formed. He knew he shouldn't care this much, but for some twisted reason he did. He wanted Tarrick to like him. It was fucked up.

He looked up to see Rosaline and Tarrick watching him. He stopped growling and bent his head back down.

"Alright, I will give him a reward for saving our lives," Tarrick said as he walked to his desk, retrieved a folder, and came back. He held the folder out to Matthew. "Here."

Matthew looked from him to Rosaline, who looked as confused as he was, and back. He reached up and took the folder, his chains rattling as he moved.

He opened it and inside was a single picture of his daughter, Lily.

It was a recent picture of her in a garden, flowers blooming around her. Her eyes had lightened from hazel to almost a bluish-grey. Her normally brown hair was beginning to look blonde. She smiled cheerfully. It delighted him to see her happy. He had been so worried she would hate her new life, that she would be scared. She didn't look it here.

Tears threatened to drop as he traced his hand across her face. He missed her so much.

Matthew could feel Rosaline studying him as he looked at his daughter's photo. He wondered what she was thinking. Did she realize that he did have a family now? Someone he cared for and loved.

Tarrick held his hand out. "I can't let you keep it."

Matthew's fangs came down, he snarled and pulled the photo to his chest. Rosaline yelped and jumped up from the chair, her heart beating faster. Matthew had scared her. Tarrick, however, hadn't moved. He kept his hand outstretched.

Forcing his fangs away, Matthew held the folder up. "I'm sorry, my lady. I didn't mean to frighten you. My control right now is…Master, may I please have some blood?"

"No," Tarrick said as he took the folder.

"When do you plan to feed him again?" Rosaline asked once she settled back down into the chair.

"When I feel his punishment has finished. A few weeks maybe."

Rosaline looked at Matthew with concern. "If he doesn't have his first feeding soon it'll damage him."

Tarrick went back to his desk and put the folder down. "Do you truly care?"

She studied Matthew's face. Matthew had a hard time looking at her. His eyes kept settling on the pulse in her neck. "I don't know. He's just a vampire."

"Is he?"

She closed her eyes. "I just don't want him to suffer."

"Then end his suffering."

"What do you mean?"

"I've already made the decision that no one under my command can feed him, which is currently everyone at Ashwood, except you. If you want him to stop suffering, you'll have to feed him yourself."

Rosaline stood and faced him. "I can get an order for you to feed him."

Tarrick shrugged. "I'm sure you could, but even for you that'll take three or four days, and if he doesn't first feed before then he'll never be able to feed correctly."

"You're a bastard." Rosaline crossed the room and stood in front of the doors. "I might not want him to suffer but I would never sleep with him. I will never let a vampire touch me again and you cannot manipulate me into doing so." And with that, she left the room.

Tarrick bowed as she left then went back to work, leaving Matthew to kneel in agony for the rest of the night.

The next night Matthew was in so much pain he had trouble sitting up. When he finally pushed himself upright he nearly cried when he saw Tarrick at his desk, still ignoring him.

He was so hungry, so desperate for food, that he would do anything to get some. His vampire side came forward and he began trying to rip his shackles off, growing increasingly more frustrated when they wouldn't budge. He tried to cut the restraints from him using his claws. When that didn't work he clawed around his bracers, shredding his skin in the process.

The scent of his own blood filled the air and his control slipped away from him.

He was lost to madness. Feral.

He sunk his teeth into his hand and began sucking his own blood, just to have the feeling of it filling his mouth.

"Stop it, Matthew," Tarrick said. He was standing before him.

Matthew took his hand from his mouth. Drops of blood slid down his chin. He surged forward at Tarrick only to be yanked back when the chains ran out of slack. He curled his lips up and flashed large fangs, then he let out a roar so fierce it would have put a lion to shame.

Tarrick sighed, then walked over and grabbed the kanabō off the wall. Matthew stilled.

As Tarrick walked towards him with the weapon, Matthew took a step away and kept backing up until he bumped into the wall. He whimpered and fell down to his knee, cowering before Tarrick.

"That's better," Tarrick said as he stood over him, dark and cruel.

Matthew hated him. Why had he saved Tarrick's life? He should have escaped during the attack. Staying here to learn about his powers wasn't worth this pain, this punishment. He no longer cared he was part incubus, he was all vampire and he should be with his people.

His eyes burned with rage and his muscles trembled as he fought to keep it together.

The doors to Tarrick's room opened.

"Get out," Tarrick yelled without even looking to see who was there.

"I was about to say the same to you," Rosaline said as she entered. She looked flawless wearing a teal wrap dress. Her nude stilettos clicked the ground as she walked. In one of her hands she clutched two jugs of blood.

Matthew could smell that it was fresh, taken from many different humans. His rage subsided when he saw her. He didn't want to scare her. With tremendous effort, he forced his vampire side away.

Tarrick crossed the room to her and bowed. "My apologies, Lady Rosaline, I thought you were a hunter."

"Give me the keys then get out." She looked past him to Matthew, who stayed kneeling on the ground.

Tarrick went to his desk and retrieved a set of keys. "This is not a wise idea right now. He needs time to calm down."

Rosaline shot him a severe glare and snatched the keys from Tarrick with her free hand. "Out."

Tarrick started to leave and paused at the doors. "Matthew, you may accept blood from Lady Rosaline as if it was from me." Then he left, kanabō in hand, closing the doors behind him.

Matthew found himself wondering again just how Rosaline outranked him. She didn't seem to have the authority to command him on some matters, but she could order him from his own room. It was strange.

He stopped caring when his eyes fell to the large containers of blood in her hand. The smell was too much. His fangs came back down and he didn't have the strength to try and put them away.

Rosaline gripped tightly to the keys and stepped forward. Matthew didn't even need to smell her fear or hear her rapid heartbeat to know she was nervous.

She stood well outside the range of his chains and studied him. She seemed to be waiting for something.

Pain ripped through him and he couldn't wait on her anymore.

"Mistress," he started, unsure if she would respond to the title, "may I have some blood?"

She nodded slowly, set the bottles down just inside of his range, and backed away.

Matthew wanted to leap over to them, rip the lids off and chug them down. But such an aggressive move might scare Rosaline. He didn't want that. She was giving him a gift, and he didn't want her to fear him in return.

Instead, he stood, picked up one of the bottles, opened it, and drank at a steady pace. The blood was a warm aphrodisiac to him. His cock grew hard while he fed. He finished the first bottle and began drinking the second.

He couldn't believe she had brought him nearly two gallons worth of blood. One gallon—the amount he could get from a single human if he drained them—would have satisfied him, but two would remove all trace of hunger. When he was done, he set the container down and closed his eyes, lost in the haze of feeding.

From outside of the room he could hear Silva and other hunter guards, along with Tarrick. All waiting in case Rosaline needed them.

He opened his eyes when he realized she was staring at him. Matthew grew uneasy as her green eyes bore into him. He forced his fangs away.

His hunger returned.

How? He just fed. But this hunger was different. The pain. It was his incubus side. He pressed a hand into his stomach.

Rosaline said nothing.

"Would you like me to kneel again?" Matthew offered.

"No."

She stood silent for a while. Matthew looked down, his eyes studied the wooden floor below him.

"I met your daughter," she finally said.

Matthew glanced up at her. He studied her face for any signs she was lying to him. He wasn't sure, she was difficult for him to read.

"I went to stay with Lord Teleclus a few weeks ago. I didn't know she was your daughter until the picture last night. Tarrick and Teleclus have kept that secret well."

"How is she?" Matthew couldn't help asking. He took a step forward.

"She's safe and happy, curious about everything. Everyone loves her. She doesn't have any idea you're alive."

"I know." Matthew brought up his arms and looked at the metal bracers and shackles on them. "I don't want her to see me like this."

"I didn't think it was possible for a vampire to resist killing their family once they were turned," she said.

"I would kill myself before seeing any harm come to her."

Rosaline took a step closer to Matthew. She brought the keys up to her chin and looked lost in thought. Every movement Rosaline made was seductive to him. His eyes studied her body and he wondered what she looked like under her dress.

Matthew grunted as a pulse of pain shot through him.

"I was nineteen when I first felt the pain you feel now. I had no idea what was happening to me. My father was an incubus and he abandoned my mother when she became pregnant. She had no idea what he was, and I had no one to explain to me what was happening to my body.

"I was a good Catholic Irish girl living in New York during the 1920s. I thought a devil had possessed me, that I was being punished for my sins. I slept through half my building and even killed a few humans on accident before an incubus showed up to save me."

Matthew wanted to go to her and reassure her. He understood her pain...when he was turned, he had no one to explain anything to him either.

"I don't like seeing incubi suffer during their transition as you are suffering now."

"Are you going to help me?" Matthew asked, hopeful she might be able to do something to end this agony he felt.

"I..." she started, then fell quiet.

"You can't. Because I'm a vampire. It's alright. I don't blame you, I know I'm a monster."

Rosaline's face dropped. There was a quiet battle going on within her.

"Why did you save my life? You had to know how I felt about you."

Why had he saved her? It had been more than just because she could further his goal to make the incubi trust him. She needed protection and he could give it to her.

"Just because you don't like me doesn't mean you deserved to die." Matthew sighed, feeling compelled to tell her more. "I'm trapped between two worlds, trying to please both. I hate what Tarrick does to me. He... teases and tortures me to the point of rage. And yet I can't help but feel drawn to him, to this place, even to you. I was alone for so long and..." He stopped.

He was admitting far more than he wanted to. Rosaline had a hold over him. For how long? He hadn't even felt it wrap around him.

Matthew could always sense Tarrick's holds, or at least he could now. But Rosaline's was subtle, nearly undetectable. He wanted to open his heart and mind to her and tell her all his secrets. He tried to break away from her hold but it seemed to chase him.

Matthew fell to his knees.

"I beg you, please release me."

She did. "I'm sorry. I didn't mean to distress you."

Did she apologize to him? No one ever did that.

"Only a handful of creatures can sense when I do that to them and each of them has at least a thousand years on you. You're much stronger than I thought you were. Stronger even than the general reports. Stand up."

Matthew rose.

"I will help you."

Twenty-Three

Matthew studied Rosaline as she stood in front of him just outside the range of his chains. She was going to help him. He wondered what had changed her mind. It was clear she hated vampires to an extreme that Matthew hadn't even seen in hunters.

"There are some rules you must agree to."

"Anything," Matthew said.

"I do not want to see your fangs or claws or red eyes. If I see them, we're done. You will do everything I say. If you fail to follow even one of my commands or you lose control, we're done. If I decide to influence your emotions or hold you, you will submit to me. Do you understand?"

Matthew was so desperate to end his pain and suffering he would have agreed to anything she asked.

"Yes, my lady, I will keep my vampire side at bay and do everything you tell me to."

"And one more thing, I want your word that you aren't going to hurt me."

Matthew nodded. "I give you my word—I won't hurt you." He hoped he could keep it. Having blood inside of him now would help him stay in control but he didn't know what his incubus side was capable of doing.

Rosaline took a step forward and paused, sucked in a sharp breath, then walked up to Matthew. She touched his chest and he trembled. Her hand felt so good resting on him.

She lifted his shirt then pressed her hand on his stomach just below his belly button. He wished she would keep moving her hand down and run it along his caged erection.

He felt an echo sensation as she scanned him.

"Your blood pouches have nearly healed. And your soavik is alive with hunger."

Matthew chuckled. "I could have told you that."

She lit up with a smile. Matthew was glad to see her smile.

Rosaline walked around behind him and unlocked the chain attached to his collar, then she ran her hands down his arms and unlocked the shackles. Once freed, Matthew rubbed his wrists. He wished she could also remove the bracers and collar.

Rosaline moved over to the bed and sat down on it. "Undress and go shower."

Matthew removed his clothes and tossed them onto his cot. She watched him undress while she slipped her heels off. If Matthew didn't know better, he swore he heard her gasp under her breath when he pulled his underwear down and allowed his hard cock to spring free.

Aware of her gaze, he strutted to the shower and turned it on. The warm water from three showerheads cascaded down around him. Matthew closed his eyes for a moment as he enjoyed the relaxing feeling it brought. He heard nearly silent vents sucking the steamy air, preventing moisture from escaping that corner of the room.

Rosaline cleared her throat.

He smiled at her and hurried with the rest of the shower. He grabbed a towel and, once dry, Rosaline motioned for him to join her on the bed. Wrapping the towel around his hips, he took a few steps at her. Her heart began to race and he could smell her fear. He took a step back.

Rosaline stood and, breathing hard, froze in place as if trying to control her fear.

Matthew hoped she hadn't changed her mind. He wasn't sure he could survive a few weeks of not feeding.

"Remove the towel and go lie down," she said.

Matthew obeyed. He tossed the towel on the ground, a small defiance to Tarrick, then lay on the silk sheets. His cock, not quite as hard as it was before the shower, rested to the side on his hip. That changed when Rosaline untied the knot on her teal wrap dress and opened it.

Underneath, she had on a black bra and a matching thong. Matthew ran his eyes down the flat plain of her stomach and over her sensual hips, his length now protruding high into the air. He desperately wanted to finish undressing her. As he sat up to go to her she took a step back, her heart racing again.

Matthew closed his eyes and sighed.

"I don't think I can do this. I can't be with a woman who fears me." He opened his eyes and looked at her. Her face betrayed the conflict raging within. Matthew needed her right now, his hunger drove him, but he couldn't stand the way she was looking at him. As if he was death. *Vampire*.

He couldn't do this. This wouldn't be enjoyable for either of them. He sat up higher.

"Lie back down," she ordered.

"No." He was done.

"You will do as I command or I'll leave."

"Then leave, have the hunters come chain me back up." Matthew pushed himself off the bed and walked back over to his cot and sat down in a huff.

She folded her arms. "Return to the bed."

"No."

"There will be grave consequences for you if you do not do what I say."

That angered him. Another incubus—*another fucking incubus*—threatening to hurt him. Matthew stood and began to stalk towards her. She backed away from him each step he took.

"Yeah? Will you have Tarrick smash me again with that spiked club of his? Maybe you'll have me imprisoned and whipped every night. Or starve me? Shackle me in silver? Collar me and take away every freedom I have? Oh! I know! You could force me to fight my own kind for your enjoyment. Or have me fight in a war I couldn't care less about. Turn me into a tool, a weapon."

She hit the edge of the bed with the back of her legs and plopped down with a cry. Matthew towered above her.

"But then again, all those things have already been done to me. I'm sure you have something new planned. There seems to be no end to the creative ways incubi can inflict pain."

Her eyebrows knitted together in anger. "I have done none of those things to you."

"You're right. You just want to put me to death for daring to exist. I've never even killed an incubus before, but I've killed plenty of vampires."

"I—" she started to say something but Matthew cut her off before she could try to refute any of his words.

"I'm starving and tired of being pushed around like a pawn." Matthew stopped. He could feel his eyes burning. She trembled at the sight of them. Good.

Wait. No. She wasn't the one he was actually angry with, that honor went to Tarrick.

He took a few steps away to give her some space and forced his red eyes to turn back to his normal brown. "And even after every pain your kind has inflicted upon me, I have no desire to hurt you. Hell, I even feel guilty about killing the humans I feed on and I'm a fucking vampire."

She sat on the bed looking up at him through her long lashes; her black bra and underwear a sinful contrast to her porcelain skin.

Matthew couldn't look at her anymore, if he did, his restraint would shatter and he'd try and take her, whether she wanted it or not. He could never allow that to happen. Never.

Breathing hard, he turned away from her and hung his head. He'd probably be forever damaged, never able to feed correctly, if he could believe Tarrick's words. The pain within him flared, he had just lost the only chance he had at feeding.

Then he felt her soft hand touch his skin. She ran her hand down his spine and let her fingers play along the dimples on his lower back.

"Perhaps—" she started, her voice soft, almost apologetic, "—perhaps I was wrong to judge you in such haste." She moved lower and gently squeezed his butt.

It was the only invitation he needed.

Faster than she could register, Matthew had her pinned under him on the bed. She mewled as she fell into the silky sheets.

His arms were wrapped around her, caging her in place. He looked for any sign she wanted to be free of him and when she gave him none, he hungrily kissed her just below her ear. She moaned.

God, it was the sweetest sound.

He wanted to know what it would sound like to have her cry his name in pleasure. He wanted to make her tremble.

Slipping his hand behind her, he unhooked her bra and tossed it on the floor. Her round breasts tumbled to the sides. Matthew pulled away from her skin and studied her perfect mounds topped with dusty pink nipples.

He pressed his mouth to one and nipped at the bud, drawing another moan from her sensual lips. His lips brushed up her body while his hand wandered down. He gently cupped her breasts before tracing his fingers down her voluptuous curves.

She squirmed under his touch and rubbed her thigh against his cock. Matthew bucked in response. He wasn't willing to let her have him yet. He seized her hip with his hand and pressed her into the bed so she couldn't do that again.

He worked his tongue over her collarbone and licked up her neck. He felt her heart quicken as he paused above her pulse and pressed a hard kiss against it. He expected fear to flood her, but instead he smelled pleasure ripple through her body. Her breathing sped with anticipation.

She wanted him to bite her. She desired it.

God, it was so sexy. Matthew's cock twitched as he dreamed of sinking his fangs into her neck.

Then, as quick as it began, the moment was over as her eyes lowered and her body became rigid under him. The smell of shame rose up from her and she pushed against his shoulders, lifting him off her.

Matthew wouldn't let this end, he couldn't.

He slid his body down so that he was lying next to her, but still pressed against her skin. He lowered his mouth to her ear. "I would never bite you unless you asked me to."

"Vampires…they…" She squeezed her eyes shut.

He kissed her forehead. "I'm not them."

Her eyes slowly opened and she looked up at him. "I suppose we'll see. Prove to me you're an incubus. Show me what you've got."

A wicked smile crossed Matthew's lips. He allowed his hand to explore the top of her black thong then he slipped under it and let his fingers slide over the warm folds between her legs. He dove deeper and ran his fingers up and down her wet crease. She felt like silk.

Her ruby lips parted and her tongue flicked out to wet them. Unable to resist tasting them any longer, Matthew leaned in and claimed her mouth with his. Their tongues danced together. Rosaline wrapped her hands around his neck and pulled him in closer.

Muffled moans escaped them both.

Matthew ran a finger across her clit and she arched her back in response. He continued to tease her by twirling his slick fingers around the nub.

He broke away from the kiss and watched her writhed and whimper with pleasure each time he stroked her. It thrilled him. He could barely take this anymore. He wanted to be in her but he wouldn't last long. Spending the last four nights in a constant state of arousal had left him too close to the edge.

As he studied her responses, her skin began to glow a soft gold. It was beautiful and unlike anything he had ever seen before. He stopped caressing between her legs and ran his hand up her abdomen to touch the glow. The light swirled around his hand. He moved his fingers through it, watching the strands dance around him.

He continued to do this until the glow began to fade and he realized that Rosaline was studying him with her wonderfully gorgeous jade eyes.

"I'm sorry I stopped, it's just…you're glowing."

Rosaline laughed. Her laugh was pure and sweet, not a hint of mockery in it. "That's sexual energy. You'll only see it if you focus. Feed on it, take it in you."

Matthew focused on her again and the golden glow appeared bright once more. He ran his hand through it and the light seemed to disappear into him. It felt amazing.

"Have you noticed your pain has eased?" Rosaline asked. She placed her hand on his abs, her gentle brush excited him and he flexed his muscles in response.

She was right—the pain was gone. He was still hungry but not agonizingly so. Relief flooded him. He wasn't going to be messed up...he could feed just fine.

Her heart skipped a beat as one moment he was lying at her side and the next he was standing beside the bed, looking down at her.

"I need more," he said, grabbing her legs and sliding her over the silk sheets to the edge of the bed. He slipped her thong off and kneeled in front of her. She hooked her legs over his shoulders and he leaned in to worship her folds with his tongue.

"You taste divine," he purred into her. Her back arched in response and he clamped down on her hips, dwarfing them in his hands.

Matthew was an amateur when it came to Tarrick, but pleasing a woman was something he had plenty of experience with and every part of him wanted, no, *needed* to bring her pleasure.

He licked and teased her nub while slipping two fingers into her heated core. She was hot and wet against his cold fingers. Her moans encouraged him to venture as deep into her as possible—he did so, then slowly retreated and entered her again.

Her hips swayed up as she rode his tongue and fingers while frantically clutching his hair.

She gasped when Matthew pressed up into the sweet spot within her while he lavished attention on her sensitive clit with the tip of his tongue. She shivered as each brush brought her closer and closer to release. Half-words fell from her lips, but many were lost between heavy breaths and moans.

"Yes, more, there—gods—*there...*" were a few that Matthew could make out.

He didn't let up, he kept the rhythm quick but steady until finally, pure bliss swelled within her and she cried out, trembling and lost in the pleasure of the orgasm. Her body squeezed his fingers and he swept his tongue over her, drawing out her gratification as long as possible.

When she slowed, he pulled away and licked his lips. He watched her as she recovered and looked down at him.

"How do you feel?" she asked, her voice alluring.

Matthew moved to sit down on the edge of the bed next to her. He flashed a devilish smile and put his hand on her hip. "Horny. I'd like to make you come again."

She blushed. He had made a sex demon blush. Matthew felt as if he had conquered all of Rome.

"I meant, how is your hunger?"

"Better, but I want more."

Matthew pulled power into his speed and placed Rosaline in his lap so that she was facing him, her legs spread around his thighs. His cock trapped between his abs and her pelvis.

She yelped once she processed what had happened. "You need to stop doing that."

"Why?" he teased and greedily kissed her neck.

She moaned and dropped her head back in response, exposing all of her throat to him.

Matthew's fangs came down, unable to hold them back anymore.

No. He couldn't let her see them. This would all be over if she did.

He picked her up by her waist and set her back on the bed. Then he rushed over to where his cot was and stood above it, his back to her. His shoulders heaved air in and out of him and, even though he no longer needed to breathe, it felt as if he couldn't catch his breath.

He heard her stand and take a few steps towards him.

His eyes burned and his claws came out. He was losing more control, not gaining it. Every side of him wanted to taste her. The incubus was satisfied but the urge to bite and fuck her as a vampire was overwhelming.

"Matthew…" she asked. Her soft voice shattered him.

"Don't. You shouldn't come near me right now. I just…give me a minute," he said.

She stood still and waited.

Matthew struggled to regain his composure. He hung his head and wished he had never been turned into such a wretched creature.

"I'm sorry," he whispered.

It was over.

Twenty-Four

It took a while but finally his vampire side receded and he turned to face her. She wore a worried expression.

Matthew was shocked when she sat back on the bed and patted the space next to her. "Come here, I will teach you something."

He thought for sure she would end this. He wondered what she was going to show him as he sat down on the bed.

"This took me a while to learn so don't get frustrated if it doesn't work."

Matthew nodded.

"I want you to touch my arm. Envision giving me pleasure through your touch. Think about drawing me to you."

Matthew reached out and touched her wrist, then slowly ran his fingers up her arm. He did want to give her pleasure. He wanted to stoke the cooling embers inside of her and make her body quake again.

She responded to him. Her eyes rolled back and her heart beat quicker, not out of fear this time but passion. Her breaths began to shorten.

He continued past her shoulder, then down to her breasts. She moaned as he caressed her warm flesh.

Her eyes snapped open and she grabbed his hand.

Matthew was worried he had done something wrong, but she released him and smiled. "The general told me that you learn abilities fast but I had no idea."

"What am I even doing? Is this a hold?"

"Close, but this is a little different. A hold evokes emotions, like fear or bliss. It's temporary. Normally, prey needs to be receptive for a hold to work but older incubi can force emotional changes onto another against their will. What I'm showing you is a chemical manipulation—a physical reaction instead of an emotional one."

She placed her hands on his chest and explored down his pecs. The ends of Matthew's nerves felt as if they were on fire and he leaned into it. His hard cock strained, desperate for attention.

Her eyes hooded seductively and she licked her lips. "See?"

Two could play that game. Matthew placed his hand on her stomach and pushed pleasure. Her eyes flared with desire, glowing bright green.

She matched him, intensifying his pleasure as she moved her wicked hands down his body. Matthew raced her, but she won when she grabbed his steel hard erection and ran her hand up and down it.

Matthew growled. He wanted more of her.

She released his thick length and shifted onto his lap, her knees once again straddling his muscular thighs. His hard sex stood ready to enter her as she lined her slick core up with him, hovering in place—teasing him with a mischievous smile and a slight bend of her neck.

"Don't offer me your neck unless you want me to bite it," Matthew warned.

She nodded.

He couldn't wait any longer. He grabbed her hips and drove her down onto him. His rigid manhood slid into her tight sheath.

She took over, riding his cock with excited intensity. He grunted with each movement, trying to fight the oncoming torrent of pleasure. God, he couldn't hold against it long if she kept doing that. He planted his hands on her divine ass to slow her down.

She got the message and began rocking back and forth, unhurried. That was better.

Matthew kept one hand on a luscious round cheek and ran the other up her back, giving her pleasure through his touch. Encouraging moans fell from her lips. "Yes, like that. You've learned so fast."

Under his fingers, he felt her wings shifting below her skin on her back. They wanted out. "I want to see them," he whispered near her ear.

She needed no further prompting; her red wings broke the skin and unfurled. They were smaller than Tarrick's and the other incubi Matthew had seen. He wasn't sure she could actually fly with them. Maybe glide.

He ran his hand along them and they fluttered in response. It was magnificent.

Matthew raised his hips up, thrusting deep inside of her each time she came down. Her speed picked up again as she neared her second climax. Her legs began to tremble and Matthew could sense her release was imminent. His was too.

Matthew ran his hand up the back of her neck and grabbed a handful of her curly red hair. He ignored his own warning to her and he yanked on it, causing her head to fall back, exposing her throat to him.

He leaned into her neck and pressed his lips against it, his cool breath flowed over her skin. He managed to hold back his fangs, but only just.

He could sense that on some level she wanted him to bite her. A vampire had hurt her in the past, that much was clear, but she enjoyed the biting even though it seemed to bring her shame. It was a forbidden fruit. The anticipation...the danger that he might bite her...it was enough to send Rosaline crashing over the edge.

Her wings flapped about and her entire body shook in Matthew's arms. Her passage clamped onto him, gripping his manhood as she orgasmed. She was tighter and more intense than any other woman he had ever been with before.

He couldn't hold back any longer. His balls drew up as he thrust into her and golden light exploded across his vision. His body quaked and he held her tight in his arms as he filled her.

When it was done, they both breathed a heavy sigh. He planted a kiss on her neck then fell to his back onto the bed. He shuddered as she moved off his sensitive length then closed his eyes and began to purr.

"Come join me," she said, already heading for the shower. Her wings retracting into her back.

Matthew didn't want to move. He wanted to grab her back into his arms and rest with her there. But this wasn't his bed. Matthew looked at the metal bracers wrapped around his forearms; he had forgotten about them and the collar while he was with Rosaline.

She had made him feel...free.

He joined her and showered off. She looked up into his eyes and her jaw dropped.

"What?" he asked.

She said nothing.

"Is it my eyes? They're red?" Matthew pressed his eyelids closed and turned from her. "I'm sorry, they probably changed when I came. I don't mean to frighten you with them. I'm not going to hurt you."

"No, it's just...here." She grabbed his arm.

Matthew opened his eyes again so he wouldn't slip and eat shit as she tugged him along. She marched him wet and naked from the shower into the actual bathroom.

Matthew had never seen the inside. It was massive, nearly half the size of the suite itself. In the center was a hot tub that could have easily fit eight people. There were lounge chairs, vanities, and more showers. All the decorations were classy and extremely bachelor.

Rosaline led Matthew in front of a mirror.

It was his turn for a jaw drop.

His irises had changed color but they weren't red. Instead, they were silver. Bright, shining silver.

"The general needs to see this," she said and started to walk out.

Matthew grabbed her wrist. "Is it necessary? Can't you just report it to him later?" He didn't want to see Tarrick right now.

Rosaline looked as if she was going to deny him the request but she seemed to change her mind when she tossed him a towel and picked up one for herself.

Matthew looked into the mirror again. The silver almost blended with the whites of his eyes, giving him an ethereal look.

"I've never seen silver before. Most of us have a shade of purple, blue, or green in our true form," she said, walking out of the bathroom. "Join me."

He pulled himself away from the mirror and re-entered the bedroom to find her already laying on the bed. He dropped his towel on the ground—that was now two of them dirtying up Tarrick's room—and joined her. Rosaline slipped into his arms, spooning with her back to him. He smiled and kissed the top of her head.

"You really are an incubus," she said as if she had finally accepted what he was.

Euphoria floated through him. Having had both blood and sex, his vampire—and *incubus*—sides felt sated. For most of his life he had felt incomplete, as if there was more of him he didn't understand, and now he realized that he had never been human, even though he had lived as one before he had been killed and turned. He wondered, for the millionth time in his life, who his parents were and why they abandoned him.

He squeezed her tighter and wondered if she knew the real worth of the gift she had given him. "Thank you for helping me."

She pressed closer, as if she understood what he was truly thanking her for. "Next time, I'll teach you how to share when you feed."

Matthew frowned. "Did I do something wrong?"

She laughed. "Not at all, you did well for your first time. I fed earlier in preparation, but you were a hungry boy. You've left me tired. If I were a human, you would have killed me."

Matthew had no idea he had taken so much. Sexual energy wasn't like blood: a physical, tangible liquid where he could monitor how much he drank. He was excited to know more and to feed more. His cock grew hard thinking of it. Her naked body next to his wasn't helping matters.

"Settle down. Rest," Rosaline said as she felt his growing need pushing into her backside.

"Sorry." He laughed and closed his eyes, wondering if they were still silver or if they had returned to his normal brown.

It wasn't even late into the night and he was tired. Satisfied and content, but tired. His senses began to drift and he heard singing coming from somewhere nearby. Maybe a succubus in one of the adjacent rooms? Her voice was light and angelic and he let the sound lull him to sleep.

Twenty-Five

*T*hump.

Matthew's eyes gradually opened. He was still in Tarrick's bed but Rosaline was gone. Tarrick was sitting next to him, his hand resting on Matthew's bare chest. Matthew tried to move away from him but his body didn't respond. He looked at the curtains, daylight bled around them.

"I had a feeling that would wake you," Tarrick said with a perfect smile.

A low growl came from Matthew's chest.

Tarrick closed his eyes.

Thump.

Damn him.

"Do you enjoy that?" Tarrick asked.

Of course he fucking enjoyed it. It set his insides ablaze with desire. But this was just another game, another tease he couldn't bear any longer.

Matthew hissed at him.

He focused on his skin where Tarrick was touching. If he could stir pleasure in Rosaline through his touch, could he do the same with revulsion? Matthew tried to push fear into Tarrick.

Tarrick laughed. "You've had your abilities less than a day, do you really think they'd have any effect on me?"

Matthew said nothing. He wished he could move.

"Not speaking to me again?" Tarrick sighed and removed his hand from Matthew. "Alright. I won't touch you if you don't want it."

He wouldn't? He had always done whatever he wanted, Matthew's desires never mattered to Tarrick before.

"I wish you knew how…hm, never mind. Get some sleep, I'm sorry I woke you." Tarrick left the bed and went to his desk to work.

Tarrick apologized to him? What the hell was going on?

Unable to stay awake any longer, Matthew would have to worry about it come nightfall.

When he woke, he expected to be shackled and back on his cot, but instead he felt silky smooth sheets rubbing against his naked skin.

Tarrick was working at his desk. It looked as if he had been there since earlier that day. He wasn't armed. Matthew could be on him before he could get to a weapon. He knew Tarrick was strong but it took him a few moments to change into his incubus form. Matthew could snap his neck before then.

But Matthew couldn't kill him. Part of him wanted to take revenge for everything Tarrick had done. Every punishment he suffered tore at him, but the incubus was the key to his survival right now. And, if he was being completely honest with himself, Matthew was still drawn to him. He hated it.

Matthew sighed and pushed himself off the bed. He kneeled before Tarrick and waited.

Tarrick looked up from his work. "Go shower and dress, you may speak if you wish."

Matthew did not wish. He stood and walked to the shower.

"You may use the bathroom showers if that will make you more comfortable," Tarrick said.

It would make him more comfortable, but going in there now felt as if it would be some sort of victory for Tarrick and he refused to give the general any easy victories. He stepped into the open shower and turned the water to a high heat.

As he showered, he felt Tarrick's eyes on him, but he resisted the urge to look. Matthew didn't loiter. When he was clean, he shut the shower off, dried, and went over to his cot, where clean clothes were neatly folded. He dropped the towel on the ground and smiled when he heard Tarrick growl.

He dressed quickly, sitting on the cot to put his boots on. When he was done, he stayed seated and crossed his arms over his chest. He had no idea how Tarrick planned to torture him tonight, but he wasn't in the mood.

Tarrick, still at his desk, placed his hand on his chin and studied Matthew. Matthew studied him right back. As time passed, he started to notice that Tarrick looked...tired. His shoulders were hunched over a little like a weight was pressing against them. His eyes looked almost sad.

He sighed and came over to Matthew, standing before him. Matthew stood as well, he didn't want Tarrick towering above.

Tarrick's mouth turned upwards into a half-smile. "You know, you are terrible at hiding your emotions."

Yeah, he hadn't had a millennium to master that.

Tarrick grasped his hands behind his back. "I don't think you are just a tool, Matthew. Or just a weapon." Matthew knitted his eyebrows, confused. "I saw how much those words hurt you when I was talking to Lady Rosaline, and I am sorry for them."

Was he sorry? Or was this just another manipulation? Matthew wanted to believe him but was so sick of being hurt. Tarrick began to pace back and forth when Matthew said nothing.

"When an incubus begins to transition, their body sends out a flood of pheromones to force food to come to them. It's extremely powerful. We needed Rosaline on our side, but she couldn't look past the fact you were a vampire long enough to see that you are an incubus, too. I needed her to be moved enough to overcome that and help you. I am sorry I had to starve you to make that happen, I didn't want to. If she hadn't come in yesterday, I would have fed you before any permanent damage was done."

Tarrick looked sincere and it made sense. Rosaline went from hating him that night to promising to help him in the future. But Matthew wasn't any less angry at him. Starved to the point of biting himself just to taste blood was a truly shaming moment in his life.

"You should know it worked. She's quite taken with you. I spent the majority of my morning being yelled at by her for my treatment of you," Tarrick said, then sighed. "She passionately pointed out that if I cannot begin to trust you in my own house, I can't expect the rest of the incubus community to trust you either."

Matthew rubbed his wrists. So that's why he wasn't shackled.

"If you want to remain unchained you'll have to control yourself. If you hurt anyone in this household, I don't care if it's a human maid or incubus, you'll be back in them and I won't give you a second chance. Do you understand?"

Matthew considered remaining silent but decided against it. Being free of the chains—even if he still wore a collar and bracers—meant he was a step closer to his goals. He'd have to prove he was worthy of being trusted, not just to Tarrick but to all the incubi. He needed to play their games if he was to learn how to defeat them one day. He needed to know what he was truly up against.

"I understand, Master."

Tarrick looked pleased. He stopped his pacing and rested his hand on Matthew's shoulder. Even through the t-shirt his touch felt good. Too good.

A soft moan left Matthew before he could stop it.

Tarrick smiled and brushed his fingers across Matthew's temple. "Your eyes are silver."

"Are they still?" Matthew touched his other temple. He wanted to go look in a mirror again.

"I don't think they'll ever return to brown. Normally you'd learn to glamor or shift yourself to hide your incubus side but I'm not sure you'll get those abilities. They're beautiful."

Matthew might have blushed if he was capable of it right now. God, he was getting hungry and it wasn't blood he craved. He wanted to slip his hand behind Tarrick's neck and pull him into a kiss but before he had the chance to do so Tarrick's phone rang.

Retrieving it from his pocket, he answered, "Report."

Matthew heard a male voice he didn't recognize on the other end. "Lord General, it's been confirmed. House Moreau has her."

Tarrick squeezed his eyes closed and swallowed several times. "Thank you, Commander Ronove."

Tarrick hung up the call. He gripped the phone so tightly that Matthew thought it would crush in his hand.

Matthew's better judgment was telling him to stay quiet but he had too many questions stirring within him. "House Moreau is a vampire house, isn't it?"

Tarrick opened his eyes, he looked nearly on the edge of tears. Matthew had never seen him this way. He nodded then backed away and went into his closet for a few moments. When he came out he carried a fresh suit on a hanger, which he draped over a chair.

"House Moreau is a particularly dangerous vampire house located in New Orleans. We control most of Louisiana, except that city and the surrounding counties. They use humans to their advantage and it makes it nearly impossible for us to get to them.

"Lady Rosaline was captured by them long ago and it took us nearly a decade to get her out of there. We lost so many in the process that I'm under orders to never carry out an assault against them without explicit approval from the High King himself. That's how powerful those vampires are."

Well, that explained why Rosaline hated vampires. Matthew wondered just what they had done to her while she was in their hands. He could only imagine the horrors. "The vampires who hurt Lady Rosaline, are they still alive?"

Tarrick nodded. "Most are."

Matthew balled his fists. He felt his eyes burning red. "Who have they captured now?"

Tarrick rubbed his fingers roughly over his mouth then down his chin. "My daughter."

Twenty-Six

Matthew watched Tarrick as he began to unbutton his shirt and walk into his bathroom, slamming the door closed behind him.

He heard the shower turn on.

Matthew felt terrible for him. From everything he had gathered about this High King, no one disobeyed his commands. If Lily had been captured, Matthew would break every rule, suffer any torture to save her. But Tarrick was a loyal general; he wouldn't dare, not even to save his own child.

Matthew listened as Tarrick entered his shower and stopped moving. A heavy sigh followed by a painful sob came from behind the door. He could tell Tarrick was fighting it back. If not for his enhanced hearing, he wouldn't have even heard it.

He wasn't sure what he should do but he didn't just want to stand here and do nothing while Tarrick suffered.

Matthew sped into the bathroom, appearing beside the general.

Tarrick had his hands pressed against the tile wall, his head hung down between them. Water cascaded down his naked body.

"Leave," Tarrick growled.

Matthew didn't move.

"Get out."

He couldn't bring himself to leave, though he should. He still hated Tarrick for everything he had done to him, but the man's child was just kidnapped by vampires and he had little hope of seeing her again. Matthew couldn't find it in him to stay angry right now. He could go back to hating Tarrick tomorrow.

He stepped into the water, still fully clothed, and brushed his fingers across Tarrick's shoulder. Muscles flexed under his touch.

Matthew knew Tarrick could resist all of his incubus abilities but he tried anyway. He tried to induce the feelings of calm and peace in Tarrick to maybe help him find a small measure of relief.

"I've made too many miscalculations lately," Tarrick said, keeping his head down. Matthew stepped closer and put his other hand on Tarrick's back. "I never expected Ascelina to attack my house directly. I knew she had allied with a witch but I didn't think she had one powerful enough to get past all the wards surrounding this place. I should have known. I've paid dearly for that mistake. So many dead, and Cullip is lost to me. He's been my friend for nearly five centuries…" Tarrick's claws came out and he balled his fists. He shook his head in disbelief. "I should have assigned more hunters to her."

Matthew knew he was talking about his daughter now. He pressed into Tarrick's back and began kissing his shoulders.

"I should have never let her become a soldier." Tarrick slammed his fist into the tile. They cracked under his strength.

Matthew stilled and minutes passed. The sound of the falling water filled the otherwise silent bathroom. Finally, Tarrick turned to face Matthew, his back leaning against the tile. A sad smile crossed his face.

"I'm risking a lot for you. I could lose everything. Don't betray me."

It was a plea. Not an order. The first he had ever heard from Tarrick.

Matthew didn't want to betray Tarrick, but he craved freedom and, once he was strong enough to ensure no one could imprison him again, he would have it. At least that was his plan. Right now, Tarrick made it hard for him to stay unwavering in his goal. Bending forward, he kissed Tarrick under his ear.

"I won't, Master," he whispered against his skin.

The lie stuck bitterly to his throat. He pushed it away and focused on pleasing Tarrick, who moaned when he pressed his lips hard into the general's neck. Matthew ran his greedy hands over the incubus' body, feeling every inch of him.

Matthew focused on seeing the sexual energy around Tarrick, golden strands of light appeared before him. He absorbed them as he worked his way down and rubbed his palm against Tarrick's magnificent cock, which grew rock hard in his hand.

Tarrick grunted. "Hungry little incubus."

Matthew smiled against his skin. "I'm not your size but I'd hardly call myself 'little'."

Tarrick chuckled. Matthew was happy he was able to distract him for even a few moments. He held Tarrick's cock captive in his hand while he ravished his neck with rough kisses. His fangs itched and he knew his eyes were red, but he was glad he didn't have to hold his vampire side back right now. The general didn't fear it like Rosaline did.

"Master?" Matthew breathed out between kisses.

"Mmm?"

"Can I...*may I*," he corrected, "bite you? I'll only take a few drops." He licked his lips then lavished attention onto Tarrick's neck with his tongue. The sound of blood rushing beneath the skin was driving him to madness. "Please."

Tarrick leaned his head to the side, exposing more of his neck. "You may."

Matthew hadn't expected him to actually give permission. Excitement washed through his body as his fangs grew. He gently licked Tarrick's neck a few times then eased his fangs into soft flesh.

The world around Matthew faded away as he sucked up a few drops of blood, which came out of a hole at the base of the fang and spread over his mouth. It was euphoric, sending him to a whole other level of existence.

The strong blood enhanced every sense. He heard music, laughter, and conversation all around him. Bright light assaulted his eyelids and he felt each individual drop of water rolling down his skin.

Time was lost to him. He left his fangs in Tarrick's neck until a hand gently tugged on his hair letting him know it was time to stop.

Matthew removed his fangs and licked the puncture wounds before the water could wash away the drops of blood that pooled there. Once he sealed the marks, he kept going, licking and kissing his way across Tarrick's neck, along his collarbone, and down his chest. He sunk to his knees and his lips roamed over sculpted abs.

Tarrick's breathing grew heavy and he rested his hand on Matthew's head, letting him know he wanted more.

Matthew forced his fangs away as he wrapped his hand around the base of Tarrick's hard length and brought it up to his lips. He teased the crown with a few swirls of his tongue, and then licked the slit, tasting him.

"Devil, you have no idea what you do to me," Tarrick said between breathy grunts.

Matthew couldn't help but smile at the comment. His own hard cock strained painfully inside his soaked jeans.

He looked up into Tarrick's eyes as he wrapped his lips around the head. Tarrick groaned with pleasure and he flexed his fingers through Matthew's hair, but he didn't rush anything, and Matthew was thankful for it since he was still new to this.

He brought Tarrick's shaft deeper into his mouth until the head bumped against the back of his throat. Matthew sucked in gently then pulled away, the length leaving his mouth with a *slurk*.

Using his tongue, he took his time exploring the massive member. Every vein. Every ridge. Every inch.

When he took Tarrick back inside of him, the incubus jerked, as if fighting the need to pump his hips.

"Grip the base tighter and stroke. Use your other hand to play with my balls," Tarrick strained to say.

Matthew obeyed.

He brought up his free hand and gently tugged at Tarrick's sac then rolled it around in his palm. Tarrick gritted his teeth, his face twisted with rapture.

Sucking harder, Matthew stroked his shaft with a tight grip. He heard Tarrick's heart pounding like thunder and it thrilled him to evoke such a powerful response from his captor.

Tarrick's claws clicked against the tiles as he used his free hand to stabilize himself. His ears turned to points and black and purple horns emerged from his forehead—one still broken.

Matthew increased the speed of his strokes, drawing heavy grunts from Tarrick's lips as he neared climax. His shaft grew thicker in his mouth and his balls drew up.

Tarrick grabbed Matthew by his hair and painfully yanked him off his dick.

Completely caught off-guard, Matthew moved his hands under him so he wouldn't fall backwards. Drops of water crashed against his face as he was forced to look up and whined at the sudden denial. He wanted to explore more of that body with his hands. He wanted to feel the steel hard cock sliding past his lips. He wanted the sounds of sex filling his ears.

"Keep your mouth open," Tarrick commanded, his voice raw.

Doing as he was told, Matthew opened his mouth wide. Tarrick stroked his own shaft with one hand and with the other gripped Matthew's hair tight, not letting him move. Not that he would now. Having Tarrick tower over him, pleasuring himself, was far more thrilling than he expected.

Tarrick's growls echoed through the bathroom as he moved his hand faster up and down the end of his cock. His hips thrust forward and he grunted as thick, creamy streams of cum exploded from him and landed on Matthew's face and in his mouth.

Matthew swallowed what he could—the water washed the rest away.

Tarrick held tight to Matthew even after he was finished. His body trembled and his shoulders heaved as he caught his breath.

He finally released Matthew's hair and ran his hand down Matthew's face.

"My magnificent vampire champion," he said and absorbed the lingering sexual energy that hung in the air between them. He turned off the water and grabbed a towel. "I won't leave you unsatisfied. Take your clothes off."

Matthew wondered what Tarrick had planned while he removed his wet clothes and soaked boots. He left them in the shower then grabbed a towel as well. As he dried off, he paused to look at himself in a mirror. Forcing his vampire guise away, his eyes returned to silver.

Tarrick was right—no more brown. At least they weren't so different that he'd draw too much attention to himself. In low light, they could pass as blue.

Tarrick had already folded his towel and was leaning against a counter, naked, watching him.

Matthew turned and reached up to touch Tarrick's horn. "Will it grow back?"

Grabbing Matthew's hand, Tarrick pulled it away as if he was ashamed of its broken state. "Eventually. Come."

The general marched from the bathroom to his bed. He pulled Matthew's towel off his waist and set it aside. The way Tarrick's sexy blue eyes turned to purple as he drank in his body made Matthew's cock throb with painful need.

In one smooth motion, Tarrick wrapped his arms around Matthew and pulled him down to the bed so they were lying side by side. The incubus leaned over and kissed Matthew with hungry possession. He drove his tongue inside and took what was his. Matthew pushed his tongue forward and dueled with Tarrick.

He felt Tarrick grow stiff against him and Matthew broke from the kiss.

"Jesus Christ, you're hard again already?" He ran his hand over Tarrick's firm cock, needing to feel it to believe it. "I know you can get hard at will but don't you need a few fucking moments to recover after you come?"

Flashing a devious smile at him, Tarrick shook his head. "No. Incubi don't."

Matthew was amazed. "So you could just keep having orgasms all night long?"

Tarrick ran his hand around Matthew's bottom and squeezed. "If I desired it."

"God, I haven't been able to come more than twice a night since I was a teenager."

Tarrick laughed. "That will change as you learn how to master your incubus side." He leaned over and kissed Matthew's neck then broke away after a minute. "Hmm, I wonder…"

He grabbed Matthew's hand and held it up between them.

"You should be able to start secreting lubricant yourself by now," Tarrick said and rubbed Matthew's palm with his fingers.

Ew. Matthew wrinkled his nose. "I'm not sure I want to."

"It is better than scrambling around for oil—or whatever is used these days—each time you want to fuck someone in the ass."

Tarrick was right. Matthew sighed. He focused on his hand and thought about bringing forward the lube. Sure enough, a clear, thick liquid oozed from his palm. It didn't stop either; he cupped his hand upwards and the entire thing filled.

"Jesus." Matthew panicked as the lube kept flowing and spilled around his hand. He focused on trying to stop the flow of liquid coming from him and it worked.

Beside him, Tarrick was laughing so hard he shook the bed. He had a towel ready, catching the excess. "That happens to everyone the first time."

"You could have warned me." Matthew snatched the towel and wiped his hand off.

"But then I wouldn't have gotten to see that panicked look on your face. And besides, I had you use your hand and not your dick, although that would have been hilarious." Tarrick was smiling wide.

"So kind, Master," Matthew feigned anger. He actually found the situation somewhat amusing, too, now that he cleaned up.

Tarrick leaned into Matthew, kissed his shoulder and grabbed his cock. He gripped it tight and ran his silky hand up and down it, coating it with his own lubricant.

Matthew bit back a moan.

"See? It's not all bad." Tarrick released him and rose to his knees on the bed. He directed Matthew to do the same then turned away, so that Matthew was looking at his back…and incredible ass.

What was Tarrick doing?

"I want you to fuck me," he said, answering the unasked question.

"Master, I- uh…" Matthew stuttered out. He never thought Tarrick would let him enter him. He just assumed he'd always be the one who was getting fucked. Wasn't that how it normally was with men…and slaves? He wasn't really sure…

"Do you not wish it?" Tarrick asked with a smirk. He knew damned well Matthew wanted him right now.

Matthew grabbed Tarrick's hips and slid him closer. His chest pressed close against Tarrick's back. "I've wanted to fuck you since the moment I first saw you."

Tarrick leaned over. "I know."

"But, I've never…with a man…"

"If I weren't an incubus you'd have to prepare me. I'll teach you later. Do you need me to explain the rest?"

Matthew could hear his amusement. No. He didn't need the rest explained. He grabbed the base of his shaft and rubbed against Tarrick's already wet entrance. He didn't want to rush this but it was near impossible when Tarrick pushed back against him, encouraging him.

Matthew tightened his grip on Tarrick's hip as he pushed forward. There was some resistance at first, then a give, and he was in—deep and fully seated.

God, Tarrick wrapped around his dick felt unlike anything he had ever experienced before. Loud grunts ripped from Matthew's lips as the tight hole clamped around his steel, gripping him in a way he didn't know was possible. Maybe this was an incubus thing…or maybe all men felt this way, but at the moment, Matthew didn't really care.

At first, he went slow, unsure what angle would feel best for Tarrick, or even what speed he should take.

Tarrick was having none of it and took over, pounding against Matthew's cock, whose eyes rolled back into his head and his fangs came down again.

He realized that even though he was the one impaling Tarrick, the incubus was in complete control. Matthew was just along for the ride. He dug his fingers into Tarrick's hips and enjoyed the feeling. The hard pounding against his cock felt incredible and his insides buzzed with delight as he fed. Thrusting his hips forward, Matthew plunged as deep as possible.

Tarrick pushed himself up and wrapped his hand behind Matthew's neck. He grabbed the loop on the back of the collar and used it to pull Matthew closer. Straining his head back and twisting his torso, he kissed Matthew—passionate and possessive.

Matthew snaked his arms around Tarrick's chest and held him tight. The skin to skin contact was too much and, as Tarrick flooded him with pleasure, he lost all control—humping like he'd die if he stopped. Loud, needy grunts and growls from both of them accompanied each quickened thrust.

Flesh slapped flesh.

Matthew's muscles locked up and his length jerked as he shot his load deep into Tarrick, coating his tight passage.

His growls turned into purrs as he ran his fingers along Tarrick's spine, exploring him and enjoying the feeling of smooth skin as his body came down from the high.

Before he completely softened, he removed himself and they both collapsed onto the bed—Matthew on his back and Tarrick on his side next to him. The incubus placed a hand possessively on Matthew's abdomen.

"That was…" Matthew couldn't even think of the right word. Incredible? Fulfilling? Astonishing? None of those seemed enough.

Tarrick's purple eyes glinted with amusement.

Matthew became aware that Tarrick was still hard. "Uh, do you need me to do something about that?"

"No need, it'll go away in a moment." Tarrick rolled onto his back as well and rested next to Matthew. He let out a heavy sigh, as if the weight of the night had finally caught up with him.

"How often do you sleep?" Matthew asked. He couldn't help himself. He wanted to know everything about everything. Always questioning. It used to drive his wife nuts.

Tarrick half-smiled. He always seemed to get enjoyment from Matthew's questions.

"Not often. A few hours each day. I can go a few weeks without if I have to. An incubus who has just gone through their first transformation sleeps as often as a human does. But the older an incubus gets, the less he needs."

"That must be nice. I hate being forced asleep the moment the sun rises." Matthew looked at the curtains and wished they were open so that he could see the night.

Tarrick grew restless next to him. His thoughts had probably returned to his daughter.

"How many children do you have?" Matthew asked.

Tarrick frown. "The total or those who still live?"

"Both I guess."

"I have had seventeen children." He paused and rubbed his hand over his forehead and swallowed what looked to be a painful memory away. Matthew thought he might not finish answering the question, but he did. "I have six children that still live, assuming House Moreau hasn't killed my daughter yet. Five males, one girl. Woman, I guess, although it's hard for me to think of her as anything but a little girl."

Matthew felt the same about Lily.

"Jesus. You've lost eleven children?"

"I raise warriors. And it has been a long war."

He'd lost so much. No wonder he wanted the war to be over. It made sense now why he was taking such a great risk by having Matthew here.

Something in the hall outside the room caught Tarrick's attention. Matthew had let his senses lapse while he was talking. He shouldn't have, Cullip had trained him to stay aware of his surroundings at all times and he still had healing lash marks on his back to prove it.

Raised voices shouted and before Matthew could make out who it was, the double doors burst open and Tane marched in.

Twenty-Seven

Tane brushed past two hunters that had unsuccessfully tried to stop him in the hall. He was wearing only black pajama pants and his hair was a mess.

"Is it true?" Tane asked. His voice concealed none of his anger.

Matthew scrambled for the silk sheet and covered his naked hips while Tarrick sat up.

One of the hunters addressed Tarrick. "I'm sorry, General, we told him you didn't want to be disturbed."

Tarrick, who hadn't bothered to cover himself, raised his hand to dismiss the hunters. They bowed and left, closing the doors behind them. Matthew wanted to sink away from this encounter. Having Tane see him naked in bed with his father was embarrassing.

Both incubi, however, didn't seem to care or notice.

"Yes, it's true," he told his son. "House Moreau has captured Lena."

Tane's nostrils flared. "And what is your plan to get her back?"

Tarrick growled and slid out of the bed. "There are orders—"

"To hell with the orders!" Tane yelled, cutting his father off. "You know what they do to captured succubi. They'll violate her."

Tarrick grabbed his underwear from off the chair and pulled them on. "I'm fully aware."

"Then you know we have to do something. We cannot leave her in there." Agitated, Tane's horns grew from his head and his eyes began to glow purple.

"There is nothing we can do for now."

"When did you become such a coward?"

Oh shit. Matthew couldn't believe Tane just said that. He wanted to be anywhere else but here right now. Even the underground prison was starting to sound good.

Anger flashed across Tarrick's face and he grew taller by a few inches. His wings emerged from his back and he stalked towards his son. Tane wisely tried to back away but Tarrick wrapped his hand behind Tane's neck and held him in place.

"Listen to me carefully: you will not disobey *his* orders. If you try to attack them on your own, not only will you fail to save your sister, you'll be put to death for your disloyalty. I will not lose another child. Do you understand?"

The vulnerability Tarrick had allowed Matthew to see was completely gone. He was back to being a general—authoritative, strong, confident. Someone whose orders were never questioned.

Tane bowed his head down and gritted his teeth. "Yes, sir."

"Do you really think I would just give up on her?"

Tane's eyes flicked to Matthew. "I do not know half of what you do anymore."

Tarrick scowled at him and dug his fingers deeper into his neck. "I'll use every resource I have to get the order rescinded but it might take some time to convince the High King to change his mind. Lena is strong, she will survive until we're able to retrieve her."

Tane jerked away from his father. "I hope you're right." He stormed over to the doors to leave the room but stopped to glare at Matthew again.

Matthew pulled up the silk sheet a little higher.

"I hope your pet is worth it, you put us all at risk by keeping it." With that, Tane left the room.

Tarrick growled. Matthew wanted to join him in the growling but kept quiet; he didn't want any of Tarrick's anger redirected at him.

As he sat watching Tarrick, Matthew came to a decision: he was going to kill all of House Moreau and rescue Tarrick's daughter. He owed Tarrick for saving Lily's life. He'd take his revenge on the vampires for what they had done to Rosaline. He would kill them for raping their prisoners.

Then again, the same thing happened to vampire prisoners in Tarrick's keep. He had seen the damage Tane caused to the female vampire, cutting her up and using her body for his own sick pleasures. They were all the same. Monsters. One day he'd punish all those who were complicit in such atrocities, but for now he could use this to prove his worth to the incubi.

Tarrick wanted a weapon—he would prove beyond a shadow of a doubt that he could be one. Killing so many powerful vampires would establish once and for all he was fighting for the incubi. They would all trust him and he could stop worrying about the death sentence hanging over his head.

Besides, it'd give him a chance to show up Tane. Matthew told himself he shouldn't be so petty but he couldn't help it. This would take some time to pull off and he'd have to plan for every possible scenario. He'd have to be patient.

His first step would be to finish his training. During the battle, he had a breakthrough when he discovered that he could use less of his energy and still get what he wanted from it, but he needed to master his skills if he was going to take on a whole house of vampires. He had no doubt there would be a vampire lord there, maybe many.

He also had to figure out a way to get down to New Orleans without hunters dragging his ass back. And, he'd have to find a way to turn off his 'death aura'—whatever the hell that was. He'd lose his element of surprise with it.

Tarrick finally settled down and returned to his human form. He grabbed his suit pants and put them on. "There's an extra set of clothes for you in the closet, to the right. Get dressed."

Matthew slid from the bed and went to the walk-in closet.

Holy crap.

It was huge. Nearly the same size as the bathroom. Hell, it was bigger than the bedroom of his first apartment. There were two standing mirrors. Matthew could only see his reflection in one of them, the other looked old. Custom dark wood cabinets lined each of the walls. Pressed suits, tuxes, and coats hung in orderly rows. Not a single thing was out of place. There was a section of rolled ties in a grid-like tie shelf. Every pair of shoes were perfectly polished, not a scuff to be seen. The center of the closet had an island table with thin rolling drawers.

Behind the table, in the back, was something Matthew had not expected: a full suit of metal armor. Depending on the lighting and where Matthew stood, it seemed to change colors from blue to purple, matching Tarrick's eyes.

The design was huge and intimidating, fitted for Tarrick when he was in his full incubus form. It had spikes along the shoulders. Hanging on the wall were metal coverings that attached to his horns, the tops of his wings, and the tip of his tail—all spiked as well.

Matthew touched the armor and his fingers tingled as if a nine-volt battery had shocked him. Magic maybe?

He looked around the back. There were gaps for wings and a tail to fit through. The armor looked heavy, but when he lifted up a gauntlet it was light, as if it had no weight at all.

Unlike everything else found in the closet, the armor was blemished. It was clean and obviously cared for but there were scratches and battle marks all across it.

"I don't don it much anymore," Tarrick said as he appeared behind him, buttoning up his shirt. "But before I became High General I wore it almost daily."

"When was that?" Matthew asked and ran his fingers down the chest piece.

"When did I become High Lord General? I was promoted when my predecessor died about three hundred years ago. I had already been a general for the European regions for many centuries before that."

"Did vampires kill him?"

Tarrick slid open one of the thin drawers in the island table revealing rows of expensive looking cufflinks. He chose a pair and put them on. "Yes. *She* was killed during a major battle. Losing our High Lady General was a huge setback for our side, and it was especially hard for me since she was my mother."

"Oh. I'm sorry." Matthew wasn't really sure what else he could say, but he did know he needed to stop assuming that everything was male. That was the second time he had made that mistake.

"Get dressed," Tarrick ordered, and motioned to a shelf where a pair of jeans and a t-shirt sat neatly folded along with a pair of boots and socks.

Matthew forgot he was still naked. He was thankful Tarrick didn't seem interested in making him wear suits. He dressed quickly.

"Come," Tarrick said, and walked from his bedroom.

Matthew followed. When he exited, he saw two hunters standing guard at the door. They both saluted and bowed to Tarrick. They kept a close eye on Matthew but took no other actions.

Matthew followed Tarrick into the elevator at the end of the hall. Tarrick pressed the button to go down a level.

"What happened to Cullip?" Matthew had been wondering that for days.

Tarrick took in a deep breath. "He's still under Ascelina's command and we know of no way to break him from it. He was hurting himself trying to get to me so we've had to keep him unconscious. I doubt we'll ever be able to wake him again, at least not until Ascelina is dead, and I've been trying to kill her for many centuries."

"That's…terrible."

"Yes."

The elevator opened to the third floor and Tarrick led Matthew back to the command center. Most of the damage done to this level during the battle had been cleaned up or fixed. He'd see an occasional hole in the marble or a mark on the wall but that was it.

It didn't surprise him Tarrick would have everything back in pristine condition right away. He was sort of anal about messes.

Inside the command center, Matthew counted fifteen hunters standing around the various tables. They were all busy reading reports, working on tablets, or talking into comms.

This time there were five humans working as dispatch in front of the monitors. Matthew heard them calling other dispatch centers, sending out orders, or receiving updates on vampire attacks. Matthew even overheard a report about a vampire attack in Melbourne.

The monitors displayed local footage around Ashwood, but also footage from estates and buildings he didn't recognize. The large screen in the center showed a map of the world with red pinpoints flaring up every now and then, coinciding with an attack.

There were two incubi in the room. One was the black incubus that had been fighting the vampire lord during the assault; the other was the fierce succubus with blue tipped horns and wings. Both were in their human guise and wearing white button-up shirts with tight black trousers tucked into polished riding boots. Having seen Tarrick wear something similar, Matthew was now certain it was a uniform.

The succubus sat in the center throne-like chair in the back of the room while the incubus sat to her right.

When Tarrick walked into the room, they both stood and pressed a balled hand into their opposite shoulder to salute and bowed. The hunters in the room did the same.

Matthew followed Tarrick and became painfully aware that the room went silent as all attention fell on him. He thought their reaction was because he was walking around unshackled, but then he noticed most were studying his eyes. None of them had seen the silver before.

Mercifully, the silence didn't last long.

"General, Lord Truax's estate is under attack. He's reporting at least twenty vampires, and half his hunters have fallen," one of the dispatchers said.

The monitors began to change to images of the vampire attack on a large estate that looked like it was somewhere in the Deep South. Matthew watched as a vampire ripped the neck out of one hunter then got staked by another.

"Have Lord Isaac send over teams Banshee and Rising Red. Shadowtalon should be near there, correct?"

A hunter standing next to the table in the center answered. "Yes sir, they're running a thumper trap with Warrior Isso about fifteen miles from that location."

"Send them too. Cassidy—"

A gruff looking man with a long scar down his face stepped forward.

"—take your team and reinforce them. Bring Fendrel and Jartha with you."

"Yes, sir," he said. His body outlined with a green light as he teleported away.

Screams and alarms bled through the dispatcher's headphones and Matthew watched as the cameras caught vampires breaking into Lord Truax's house. A magic ward flashed green and incinerated the first vampire to cross the threshold.

In a courtyard outside of the estate, a giant stone covered in runic symbols began to glow bright green. Three teams of six hunters appeared, runes burning the grass below them. Matthew guessed the stone was some sort of long-range teleport seeing as Cassidy was with them.

The knight-looking hunter Matthew had seen during the assault on the keep was also there. He didn't seem to belong to any team. A fully armored warrior incubus—bigger than Tarrick in his full form—was part of the group. Matthew wondered which one was Fendrel and which was Jartha.

A group of vampires ambushed them, and three hunters went down before they countered, taking the vamps out.

Another group of six hunters teleported to the other side of the estate, they looked as if they were using their normal teleports. What was the range of those? Shortly after, a succubus flew in and landed next to them. She wore dark shorts and a halter top showing off her neck. Except for the sword in her hand, she looked as if she was about to go clubbing. That must have been the team called 'Shadowtalon' and she must have been the bait in the thumper trap.

Matthew watched the battle, studying the moves of each of the hunters and how the vampires attacked back. Grossly outnumbered at this point, the vampires retreated. It wasn't long before the estate was clear of them. The entire attack from start to finish took less than fifteen minutes.

Hunter Cassidy walked up to a camera, his comm to his mouth. "General, we're clear here."

Tarrick pressed a button on the table. "Losses?"

"Five hunters from our group. I'll find out the rest of the numbers from Truax's commander. At least three incubi are dead, but I didn't recognize them. Banshee and Shadowtalon are tracking the runners now. We have two staked vamps I'll bring back for questioning."

"Keep me updated," Tarrick said.

"Yes, sir."

Tarrick pressed the button again and motioned the two incubi over.

Matthew was thankful the rest of the room returned to their tasks and no one was blatantly staring at him anymore.

"Matthew, this is Lady Dennith, she is my right-hand. She fights as my eyes and ears in battles and if I fall, she becomes the temporary High General until a new one is promoted. You are to follow her orders as if they were my own," Tarrick said.

Matthew nodded as she studied him with dark brown eyes. She stood tall, built like an Amazon, and sported short dark hair. Based on what little he had seen, most warrior incubi were physically bigger than the social ones. It was fascinating.

"And this is Lord Vassu. He is one of my best warriors and usually fights in vampire territory."

Vassu nodded to Matthew. Seeing him this close, Matthew could truly appreciate his large stature. He had to be nearly seven feet tall in his human form and he looked as if he spent most of his day in a gym.

He wondered what sex with him would be like; was he a gentle giant or did he dominate whoever he was with? His cock had to be massive. Matthew's thoughts turned dirty as he imagined being rammed by Vassu.

Damn it, Tarrick wasn't the only man turning him on all the time anymore. It seemed that being around incubi—and going through this transformation—had certainly shifted his preferences to become a bit more all-inclusive.

All three incubi grinned at him.

"What?" Matthew asked. "Did I do something?"

Tarrick laughed. "You're throwing off pheromones, trying to draw in prey. Until you learn how to control that, it'll happen whenever you start thinking about sex."

For once, Matthew was glad he hadn't fed on any substantial amount of blood in the last few hours—if he had, his face would have turned beet red as embarrassment flushed through him. He rubbed his eyes and forehead with his hand.

"Oh my god, seriously?"

"Which one of us were you thinking about?" Dennith asked, smirking.

"Don't tease the young one. First transformation is hard on us all. Although, you are so old you've probably forgotten," Vassu said with a deep rumbling voice.

Dennith scoffed at him.

"Matthew, I brought Dennith and Vassu here to train you to fight. Silva will be training you as well. Because you came to the defense of the keep during the attack, you've been given some more time. We need to make the most of it."

Matthew nodded. "When do I start training?"

"Tomorrow. Come with me," Tarrick said.

Tarrick led Matthew out of the command center and down a corridor. They arrived at a set of double doors and Tarrick pushed them open to reveal a long hallway lined with more doors. The scent of incubi and hunters he recognized lingered in the air. These were bedrooms.

Tarrick entered the fourth door on the right.

Matthew followed.

Inside there was a queen bed, a bookshelf full of books, and a nightstand. There were doors leading to a small bathroom and closet. The room had no windows.

"This is where you will stay from now on. There is a lounge at the end of the wing, you are permitted to go in there but nowhere else unless you are requested or ordered to do so. For the time being, you may accept blood from Commander Silva, Lady Rosaline, Lady Dennith, or Lord Vassu. There are always two hunter guards in this wing, if you need something you may ask them and they will relay your request. Do not enter any of the other rooms, even if you are invited in. All of them are warded against vampires."

Matthew was in awe. He assumed he'd be sleeping on the cot in Tarrick's room or back in the cell. He didn't expect to have his own space.

"I...thank you, Master."

"The rooms on this level are for warriors and top hunters. Most have spent their lives killing vampires. None will disobey me, but not all of them have accepted the idea of fighting or living alongside you. Don't expect the warmest reception here and control yourself. I don't want to have to put you back in the cage because you lost your temper with one of them."

"I won't let them get to me." Matthew was growing used to people not accepting him anyway.

"Good. I will be away for a while. I expect to only receive reports about your perfect obedience while I'm gone."

Matthew wondered where he was going, but Tarrick didn't look like he would tell him if he asked. "Then that's what you'll get." Now that he was unchained and had his own room, he didn't want to take steps backwards.

Tarrick placed his hand on Matthew's shoulder and squeezed. "Get some rest, you won't find much over the next few months."

Twenty-Eight

When Tarrick left him alone the first night, Matthew explored his small room. The bathroom wasn't big, but it had a toilet and a standing shower. The closet was full of t-shirts and jeans. There were also a couple of pairs of black tactical pants.

Matthew wondered if he would have to do his own laundry when he noticed the hamper for dirty clothes, but that question was answered the next night when he found the hamper empty. He smelled a maid had been in his room at some point during the day.

The bookshelf was filled with interesting books covering all different subjects. The topics spanned from modern and ancient war and strategy to classics from Twain to Shakespeare. But the books that interested Matthew the most were the ones on supernatural creatures. Incubi scholars wrote most of them, but there were a few in the mix written by vampires.

Over the next few months, Matthew spent every free moment he had reading and studying the tomes, astounded by the sheer number of other creatures also sharing this world; it didn't just end at dragons and gargoyles.

He read about demons sealed away in a place called the Pit—or what humans named Hell—and hadn't walked the planet in thousands of years. One scholar speculated vampires and incubi descended from demons while another scholar was adamantly against the idea.

There were entries about shapeshifters, rakshasa, sirens, trolls, oni, elves, jubokko, the list went on and on, he even read about faeries. Small. Glowing. Faeries. If Matthew wasn't a vampire living among incubi, guarded by magically enhanced humans he'd think this was all bullshit.

The first night, as he lay in his bed, waiting for the sun to rise, he heard the woman singing again. Matthew listened to her sweet song until his body shut down.

As the weeks went on, each night near dawn he heard her song. Curiosity plagued him. Who was singing? He opened the door to his room and the two hunters standing guard watched him as he walked down to the double doors leading out of the wing.

His guards drew their stakes.

"You are not permitted to leave," one warned.

"I know, I'm not. It's just...do you hear singing?" Matthew asked.

The guards glanced at each other then shook their heads.

The double doors opened and Silva appeared. She looked tired, coming off a long shift. The top of her leathers were already unlaced. Matthew knew she had a room on this wing, but he had never seen her returning to it.

Not expecting him to be standing on the other side of the door, she nearly ran into him. He looked past her, there was no one else there and yet he still heard the singing coming from that direction.

"What the hell are you doing?" she asked.

"I'm sorry, Commander. Do you hear singing?"

"No. Go to your room. The sun is about to rise and I don't want to have to drag your dead ass back to your bed."

Matthew grumbled but did as she ordered.

The singing continued through the months, but he never could find out who it was. Everyone he asked looked at him as if he was crazy.

Besides reading and trying to solve the mystery of the singing, Matthew's nights were full of training. Ten minutes after sunset he'd be collected by a hunter or summoned to a location. He learned to shower and dress quickly so he'd have a few minutes to read before training started.

Usually, his night began when Rosaline summoned him up to her room for a few hours. She'd give him bottled blood—Matthew was happy he wasn't killing humans anymore but he still wished he could drink directly from a vein.

Once he finished the blood, Rosaline taught him how to control his new incubus abilities as he fed sexually from her. He never bit her. He teased the hell out of her neck each time they made love, hoping she would ask him to, but she never did.

After a few weeks, he learned how to stop throwing out pheromones every time his thoughts turned to sex. He was thankful for that since the other incubi and hunters always knew what was happening and would smirk at him.

Under Rosaline's tutelage, he learned to control the amount of energy he took from his partner, how to better push pleasure, even how to reach out and manipulate a person, to hold them under his command.

The incubus hold was much different from the vampire compel. It was subtle and influencing, a gentle redirection of emotions. A compulsion was a domination of will and gave complete control over a person.

He wasn't good at holding, any incubi sensed it right away. Even the hunters could resist him. Normal humans didn't notice but the effects didn't last long, and besides, he'd rather just compel them because it was easier.

Matthew's vampire skills were off the chart but his incubus ones weren't impressive. Rosaline assured him it was only because he was young and new at this and, in time, his power would grow.

Matthew wasn't so sure.

He had a feeling that because he was killed and turned into a vampire before he finished his transformation, this side of him would always be weaker. He never did end up getting incubus horns or wings at any point during the months of his training. His only physical change was the silver eyes.

In addition to learning to control his incubus powers, Rosaline also taught him all about incubus society. She brought photos and had him memorize the lords and ladies of each house, along with their families. Most incubi didn't actually hold any rank or title; he had just been around a disproportionately large amount of those who did because of Tarrick.

In fact, Tarrick's household had a handful of lords and ladies that lived there and in exchange worked to improve the strength of the house and served Tarrick. Most seemed curious when they would interact with Matthew, but a few clearly didn't approve of him being there.

Like Lord Darius, who was the same age as Tane but looked nothing like him. Dark haired with equally dark eyes, he was handsome but thinner. He was a social incubus, not a warrior, but Matthew would have never guessed it by the way Darius glared at him each time they passed each other, as if he wanted to challenge him.

Matthew was more than happy to go out of his way to avoid him. Him and Tane.

Along with learning how to navigate the social structures of the house, he learned which incubi outranked Tarrick so that he'd know to kneel to them. And he was instructed on how to bow properly to lords and ladies. Bowing was far more nuanced than Matthew expected—arm placements, how low the head dropped, and the deepness of the bend were all important.

He did find it interesting that Tarrick was the only one he had to address as 'master'. Even the High King was addressed as 'Your Majesty'. Slaves only ever had one master even if others could issue him orders.

Matthew asked Rosaline to show him a picture of the High King but she told him it wasn't necessary, that he'd know who he was if he ever saw him. It left Matthew disappointed.

Rosaline also taught him how to dance in the massive ballroom in Ashwood Estate. He hated it at first; he had never danced much beyond clubbing and the occasional swaying slow dance. This dancing was formal, like the kind found in period movies. He was terrible at it for a while. But Rosaline was patient, and before he knew it he actually became quite good. He found himself looking forward to dancing with her every night.

One night he was summoned to Rosaline's room, only to find it empty. As he looked around for her, Silva appeared behind him and staked him through his back. When he came to, she was standing above him holding the bloody stake in her hand.

He learned the hard way that hunters had runes masking themselves from vampires and other creatures so long as the hunter didn't move. That meant he always had to expect an attack coming from just a few feet away. He kept his senses sharp and learned to keep his guard up.

After he spent a few hours with Rosaline each night he'd train with Dennith, Vassu, or Silva.

Dennith trained Matthew on how to use his vampire abilities to counter her attacks. Over time, Matthew learned just how much blood energy he needed to sustain a power. He could run fast for hours, whereas before, he'd throw so much energy behind his speed that he burned out in a few minutes. Having all four blood pouches working helped too.

The warrior succubus seemed to enjoy sparring with Matthew as much as he enjoyed sparring with her. She most likely had never worked so close with a vampire before and even her own skills seemed to be improving as they fought.

Matthew grew to respect her. She was old—nearly eight hundred—a skilled fighter, strict, and possessed an even temperament with an air of authority about her. She loved to tease Matthew whenever he fumbled, but she wasn't overly malicious about it.

He found out she believed as Tarrick did, that Matthew could end the war, and she accepted him as an incubus while respecting his vampire side. Matthew only trained with Dennith once or twice a week. With Tarrick gone, she was busy running the command center.

Most nights he trained with Vassu, who focused on teaching Matthew weapon and close quarter combat. Unlike Dennith, Vassu had not been so quick to accept Matthew for what he was. The reason he was there the night Matthew had fought the vampires in the arena was to see if he was worthy of being trained by him.

Vassu had not been convinced until after the attack on the keep when Matthew kept his word to Silva and returned before daybreak. He was just over three hundred and, according to hunter gossip, he had recently gone through his third transformation. He had come out the other side of it as one of the biggest incubi around.

Matthew saw his true form when they sparred and it was awe-inspiring. He was black as night from head to toe except for the white tips on his horns and wings, just over ten feet tall and a wingspan that could cross a room. He was as strong as a vampire and had the sensitive hearing to match. For such a large creature, his reflexes were quick. Matthew moved faster but Vassu always anticipated his moves and was there waiting for him.

On more than one occasion, Vassu smacked him around so bad during training that he had to be dragged back to his room by hunters and it wouldn't be until the next night he'd get enough blood or sex to heal his wounds.

Sometimes he'd overhear Rosaline scolding Vassu for riding Matthew so hard but Matthew didn't mind it. Vassu was forcing him to think and react faster. His foes wouldn't be kind enough to leave him alive at the end of a fight.

He mastered weapon fighting while training under Vassu, but Matthew's favorite nights were with Silva. She'd summon him to Ashwood VHA but she'd let him run the miles there by himself. He enjoyed the sense of freedom that running in the forest, under the night sky, brought.

Training with Silva meant training with hunter cadets and he loved it. She set up obstacle courses where Matthew had to make it to the end without getting shot by a bolt, or sometimes he'd have to locate all the cadets in an area and steal flags they had tucked into their belts before they could stake him. The training was more for the hunters than it was for him, but he learned a great deal.

Once, she released three vampires into the forest and Matthew had to stake them all before they escaped, and before the hunters got to them. To make it more challenging, she gave him no stakes. He ended up using a tree branch on one vampire and stealing stakes from hunters to use on the other two.

Just as Cullip had, Silva quizzed him with twenty questions at the end of most nights. Unlike Cullip, she didn't whip him, she just expected him to answer correctly. And he did. It became rare for him to miss a question.

One night a team of veteran hunters he didn't recognize ambushed him while he was on his way to the academy. He dodged their initial attacks but they chained him in silvers before he had a chance to counter.

They left him there all night until just before sunrise when Silva came and let him free. He had to rush back to the keep to avoid the sun and collapsed on the stairwell up to his room as day broke. That event knocked him down a few pegs and served to remind him he had been training with mostly novice hunters.

When he woke he was back in his bed and Silva was there holding a bottle of blood to his lips. She fed him and he healed the deep wounds the silver chains had seared into his skin.

"Why did you run back to the keep last night?" she asked once he was finished drinking.

Matthew was confused. "Um, I really didn't want to die...?"

She shrugged. "You almost didn't make it. You should have sunk into the ground."

Matthew eyed her, unsure of what the hell she was talking about.

She smiled at him. "Vampires can return to the earth when they wish it. Tonight we'll see if you can figure out how to do it."

Out in the forest, Matthew heard hunters stalking around from time to time but she told him to ignore them.

"I have no clue how vampires do it, so you have to figure it out on your own, but you have the rest of the night to do so. I suggest lying down, that's how the younger ones do it."

Matthew lay down on the forest ground. He thought about his body sinking into the ground but nothing happened. He concentrated on reaching out with his senses, focusing on the ground below him. After a few hours, he could pinpoint every bug within three feet of him but still no sinking.

Silva waited by him the entire night in silence. Matthew finally sighed and stood as dawn approached.

"What are you doing?" she asked.

"I don't think this is happening, I've been trying all night and nothing is working. I need to get back."

The sky lightened around them.

She crossed her arms. "Lie back down."

Matthew just stared at her. She couldn't be serious.

"Those hunters I told you to ignore earlier are the same group that took you out last night. I've ordered them to stop you if you try to run back to the keep."

Fear rose within Matthew. The sun would be breaking the horizon any moment. "Why would you do that?"

"Because you always figure out things fastest when your life's in danger. And I'm telling you that every vampire, even fledglings, can sink into the ground. So lie back down and do it."

Matthew growled at her but she didn't flinch. He looked at the sky, it was frighteningly bright to him now. He noticed his breathing had gotten harder as his instincts screamed at him to get to a safe place before the sun rose.

Lying down, he watched the horizon. There was no way he could do this. All night he had been trying and nothing had happened.

The sun broke above a hill. Matthew forced himself to stop breathing, focused below him, and let the ground swallow him up. He sunk deep into it, the dirt moving around his body and covering him.

He fell asleep in the ground.

When he next woke, he panicked and dirt filled his mouth.

He wasn't sure how to get out at first, but then calmed himself and focused. He felt attuned to the earth around him. It yielded to his command to lift him up.

He broke through the surface, dragged himself out, and began coughing.

Silva was there waiting for him. "Nicely done. You have about—" she looked at her watch, "—seven minutes before Lady Rosaline summons you, and I don't think she'll appreciate you arriving in your current condition."

He scowled at Silva then bolted back to his room to shower.

Over the months, his training went somewhat smoothly. He lost his temper a few times during a sparring match, or when a hunter or Tane—who ran the household in his father's absence—directed a rude comment his way, but he pulled himself together before it went too far. That or Vassu tossed him around until he cooled down.

When he next saw Tarrick, four months had passed. It wasn't quite the reunion that Matthew had been expecting.

Twenty-Nine

It was summer now, and the nights were warm. Matthew walked the grounds with Lady Rosaline while she taught him the art of conversation. She forced him to try to seduce her into his bed. As if he could actually seduce a woman like Rosaline. But still, he enjoyed sex with her even if he wasn't entirely hungry, so he gave it his best shot.

He was terrible at it. She seemed to find it endearing and rewarded him with a kiss.

In the keep, the usual sounds of routine—hunter rotation, scheduled dinners, even the servants cleaning—changed and there was a rush of activity. Something was wrong. He broke away from her.

"What is it?" Rosaline asked.

"Dennith and Silva are on their way out here, they're both agitated." He could hear their hearts beating fast.

Silva teleported beside them and thrust a sheathed longsword at Matthew. "You're up."

Was this a new training exercise? They rarely ever pulled him away from his time with Rosaline.

"What do you mean?" he asked as he buckled the sword around his waist.

Dennith ran into the garden fully armored, but not yet in her incubus form. "It means training is done, there's a major battle going on in Northern California right now and we need to be there. The High King himself has ordered you to hit the field."

Concern flashed across Rosaline's face.

"We need to get to the academy. How fast can you run there with me?" Dennith asked.

"About under a minute if I push it," he answered. Matthew thought he could go even quicker but it'd mean burning away all his energy.

"That's faster than I can fly. Let's go."

Matthew scooped up Dennith and booked it to the academy. By the time they arrived, Silva—who had teleported—stood waiting for them, holding two large jugs filled with blood.

She led them to the teleport stone hidden in the basement of one of the dorms. During his months of training, Matthew learned that Tarrick didn't have a stone at his estate for security reasons.

Waiting at the academy's stone were twenty-five hunters: four teams along with Fendrel, the knight hunter. Matthew found out he was a special brand of hunter that specialized in taking down different monsters besides vampires.

Fendrel was a dragon slayer. A *for real* dragon slayer.

However, because dragons were sleeping and rarely woke, he was sent to join just about any fight happening. Some cadets had told Matthew that Fendrel was once a true knight during the middle ages, but Matthew was skeptical about that.

The trainees loved to tease him. For an entire week they had him convinced Dracula was a real vampire that was still alive. Vassu eventually told him Dracula was fiction and disciplined the cadets once he learned what was going on.

"Don't bother kneeling to anyone until the end of the battle and you are free to take whatever blood you need from our enemies," Dennith told him as she checked over her weapons to ensure they were all in place.

"Many of the hunters and incubi fighting don't know who you are, they might try to attack. If they do, just fall back to our group," Silva said.

"Yes, Commander," he said.

Silva turned to address the rest of the group. "We're going in hot, vampires are at the stone."

All the hunters had weapons drawn and they circled in a defensive position.

"Matthew, teleporting for the first time is rough, you'll probably lose your dinner." She lifted up the jugs in her hand. "Recover as fast as possible. Teleport in three, two, one." She put her hand on the stone and a bright green light flashed around them.

When it faded they were in a roofless courtyard surrounded by walls of a modern mansion.

Matthew's stomach twisted and he fell to his knees. He began to vomit black blood while the hunters moved around the area, engaging a handful of vampires that had been waiting for them. The sounds of battle filled the air.

When he finally stopped puking his brains out, he grabbed one of the jugs of blood and chugged it. His senses came back to him and he watched as a vampire lord flew overhead. Dennith brought her wings out and took to the air, giving chase. The two creatures disappeared over the house, out of Matthew's sight.

Matthew counted eight more vampires coming over the top of the roof, making their way to the courtyard. One jumped down, rushed in and sank its claws deep into a hunter's neck.

Drawing his sword, Matthew sliced the vamp in two before it hurt anyone else. New screams drew his attention and he turned around to see a female vampire clutching a hunter by his ankle and dragging him away.

He rushed at the vampire and slammed into her full force. They went tumbling down but Matthew ended up on top, pinning her under him. She hissed and clawed but he held her tight and looked her in the eyes.

"Fight for me. Kill vampires."

She struggled at first, but she was young and not much of a match for Matthew. Her will collapsed to his and he released her. She sprang to her feet and launched herself at the other vampires, attacking them. Matthew repeated the process with a second vampire: capturing him then compelling him to fight his people.

"I won't be holding them long," Matthew told Silva when he rejoined her. She had taken up a defensive position behind a planter.

"I'll kill them once we're clear," she said as she shot an approaching vampire in his blood pouch with a bolt. It screamed and retreated. "We have this under control. Get to the front."

Matthew nodded and sped through the house—owned by incubi, he didn't need to be invited in—and out the front doors. When he exited, he skidded to a halt and gasped. He had never seen anything like it before.

Tarrick had told Matthew vampires and incubi fought in battles, but he always assumed it was skirmishes or assaults like the one on the keep. This was nothing like that. This was war.

There were thousands of vampires, incubi, and hunters fighting.

The battle took place in the fields of the surrounding vineyards—all the grapevines trampled to nothing. Huge smoldering pits littered the field. Some distance away, thick smoke billowed out of neighboring houses.

Not far away from him, a group of hunters went flying into the air, launched up by waves of vampires trying to cut through their line. Their bodies tumbled like ragdolls. Those who weren't killed immediately teleported away. Matthew dodged as a body flew past him and hit the wall with a sickening *thuck*.

There were groups of hunters on the roof above him, raining a hail of arrows and bolts down upon the vampires.

In the distance, he saw a swarm of bats surrounding a hunter, each one tearing at his flesh. As the hunter turned green to teleport away, the bats formed into a vampire, who ripped the hunter's heart out then turned back into a swarm of bats.

Wolves howled. Coming up the flank were thirty or forty massive wolves, bigger and mangier than any Matthew had ever seen. Shifters, fighting for the vampires. Matthew watched them rip apart any hunter or incubus they could separate and pin down.

High above him, incubi and vampire lords clashed in the air.

Dead hunters and incubi littered the ground, as did decaying vampires. The smell of blood was pungent.

This battle had been going on for a while, and it was surreal.

The monster in Matthew rose up and a smile crossed his face. Both sets of his fangs came out, his eyes burned red, and his fingers became claws as he gripped his sword tightly.

He pushed power into his speed and joined the fray.

In less than a minute he killed five vampires and stabbed three more in their blood pouches. None had touched him. He stopped to revel in his power only to feel a clawed hand penetrate his skin and dig deep into his lower abdomen. A vampire grabbed onto one of his blood pouches and squeezed, bursting it.

"What the..." The vampire's eyes grew wide when he realized that Matthew had four blood pouches inside of him.

Matthew answered by cutting off the vampire's arm, then his head, in one swift motion. He yanked the arm out of his body before it could decay inside of him. Because that would be nasty as fuck.

Before he had a chance to recover from the wound, a striped wall of muscle and fur pounced on top of him. Matthew toppled down into the dirt and vines, sword flying from his hand.

He rolled out of the way as a tiger's claw swiped at him, coming so close he could feel the air rushing by.

The tiger, with scorching yellow eyes, snarled and lashed out with a second powerful swipe of his claw. This one hit Matthew in his side, cracking ribs, splitting skin, and sending him rolling across the ground. His body slid under the feet of a vampire and hunter who were dueling, toppling them both over. All three became a tangled pile of limbs and weapons. They scratched and clawed, trying to escape from each other.

The vampire, ending up on top, thrust a dagger at the hunter. The hunter teleported away before it hit him. Unfortunately for Matthew, he was underneath the hunter and took a dagger to his chest.

Matthew roared and tossed the vampire off him.

As soon as he was up on his feet, he was knocked right back down again, pinned under the tiger's huge body. Its claws dug into his shoulders and teeth clicked against Matthew's collar as it attempted to gnaw at his neck. Its hot breath belted against Matthew's cool skin.

Matthew kicked and clawed but the tiger's skin was thick and he could not prise the big cat off.

Unable to do much damage to Matthew's neck, the tiger raked a claw down Matthew's front and bit at his shoulder.

Desperate, Matthew pulled out the dagger still stuck in his chest and drove it into the tiger's eye.

The tiger reeled back, taking a chunk of Matthew with him. It roared, spitting out the piece of decaying meat that was once Matthew's deltoid.

Matthew's pride took a hit as he admitted to himself this was a fight he couldn't win. His abdomen was bleeding from the vampire that had popped a blood pouch, he had deep gashes and a stab wound in his chest, and half of one shoulder was missing. Matthew needed time to recover.

As the tiger lunged at him, Matthew pulled all the power he could muster into his speed and ran the hell away. Dust flew into the air as the tiger's paws slid in the dirt, trying to redirect its mass but there was no one for him to fight—Matthew was long gone.

He retreated to the teleport stone, grabbed the second jug of blood, and downed it.

Silva cut off the head of one of his compelled vampires. "You look like shit."

"Tiger," Matthew said, his voice raw from the tiger's bite marks around the collar.

Matthew looked above him and had an idea, but he waited a few minutes before voicing it, giving his body time to repair his arm and close his wounds. "Can you bring one of those lords out of the sky?"

Silva raised her brow. "You think you can take a lord on?"

"Don't know, guess we'll find out if your training was any good," he answered with a smile.

"The training was fine, it's the student I'm unsure of. He just got his ass handed to him by a tiger shifter," she said smiling back.

Matthew scowled.

She ignored it as she summoned the other Wardens over, giving them quick commands. Her team waited patiently until a vampire lord passed overhead.

All the hunters flicked their arms and silver-coated chains from a device under their sleeves shot upwards into the sky. Three of them hit their mark and hooked onto the lord. The hunters were lifted up off the ground as the lord tried to fly away.

Matthew grabbed one of the silver chains to help them out, burning his hand in the process.

"You're buying me gloves after this battle," he said to Silva and yanked hard, sending the lord plummeting to the ground.

The vampire struggled to his feet as the hunters shot more silver chains at him. Matthew leaped on top of the lord, driving his knees into his abdomen. The lord hissed and tossed Matthew away like a doll. Damn, this fucker was strong.

The lord pulled on the chains sending the hunters tumbling to the ground.

Matthew received a small opening when Fendrel sliced into the lord's wing with his sword and bashed his shield into the back of the vampire's head, stunning the lord for a moment.

Matthew didn't give him a chance to recover. He drove his foot into the back of the lord's knee, his legs collapsed out from underneath him and he was back on the ground. This time Matthew was on him faster. He grabbed the lord's hair and looked into his eyes. "Fight for me."

The hunters in the area stilled as they waited to see if Matthew could really compel a lord.

"What are you?" the lord asked as he struggled against Matthew's will.

"An incubus," he replied and winked. "Now, fight for me," he repeated the command and touched the lord, nudging his emotions just enough so that he'd want to surrender to the compulsion.

The lord lost the battle of wills and belonged to Matthew now...so long as he could keep his concentration, but it was taking most of his focus to keep the compulsion up.

"I have him," Matthew told the hunters. They released the lord from their chains.

"Kill the other lords," Matthew commanded. The vampire's wing mended before their eyes and he took off back into the sky.

Silva picked up a sword from a dead hunter and tossed it to Matthew. "Didn't take you long to lose your weapon."

Matthew snatched it from the air and sheathed it. "I told you...*tiger.*"

She pointed to the neighboring mansion. "Go clear the two neighboring houses. They're full of vamps and we can't get in."

Matthew sped away and hoped he wouldn't face anything too challenging. If something hit him hard enough, he'd lose the lord fighting for him.

On his way to the house, he spotted Vassu fighting on the ground, full-sized and armored in thick metal plates. Vampire bits piled at his feet. He cleaved a vampire in two with his double bladed sword then took to the air to face a lord.

Matthew jumped a fence and ran towards some broken double doors. He sensed seven vampires in the house.

He slammed into an invisible wall as he tried to enter and fell backwards on his ass, snarling at the air. One of the home's human owners must still be alive. The vampires already in there had likely compelled one of the owners to invite them in before killing them.

He extended his senses and smelled a frightened human girl on the other side of the house. He rushed that way.

The girl—a teenager—was in the middle of a group of four hunters who were fighting off a vampire.

The hunter's looked a little different from the ones he normally saw. This team had matching uniforms, black hooded cloaks and dark masks covered their mouth and nose. All of them fought with great agility. They looked like a team of assassins. They didn't speak much but when they did it was Japanese to each other and English when reporting into their comms.

Had they been called here from Japan? Matthew wasn't sure of the range of the teleport stones but maybe they could move someone around the world in the blink of an eye.

As he watched them take down the vampire and engage a second one that had entered the area, he wondered if they were protecting the girl because they cared about her, or if it was to keep her alive and make it so no other vampires could enter the home. Or both.

Before Matthew could get over to her, a stake punctured one of his blood pouches from behind him. Matthew roared as he turned and swiped at the hunter who stabbed him. The hunter dodged out of the way. He was small and fast. He looked like a fifth member of the assassin group, except his mask was red. Matthew guessed he was probably their leader.

Leaving the stake embedded in Matthew's back, the assassin reached under his cloak, pulled out a silver grenade, and chucked it at Matthew while tumbling away.

Matthew snatched it from the air and threw it at the other vampire the group was fighting, covering the vamp with silver dust. The assassin hunters took the opportunity to stake and kill the creature.

The red-masked leader teleported away. His teleport was different: he left in a white glow, not a green one. And now, Matthew could no longer sense him.

Damn it. He didn't have time for this shit.

He approached the hunters and throwing stars went flying at him. He dodged them easily only to feel a sharp burning sensation in his back. The leader had driven a dagger into his ribs, the weapon coated with the burning liquid that slowed his healing.

Son of a bitch.

Matthew grimaced as he tried to pull the dagger from his back, but he couldn't reach it. He poured more power into his speed, ran to a dead hunter, and grabbed the comm from off the body.

The assassin teleported behind him. Matthew rolled away as the tiny man tried to stab him with a new dagger. Just how many fucking weapons did this little shit have?

A silver chain went flying past him. Matthew was doing his best to dodge these attacks but this group was quick. The hunter on his ass had reflexes faster than Silva, and the other four were definitely seasoned.

Matthew pressed a button on the comm. "For the love of god, please tell these hunters on the south side of this pink stucco mansion to stop fucking attacking me."

He tossed the comm away and hoped that would work. A small throwing knife lodged itself into his belly and pierced another blood pouch. Matthew pulled it out and poured red threads of energy into healing the wound to prevent it from gushing blood. Still poisoned with a dagger in his back, it took him longer than normal.

Three of his blood pouches had been damaged in this fight. He had stopped the bleeding in two but the stake was still lodged in one. He needed more blood. And soon. His concentration faltered and he felt the vampire lord fighting against him, trying to free himself.

The red-masked assassin leader appeared in front of him and Matthew barely moved away fast enough to avoid getting staked in the heart.

A female voice came through the hunter's earpieces: "All warriors, be advised there is a vampire fighting on our side. Brown hair, silver eyes, six-two. He is collared and armed with a silver longsword. By order of the High Lord General he is not to be attacked."

Matthew forced his irises to change from red to silver.

The leader froze, his eyes widened.

"Yeah, I'm on your side here. Get your damn dagger out of my back," Matthew said and batted the stake away the hunter was holding.

The assassin teleported behind him and yanked both the dagger and the stake out. Matthew growled and forced the wounds to close. Blood. He needed blood.

Matthew approached the group of hunters. They had heard the order, but all their weapons trained on him anyway.

He ignored them and went for the girl. She was terrified of him and he hardly blamed her: he was covered in blood, most of it his own, his shirt was ripped to shreds thanks to the tiger, and he had raw pink scars all over his neck and chest. Not to mention his claws and fangs.

He took a deep breath and forced his vampire side away. When Matthew took a step at her, the girl stumbled backwards, bumping into a hunter.

Faster than she could see, Matthew moved to her and put his hand on her face. He couldn't compel her right now because he didn't want to risk losing control of the lord, but he had other ways to get what he needed from her.

"You don't need to fear me, dear. I won't hurt you," he said, using his incubus abilities to wrap a hold around her. The girl relaxed. "Is it okay if I enter your home?"

"Yes," she said with a nod.

That was the only invitation Matthew needed. He released her and reached out with his senses.

"You're an incubus," the leader assassin said. It wasn't a question.

Matthew nodded and let his vampire guise out again. "There are four vampires on the ground floor, three on the top. Give me three minutes and I'll have them cleared."

Matthew drew his sword and pushed all his remaining power into his speed. He surged into the house and went to the top floor, passing over the bodies of at least eight hunters and the girl's parents on his way up.

He moved with such speed that the first two vampires didn't even see him as he took their heads off. The third, a bit quicker, clawed at Matthew's shoulder. Matthew slammed him against the wall and sank his fangs into the vampire's neck. He drained him fast and the vampire fell limp. The vamp wasn't permanently dead, but it sure looked that way. He wouldn't be getting back up until someone gave him blood.

With four more vampires to take care of, he went to the landing above the stairwell and jumped down next to a vampire below. He brought his

sword up and sliced its body in two. The two young vampires waiting
there took several steps away and their eyes grew wide when they saw
Matthew.

"Death," one gasped. They ran from him, out of the house.

His aura. It had to be.

Others had shied away from him as well but their actions were lost in
the fervor of battle. Now it was an issue. He needed to figure out a way to
suppress his aura. Not that he had time right now.

The last vampire, at the back of the house, didn't run when Matthew
entered the room. Instead, the vamp stood ready with a sword in hand. He
charged at Matthew who deflected his blade with his bracer and countered
with his sword. The skilled vampire blocked him.

The two of them dueled.

Matthew was faster with and had more raw power, but this vampire
was experienced with his blade and deflected each of his attacks. The combat went on for several minutes until a white glow appeared behind the
vampire. The red-masked assassin drove a stake into the vampire's back.

Before the body hit the ground, Matthew had his fangs in its neck, replacing more of the blood he had lost.

The hunter watched as he fed, studying Matthew's collar and bracers.
"You took longer than three minutes."

Matthew dropped the body and scoffed at the hunter. "Cut me a little
slack, this is my first real battle. The rest of the house is clear."

The hunter pushed his red face mask down but left his hood up revealing his Japanese heritage. He looked young, maybe eighteen. Matthew
guessed he was older than he looked given his skill and rank. Matthew
easily stood a foot taller and tripled his mass, but even as he towered over
the small hunter, he found himself strangely attracted to the man.

He blamed his incubus side for that. Some days he wanted to fuck everyone in sight and it took all his self-control to settle down.

The assassin hunter stuck out his hand. "Commander Hiroto of House
Kōki."

No hunter had ever offered Matthew their hand, and incubi didn't greet
each other that way. Matthew smiled and shook his hand carefully so that
his claws didn't scratch him. "Matthew, the incubus vampire."

Hiroto chuckled. "That's a new one. Where have they been hiding
you?"

He was awfully inquisitive for a hunter and far more talkative than Matthew would have thought him to be. He always imagined assassin types

would be quiet...broody.

"Lord General Tarrick is my master," he said and tapped his collar. Matthew wasn't sure he should be telling him that but he had never been ordered not to and right now he didn't really care.

Thump.

Damn it. Feelings of pleasure surged in Matthew and he felt drawn to the source.

"Speaking of...please excuse me," Matthew said.

Hiroto nodded as Matthew ran from the house.

Thirty

Matthew made his way across the gardens that served as part of the battlefield, killing a handful of vampires who got in his way and dodging a few hunters who tried to attack him.

Thump. Thump. Thump.

There was more than one incubus thumping. The vampires around Matthew paused, the feeling flooding them as well. Many of them fell as hunters and incubi took advantage of the distraction.

Matthew kept going until he saw Tarrick.

He was on the second story balcony, overlooking the battle. Surrounding him were commanders and other important looking incubi. Just inside the house, Matthew could see what looked like a mobile command center, complete with dispatchers relaying information.

Tarrick, in his full incubus form wearing his iridescent spiked armor, appeared intimidating and magnificent. His wings stretched behind him and Matthew watched as he impaled a vampire through the belly with his massive sword and kick him off the balcony.

Three smaller incubi were off to the side. They all had their eyes closed.

Thump. Thump. Thump.

A vampire lord crashed down into one of the incubi and crushed her. The lord clawed the face of a second one.

Matthew crossed the remaining distance and leaped up to the lord. He landed behind him and ripped off one of his wings. The lord howled, grabbed Matthew by his arms, and tossed him so far across the battlefield he was nearly back at the neighboring house.

Matthew bounced and slid towards a group of hunters that teleported out of his way. He careened through grapevines before finally crashing into a short retaining wall.

By the time Matthew made his way back, the lord was locked in battle with Tarrick. Tarrick slammed the hilt of his sword across the vampire's face then reached out and touched him.

The lord fell under Tarrick's hold for a moment. Silva teleported in and staked him through the heart.

"Don't you have some houses to clear?" Tarrick asked as Matthew jumped back up.

Tarrick didn't wait for Matthew to answer. He turned and barked orders at a group of hunters standing on the roof, covering the north side of the house.

Tarrick may have been busy commanding a battle, but Matthew hadn't seen him in four months. He dared to linger for a long moment.

Chaos ensued around them: information was being called out by many dispatchers all at once, a hunter flashed in to give a report, medics rushed in to help the incubus that had been injured by the lord, and the battle raged below them, but Tarrick—the High Lord General—was phased by none of the madness.

Matthew watched as Tarrick processed every bit of information thrown at him and in almost a dispassionate manner relayed new orders. Calm. Collected.

Tarrick sidestepped as a stray bolt went flying by his head then ripped open a missive a dispatcher handed him. He in no way acknowledged or even seemed to notice he had just narrowly stepped out of the way of death.

How was it that this man could fill Matthew with such fear and desire at the same time?

Matthew reluctantly broke away and left to clear the other house. It didn't take him long, the owners of the house were dead and there were only a couple of vampires still alive inside. To his surprise, a group of cadets from Ashwood he trained with often had cleared the vamps. They were exhausted—it was their first battle also—but they handled themselves well, although he got the sense they weren't supposed to be here.

Thump.

Fucking hell. Matthew returned to the balcony, crouching on the thick stone railing.

"You keep thumping and I'm not going to be able to keep control of that vampire lord," Matthew said and pointed up at the sky.

Tarrick spoke an order into his comm for Vassu and another warrior incubus, whose name Matthew didn't recognize, to take out a group of vampires trying to destroy the teleport stone.

The general checked the time—sunrise was still a long way off—then he watched the compelled vampire lord fight another vampire in aerial combat for a moment. Tarrick seemed to be weighing which was more important: the distraction that the thump caused some of the weaker vampires or having the lord fight on their side.

"We'll stop the thumping for now," he said as he made his choice.

Two fully armored incubi swooped down from the sky and landed next to Tarrick. One was Tane, whose incubus form was only six feet tall right now—small for a warrior incubus—and the other had to be a son of Tarrick's as well. His face and hair looked just like his father except his horns curved forward, not back, into frightful points and his coloring was a dark green, not purple. He was nearly eight feet, in his full form—taller than Tarrick.

Matthew could sense he was powerful.

"We've cut off their route for reinforcements," he said as he landed. He had just a hint of a Russian accent.

"Good. Tarquin, join the hunters in the—"

"Sir!" a dispatcher cut him off. "The veil covering the south is failing. A human just called emergency services reporting noises from the battle."

"Go handle that instead," he said to Tarquin. "Afterwards, join Ashwood Blue and flank those wolves. We need them pushed back. Tane, rejoin the main battle."

Tarquin. Rosaline had mentioned him once. He was a general in his own right, favored to replace Tarrick should he ever fall. He had the near-impossible task of trying to fight the vampires in Russia.

The eldest son took to the air while Tane stepped forward next to Matthew.

"Twenty-three," he said, telling Matthew the number of vampires he had killed.

Matthew narrowed his eyes and growled, not wanting to be drawn into such a petty, cliché game.

And yet he couldn't help it. "Fourteen, but I was late."

A vampire lord fell from the sky and landed on the ground below the balcony. Matthew's compelled lord landed on it and began to feed.

"That's not including the ones he has killed," Matthew said.

"Those don't count."

Matthew scoffed and jumped down. He had some catching up to do. Tane followed behind, clearly determined not to let Matthew get ahead of him in numbers. The two clashed against the vampires, taking down any that stood in their way. Matthew even killed a few wolf shifters. To his disappointment, he wasn't able to find the tiger. Either it had died and reverted to a human form or had moved away from the front of the vineyard.

The battle raged for hours.

At one point during the night, Matthew broke away from the fighting and found an empty location around the back of the house. He called his compelled lord to him. The lord landed, trembling, still trying to break away.

"Do you know how to suppress an aura?" Matthew asked it, once he was sure no one could overhear.

"Yes."

"How?"

"Release me and I'll show you."

"No. You are going to show me now," Matthew said and poured power behind his command.

The lord growled. He held his wrist up to Matthew. "My blood will show you."

Matthew grabbed the wrist and sunk his fangs into it. When he pulled the powerful blood into him, he began to see things...memories in the blood. He saw the lord learning how to mask himself to other vampires. He didn't have a death aura like Matthew, but rather he was suppressing his power so that younger vampires wouldn't become overwhelmed by it.

Understanding came to Matthew and he knew what he had to do now. He reached into himself and felt the aura coming from within, then he turned it off.

He withdrew his fangs and licked the wound to cover up the bite marks. "Do you still feel the death aura around me?" The vampire lord shook his head. It had worked. "Tell no one what I asked of you. Return to fighting."

When Matthew rejoined the battle, no one seemed to have noticed he had been missing.

A few hours before dawn the vampire forces retreated. Matthew, having sustained many wounds during the fighting, called his compelled lord to him and nearly drank him dry. After the lord fell unconscious, he sliced off his head.

Matthew wasn't quite sure what he should be doing now that the battle was over. He extended his senses and listened up at the balcony where Tarrick's mobile command was set up. The general was busy issuing orders and Matthew would just get in his way.

He did overhear Tarrick order the evacuation of this estate by next nightfall. This was in vampire territory and the losses they sustained didn't make keeping this place worth another battle. In that way, this was a vampire victory…but looking around, Matthew didn't think either side had won. Each suffered massive losses.

Matthew went into the house. The sounds and smells of sex were all around him. Wounded incubi were fucking so they could heal. Their partners were mostly hunters.

Being a hunter was a hell of a job. Some days they killed vampires, some days they fucked their boss to heal them. And today, for a handful of them, it was both. At least each of them seemed to know what they signed up for and had a choice in the matter.

Matthew rubbed the bracers that served as a reminder that he was nothing more than a slave whose choices had been taken from him.

He found a bathroom, ripped off what was left of his shredded shirt, and looked at himself in the mirror. Blood was caked on his skin and his eyes were red, his fangs long and ready. The battle had thrilled him more than it should have.

He knew he was a monster, but did he really have to enjoy killing so damn much?

Matthew, unable to force his vampire guise away, carefully washed his face and claws just to clean up a little.

On his way out of the bathroom, Matthew saw three dead incubi that had been dragged into a sitting room. He recognized them from the photos Rosaline had shown him. They were the lord and lady of this estate, along with their daughter. Their bodies smelled as if they had been dead for hours. They must have been killed in the initial attack. Maybe that was how this battle started.

As he stood there Matthew could hear the singing again.

It wasn't even dawn yet. And they weren't at Tarrick's keep, which meant whoever was singing was here. Determined to find her, he left the sitting room and moved towards the voice. He followed it up the stairs and down an abandoned wing of the house where he came to wooden double doors. Whoever was singing was in the room behind them.

Finally. Answers.

He pushed the doors open and looked around.

There was no one.

Inside, the design was akin to a shrine. Unlit candles lined the walls. Plush chaise lounges and pillows covered most of the floor. At the other end of the room, the wall was painted with elaborate symbols Matthew didn't recognize. There was a full-size marble statue of the incubus goddess, Ilertha, in the center against the back wall. At her feet were offerings of incense, gold, and various trinkets. This entire room appeared to be set up to give her praise. Matthew could smell that a lot of copulation happened in here. Was that how they worshiped her?

Matthew couldn't take his eyes off the statue; she was flawless.

And she was singing to him.

The statue wasn't moving but the song was coming from her all the same.

Matthew moved into the room and stood before her. He bowed his head and swallowed hard. The music moved him to tears.

"Why do you sing to me?" he asked, his voice barely a whisper.

There was no answer other than the song.

The world around him faded away and Matthew let the tranquility it brought wash over him. It calmed him, the high of battle faded, and his vampire form melted away. He lost himself in her voice.

The next thing he knew there was a hand on his shoulder. Matthew blinked hard as he came out of his trance, but the singing didn't stop.

Tarrick stood by his side. He was in his human form but still in armor, which had shrunk to fit his human size, proving without a doubt magic laced the metal.

Silva was standing at the door, her skin covered with scratches and bruises, and she looked exhausted. Matthew sensed a couple teams of hunters waiting out in the hallway. Did they expect him to put up a fight?

The sun would be up soon. Just how long had he been standing here? An hour at least. It felt as if only moments had passed.

Matthew sunk to his knee before Tarrick.

"It took us a while to find you, we thought you had run away," Tarrick said.

"No, Master, I didn't run."

"Why are you in here? You may rise."

Matthew looked up at the statue as he got back to his feet. "She is singing to me. Can you hear it?"

Tarrick shook his head. "No, but I've read plenty of reports saying you've been asking around about singing. Can you repeat the song?"

Matthew nodded. He was happy Tarrick wasn't mocking him and didn't seem to think he was crazy. He began to sing along with the voice. It was the same song every night and he had it memorized. Although, he had no idea what it meant since it was in a language he didn't speak.

Tarrick smiled. "That is an incubus nursery rhyme we sing to our children. You are singing it in our old tongue."

"What is it about?" Matthew asked.

"It is about a lost boy who journeys far and has many adventures before one day reuniting with his family."

"Sir, the sun is up in less than two minutes," Silva said.

Tarrick motioned behind him. "There's a coffin in the hall for you."

"A coffin? Seriously?" Matthew asked and eyed Tarrick.

"The teleport stone was badly damaged. We have to fly you back east. We do have better light-proof containers for vampires, but none of them are here at this estate so we're stuck with a coffin." Tarrick flashed a devious smile at him. "Don't worry…it's never been used before."

Matthew gave a heavy sigh. He took off his belt with the sword and handed it to Silva, then walked out into the hall. All of the hunters out there looked just as tired as Silva.

Matthew got into the coffin and waited for the sun to rise.

Tarrick stood over him and pressed his hand on Matthew's bare chest. As always, his hand against his skin felt so damn good.

"You did well tonight," Tarrick said.

Matthew tried to smile but the sun rose and he was out like a corpse.

Thirty-One

Matthew woke in his room. On the nightstand next to his bed was a small box with a ribbon around it. He opened it and inside was a pair of fingerless leather gloves with a note that read:

Enjoy.
—Silva

Matthew smiled.

He showered and dressed, then picked up The Book of Five Rings to read while waiting to be summoned. Ten minutes later no one had come to collect him.

Some nights that happened. He didn't mind, it meant more reading time for him.

Three hours later he smelled Tarrick's scent outside of his room. He set down his book and kneeled as Tarrick entered. He was back in his usual attire—a fitted suit. Matthew couldn't help but notice just how flattering it looked on him.

Tarrick shut the door behind him and studied Matthew in silence for a few moments.

Matthew half-smiled when he realized what Tarrick was waiting on.

"May I have blood, Master?" It had been a while since he had to ask for blood this way because it made Rosaline uncomfortable and she had been the one to feed him most nights.

"You may," he said and pulled out his cell phone to call for some.

"Master…?"

Tarrick paused his call. "Yes?"

"I don't really want to kill anyone. May I have bottled blood or just not kill the human?" Matthew wasn't sure if Tarrick would grant him the request.

While battling, he enjoyed the thrill killing brought him. He reveled in it actually. He still wanted fresh blood but a human that couldn't even put up a fight…he had grown to hate the idea ever since learning how to stop himself in the middle of a feed. Even the vampire clawing under his skin wanted a challenge.

Tarrick nodded and raised the phone to his ear. "Quart of blood, Matthew's room." He hung up. "Rise."

Matthew stood.

Tarrick circled around him, studying him. "Take your shirt off," he ordered. Matthew pulled off his shirt and Tarrick ran a finger over his shoulder where the tiger had bitten him. The skin still showed a little pink, but had otherwise repaired. "You've healed well."

"How long has it been since the battle?" he asked as he tossed his shirt onto the bed.

"You tell me."

That was always a hard one for Matthew. All the damage done to his blood pouches was fully healed. He only had a few scars left, and he was hungry enough that he wanted more blood but not hungry as he should have been considering all the healing his body went through, meaning he was probably given blood through an IV at some point. It could have been two days or two weeks for all he knew.

"I'm not sure," he admitted, "I don't know when all these wounds healed."

Tarrick ran his fingers across Matthew's stomach; the touch electrified his nerves and went right to his cock. "You have another way to measure."

Ah, his soavik, he knew just how much his body used up each day. "Six days."

"Correct." Tarrick looked pleased.

"Why was I kept out so long? Was there a new council on what is to be my fate?"

"Yes."

There was a knock at the door. Tarrick opened it, took a bottle of blood from the hunter, and handed it to Matthew. Matthew wanted to know what decision had been made about his future but he drank his blood first.

Tarrick waited to speak until Matthew had finished drinking. "You performed admirably, better than I anticipated you would after only four months of training. But I should know by now not to underestimate you. Compelling the vampire lord was extraordinary and completely unexpected, but most importantly you killed more vampires that night than any other single person did. I'm extremely proud of you."

Matthew couldn't help but smile. He reminded himself for the millionth time that he shouldn't be so damned petty but he wished Tane had been around to hear that.

"Your actions did not go unnoticed. Rumors about who and what you are began flying the moment the battle ended. The High King rescinded his order to keep you a secret and now every member of our society knows that a vampire incubus exists and is fighting on our side."

"Is that good or bad?"

"A little of both. The hatred of vampires runs deep in my people and many think you should be killed now before you have a chance to betray us. Others are okay with you so long as you are kept as a slave, and then there are those who feel as Lady Rosaline does, that you should be embraced as an incubus with no restrictions."

Matthew rubbed his collar absentmindedly. "And you think I should be a slave?"

"For now. I hope one day you'll be trusted enough and that will change. But, the protection of my people is my sworn duty and I cannot ignore that your vampire nature gets the better of you sometimes. Until you learn to control it, and until we understand everything you are capable of, it wouldn't be responsible for me to allow you total freedom."

Matthew frowned. He had much better control of himself as of late. During the battle he hadn't hurt anyone that wasn't a foe. Well, he did have to break a hunter's hand who kept trying to stake him while he was busy fighting a wolf shifter, but that was it. He had actually saved several hunters by pulling vampires off them...he even carried a few wounded over to the triage area.

Tarrick rested his hand on Matthew's chest. Again it was electric, reminding Matthew how hungry his incubus side was right now.

"I know my position might seem harsh, but always remember that even I have people I kneel before and must give my allegiance to. Collar or no, we all have our masters."

One day, that would be different for Matthew. One day, others would kneel before him.

"What's next? I keep training?" he asked.

"Of course, that will never end no matter how good you get." Tarrick laughed at something. His hand was still on Matthew's chest. "That night I trapped you, I was out there because I wanted to keep my abilities sharp. I don't normally run thump traps, not since I was young."

"Lucky me," Matthew said, the sarcasm dripping from his words.

Tarrick's eyes turned from blue to purple as he ran his hand down Matthew's chest and across his abs. "Lucky me," Tarrick echoed the words with his deep, sexy voice.

Matthew bit his lower lip as his cock strained.

Tarrick took a step closer and his hand traveled lower down Matthew's torso. Matthew wasn't in the mood to be teased right now, he was too damn hungry.

Before Tarrick could register what happened, Matthew grabbed him by his arms and had him pinned with his back against the wall.

Matthew brought out a single clawed finger, sliced off Tarrick's tie, and tossed it aside. Tarrick gasped as his suit shirt was ripped open, the buttons popped off and bounced around the room. Matthew planted his mouth on the dip in the general's lower neck.

Tarrick moaned and his breaths shortened. "Do you have any idea how expensive these shirts are?"

"Send me the bill," Matthew said between licking and kissing Tarrick's skin.

Tarrick grabbed Matthew's hip and in a single graceful move, the incubus slipped out of his grasp and was behind him, shoving him against the wall and gripping his hair, forcing him to tilt his head back.

"I can think of another way you can repay me," Tarrick whispered into his ear.

Matthew groaned and a shiver went through his body. Damn it. Tarrick was so fucking sexy. And confusing. He should hate everything Tarrick represented, and yet with one touch Matthew was his. Tarrick worked his hands downwards and grabbed a handful of Matthew's ass, massaging it through his pants.

Matthew's need grew. He undid his belt while Tarrick unzipped his own suit pants.

The moment Matthew pulled his pants down, Tarrick's cock was on him, rubbing the middle of his ass. He made sure to release enough silky wet liquid because it didn't seem Tarrick was going to wait much longer before entering him.

He was wrong.

Tarrick teased his cock against Matthew's skin with slow stroking motions. It was maddening. Both of Matthew's claws came out in full and he scratched at the stone wall in front of him.

Tarrick nipped at his shoulders with his teeth, and Matthew's chest rumbled. If the teasing continued, he'd overpower Tarrick and take him. Consequences be damned.

When he couldn't stand it any longer, Tarrick pressed him hard against the wall and slid his thick shaft inch by inch into Matthew's tight hole. It slowly stretched to accommodate Tarrick's huge length. The burn subsided after only a moment and both men grunted.

Once he was in, Tarrick set a quick pace behind him, breathing hard with each thrust.

A tail snaked around Matthew's torso and squeezed tight. His eyes rolled back into his head as Tarrick slammed into him. Trapped in place, he let himself surrender to Tarrick's control and fell into pure pleasure. He lost himself in the moment. His mind felt as if it was floating, that is until Tarrick unexpectedly pulled out of Matthew and uncoiled his tail.

Before he could figure out what was going on, Tarrick grabbed him and sent him flying across the room. Matthew crashed into the wall with an 'oof' and slid down onto the bed, ending in a seated position.

What the fuck? If Tarrick wanted it rough tonight, Matthew was all too happy to oblige. He growled and flashed both sets of fangs.

Tarrick's horns emerged—the right one still broken—and his wings came out of his back.

"Stay," he commanded.

Matthew didn't want to but he obeyed.

Tarrick pulled his own shoes and socks off. Then slipped out of the rest of his suit. Matthew did the same, tossing clothes and shoes across the small room.

When he was done undressing, Tarrick pounced, grabbing Matthew's feet and yanking him down the bed so that he was flat on his back. He kissed Matthew's knee and began to crawl up Matthew's body, his mouth leading the way across his skin.

Matthew arched his back as Tarrick's wet tongue skimmed the length of his cock, from balls to tip. It was a tease. Cruel and wonderful all at once. His claws dug into the bed, ripping apart the sheets, in an effort to stay grounded.

Tarrick grabbed the base of Matthew's shaft and brought the head close to his mouth. He circled his tongue around the crown.

"More," Matthew pleaded.

Tarrick pushed himself up Matthew's body and leaned in, brushing his lips against his ear.

"You'll get what I give you," he whispered seductively. His hand, which he hadn't removed from Matthew's cock, moved up and down at an unhurried pace. His wet tongue flicked against the skin, below his ear.

Matthew whimpered and thrust his hips trying to end the torture.

Tarrick clamped his hand around his base and pushed Matthew's hips back to the bed, not letting him have any pleasure he hadn't been given.

A desperate moan left Matthew. Tarrick had all of him right now and, god, he needed release.

Tarrick pulled himself off Matthew and sat up on his knees. He pushed Matthew's legs farther apart and upwards to gain access to his entrance. He was slow to re-enter, studying Matthew as if he took great pleasure from every whine and moan he drew from his vampire slave.

Matthew arched his back off the bed to try to speed things up, but Tarrick's tail wrapped around his neck, holding him in place, forcing him to accept what was happening. He stroked Matthew's cock and only after he was fully seated, pulled out then drove back into him, setting a pace that would have them both coming before too long.

Tarrick looked magnificent. Each time he plunged into Matthew's hole his muscles flexed and his wings stretched out. His eyes drank in Matthew's hard body with intense hunger.

Matthew fed on him, the golden energy filling his soavik.

As he came close to release, Tarrick stopped stroking and grabbed Matthew's index finger. Tarrick pressed the clawed finger into his wrist and cut himself.

"Open your mouth."

Matthew opened his mouth wide. The promise of blood had his fangs long and ready in anticipation. Tarrick kept the cut facing upwards, the blood pooling on his wrist. With his other hand, Tarrick resumed stroking Matthew while thrusting, bringing them both close to the edge.

"Master, I'm…" He didn't finish his sentence as Tarrick tipped his cut wrist over Matthew's mouth, filling it with blood. His dick jerked in Tarrick's hand and his balls drew up.

The most intense orgasm he'd ever experienced ripped through his body.

If Tarrick found his own release, Matthew didn't notice. He was too far lost in bliss as his body quaked with each wave of pleasure. The blood dripping into his mouth, the feeding, the touching, the pounding between his legs…it was extreme. Every inch of his skin rippled with pleasure and his insides heated like a furnace.

Pure ecstasy.

When it was done, he sunk into the bed, closed his eyes, and lost time as he recovered.

"You aren't going to fall asleep on me, are you?" Tarrick asked, sitting up next to Matthew in the bed. Matthew hadn't even felt him leave his body.

Matthew smiled and blinked hard to chase the sleep away. He looked down, his abs were covered in his own cum. He needed to shower. "That was…" He found himself lost for words again.

Tarrick only answered with a satisfied, "Mmm."

Matthew returned to his human form and looked around the room. It was a mess. Buttons, clothes, and shoes were everywhere. His sheets were shredded. Tarrick frowned at the disorder, and Matthew laughed at him. It was his own damned room; he was going to leave it messy.

He pushed himself off the bed to his shaky legs and stumbled into the bathroom. He entered the shower and heard Tarrick ordering someone via cell phone to bring him a new shirt and tie, and for the maids to come change the bed sheets in about an hour.

When the call was done, Tarrick, back in his human form, joined him in the small shower. Matthew eyed the still-bleeding wound. It wasn't deep, Tarrick could have healed this on his own. Did he want Matthew to heal it for him? He grabbed Tarrick's wrist and brought the cut to his lips.

A low warning growl came from Tarrick.

Matthew got the message. "May I heal it for you, Master?" The scent of the blood was delightful.

Tarrick stopped growling. "You may."

Matthew licked away the blood, its intoxicating taste filling his mouth and warming his body. The skin stitched together, and Matthew lowered the arm but didn't release it. He wanted to be closer to Tarrick. Tarrick didn't move away when he stepped in, their bodies brushed against each other as he showered off.

Matthew watched the water stream down Tarrick's skin. It was mesmerizing.

All incubi were gorgeous, perfect even, but Tarrick's body interested him as none other had. Matthew began tracing the muscles on his arm and shoulder. He wasn't even doing it because he was turned on, he just wanted to feel him.

Tarrick raised an eyebrow. "You are awfully quiet. I'm usually barraged with questions by now."

Removing his hands and looking away, Matthew was…embarrassed. But not because of what Tarrick had said; it was because he realized that he cared for Tarrick. Craved him…longed for him when he had been gone.

Matthew had been a fool to think he could overpower a thousand-year-old incubus. Sure, he could kill Tarrick right now, break his neck before anyone could come and help him, but he wasn't doing that. He was standing in the shower, desiring to be closer to Tarrick. And not just physically.

He belonged to Tarrick the moment the first collar snapped around his neck. He just hadn't realized it at the time.

"You don't have to stop," Tarrick said, brushing his hand against Matthew's hip.

Matthew didn't want to stop but he didn't want to continue either. He was so torn. Scared. He was part of a world that he was only just beginning to understand and his guide was a man who didn't even trust him. His master.

He rubbed at the metal around his wrist and grew agitated, upset by the bracers and collar. Upset he wasn't trusted. His fangs dropped and claws came out. He closed his burning eyes and tried to push it all away.

Tarrick sensed what was happening, that he was in danger, and began to move out of the shower but Matthew ensnared his wrist to stop him. The tips of his claws pierced Tarrick's flesh and pinpoints of blood appeared.

"Please don't leave. Please don't call the hunters. I swear I won't lose control," Matthew begged.

Tarrick's eyes grew dark.

Matthew released him and retreated back into the water.

Tarrick was right, Matthew's vampire nature did get the better of him. No. All of his nature got the better of him. Could anyone blame him? Who wanted to be a prisoner? A slave?

If he was ever going to be completely trusted, if he was ever going to get out of here and live life on his own terms, he needed to keep himself under control. But his feelings for Tarrick were complicating matters. Some nights, escaping didn't seem so important anymore.

He might be a slave for now, but Tarrick was offering him a future. A place among his people. Ascelina had helped him, but Matthew wasn't sure what she'd expect in return. If she saved him, if he got out of here, would he end up on the other side of the battlefield?

He wanted...*fuck*...he wanted to be powerful but he didn't want to be a pawn. This wasn't his war. Conflict raged within him.

Matthew forced his fangs back into his gums and put his claws away. He hung his head and whispered, "I'm sorry, Master."

He was surprised when Tarrick didn't leave or threaten him.

Tarrick reached over and rested his hand on Matthew's waist. "What has you so upset?"

"I…" Matthew swallowed the lump that formed in his throat. What could he tell Tarrick? Not the truth about his feelings and he already knew Matthew wanted his freedom.

"You're falling for me," Tarrick said. The shock of the realization laced his words.

"Fucking incubus." Matthew knocked Tarrick's hand away from him. He had completely forgotten Tarrick could read his emotions through touch. His eyes were back to burning red again and he snarled. "No. I hate you."

"That might be true but one feeling does not negate the other. If you do not wish to talk about your feelings right now, I won't force you. We'll speak when you're ready."

Matthew was thankful Tarrick wasn't going to force him to face how he felt. Tarrick put his hand back on Matthew's waist.

"Don't be so hard on yourself, young one. Everything has a way of sorting itself out." He pressed a kiss to Matthew's shoulder then flipped off the water. "Go get dressed, we need to get you fitted."

Matthew was thankful for the change in topic. "You aren't going to make me start wearing suits, are you?"

Tarrick laughed. "Suits? No. But you are going to wear a tux. It's time you were properly introduced to our world. Next week, you're going to a ball."

Thirty-Two

Matthew shifted around in his seat in the limo for the tenth time in the last minute while he waited for Tarrick. The tux he wore looked great on him, but it was uncomfortable. It wasn't the material or the fit, all that was perfect, it was what it represented: the ball.

Not just any ball either. It was one of the biggest of the season. Anyone who was anyone would be there.

During his training, Matthew had learned a great deal of incubus protocol from Rosaline, but he found out that she had only scratched the surface of the rules for polite society. He had spent the last week in an etiquette crash course.

Both Tarrick and Rosaline spent the nights teaching him the current popular dances, rules, and even worked on conversation with him.

There were rules for everything: when and how to arrive at an event (it was all a show), how to eat (not that it mattered for Matthew), what topics were considered off limits (at this event it was considered in poor taste to talk about the war), who it was okay to have sex with (on duty hunters and claimed humans were off limits), where to go to have said sex (Matthew was allowed to take a willing partner), the list was endless.

He found it interesting that there were rules about leading for when two men or two women danced together—it was who held a higher position in their society. Opposite sex couples were usually led by the men unless a higher ranked woman insisted on taking the role. It was rare but it did happen.

Matthew had to hand it to the incubi, they really didn't care what gender they fucked so long as an attraction existed.

The class and rank system for the incubi fascinated Matthew. There were actually only a few unique titles, mostly everyone who would be there would be a lord or lady, but everyone fell into a ranking order of sorts. It wasn't really official or even discussed, but every incubus was expected to know who was higher or lower in rank than them and stay up to date on any changes, such as when an incubus gained more power, wealth, or influence.

Acquiring a Fortune 500 company, for example, might shoot an incubus right to the top of the social ladder, where they would be responsible for maintaining hunter teams and employing other incubi. Matthew was astounded at just how much wealth the species controlled—and how many companies they owned. Half the damn planet belonged to them. And humans had no fucking idea.

The ranks could also change based on the situation or events. A king or queen outranked Tarrick most of the time unless they were on a battlefield. In those situations, Tarrick, as the High Lord General, had absolute authority. If he ordered them to fight, they would, even if they were not warriors.

There was no kneeling at parties unless the High King showed up, and then everyone kneeled to him.

Matthew had been relieved to learn that the High King wasn't expected to be there tonight. He didn't venture out of New York and this party was in Virginia, hosted by Queen Agleea, who was the High King's granddaughter, and her consort Lord Ennius, who was not a king but high-ranked and respected all the same. Queen Agleea ruled most of the East Coast.

Matthew fell under intense pressure to perform perfectly at the party. It was literally life or death for him. Convince the incubi to like him, and he had a chance at living.

He tugged at the bow tie, loosening it by mistake. Great, now he'd have to retie it. He growled in frustration, pulled it off, and tossed it across the limo. It landed at the feet of a hunter.

There were four of them, including Silva, in the limo and a few more in the two cars traveling behind them. They weren't here for Matthew. Lords and ladies traveled with at least one team of six hunters at all times, Tarrick was no exception.

And tonight, with such a major grouping of incubi, those numbers were increased.

The plan was to drive to the teleport stone at Ashwood and teleport to the estate in Virginia.

At one point during the last week, Silva had stolen Matthew away for a few hours and had him teleport between two stones until he could go back and forth without feeling queasy. Matthew spent most of that time on his knees, vomiting his guts out. They both celebrated the first time he managed to keep everything down.

Silva picked up the bow tie from the limo floor and sat down next to Matthew. She wrapped the strip of cloth around his neck and began to knot it for him.

Tonight, the hunters wore their normal leather uniforms but had a sigil pinned on them to represent House Tarrick. The sigil design featured a shield with two swords and a crossbow behind it; incubi wings expanded out from the sides, and in the center was a starburst pattern. Silva wore a second pin, a metal bar, identifying her as a commander.

"Nervous?" she asked.

He glared at her. She knew the answer to that one.

"I was too the first time I had to guard one of these."

"That's hardly the same. Hunters are welcome. I'm a vampire walking into a ball with thousands of incubi. And most of them want me dead."

"I don't think as many want you dead as you think. They want to see you and gossip about you. When you deal with creatures that live so long, very little is new and exciting…you are new and exciting," Silva said and finished with the bow tie.

Matthew scoffed.

"I'm serious. You have to know by now that there is something about you that incubi find appealing. It's not just the general or Lady Rosaline—I've seen how others react when you walk by them. They hunger for you. Maybe you give off some sort of pheromone they can't resist or maybe it's because you're sexy, but I'm telling you this won't be as bad as you think."

Matthew grabbed Silva's hand and held it. "Thank you."

Silva smiled and squeezed his hand.

"Now, go back to the part where you think I'm sexy," Matthew teased, and moved his hand up her arm. There was something he found appealing about her small frame and commanding presence. The idea of such a petite, dangerous thing taking charge of him in bed had its allure.

Silva laughed. "You act more and more like an incubus every day. But I don't sleep with anyone I might have to kill."

Ouch.

"Do you need more blood?" she asked.

Matthew rolled his eyes and groaned. No one wanted him to get hungry during the ball so the past few days they had given him so much blood he was nearly bursting. He also fed sexually from three humans yesterday to sate his incubus side. "No. Jeez. You could cut open a vein right now and I wouldn't be interested."

"If you get hungry during the ball, just tell any hunter…"

Matthew held up a hand and cut her off. "I know. You can stop telling me. I promise I won't be going into a blood rage."

A voice came through Silva's earpiece. "Commander, the Lord General is on his way out."

Silva scooted to the door and exited the car to wait for Tarrick. Matthew watched as her eyes swept the area, looking for any potential dangers.

Tarrick emerged from the keep a moment later. He rushed to the car while adjusting a cufflink and slid into the seat next to Matthew. Silva followed behind him and shut the door.

"Let's go," Tarrick said. He seemed bothered by something.

The caravan of cars took off to the academy.

"Everything okay, Master?" Matthew asked. In the week leading up to the ball, they had stressed to him that he had to get ready quickly because they'd be late since he couldn't leave until after sunset.

"There's a vampire attack in South Africa. Dennith is handling it now." Tarrick probably wanted to be the one handling it seeing as it was obviously on his mind.

"Well, we can always skip tonight. You can go back to the command center and direct the attack," Matthew suggested with a smile.

Tarrick's mood shifted slightly as he chuckled. With his nerves as frayed as they were, Matthew hardly noticed how good the general looked in his tuxedo and he fidgeted around in his seat.

"You'll do fine tonight. Just stay confident. Feign it if you have to, and you'll get through this," he said and placed a reassuring hand on Matthew's shoulder. "Did you get enough blood?"

"Gah! Yes. So much blood that I could open my own god damn blood bank."

Several of the hunters had to stifle a laugh.

Matthew raised his hand to tug at his bow tie again but Tarrick caught his wrist. "Stop touching it."

"Can't you just send me to go fight some vampires? I'll even take on a few lords at once. I think that would be easier."

"No. The ball will only be uncomfortable for a little while and then you'll get the hang of it. You excel at adapting to new situations. This is no different."

Matthew sighed and sank back into his seat.

Tarrick and Silva began discussing hunter positioning around the estate. Bored, Matthew tuned them out and ran through the names and faces of the people who would be there tonight. His memory had always been good, but ever since becoming a vampire—and thanks to Cullip's whippings—it had become nearly photographic.

They arrived at Ashwood Academy. Matthew trailed behind Tarrick as they walked to the stone.

"Ready?" Silva asked once they arrived. Three teams of hunters were standing there waiting.

"Not even a little," Matthew said and fiddled with a button on his tux.

Tarrick grabbed Matthew's hand. "Still yourself, young one. You can do this."

Matthew closed his eyes and took a deep breath in. Old human habit. It calmed him. That and Tarrick nudging his emotions just a bit. Matthew didn't resist him; he could use the help to relax his nerves. If he didn't pull it together everyone would be sensing how he felt and he'd be devoured, socially speaking.

Tarrick was right, he was good at adapting and he could do this. He just needed to think of it like going into battle. Shit needed to get done and he was going to do it. Matthew pushed his anxiety away and masked his feelings.

He stood up straighter and confidence crossed his face. "The night's not getting any younger, let's go."

Tarrick released Matthew's hand. Silva counted down and pressed the stone. Green light flooded them and a second later they were in the front yard of Queen Agleea's estate. No, not an estate, it was a god damn castle. It was massive, easily four or five times bigger than Tarrick's keep and just as impressive. It rose six stories high and Matthew sensed an entire underground network going down three, maybe four levels.

Matthew filtered out the thousands of heartbeats drumming in his ear. Once he could focus, he realized that this castle was in the middle of a forest with no neighboring houses or facilities for miles out. Many hunter teams patrolled the surrounding area.

There were two teams of Agleea's hunters standing guard at the stone. Each had their hand on their weapons the moment Matthew teleported in. Around him, Tarrick's teams of hunters moved off, except Silva who stayed with them.

A young incubus stood nearby with a tablet in his hand and a headset on. He bowed to Tarrick then spoke into his headset. "High Lord General Tarrick has arrived along with…" he studied Matthew and his heart sped, "…Matthew of House Tarrick."

House Tarrick? Was Matthew part of his house now? He liked that idea.

Tarrick didn't wait for any type of instruction. He marched past the hunters and the incubus towards the castle. Matthew strode after him and Silva took up the rear.

Every hunter they passed saluted to Tarrick, but their feet instinctively fell into a defensive posture when they saw the vampire. Their eyes glued to Matthew as he crossed the grounds. Any incubi they passed fell silent, watching with timid curiosity.

Matthew ignored them the best he could.

When they got to the main doors the incubi greeters took a step back when they saw Matthew.

Matthew stopped. A wave of emotions crashed into him: pleasure, desire, lust. He felt dizzy.

Tarrick turned. "Is everything alright?"

Matthew struggled to shut out the emotions. "I've never been so close to this many incubi. I feel like my insides are being crushed."

"Ah, that happens to every young incubus at gatherings as large as this one. Will you be okay?"

"Yeah, just give me a sec. I'll adjust."

Tarrick patiently waited while Matthew worked out how to keep the pheromones of other incubi from bombarding him. Once he shut them out, he nodded to indicate that he was ready to go.

The general led the way through the front doors. Inside was a long hallway with a high ceiling, tall marble pillars, and a deep red carpet running the length of it. There was a double staircase at the end and a door leading onwards. There were a handful of incubi inside. They all stopped chatting the moment Tarrick entered and they bowed to him, but their eyes were fixed on Matthew.

As he marched on, Tarrick seemed to take no notice of them. Matthew hardly paid attention to where they were going as smells and sounds battered against his senses. Orchestral music and conversation filled the air as they approached a thick velvet curtain. Tarrick pushed it aside and led them into a private passage.

At some point, Silva had broken away and was no longer with them but Matthew hadn't noticed when. Tarrick came to a halt in front of another thick curtain. He grabbed Matthew's elbow. "Do you remember what you're going to do once we enter?"

Matthew nodded. He could sense thousands of incubi on the other side of the curtain. "I follow you. You'll introduce me to Queen Agleea and her mate Lord Ennius. I bow. Then we mingle. I remember."

"If you get overwhelmed or feel yourself losing control during the night, the third outside balcony on the second floor is being kept clear for you, go there. If you need to find me, ask any hunter. And remember, there are ears everywhere. Nothing you say will be private—guard your words."

"I understand."

"I know you do." Tarrick whipped the curtains open. He stepped out onto the landing above a sweeping double staircase that joined and led down into a ballroom.

Matthew's eyes grew wide, unable to believe what he was seeing. The ballroom before him was larger than he could have imagined.

The ceiling, covered in an impressive painted mural, was six stories above him and balconies lined the walls the entire way up. Some looked like private booths while others were open to anyone and crowded with incubi who were chatting, drinking, or watching the scene below.

Looking down the stairs, the ballroom floor was packed. Everyone was dressed in modern formal wear and the incubi were showing off their horns and brightly colored eyes. For some reason, Matthew had envisioned they would be a little more old-fashioned in their attire…but their style was more red carpet than regency.

A large orchestra filled the air with music and the center of the ballroom brimmed with couples dancing across the floor with flawless, synchronize precision. It was incredible.

The music stopped abruptly and the dancers halted. Hushed whispers crossed the crowd and the moment Matthew dreaded was upon him as every pair of eyes in the room turned his way.

Thirty-Three

Everyone in the ballroom studied Matthew. He swallowed away a lump that formed in his throat and pushed away the urge to run out of here.

In front of him, Tarrick—who exuded endless confidence—began descending the stairs as if nothing strange was happening.

Matthew followed, keeping close. In an effort to calm his nerves, he fell back to his training and began studying the room. With one sweep of his eyes, he recognized hundreds of incubi from the photos Rosaline had shown him.

Hunters were discreetly posted around the room, standing guard. These were the most elite—each wearing a commander bar on their uniform. Not a group Matthew wanted to piss off. Actually, he didn't want to piss off anyone. His goal was to make it through the night without being staked.

Matthew returned his focus to following Tarrick, the last thing he needed right now was to trip and fall because he wasn't paying attention. The descent down the stairs seemed agonizingly slow, and when they finally reached the bottom, the sea of incubi parted—no one stood in Tarrick's way.

On the far side of the ballroom, opposite the stairs, was a multi-tiered stone dais. At the top, an empty golden throne. Matthew had learned that each major event hosted by the incubi always had a throne ready for the High King, in case he showed up. And even if he didn't make an appearance—which was most of the time—it served as a reminder of his authority.

Below the golden throne, but just as impressive, were two occupied thrones. On them sat Queen Agleea and Lord Ennius. They were both attractive. Queen Agleea was tall, with sharp features. Her dark hair pinned by diamond and royal blue sapphires. The top of her jeweled blue dress hugged her body while the bottom flowed long and free. It parted, showing off long, gorgeous legs. Her eyes glowed teal.

Lord Ennius was shorter than his mate but no less impressive looking. He had a goatee with slicked back hair that complemented his dark green eyes. He was slender but carried it extremely well. His tuxedo vest and bow tie matched the blue of Agleea's dress.

Both were extremely old and powerful. Matthew sensed their presence above all the others in the room from where he was standing. It reminded Matthew just how young he was.

As Tarrick walked through the gap in the crowd, most incubi he passed bowed. Only the kings and queens of other regions or high standing lords and ladies refrained from doing so, but even they gave a nod of respect to the general.

Matthew trailed behind and smelled fear coming from some of the incubi, anger from others, but felt relieved when it seemed most were simply curious. Every now and then, he'd feel desire directed his way. Despite what Silva had told him, it caught him a little off-guard.

A line of people waited to greet the Queen. No one objected as Tarrick marched past them and came to stand before the thrones, Matthew at his side.

Tarrick crossed his right hand in front of his waist and bowed to Agleea, then he motioned to Matthew. "Your Majesty, please allow me to present Matthew of my own house."

Matthew pressed his open palm to his opposite shoulder and bowed deeply, just as he had practiced a thousand times with Rosaline. He kept his hand steady, concealing his nerves, and after several long seconds, he stood upright.

Agleea stood. Ennius as well, mimicking his mate.

She walked down the steps of her pedestal and stopped in front of Matthew. He had no idea what to expect but undressing him was right at the bottom of his list. Completely taken off-guard when she began to unbutton his vest, he said nothing as he watched her slender fingers work their way down.

He felt eyes boring into him and Matthew glanced up at Ennius, who stood in front of his throne looking displeased. Matthew hoped the displeasure wasn't aimed at him; it's not like he had asked the Queen to begin removing his clothes.

Matthew returned to watching her. When she was done with his vest, she unbuttoned the lower half of his shirt and he had to suppress a gasp as she slipped her hand inside.

Her warm fingers pressed against his abs and he felt a familiar echoing sensation. Scanning.

"You are purring," Agleea said, her voice deep and sultry.

Matthew hadn't even realized, nor was he sure how to respond. His first impulse was to say nothing, but he didn't want to come across as shy—he wasn't shy, just nervous—and he needed everyone to believe he was as much an incubus as any of them.

Matthew leaned into her and kept his voice deep and personal. "Can you blame me, Your Majesty? I just went through my transformation this year and now I have a gorgeous succubus queen massaging my lower abs."

She chuckled in response, as did others around them, and she slipped her hand out from under Matthew's shirt. She reached up and ran her finger over Matthew's collar then motioned for him to button up his clothes.

"His lineage?" she asked. Her eyes didn't leave Matthew as she spoke.

Tarrick shook his head. "We still don't know, Your Majesty. I was hoping someone might come forward after knowledge of him was made public, but that hasn't happened."

"His sire?"

"Unknown, he has no bond to him or her."

"And his transformation would have happened when he was thirty-two had he not been turned?"

"Yes, Your Majesty."

"So late. And these eyes…" Agleea ran her fingers across the skin just under Matthew's eyes. "I have never seen the like. What a puzzle you are."

The Queen called him a puzzle, but what it really meant was abandonment: first by his parents who dumped him at a hospital, and then by his sire who left him to fend for himself, alone. The guilt he felt about abandoning his own family after he had been turned still clung to him.

He hid his pain with a smile. "If you find any of the pieces, Your Majesty, please let me know."

Agleea ran her teal eyes up and down Matthew. "I've read the reports on you and you are not quite what I expected."

"I hope I'm not disappointing you, Your Majesty."

"Not yet. You are more incubus than I anticipated." She paused, thoughtful for a few moments, then continued. "When a young incubus is formally introduced to our society for the first time it is customary for them to display a show of skill."

"Your Majesty, Matthew has not—" Tarrick stepped forward to object, but Agleea held up her hand. He snapped his mouth shut and stepped back. Normally Tarrick was a master at concealing his feelings but the edges of his eyes creased with worry.

She continued addressing Matthew. "I would like you to impress me with your skills."

Matthew's brows knitted together, confused. Neither Tarrick nor Rosaline warned him about this. "You wish for me to fight someone?"

"Most young warriors do indeed choose to spar or exhibit their skills with a blade but it can be anything. The choice is yours."

Matthew didn't want to fight tonight. Besides ruining his tux, it'd just make the incubi watching fear him. When he fought, he didn't hold back and it always ended up brutal and bloody. Also, if every warrior showed off their fighting skills he doubted it would actually impress the Queen.

The room fell silent while every incubus watched the exchange. Matthew wondered how many of them expected him to make a fool of himself.

Matthew took a deep breath. There had to be some other way he could impress her beyond running really fast or punching someone really hard, as he was sure they all expected him to do.

He studied the ballroom for a moment. Large paintings and banners adorned the walls, and marble sculptures and statues took up corners and alcoves. The back of his neck prickled when he sensed something and an idea came to him...

"Would you allow me to escort you around the ballroom?" he asked and held out his arm for her to take.

She looked both perplexed and amused as she nodded and slipped her arm in his. Matthew began to walk the room clockwise, the incubi moving out of the way as they walked. Both Tarrick and her mate, Ennius, followed behind them. Matthew sensed hunters moving to better positions as well.

He stopped in front of a massive painting that went from the floor up until just below the balcony above it. It depicted roman soldiers battling in front of a burning city.

"The fall of Jerusalem in 70 AD to the Roman emperor Titus. This piece is called The Siege, painted in 1847 by Stevens Roberto. But this one is a fake."

"How can you tell?" Agleea asked.

"Stevens Roberto was left handed. Half these strokes are backwards and that ship in the water is off by a few centimeters." Matthew pointed to the flaws as he spoke.

She lifted an eyebrow and nodded. "You are right, I had the real one put away because I feared someone would accidently spill wine on it." Laughter filled the room as if everyone was in on a joke Matthew didn't understand.

Once it died down, Matthew motioned forward to see if she was ready to continue. She walked with him as he correctly named all of the art that came from human artists that were hanging from the wall. Each piece was famous, worth millions. Matthew was unable to identify the paintings featuring incubi, but the Queen seemed to enjoy naming them for him.

"How do you know so much about art?" she asked when they were halfway around the room.

"Someone I once cared for loved art. It rubbed off on me."

God, his wife loved art and music. She was cultured in every way Matthew wasn't. Every vacation they took, she would drag him and their daughter to all the art museums and talk endlessly about each piece. Matthew always humored her, even though he would have rather been lying at the beach with a beer.

When he became a vampire, it was as if his brain adjusted fuzzy memories of those trips back into a sharp focus. And thanks to his training, he could recall everything she told him, even the smallest detail. He wished he could thank her for it.

Matthew halted in front of a large alcove. Inside was a full-sized statue of Ilertha. Matthew dipped his head to her, then continued on, worried he might lose time or it might start singing if he looked at the statue for too long.

Agleea eyed him curiously but said nothing.

Matthew knew none of his knowledge could really impress her, even if she did seem mildly entertained, but there was one thing he thought just might work. He hoped.

He led her to a marble statue of Pan, a Greek god who had the legs and horns of a goat. He was sometimes associated with male virility and sexuality. Fitting.

"How long have you owned this, Your Majesty?"

"Hm, at least twelve hundred years I think. It's traveled with me my last four major moves. I've always been fond of this statue."

Matthew looked at the statue and smiled. "Did you know that this statue is a gargoyle?"

She studied it for long moments then she shook her head. "It can't be. Gargoyles do not look like this. And even they have to move from time to time. I've never seen it so much as budge in all the years I've owned it."

"I don't wish to challenge you, Your Majesty, but I give you my word this statue is alive."

"And why do you think it's alive?"

It didn't have a heartbeat or blood, but the moment he reached out with his senses he had felt its…essence…and he knew it was a living creature.

"I can feel its soul."

The Queen laughed—as did others. "Only gods, guardians, and demons can feel souls. Come, you do not have to try to impress me anymore, you've amused me and I am satisfied."

But Matthew wasn't satisfied. He wanted to impress her and everyone watching. He touched the statue but nothing happened. He dropped his hand.

Agleea stopped and turned back to him. Matthew could feel irritation growing from both Tarrick and Ennius.

Hm.

An idea came to him. He stopped suppressing his aura and pushed power into his hand, focusing his fingers. He only had one shot at this before the irritation directed at him turned into full-blown anger.

He touched the statue.

Its face twisted into a snarl and it lunged forward.

Matthew's vampire side came out as he stepped between it and the Queen.

Tarrick was already there; his claws and horns out and ready. Every hunter in the room was drawing their weapon. Panicked cries came from incubi.

"*No!*" Matthew yelled at the statue.

It froze in place.

Matthew suppressed his aura. "I am sorry I disturbed you, go back to sleep."

The statue stepped back and its face and body relaxed. It froze back in the same position it was before as if nothing had happened.

Around him, many incubi had clawed hands, ready to attack. A few had wings out, their clothes ripped and ruined. All the hunters stood ready. Ennius was next to his mate to ensure she was okay. Tarrick looked angry. So much for not pissing anyone off…at least Matthew hadn't been staked yet, but the night was young.

Matthew forced his vampire side away as fast as possible.

Queen Agleea pushed away from her consort. She looked composed, not even a little rattled or shaken. She smiled at Matthew and he smiled right back at her, puffing his chest just a little. He couldn't help it. He loved being right.

"Why didn't you flinch from it?" she asked.

"What would be the point? If it wanted to kill me, it would have. There would be nothing I could do to stop it." Matthew chuckled. "It is the same reason I do not flinch from you I suppose."

She joined him with a playful laugh. "Alright, Matthew, you've impressed me. Let's resume this ball." She held out her hand to him. "Come, dance with me."

The center of the ballroom emptied and the orchestra began playing a few bars of music.

"Would you like me to lead?" she asked him as he put one hand on her hip and took her hand with the other. He hoped she didn't pay too much attention to his crotch...being so close to such a powerful succubus was turning him on.

"Only if you wish to. I know the dance for this song."

"Then by all means."

Matthew waited for a beat then began leading her across the dance floor. He was perfect in every move. With all eyes on him, he had to be.

After a few minutes, others joined them in dancing and before too long the entire dance floor was packed. The incubi not dancing resumed their conversations; the topic of the moment was Matthew and he heard the word 'vampire' uttered often.

When the song was nearly over Ennius appeared beside them, indicating his wish to cut in. Matthew released Agleea and bowed deeply to both of them.

He turned to walk away from the dance floor only to have a woman press into his arms and continue the dance.

"Lady Rosaline," Matthew grinned at her. She had arrived at the ball before Matthew even awoke and this was the first time he had seen her tonight. She looked lovely in a long green dress and matching jade pins in her hair.

"That was...I haven't seen Queen Agleea dance with anyone but Lord Ennius for as long as I've been alive. I think he's a little jealous of you."

Matthew looked across the ballroom at the couple. Both of them looked sexy as hell. If either of them offered to bed Matthew he'd jump at the chance. "Him? Have you seen that guy? He has nothing to be jealous of."

Rosaline laughed as Matthew spun her and pulled her back into him. For the first time tonight he truly felt at ease.

"Tell me honestly, how mad do you think the general is at me?" Matthew had no idea where Tarrick had gone. He wasn't on the ballroom floor anymore.

Rosaline shrugged. "No one was hurt and the Queen seemed thrilled. I think in a few moments he'll calm down and you'll be safe."

"I hope so."

"I'm going to dump you into the arms of Lady Cristin. She's shy but she's had her eyes on you since the moment you walked in."

This whole room had their eyes on him since the moment he walked in. But before Matthew could point that out, she broke away and a new woman, wearing a flowing peach ball gown and diamond earrings that reminded him of chandeliers, filled his arms.

"Lady Cristin, it is an honor," he said with a smile.

She blushed in response and Matthew led her across the dance floor.

Thirty-Four

Matthew was stuck dancing for the next three hours. Every time he'd be free of one incubus, another took her—or his—place.

The conversations he had with his partners all followed the same beats. They'd be timid at first and start with a few innocent comments. Usually about his silver eyes, or how surprised they were that his skin wasn't as cold as they expected, or that they couldn't believe the statue had been a gargoyle.

Then they'd move into questions about what it was like to be both a vampire and an incubus. Sometimes they'd ask him what blood tasted like or what it had been like to die. Matthew tried to guide each conversation away from the vampire questions and focus more on the incubus side.

By the end of the dance they'd be relaxed and flirting with him. A few even propositioned him outright. Matthew was tempted but he didn't feel he should be sneaking away to have sex right now. He was here, after all, to make a good impression on as many people as he could.

Or that was his policy until he saw Lady Naveeda enter the ballroom.

She was the daughter of a king in South India. Matthew recognized her right away from the picture Rosaline had shown him, but the photo had done her no justice. She wore a red and gold silk sari, the long strip of cloth that made up the garment draped her body in all the right places. Her kohl-lined eyes were as dark as her hair. Her skin was the color of toffee and Matthew wanted to taste every inch of it.

His mind flooded with images of her dark body pressed against his pale one. He didn't particularly enjoy being so pasty, but tanning these days would give him a quick case of death.

His current dance partner commented that he wasn't breathing. Matthew looked down and gave some appropriate response that he immediately forgot. He tried to focus on his partner, to give her the attention she deserved, but his eyes kept drifting back to Naveeda.

Then, he watched as Tane walked up behind her and wrapped his hands around her waist.

"Are you growling?" the woman in his arms asked him.

He had been. He started the moment he saw Tane.

"No, sorry, just a purr," he lied and flashed the most convincing smile he could muster.

She seemed to buy it. When the song finished he excused himself and bolted away before anyone could snatch him up.

He ended up in an empty hallway and he sighed heavily as he rested his back against the wall.

Silva entered the hallway.

"Commander," he nodded to her.

"That was a fast exit," she said and crossed her arms as she leaned against the wall opposite of him.

"I need a break. Even I can't dance all night long."

"Ah, so it wasn't because you're crushing on the succubus in Lord Tane's arms."

Matthew growled at Silva.

She laughed. "I thought so. You know, I think I just overheard her say she was going up to the third floor. And I think Lord Tane got stuck dancing with someone else."

Matthew's eyes narrowed, suspicious. "Why would you tell me that?"

Silva shrugged. "You're a smart boy, you figure it out."

"You don't like Tane, do you?"

"Lord Tane is an excellent warrior," she said, and pushed off the wall. "Do what you want with the information but be careful, he can bite."

"So can I."

Silva laughed again and left the hallway.

Matthew found a stairwell not far from him. He went to the third floor and looked over the edge of a crowded balcony.

He noticed that the statue—well, gargoyle—of Pan had been removed from the dance floor. He caught sight of Rosaline. She was in the center of a large crowd of incubi, mostly men. They all seemed to be fawning over whatever she said.

Matthew didn't see Tarrick, but he did see Tane dancing with a lovely woman. Tane seemed to be enjoying himself but for all Matthew knew, it was a front. Just like his father, he was great at putting on a mask.

The incubi around him were whispering to each other. This floor seemed to be where a lot of alcohol was being consumed. Every balcony had buckets of ice filled with red or sparkling wine bottles. Matthew wished he could drink some and feel even a small buzz.

When he picked up Lady Naveeda's scent—fire and turmeric —he bowed to the incubi around him then followed it down a hallway, away from the ballroom.

After a few moments of stalking the smell, he realized that the wing he followed it to was strangely empty. A few of the rooms had occupants but it was quiet. If Matthew ran into her here, alone, he'd scare her. He stopped. His desire for her didn't outweigh his worry that he'd frighten her.

He started to walk back the way he came when a door opened behind him and Lady Naveeda exited the room. She gasped when she saw him and her heart raced.

Matthew pressed his hand to his shoulder and bowed deeply. "Lady Naveeda. I did not mean to frighten you."

"I'm not frightened," she said and closed the door to her room behind her as if to prove it. Matthew detected traces of adrenaline running through her blood.

"May I confess something to you?" he asked.

She nodded, her eyes wide.

Matthew leaned in just an inch and lowered his voice as if he was going to tell her a secret. "I'm a vampire."

She looked confused. Of course she knew he was a vampire.

"It's unbelievable, I know, but it's true. I managed to sneak past thousands of vampire hunters and incubi warriors to break into this ball. But I think they're on to me. There are some hunters stalking me right now in this very hallway. I bet if you asked them to show themselves, they would."

She looked around and saw no one.

"Show yourselves," she called out.

Six hunters appeared out of nowhere. They had been standing still, masking themselves, effectively making them invisible, but Matthew had felt them move into place before he entered the hallway. In fact, they had been watching him all night. Every time he went somewhere he'd feel them move into position then disappear from his senses.

The only hunter Matthew recognized was Hiroto, the masked assassin he encountered on the battlefield. He could only assume that the five others were at least as skilled as he was.

"Imperator Prescott," Naveeda said and bowed to one of the hunters. Matthew had never seen an incubus bow to a hunter before.

Prescott...the High King's commander and leader of the Argonauts—consisting of the six best hunters in the corps.

Or so the trainees at Ashwood had told Matthew. He was inclined to believe them considering Imperator Prescott was one of the four people

Matthew couldn't compel without his collar blowing up. And it made sense to him that he'd be watched by the best tonight.

Matthew studied the Imperator.

His uniform was ancient Greek influenced with a form-fitting breast-plate, heavy arm and leg guards, and leather straps that formed sort of a badass skirt. It looked as if it was made of metal, but it didn't seem to hinder his movement. He wore a helmet that concealed his face; on the top were large, intimidating horns curling backwards. It was strange, though, he had no weapons on him, at least none that Matthew could see.

The magic rolling off Prescott—probably from his runes, or maybe his armor—made Matthew's skin prickle.

The sigil he wore consisted of a shield with a large ruby in the center with a crown above the gem. What looked like an incubus tail coiled around it. He also wore the pin identifying him as a commander and a third one that looked like a sword—*Imperator*.

Prescott nodded to Naveeda, then the hunters vanished again.

Matthew turned his thoughts away from the hunters, trying to ignore the fact they were still watching him.

Naveeda relaxed. "Is it true what they say about you?"

He had overheard some of the most ridiculous rumors about himself tonight. Like that he was already a vampire lord, or that he needed four gallons of blood a day or he'd go into a blood rage, or he could walk on walls like a spider. He wondered if the incubi would be so chatty if they knew he could hear them. "You're going to have to be far more specific, my lady."

"That your appetite for sex has been insatiable ever since your transformation?"

Matthew laughed. "No. I don't think that's the case. My appetite has certainly been healthy but it's not insatiable."

"Oh, what a shame," she said, her eyes taking the time to trace his body.

Pleasure stirred within Matthew. "Lady Naveeda, do you think it's wise to try to hold me?"

Her lips curled up into a devious smile. "Wise? No. Fun, absolutely. And I think you'll enjoy it." Her eyes flicked down to Matthew's growing bulge.

She was right—he would enjoy it. It was a weak hold and Matthew could break it easily if he wanted. But he was willing to play along. He wanted her and if she needed the illusion that she could control him, he was fine with that.

Matthew took a step towards her and her heart sped with excitement.

"Have you ever been with a vampire?" he asked, his voice deep, masculine.

He already knew what her answer would be. During his training, Rosaline had told him that sex with vampires was forbidden unless it was for reasons of capturing or breaking one. The two species were, after all, at war.

Matthew was an exception because he was also an incubus. In their eyes, he was the vampire they were allowed to fuck. That was the reason he had been propositioned so many times tonight. Not many incubi ever got the chance to sleep with a vampire.

She shook her head. "No."

"We aren't exactly gentle," he said, closing the distance between them. Matthew was lying...of course he could be gentle, and often was with Rosaline. But Naveeda wasn't Rosaline.

"I don't want you to be," she looked up at him. Her dark chocolate eyes turned to a cloudy blue as she grew aroused.

Matthew leaned down and captured her lips. They parted for him and he swept his tongue through her mouth. She moaned in response.

Matthew grabbed her hips and lifted her. Pressing her against the door, their kiss heated like a volcano ready to erupt. His hand wandered her body, possessive and unable to pick just one part to focus on. He reached the bottom of her sari and pulled it up so that she could wrap her knees tighter around him.

He slid his hand up her leg and grabbed the soft mound of her ass. Matthew bit back a moan when he discovered she wasn't wearing any underwear.

She turned the knob on the door, sending it flying open. Matthew pushed power into his speed and had her against the far wall before she even knew what happened.

The bedroom wasn't huge but it was lavishly decorated. It seemed all incubi enjoyed excessive opulence. It wasn't to Matthew's tastes; he preferred a warm, practical design, although he had developed a fondness for silk sheets.

But right now he wasn't paying attention to the room.

Instead, he kept one hand under Naveeda to steady her against the wall while his other hand roamed up her silky dress. He stopped only when he made it to her breast and weighed it in his palm.

Naveeda broke from the kiss and gasped. Her knees squeezed tighter around his hips. She ran her fingers along his lips and he licked them, inviting them into his mouth. She accepted the invitation, pushing them in and he sucked them eagerly, feeding off her desire. His gums began to itch.

"I want to see them," she said and touched his teeth.

If the lady wanted to see Matthew's vampire side, he was all too happy to accommodate her. His eyes burned and his fangs came out, both the bottom and top set. He playfully snarled at her.

She laughed as a release for some nerves.

Grabbing her wrist, he pinned it hard against the wall. Her breath quickened and she pawed at Matthew's zipper with her other hand. When she wasn't able to undo it one-handed she began stroking his hard cock through the tuxedo pants.

Matthew seized both of her wrists and wrapped her arms around his neck. He let go of her, had his pants unzipped, and pulled his hard rod out before her muscles had a chance to flex in reaction.

He pushed her dress up higher around her waist and slipped two fingers between her wet folds. She was moaning and ready for him. This wouldn't be a slow fuck.

Matthew removed his fingers and grabbed the base of his cock. He lined it up to her entrance, pausing to tease her with the thick head.

"Vampire," she gasped, *"please."*

He grinned at her and pushed himself in a few inches before taking it back out again.

She growled and her hands dropped to his back to pull him into her. He yielded to her desire and sunk deep into her body. Her hot, heavy breath licked his ear.

Matthew thrust hard over and over again. Each push drew a moan from her mouth and a grunt from his. He sucked and licked her neck with gluttonous fervor.

"Bite me," she said, her voice low and torrid.

Matthew winced. God, he wanted to sink his teeth into her neck and steal a few glorious drops of blood from her. But he hadn't thought to ask Tarrick if it was okay for him to bite others during sex. He couldn't risk it; he feared Tarrick's wrath too much.

Naveeda squeaked when Matthew tossed her over to the bed. She landed on her knees. Before she could move, Matthew was standing behind her. He grabbed her hips and pulled her up slightly, closer to him. Pushing her dress up to expose her two magnificent round globes, he ran his fingers up and down the split between them, drawing enticing whimpers from her.

He grabbed the cheeks and spread them slightly.

The view was incredible.

He needed to be back in her, filling her completely. He lined his cock up to her warm entrance and watched it disappear inside as he impaled her. Once his large manhood was fully seated, he slid out again, and back in; slow and deliberate.

"Harder," she demanded. He obeyed by slapping her ass and setting a fast pace.

He leaned over her with the intention of giving her clit attention, but before he even touched it, she screamed his name and began to tremble under him as an orgasm ripped through her.

Matthew smiled. Guess she hadn't needed that extra stimulation. He continued to pound into her as her core pulsed tightly around his dick.

His hands clamped down on her hips and he roared as he exploded inside of her. Every muscle he had convulsed as pleasure crashed through him.

When he began to soften, he carefully pulled himself out.

She collapsed forward on the bed in front of him. Matthew lay down beside her and rested a hand on her hip.

"You taste wonderful," she said. Matthew had felt her take small sips of his energy throughout the encounter.

"You too."

They rested together for a bit before she slid off the bed and straightened out her dress.

"Hm, disappointing," Matthew said as he watched her.

Naveeda turned and tossed him an offended glare, no doubt thinking he was insulting her body or performance.

"It was my plan to make you orgasm at least three or four more times. But if you aren't up for it, I understand. Incubi don't seem to have as much stamina as vampires do."

"My stamina is just fine. It's just that…" She looked at the door, "…we'll be missed…everyone will notice you gone."

Matthew chuckled. "How can I possibly care about everyone when I'm here with you?"

He must have said the right thing because she licked her lips and began to remove her sari. Matthew was happy she was the one removing it because he had absolutely no idea how to take that thing off her and would have ended up shredding it in frustration.

He busied himself by removing his tuxedo and got ready for round two.

Thirty-Five

Matthew watched Naveeda sleep naked on top of her bed as he finished buttoning up his vest. She looked like a goddess.

She had fallen asleep while he showered and Matthew didn't dare wake her. She needed rest after their sexual activities. He had spent the last hour pleasing her many times, and both were satisfied.

He finished dressing and cracked opened the door as quietly as possible. He looked back at her one last time.

A familiar scent from outside of the hallway filled his nose.

"My apologies, Naveeda. Every damn girl from House Laike wanted to dance with—"

Matthew opened the door all of the way and came face to face with Tane.

Tane's eyes widened. Then he glanced at the bed, where Naveeda moaned and turned over in her sleep.

Matthew smirked as he bowed. "Lord Tane."

Tane's jaw clenched as Matthew walked past him and closed the door, making sure it locked behind him. The rage coming from Tane was palpable. The smirk didn't leave Matthew's face as he walked down the otherwise empty hall, leaving Tane alone. Angering Tane hadn't been why Matthew slept with Naveeda but, damn, it was such a sweet cherry on top. He swelled with satisfaction.

Matthew walked over to one of the many balconies on the third level. The drunk incubi who filled it all acted friendly as he approached. Someone shoved a glass of alcohol into his hands. Matthew thanked them then passed it off to a different incubus who gratefully took it from him.

Couples making out on a plush bench that lined the side of the balcony drew his attention. They looked like they might begin ripping each other's clothes off right here.

It amused him when he realized he wouldn't mind if they did. The energy flowing from all of them was exhilarating. Just over half a year ago, the idea of watching people have sex so publicly would have made him shy away with embarrassment, and no one seemed to mind him watching. He felt welcome here. Accepted. Right now, the idea of one day escaping felt like a silly memory to him.

That, combined with the intoxicating aromas that filled the area, had him lost in thought.

He didn't sense Tane approach him until the moment before Tane's fist connected with his jaw.

Matthew went flying back over the edge of the balcony. He plunged down three stories and landed on his back, narrowly missing a dancing couple. Around him, the music stopped and cries rose up as people rushed to clear out of the way.

Rage swept through Matthew, but when he saw the incubi couples surrounding him—most scared out of their minds—he managed to keep his vampire side suppressed and sped healing to the broken bones he suffered.

Still on his back, he looked up at Tane whose eyes were glowing purple and his horns and claws were out. In his hand was a silver longsword. He jumped over the balcony railing and aimed for Matthew. The look of rage plastered on Tane's face made it pretty damn clear his goal was to kill him.

Matthew rolled out of the way as Tane landed on his feet, his sword impaling the wooden parquet floor where Matthew had just been.

Tane yanked the sword out of the wood and lunged at Matthew.

Matthew pushed power into his speed and got to his feet. He wasn't quick enough, the end of the blade sliced his shoulder.

Great. Now his tuxedo was ruined.

Roaring and flashing his fangs, Matthew's vampire side came forward. His claws were long and his eyes raged red.

Tane came at him again and Matthew blocked two swings with his bracers. He countered by stepping in close and raking his claw across Tane's chest, shredding Tane's tux and drawing blood.

Tane swiped his own clawed hand across Matthew's face, leaving behind five deep red cuts. He kicked Matthew in the stomach and sent him tumbling across the room.

"She was mine," Tane yelled and stalked after him.

It wasn't Tane's name she had screamed out tonight. But Matthew would never say something so crass about a woman who had welcomed him into her bed. Instead, he laughed at Tane, which only served to anger him more.

At this point, most of the incubi on the ballroom floor had pressed up against the walls, as far away from the two of them as possible. The hunters and a few warriors had weapons ready but none stepped in. As Tane came at him again, he didn't have time to figure out why they weren't stopping this. Matthew didn't want to lose all of his control, but Tane was making it damned hard.

Matthew pushed himself up and appeared behind Tane. He heard gasps from the crowd.

Before Tane even knew he was there, Matthew punched him in the side of his ribcage, sending him flying into a wall. Works of art crashed on the ground, their heavy frames shattering.

Tane stood and grasped at his side, ribs broken.

He snarled at Matthew and came at him again. Matthew dodged another swing only to be kicked in the shin, his tibia snapped.

Howling, he grabbed Tane by the throat, his claws digging deep into flesh.

Tane swung his sword into Matthew's neck, just above his collar.

"Stop," a harsh command rang out.

Tane's sword stopped its swing. The blade pressed against Matthew, sizzling as it burned his skin, and Matthew's hand clasped Tane's neck so tight, that the young incubus couldn't breathe.

It had been Queen Agleea who had told them to stop. Disobeying her would mean a great deal of punishment, if not death. But Matthew didn't want to obey her command. He wanted to rip Tane apart.

Tane was turning blue but he didn't panic. Both men narrowed their eyes at each other.

"Let each other go," Agleea said from her throne.

Tane lowered his sword and Matthew released his neck. Tane gasped for air once he was free.

Neither broke eye contact with the other.

Matthew began pouring energy into healing his broken tibia and the scars on his face.

Once Tane had caught his breath, a hunter tossed him a vial of vampire blood and Tane downed it to heal his own wounds.

Matthew could smell fear around him. He felt bad for all the social incubi. To them, the fight probably looked terrifying. *He* was terrifying. The vampire. The very thing they had been conditioned to hate their whole lives.

The fear he felt coming from them wasn't helping him calm down. His vampire side wanted to finish the fight. He was confident he would have ripped Tane's neck apart before the sword could have severed his head.

"Both of you, come here," the Queen ordered.

Tane and Matthew snarled at each other then stomped over to Agleea, who was high above them on her dais.

Algeea laughed. Matthew wondered what the fuck was so funny.

"You two are hardly the first young men to fight over a woman." Her smile dropped. "Although I don't think I've ever seen it get so violent so fast. Your house will have to pay for the damages."

Matthew cringed. In a few seconds, they had managed to destroy literally millions of dollars in artwork. He wasn't looking forward to facing Tarrick…who he was unable to sense right now.

"In the future," she continued, "if you boys wish to fight over a woman, you can take it outside. Do you understand?"

"Yes, Your Majesty," they both said in unison.

Matthew wasn't allowed outside without an escort but she wasn't saying it for Tane or Matthew's benefit, but rather to reassure the other incubi in the room. It made the fight seem as if it was just two hotheaded boys going at it and not a warrior incubus and a vampire trying to kill each other.

"Matthew, you're dismissed to go wait for the head of your house on the second floor." She pointed upwards. He knew where he was going, the third outside balcony that had been kept clear for him.

Matthew bowed to her and ran up to the balcony at a lightning speed. He didn't want to stick around any longer than he needed. His control was thinner than he cared to admit. Even the wrong comment right now might push him too far.

His vampire side still hadn't receded, no matter how much he wanted it to go away.

The balcony was large and secluded between two stone walls with no windows overlooking it. There were two lights on the wall next to the door illuminating the area.

Matthew looked over the edge, less than twenty feet to the ground. There were scenic gardens surrounding the castle and beyond was a wall. Then the woods, where thousands of hunters were patrolling.

"Thinking of running?" a young voice asked. Leaning against the railing was Hiroto. The hood of his cloak was up and his red mask covered the bottom half of his face.

Matthew glanced behind him. He couldn't sense or see the other five Argonauts but he assumed they were here watching him.

He growled at Hiroto and began to pace back and forth on the balcony, eyeing the hunter. He flexed his claws. Part of him hoped Hiroto might try to attack him just so that he could finish a fight.

But Hiroto crossed his arms and eyed him right back.

Matthew needed to calm down before Tarrick arrived. "No," he said. Maybe talking to the hunter would get his mind off fighting. "I've seen what you can do, I don't want to find out firsthand what the other five are capable of."

Hiroto nodded and accepted the answer. He reached up and pulled his mask down around his chin.

Matthew went back to the railing and looked over. "How far do you think I could make it before you guys could stop me?"

"Hm." He looked down over his shoulder. "If you jumped over, I don't think your feet would touch the ground."

"Seriously?"

Hiroto nodded.

"Now I'm half tempted to do it just to see if you are all really that good."

"Do it—it'd be fun for us. But painful for you."

"Yeah, I wouldn't expect otherwise." His whole life was painful for him. Matthew closed his burning eyes. Silence passed between the two men and Matthew's mind began to drift to thoughts of what Tarrick was going to do to him.

"You have a nice dick," Hiroto said, breaking the silence.

Matthew choked on air as he laughed and raged all at once.

Hiroto laughed at his reaction.

"Please tell me you weren't in the room when I was with Lady Naveeda," he said.

Hiroto answered only with a wide smile.

Matthew wanted to bury his face in his hands but he'd probably cut himself on his claws. "Jesus Christ. Really?"

Hiroto shifted a little to get more comfortable on the railing. "Had to make sure you weren't going to hurt her."

"I would never have hurt her. And I'm not a damned exhibitionist." He was a voyeur maybe, thinking back to the couple on the balcony, but he didn't want others watching him.

"Really? You should be. You have the body for it." Hiroto eyed Matthew up and down.

"Gah, please shut up."

Matthew returned to his pacing. He studied Hiroto as he walked back and forth. He was thin, short, and Matthew found his face appealing. He had high cheekbones and soft features. His eyes always seemed to smile.

If Matthew couldn't fight anything right now, he wanted to fuck something. He cursed under his breath. Being an incubus was turning out to be a real pain. Ever since his transformation, he wanted to have sex all the freakin' time.

Maybe his appetite was growing as insatiable as the rumor went.

"You're a strange hunter," Matthew said.

Hiroto frowned. "Am I?"

"Yes. Most hunters are…rigid. Why are you talking to me?"

Hiroto shrugged. "You needed someone to talk to."

Matthew shook his head. "You're wrong. I need something to fight or fuck right now."

"If you attack me, I'll fight you." He patted a dagger on his belt. The offer was so tempting. Matthew looked down at his ripped tux. There were cuts above the bracers where Tane had swung at him. He was in enough trouble already. "But I can't fuck you right now. I'm on duty."

God, that made Matthew want him more. The things Hiroto said shocked him and aroused him all at once. He imagined taking him slowly in a large bathtub, Hiroto sitting on his lap with Matthew's arms wrapped around him. "And when do you get off duty?"

Hiroto sighed. "Not until this vampire I'm babysitting goes to bed."

Matthew grinned. "Man, that's the worst."

"Yeah, tell me about it."

Calmer now, Matthew's hands returned to normal and his fangs went back into his gums.

"You good?" Hiroto asked.

"Well, I don't want to fight anymore," he said and winked at the hunter who smiled. Leaning his butt back against the railing, Matthew wondered where the hell Tarrick was. He wanted to get this over with. He closed his eyes and reached out with his hearing. He scanned the castle level by level, wing by wing trying to find Tarrick.

He finally heard his voice far below him in the underground levels.

"You are wrong about this," he overheard Tarrick say. He sounded as if he was in the middle of a heated conversation.

"Lord General, you've lost your mind. It is an abomination," a male voice spoke. Matthew couldn't identify it.

Whoever this guy was, Matthew didn't appreciate being called an abomination.

"He is not an abomination," Tarrick responded to the man.

"It is, and it should be locked away, not dancing with our sons and daughters. You'll lose your position if this goes bad."

"I know the risks, and I'm telling you he's worth it. You've seen what he can do, and he's still improving every day," Tarrick said.

Matthew's chest filled with delight upon hearing Tarrick stand up for him.

"I can't support your bid to rescue your daughter if you continue to treat it like it's one of us," the unidentified voice said.

"You are making a mistake," Tarrick growled.

Someone with light footsteps entered the room. "I have the fight queued up." It was Silva's voice.

She must have handed him a tablet or something because Matthew could hear Tarrick watching a video of the fight between him and Tane. Now his reasoning for being late made sense. Tarrick always wanted to know all the facts before making a decision.

Matthew hoped that decision didn't involve him being whipped, chained in silver, or shackled again. And he really didn't want to be stuck alone in a cage. That prospect scared him the most.

When he opened his eyes Hiroto's face was inches away from his. Matthew jumped. "What the hell?"

Hiroto took a few steps back. "Just wanted to see how close I could get before you noticed me. Who were you eavesdropping on?"

"No one," Matthew said and slipped out of his tuxedo jacket, setting it on the railing.

"You should learn to lie better."

"I don't answer to…" Matthew stopped speaking when he noticed Hiroto's shadow. The lights at the door had Hiroto backlit, his shadow—upside down from Matthew's perspective—was that of a small four-legged creature. It had pointed ears and bushy tails. Many bushy tails.

Matthew stood and walked beside Hiroto to look at the shadow upright. It was a fox.

"Holy shit, you aren't human."

A sly smile crossed Hiroto's face. "Never said I was."

"I thought all hunters were human."

"Nope."

Matthew studied Hiroto closer. He was standing only a foot away from him. He smelled like incense and cherries. He looked and sounded human, except maybe for a heartbeat that was slightly faster. Matthew had no idea what kind of creature cast a shadow of a fox. There had been nothing in the books he read, although there were still a few untouched ones on his bookshelf.

Hiroto seemed amused as Matthew walked around him.

"What are you?"

"Should I tell you? I kind of like the idea of you not knowing. It'll drive you crazy."

Matthew huffed, went back to the railing, and leaned against it. He wasn't in the mood to be teased right now. "You're cruel."

Hiroto joined him on the railing. "I do not mean to be." Hiroto reached up to his hood that clung to him and he pulled it back.

Neck length pure white hair fell free and framed his face. Matthew's jaw slacked when he saw two pointed, fluffy ears atop of his head.

"I'm called a kitsune. A fox spirit."

A million questions flooded Matthew. He wanted to know everything about him now. What did being a spirit mean, did he use the same runes as other hunters, was that why his teleport was white and not green, why did he have so many tails in his shadow, could he shapeshift or did he just have the ears?

But instead of asking any he just sat there, his mouth gaped.

"You can touch them if you want," Hiroto offered.

Matthew laughed at himself. He was being a fool…a fool who wouldn't pass up the opportunity to touch Hiroto's white fox ears.

He reached over and gently ran his hand along one. It was soft and twitched back and forth when he touched it.

Red markings, that looked as if they were painted on with broad brush-strokes, appeared across Hiroto's cheeks.

Matthew ran his fingers across the red lines on Hiroto's face. He almost expected paint on his fingers when he looked at them but there was none. Hiroto laughed. It was friendly and warm.

"How old are you?" Matthew asked.

"He's older than me," Tarrick said behind them.

Thirty-Six

Tarrick dismissed the hunter with a wave of his hand. "Thank you, Commander."

Hiroto bowed and disappeared from the balcony in a flash of white light.

How long had Tarrick been standing behind him? Too many times tonight Matthew had let his senses lapse. He kept his eyes averted from Tarrick as he pushed off the railing and sunk down to a knee. Matthew didn't need to look at Tarrick to know he was angry.

"You two nearly killed each other tonight," Tarrick said.

Matthew had no response. Tarrick was right, they had both come close to killing each other. Now that he was composed, he could acknowledge that Tane's blade had come closer to slicing off his head then he cared to admit.

"Why did you sleep with Lady Naveeda?" Tarrick asked.

Matthew could feel Tarrick's eyes on him. "Master, I...she caught my eye from across the room. From the moment I saw her I desired her."

"And her being with Tane had nothing to do with it?"

"No, Master." Matthew sighed. "It's obvious that Tane and I do not like each other. He...infuriates me. But I wouldn't sleep with someone simply to spite him."

Tarrick was silent for a bit then finally said, "I believe you."

Relief flooded Matthew.

"But if you and Tane fight again, you will be punished. Do you need details on what I will do to you?"

By now, Matthew had a pretty good idea of the punishments that Tarrick could dish out. "No, Master. I won't fight him." But Tane better not sucker punch him again.

"You are extremely lucky that Queen Agleea likes you. This entire night would have gone completely different without her support. Stand up."

Matthew rose and faced Tarrick, who looked stern.

"This has been an extremely expensive night for me."

"I'm sorry, Master." He felt terrible about that.

"You'll be making it up to me soon enough."

Matthew had no idea what his future would be like but he was still going to rescue Tarrick's daughter from the vampire house. He had been unable to do anything while he was training and he still needed more information before he could formulate a plan and save her.

"Why didn't you choose to fight when Queen Agleea wanted you to impress her?" Tarrick asked.

Matthew smiled and his finger looped into a rip on his sleeve. "I didn't want to ruin the tux."

One side of Tarrick's lips curled up into a half-smile.

"And I got the feeling that fighting wouldn't impress her," Matthew added.

"Your instincts were correct, not much impresses her anymore. How long have you been able to sense gargoyles that way?"

"I'm not sure, Master. I spend a little bit of time each night trying to extend my senses farther out. Uh, maybe a few weeks ago I started being able to feel the ones on your keep."

"I expect you to report any new abilities that emerge."

"Yes, Master. I didn't mean to keep it from you. It just felt like something I always had the ability to do. It's hard to explain but I didn't even think about it." It was true. Feeling the gargoyles on the roof above him had felt normal and he hadn't given it a second thought at the time.

Tarrick gave a slow nod, accepting Matthew's explanation.

"Why didn't you bite Lady Naveeda when she offered you her neck?"

Damn it. Did everyone know everything he did with that woman? It was embarrassing. Matthew ground his teeth together and turned his gaze away from Tarrick.

"You're getting upset, Matthew. Why?"

His fists balled. "I am not used to people watching me have sex."

Tarrick reached out and touched Matthew's face, tracing along his jaw line, and scraping his slight stubble. Matthew looked back to him.

"You are so modest. And young. Over time it'll stop bothering you," Tarrick said.

"If you say so, Master." Matthew looked away again. "I wanted to bite her but didn't because I feared what you'd do to me if I took blood without your permission."

Through the touch, Matthew could feel how pleased that made Tarrick. He wondered if Tarrick knew how ashamed he felt. How broken inside he was.

"In the future, you may bite only if they ask for it and may only take a few drops of blood. And you have to heal the wound. I don't want to see a parade of incubi with bite marks walking around."

Matthew nodded.

"You did extremely well tonight. Had Tane not attacked you, it would have been perfect." Matthew wondered if Tane would be punished for his actions. He doubted it. Tarrick pulled his cell phone from his pocket and checked the time. "I hope you'll be able to repeat the performance."

"Master?"

Tarrick flashed a knowing smile at him. "This was just the first of many events you'll be attending in the coming months."

****

Tarrick hadn't been exaggerating about the number of events Matthew would be attending. Nearly every night during the next few weeks Matthew was brought to a gathering or party by Dennith or Rosaline. Vassu had been redeployed back to the West Coast and Tarrick was busy most nights.

None of the events were as big as Queen Agleea's ball.

A few of the dances had upwards of four hundred guests but most were smaller gatherings anywhere from ten to a hundred incubi.

At first, the reception of Matthew was always similar to the one he had received at the ball. Most people were both hesitant and curious around him, but he always kept his attitude friendly and by the end of the event he'd have incubi surrounding him.

Silva had been right…it was as if they were drawn to him. After a while, he found himself enjoying the attention.

Sometimes, Tane would show up to the same party. The two of them never spoke to each other, but Tane took great pleasure in stealing away and bedding any incubus that caught Matthew's eye. It'd piss Matthew off but he forced himself to let it go. He had to or he'd end up ripping out Tane's throat.

Matthew never saw or felt Hiroto or the other five Argonauts again. It seemed as if everyone was satisfied he wasn't about to go on a murderous rampage through the incubi community. He still had hunters watching him but the duty fell to the Wardens.

He was happy for it. It would make things easier. Silva was a great hunter, but Matthew knew how to fight her since he had spent so much time in training with her. He also liked that she stayed out of the room when he was fucking someone.

Matthew spent any free time he had plotting to take down House Moreau. He became obsessively focused on the idea.

Each party he attended he worked to gain more information about the vampire house. He'd mention the house offhandedly during pillow talk with a succubus or lead the conversation that direction with a drunken warrior.

He learned that vampires didn't often sleep together in large groups. They usually scattered before sunrise, making it so hunters couldn't go in and clear up nests of them.

But not the vampires of New Orleans. Their estate was protected by compelled human thralls, hired mercenaries, guards, and gargoyles that followed the commands of a vampire lord who lived there. They even had the local law enforcement in their pockets to help keep incubi out of the area.

During a dinner party, Lord Evan had told him that House Moreau consisted of at least six vampire lords. It was during that same dinner party that Matthew began to formulate a plan. He was there to make an impression on Lady Sabine. She was just under 400 years old and had a small private home in a secluded location on the east side of the Rocky Mountains in Colorado. She was a warrior who didn't seem to enjoy the extravagant lifestyle most incubi reveled in but she was still respected by their society for her ability to entertain.

That night, she encouraged everyone to drink copious amounts of alcohol while she recounted stories of glorious battles and deeds. Sober, Matthew listened as she recounted humorous tales of hunters or incubi caught in embarrassing situations. He enjoyed her tales.

Late into the party, while the group—ten incubi and two human companions—were sitting around in Lady Sabine's living room laughing and talking, Matthew abruptly stood up. His eyes turned red and his fangs came out.

Two hunters standing guard in the room drew crossbows and pointed them at him. Sabine stood, a sword in her hand. Matthew had no idea where it had come from. Silva had her hand on a weapon under her cloak but she hadn't drawn.

"What is it, Matthew?" Rosaline, who was his escort, asked. Matthew was happy she hadn't assumed he was about to attack them. Over the months they had spent together she had come to trust him.

"There are twenty-eight vampires approaching from the west side and an additional four coming from the north. They are about two miles out and moving fast. Really fast."

Looking around, Matthew grew concerned. Of the incubi, Sabine looked sober enough to fight but the rest were completely drunk and they weren't warriors.

There were eighteen hunters here tonight. The Wardens; Lady Sabine's team of six, the Crypt Killers; and another six who came with Lord Evan, Pardwell Green. The other incubi weren't lords or ladies and didn't command hunter teams.

Sabine growled. "Damn it. We're too outnumbered—we won't be able to hold this. Get to the stone."

Silva reported the situation to Tarrick via her comm as the entire party rushed to the basement of the house, where the teleport stone was hidden away. Matthew kept Rosaline close to him.

Matthew overheard Tarrick's voice over Silva's earpiece: "Belay the order to retreat—you will stay and fight. No one is to use the teleport stone."

"Acknowledged." Silva turned and held up her hand, stopping the group. "Lady Sabine, we've been ordered to stay. All of us."

Sabine grabbed a comm from a nearby drawer. She slapped it on her wrist and set it to speaker. "General we're outnumbered. This house isn't worth a battle that's not in our favor."

"My order stands. Everyone stays," Tarrick said.

Why the fuck wasn't Tarrick letting Rosaline go home? She trembled in Matthew's arms.

Sabine clenched her teeth. "At least let me send the non-combatants out of here."

Over the comm dozens of voices were shouting out information to Tarrick about attacks happening. It sounded like pure chaos over there. "No," he said. "The leylines have been disrupted. We're working to pinpoint the problem now. The last three teams that teleported ended up as a liquid puddle when they arrived at their destination."

Sabine gripped her weapon tight. "Is there anyone close enough to provide backup?"

More chaos from the other end. Tarrick got back to them after a few moments.

"No. This is a coordinated attack. Other estates are under assault right now and I can't send backup to anyone. You are on your own, but you are better off than most right now. Use Matthew."

"Understood."

Sabine cut the transmission and growled. "Everyone but Matthew and hunters get to the stone. There is a chest down there with weapons in it, lock the door and arm yourselves." She ordered one of the hunters to stay with the group. "As soon as the leylines are working get out of here." She turned to Silva. "Set up the defenses, I will be right back."

She disappeared down a hallway and Silva began ordering hunters into strategic spots around the house.

Matthew slipped off his suit jacket—Tarrick had finally gotten him into one since tonight wasn't formal enough for a tux and he couldn't show up in jeans—and began to unbutton his shirt.

"Can you sense any lords among them, Matthew?" Silva asked.

Matthew closed his eyes and scanned the vampires. "I don't know. It's hard for me to tell lords apart because they can mask their power. Does this house have alarms like back at the keep?"

"Yeah. We already turned it off because of you. I'll keep it off for now but I might have to turn it on if they make it inside. Once you're outside I'm going to activate some wards. Don't cross the thresholds until I tell you it's safe."

Matthew nodded. "They're close."

Sabine returned looking imposing in her armor and full incubus form. Looking down at Matthew, she held out a sword. "Then what the pit are you waiting for? Go kill them."

Matthew snatched it from her and rushed outside. The vampires clearly weren't expecting him to be there or moving as fast as he was. He cut the heads off the first three before they even saw him.

They were young. Weak. If these attacks were as coordinated as Tarrick said, the more powerful vampires would be at more strategic locations.

A volley of silver bolts flew past him and two vampires rushing at him were turned into life-sized pincushions. They screamed as the silver burned their skin. The hunters could finish them off.

Matthew went for the most powerful vampire he could sense. As he got close, the vampire sprouted wings and took to the air. Sabine would have to deal with him, much to Matthew's disappointment.

None of the vampires around him were challenging. He ended up with handfuls of claw marks and one managed to bite him and take a chunk out of his shoulder, but he healed it all back easily. He wished he was fighting the lord and not just cutting down young vamps. The worst injury he sustained was when a stray silver bolt caught him in the ribs.

Friendly fire.

Or maybe an asshole hunter who took the opportunity to ping him.

Not every hunter was thrilled to be working with a vampire.

Matthew broke away from the main fighting to stop a group trying to flank the house when he realized he was alone with four of them. He pushed power into his aura and as soon as he did, the vampires cowered away.

Matthew smiled as he chased one down. He grabbed it by the neck. "Answer my questions."

The vampire nodded, falling to his command.

"What do you know about House Moreau?" Matthew asked.

"Not much. Old vampires. Lots of rules. I stay away from them."

He was useless. Matthew released the vamp and let it run away. He chased down another, a female, and repeated the process. She knew more. She gave Matthew the address to the house and told him that every Friday the important vampires of New Orleans gathered there. Also that any vampire who traveled to the area had to get permission from them to hunt. Failing to follow their rules meant death.

Matthew released her and watched the other vampires flee. They were weak and helpless and no longer a threat to the house. Fighting them would have been like stabbing kittens, an act Matthew would find no pleasure in. Tarrick would be pissed if he found out but no one was around.

With the threat gone, Matthew returned to the house. He could smell blood as he approached. Three hunters were dead. Another was clawed up pretty badly but he'd live. Others had non-life-threatening injuries and were downing vampire blood to heal up.

He smelled incubus blood inside the house.

It was intoxicating. Fighting always made him hungry...even if he had just eaten.

He stopped at the front door and a hunter disabled the ward for him, the green glow draining away.

In the living room, Sabine was laying on the couch, surrounded by hunters. Blood dripped out from under her armor.

Matthew set his sword down on a table and watched as Silva whispered a command to the armor and it folded down into a chest piece. She peeled it away from the incubus.

Sabine had a serious claw wound in her neck and several deep stab wounds in her side. She was fighting to stay conscious.

Silva leaned over and began kissing her but Sabine passed out before she could respond. Silva shook her to try to get her back. "Lady Sabine? Come on, wake up."

Matthew approached and put his clawed hand on Silva's shoulder. "Let me try."

She looked at him then back down to Sabine.

"Trust me, I've done it before," Matthew said.

She shifted over to give him space.

He kneeled down beside the couch and pulled Sabine into his arms. He pressed his lips to hers and forced energy to flow from him into her.

It wasn't long before her lips began to respond to his. She wrapped her arms around him and took over, stealing his reserves away at a rapid pace. Unlike the first time with Tarrick, Matthew didn't resist. He let her take whatever she needed.

While it would be painful as hell, he could live with an empty soavik—she could not.

Sabine broke away from him. Her wounds stitching together.

"Did you force energy into me?" Sabine asked with a raw cough as she sat up on the couch, astonished.

Matthew nodded. "What happened with the vampire lord?"

"He got away," Silva answered.

"I wish I had wings, I'd have much rather fought him. Those weak vampires weren't much of a challenge."

Silva tossed him a container of blood and scowled. "Those 'weak' vampires killed three of my men, Matthew."

He winced. He hadn't even considered that and now, because he respected Silva a great deal, he felt terrible for upsetting her. "I'm sorry, Commander, I didn't mean to offend you."

The rest of the night was uneventful for their group. Matthew spent it comforting and gently reassuring Rosaline that everything was okay now.

The leylines were fixed half an hour before sunrise and Matthew returned to Tarrick's keep and collapsed into his bed. He listened to Ilertha sing to him as he planned his attack on House Moreau.

He had a location now. He just needed a few more pieces to fall into place...then he'd go rescue Tarrick's daughter and the incubi would accept him as one of their own.

Thirty-Seven

Matthew paced back and forth on the balcony of Lord Brodeur's keep. There was a party going on inside and he had been kicked out for losing control.

A large number of hunters were patrolling the grounds below, but Silva was the only other person on the balcony with him. He felt bad for what he was about to put her through, but it was the only way he could escape without hurting anyone.

Matthew had carefully planned every moment of this night and, so far, it was going perfectly. House Moreau would fall by his hand in a few hours.

Weeks ago, he convinced Rosaline to tell him about every event he'd be attending. None were in Louisiana. He had to change that.

He got her to tell him about the different events he wouldn't be attending. Lord Brodeur's party in Baton Rouge was on the list. It was large, over two hundred elite incubi would be in attendance, and it was on a Friday. Perfect.

The problem was that Lord Brodeur—and most of his friends—hated Matthew. They wanted to see him chained or killed. Matthew could hardly blame them, most of these incubi lived relatively close to vampire territory and had all lost homes and loved ones in the war.

Matthew begged Rosaline to take him anyway but she wouldn't budge. She didn't like this circle of incubi. In the end, he had to convince Tarrick to bring him, but it was a while before Matthew even saw him.

Tarrick was busy cleaning up the aftermath of the massive vampire assault that had taken out the leylines. The attack on Lady Sabine's house was nothing compared to what happened elsewhere. The vampires had killed hundreds of incubi and hunters that night.

It was a major blow to them.

Tarrick had been summoned to New York to answer to the High King and was gone for a week. When he returned, he sent for Matthew.

When he arrived at Tarrick's room, Tarrick said nothing to him before ripping off Matthew's clothes and taking him. He was rough, letting off steam, and Matthew enjoyed every moment of it.

When they were both lying naked on the bed, Matthew kissed Tarrick's neck, trying to rouse him for another round.

"I take it New York didn't go well for you," he said, moving to Tarrick's ear lobe and sucking on it.

"Not really. No." Tarrick didn't respond to Matthew's advances—his mind already onto something else.

Matthew gave up and rested his head on Tarrick's shoulder. He hadn't expected Tarrick to wrap his arm around him and pull him in closer. It felt nice.

"I want to go to the Lord Brodeur party," Matthew said after a while had passed.

"Lady Rosaline told me you've been bugging her about that. Why do you want to go so bad?"

"All the parties and dances you are sending me to are full of incubi who are either indifferent towards me or like me already. But Lord Brodeur hates what I am. Maybe I can convince him to change his mind or at least sway some of the opinions of his entourage. It'd be a fun challenge." Matthew was only partly lying. He was going to sway their opinion, but it wasn't by his skills in conversation or dancing, it was by wiping out the vampires that controlled the neighboring region.

"You really do enjoy challenges, don't you?"

Matthew pressed a kiss onto Tarrick's chest and smiled against his skin. "Yes I do, Master."

"Tane will be there. He and Lord Brodeur's son are close."

"I've gotten good at staying out of Tane's way. Do you think Rosaline will come if we both go?"

Tarrick shrugged. "I'll ask her."

Matthew sat up on his elbow, excited. "Then that's a yes?"

"Yes. But you better impress me."

"I will, Master. Don't worry about that."

Getting to the party was only step one. He needed help if he was going to take down a house with so many vampire lords. Help from a hunter or incubus was out of the question, but there was someone else he could turn to that was close by.

For about thirty minutes each night, after he'd arrive home from some event, he sat on the roof of the keep and read books by moonlight. The hunters thought it was odd behavior but Tarrick allowed him to do it. It was nice to be out under the starry sky, smelling the air, and listening to the night's sounds.

The real reason he was out there, however, was the gargoyles. He'd talk to them. He said nothing important, he'd just talk about a party he had just attended or something he found exciting in a book. He could feel them enjoying it even if they never talked back or even moved.

A few nights before the party he addressed Asper, the first gargoyle he had ever seen. Tarrick's gargoyle.

He told her about his plan to attack House Moreau, and that he was doing it to get Tarrick's daughter back. He told her the entire truth and asked for her help. She didn't move. Matthew had no idea if it would work. He'd find out soon enough.

One of the more impressive things he did in preparation, at least in his mind, was when he woke during the day while the human maid was in his room cleaning. He was tired and couldn't move but he could speak. He waited until the maid was near him and snapped his eyes open. She looked down at him and gasped. The daytime maids didn't wear those fucking contacts that prevented him from compelling.

"Go close the door and come back here," he whispered a command to her so that the guards in the hallway couldn't hear him. She did as he told her to. "If I ask you to get me a few things and have them waiting for me at Lord Brodeur's keep, do you think you could do it?"

She nodded. "I know the head housekeeper there. She can get what you need if I say that the Lord General is requesting it."

"Good. Here's what I want you to get for me…"

The night of the party had come at last. Matthew planned every moment. He arrived with Tarrick and Rosaline. He bowed to Lord Brodeur and took the predicted verbal beating from him. After, he mingled and danced with a few incubi who actually liked him.

At ten o'clock he stumbled in front of Tane, knocking the drink Tane was holding onto his tuxedo. Tane growled and launched himself at Matthew.

Matthew darted behind Tarrick, his vampire guise out, snarling at Tane.

Tarrick put an end to the fight before it even began by ordering Tane upstairs to change and Matthew out to the balcony to calm down.

Having faked the whole thing, Matthew was already calm. Tane and Tarrick had both reacted exactly the way he expected them to.

At five after ten, Matthew stopped pacing and grabbed a black duffle bag that was waiting for him on the balcony.

"What is that, Matthew?" Silva asked when she saw the bag.

"Change of clothes," he said and began stripping from his tux.

Silva's brows knitted together. "Why are you removing your tuxedo?"

Matthew peeled out of his coat and shirt. "It's hard to run in a tux."

"I don't understand." She watched him change but did nothing to stop it. She looked as if she was in a haze. Confused.

"You will in a few moments."

Once he was down to his underwear, he got dressed in black jeans, heavy black boots, and a black turtleneck that hid his metal collar. All the black made his pale skin stand out like a beacon but it seemed fitting, if not a little cliché, for a vampire.

There was a silver sword inside the bag with a belt sheath. He put the belt on and adjusted the sword so that it correctly sat at his hip. He folded the tux best he could and put it in the bag.

Two minutes.

He walked over to her and removed Silva's sash of throwing daggers.

"Matthew, why can't I move?" she asked, her body frozen in place.

He put the daggers on over his own chest and slipped on a leather jacket and zipped it up to hide the weapons. "Because I compelled you three days ago and you are under my command."

Her heart was racing.

He reached up and touched her face to nudge her emotions slightly so that she wouldn't panic. "Please don't be scared, I'm not going to hurt you. You'll be released from the compulsion in about twelve minutes. I know this will probably be a black mark on your record, and for that I am sorry."

He took four silver powder grenades, three stakes, her crossbow, a vial of the brown liquid that slowed healing in vampires—during training he learned it was foxglove—and her silver chain from her belt and put them into the duffle. He then took her cell phone and pocketed it.

"How did you compel me? I don't remember it," she asked, her voice distraught.

"I took your contacts out the other night when we were in the lounge alone together. I made you forget what I had done. All you're going to do is create a distraction. Once it's over you'll be released."

Matthew had taken a page from Ascelina's book. Almost every night Silva would come off her shift shortly before sunrise. She had a routine where she began undoing her uniform and taking off her weapons. She'd toss them into her room then go grab a yogurt or fruit from the lounge.

Matthew would join her to ask her questions about supernatural species, fighting techniques, or just to chat. She was always happy to answer; it seemed to help decompress her before she headed off to bed.

He learned that she was sixty-three years old, though she looked as if she was in her mid-twenties. Tarrick was extending her life. He didn't need to sleep with her to do it, but it was sort of like an energy transfer she had to go through every year. Vampires could stem a human's aging as well by feeding the human their blood every month or so.

Matthew really enjoyed talking to her. She was a sassy human and some mornings he'd go to sleep laughing due to their ribald banter.

It pained him that he was doing it so she would drop her guard enough and relax around him. One night when they were alone in the lounge, he pushed power into his speed and plucked the contacts out of her eyes. He pinned her down so that she couldn't sound any of the alarms like Cullip had done when Ascelina compelled him. Before she could teleport away, he sunk his claw into her rune to disable it.

The look in her eyes when she realized that he had tricked her—betrayed her—crushed his heart. He almost couldn't go through with it. But he did, and feeling her will slip away as she tried to fight him had been devastating for him.

He would have rather compelled any other hunter besides her but she was the only one he could guarantee would be here tonight. And, as a commander, no one would question her orders if she sent Matthew off to fight.

One minute.

"You're running away?" she asked. Her face twisted as she tried to fight against the compulsion. If Matthew could hold a vampire lord, a human—even if she was a hunter—had no hope of breaking it.

Matthew didn't answer her question. It was better she thought he was trying to escape for now.

"Don't run, Matthew. We can track you with the collar. You'll just be recaptured and every freedom you've worked for will be taken away from you."

He was touched that Silva showed concern for him. She had told him once that she always thought of him as a warrior, even when he was kept caged. Matthew rubbed a gauntlet under his shirt. "I don't have as many freedoms as you think."

Thirty seconds.

Matthew slipped on a pair of fingerless leather gloves and grabbed some heavy-duty earplugs from out of the duffle bag.

"I'm sorry, Silva, you are the last person I wanted to do this to. You have always been fair to me. I hope you will forgive me. And tell Tarrick…"

Matthew paused for a moment. "...tell him I'm sorry too."

"Release me and—" she didn't finish. It was time. Another command he had given her took effect. She raised her comm to her mouth and Matthew put the earplugs into his ears. "Multiple contacts north side. Matthew has reported at least fifty vamps incoming, three miles out and moving in quick."

Alarms in the keep sounded and the hunters below rushed about as they prepared for incoming vampires.

He ignored the urge to apologize to Silva one more time and jumped over the balcony railing, duffle bag in hand.

Silva would tell them that she was sending Matthew out to go fight. No one should find it odd that he was running around alone but he didn't risk it. He pushed power into his speed, moving fast enough to blur.

He needed the hunters to be distracted for ten minutes. That was how long it would take him to run from Baton Rouge to New Orleans. He'd burn a bunch of blood pushing himself at max speed but there would be plenty of humans in New Orleans he could refill on.

He kept close to the I-10 as he ran. Cars appeared to be crawling along as he passed them. He kept his senses open for any hunters that might teleport in front of him.

None did.

He made it to New Orleans without seeing a single incubus or hunter. Using Silva to falsely report incoming vampires as a distraction had worked.

Matthew jumped into a parked car with a young couple making out in it. He compelled them to stay calm while he fed on their blood. When it was done, he compelled them to forget what had happened and told them they would be walking home tonight.

As he slid into the driver's seat of the now otherwise empty car, the phone he had taken from Silva buzzed in his pocket. He pulled it out and looked at the caller ID.

Lord General.

Matthew debated answering it. Every part of him screamed to let it ring through but he couldn't help himself. He answered but said nothing as he held the phone to his ear.

"Matthew—" Tarrick growled. "—you've made a mistake tonight."

Matthew swallowed. He could hear anger laced in every word.

"You might think you are being clever by running into an area where I cannot send hunters, but I will recapture you in time. If you come back now, I promise you will only be physically punished for your lapse in judgment. But if you don't return, when I capture you again I will break you down until there is nothing left but a mindless weapon for me to use. Every part of you will be gone."

Matthew wished he hadn't answered the phone.

He knew Tarrick wasn't making an idle threat and it scared him. He had to be successful tonight or he could never return. And the idea of never seeing Tarrick again hurt far more than he cared to admit. He had spent months ignoring the feelings he had for the incubus general, but right now they were at the forefront of his mind.

It had always been his intention to escape once he had learned what he could from the incubi, but lately he found himself wanting to stay.

He enjoyed the parties and the dancing and the conversation. He enjoyed talking with Silva, training with the hunters, spending time with Rosaline, sparring with Dennith, and sleeping with Tarrick. These were all things he didn't want to lose.

He was beginning to feel as if he had a family again. It was a place where he belonged. Ashwood was home to him now. House Tarrick.

And that was why he had to take out House Moreau. Those vampires had hurt people he cared for and he couldn't let that stand. He just wished he wasn't a slave.

"Master, I…" He wanted to explain what he was doing but he couldn't tell him, not until it was over.

Matthew ended the call.

He put the address into the phone and decided to drive over since he wasn't sure how the vampires would react to him speeding in. His plan wasn't to just show up and start killing, he wanted to try and gather information on what he'd be facing—something he had learned from Tarrick.

He drove to the address and parked a street over. Taking the duffle bag with him, he approached the location.

It was a large, white mansion in the Garden District. It had a sizable staircase leading up to the front door, bold pillars and balconies that wrapped around the house, and a black iron fence surrounded the property. The inside was dark and looked empty.

Matthew couldn't sense anyone, either.

He cautiously touched the front gate. Magic sparked across his fingers. He had to fight the feeling of uneasiness. If he were human, he'd want to move away from this location. He pushed open the gate and his skin tingled as he passed through a magic veil. Once on the other side, his senses were assaulted as everything changed.

The cold, empty looking mansion lit up with warm lights. Gargoyles, resting on every corner, became visible. Lively music and laughter filled the air.

Matthew could sense easily a hundred vampires in the area and quite a few humans. There were five incubi nearby as well. One inside and four behind the house, in what Matthew could only assume was a second structure.

The garden and balconies were full of vampires. The clothing varied from formal to casual, dated to modern; anything seemed to go. It was a feast for his eyes to see such an array.

The vampires glanced at Matthew, studied him for a moment, then went back to whatever they were doing before he entered. There were vampires feeding or playing with humans, a vampire couple was making out on a stone bench under a tree, and there were groups lost in conversation. None seemed alarmed that Matthew had shown up.

Matthew walked up the stairs to the open front doors. He caught the scent of blood as he looked inside. It was packed.

There were vampires dancing, laughing, talking, and drinking from compelled humans. With the exception of the fangs and feeding, it looked and felt just like any normal party might. It was less rigid and formal than anything he had been to with the incubi.

As Matthew went in, a strong hand grabbed his shoulder.

"Stop right there."

Thirty-Eight

Matthew's hand dropped down to his sword.

The vampire gripped Matthew tighter. "You don't want to do that, kid."

Kid? Matthew yanked his shoulder away from the hand and turned to see who had grabbed him.

The vampire was tall and well-built but he had been young when he was turned, maybe twenty…chances were he was much, much older. He looked like he was working the door as a bouncer of sorts.

"Whoa. Your eyes…crazy." Matthew had no way to hide them other than turning them red but he was worried it might come off too aggressive. The bouncer looked around. "Where's your sire?"

"I don't have one," Matthew answered. He forgot just how young he would seem to all these vampires. He was only eight now—he had a birthday…hm, deathday…a few months ago. Vampires were bonded to their children for about a hundred years before the connection faded.

Matthew had never felt even a single moment of what that bond was like.

"He's gone," Matthew added to make it sound as if his sire had died.

"Tough break. No weapons in the house," he said and held out his hand for Matthew's sword.

Matthew considered drawing the sword and ending the vampire's life but he wanted to see more before he attacked. He undid the belt and handed the sheathed sword to the bouncer. The vampire pulled the sword out and when he saw it was silver, he raised an eyebrow.

"Took it from a hunter," Matthew said with a shrug.

He seemed to accept the explanation. "You can get it back when you leave."

"No. When I ask for my sword back, you will give it to me," Matthew said, compelling him. None of the vampires surrounding them took any notice.

The vampire nodded. "What's in the duffle?"

"No need to worry about it," Matthew said.

"New in town?" he asked, not even realizing he had been compelled.

"Yes."

"Then you need to see Victor before you hunt. There are rules. For tonight, the lower level has humans you can kill if you are hungry, the ones up here are for tasting only. They aren't for young ones who can't break away from a feed yet."

"I can break from a feed."

"Yeah. Okay." The vampire didn't believe him.

Matthew was getting annoyed by this guy. "Are all the lords of New Orleans here tonight?"

"Yeah."

Good. "Where do I find Victor?"

The bouncer waved someone over to take his spot and said, "Follow me."

Matthew followed the bouncer into the house. Along the way they passed by large groups of vampires and dazed humans wandering about, their skin littered with bite marks. Matthew watched as a vampire bit one, filled his mouth with blood, then turned and kissed another vampire to share the blood. Sire and child. A sense of longing filled Matthew's heart.

The bouncer led Matthew into a large central room full of plush red couches, fine artwork, and statues.

There were eight vampire lords in this room. None made much of an effort to mask their power. The room was packed with other vampires as well, but Matthew noticed that many of the younger ones stayed out; the power coming off the lords was overwhelming even to him.

Shackled atop a heavy wood table was a naked succubus. Vampires were feeding off her. She was young, with dark hair and striking features. Her skin was covered in bruises and bite marks. She wasn't Tarrick's daughter—this one wasn't a warrior.

A large male covered with tattoos—a lord—bit her arm and thrust his fingers into her vagina. As he moved them in and out, she whimpered in pain.

Matthew's eyes turned red with anger.

"What have we here?" a deep voice with a French accent asked. The room went silent and Matthew ripped his burning eyes away from the succubus to see who had spoken.

At the far side of the room stood a massive dark wood chair with a vampire lounging in it.

Victor Moreau.

He wore a black and red leather outfit that made him look imposing and he was surrounded by vampires who were trying to garner his attention.

"He's new in town," the bouncer answered.

"Sire?" Victor asked.

The bouncer shrugged. "Says he doesn't have one."

Matthew dropped the duffle onto the ground. "I can answer for myself."

The bouncer laughed. "Can you now? Most children are too scared."

"Who was your sire?" Victor asked him directly.

Matthew started to doubt his plan. This room reeked of power. He wasn't sure he could take them all on. The only lord he had ever killed was the one he compelled during the battle in California, and even then, it had been a weaker lord. Victor Moreau was not weak. And with the other lords in this room Matthew had no idea what he could realistically do here.

"Does it matter? He's dead," Matthew said.

A sickly looking male vampire, turned sometime in his teens, stepped forward and pointed at Matthew. "He lies."

A vampire that could sense when someone lied? That wasn't good for him.

Victor stood and Matthew took a step back. He couldn't help it. Victor stopped suppressing his aura. He had felt powerful before but now it was crushing. Is this how other vampires felt around him when he stopped suppressing his own aura?

"Lying to me is not wise. Who was your sire?"

Matthew frowned. He hadn't come here to explain his story. He came here to kill them. "I don't know. I was turned and abandoned. I have never shared a bond with a sire."

"And you survived? That is uncommon," Victor said and sank back into the chair. "What is your name?"

"Matthew."

"Last name?"

"I don't use it anymore." Incubi didn't have last names. They just used whatever house they were part of—Matthew of House Tarrick sounded good to him, but it wouldn't get him far in this crowd.

"Unfortunately for you, Matthew, I cannot permit a child to feed in my city without a sire. We limit the number of humans that are killed to avoid the attention. You may stay here for the night but you'll leave tomorrow."

"He told me he can break a feed," the bouncer said.

The room filled with laughter. Matthew narrowed his eyes.

"Child, if you can break a feed show us," a female lord, wearing a black skirt and matching corset, said. She motioned to the succubus.

"Savass," Victor growled the woman's name as a warning to her.

Matthew ignored them and approached the succubus. Savass grabbed Matthew's shoulder to stop him. "I am only playing, child."

"You don't wish me to show you, then?" Matthew asked, confused and pissed off that the room full of vampires assumed he was weak.

Savass laughed. "Male pride is the same no matter how old or young the vampire is. Even if you've been able to break from a human once or twice, no child your age can stop feeding from an incubus once they start."

Matthew growled. "I can."

"Fine, let him," Victor said, "but, young one, if you do not break I will have you staked and dumped in incubus territory."

Matthew nodded and took off one of his gloves. He ran his hand down the face of the succubus. She squirmed under his touch.

"Darling, I won't hurt you," Matthew reassured and nudged her emotions to relax her. Her eyes widened when she felt him use incubus abilities. Matthew winked at her as he leaned down and sunk his fangs into her neck. He took a few intoxicating drops then removed his fangs. He gently licked her neck to close the wound.

When Matthew looked up Victor was watching him closely. "I've never seen one so young do that without their sire. Alright, you may hunt so long as you do not kill and after you must compel the human to forget. If you kill a human by mistake you must report it right away."

"I didn't come here to ask for your permission to hunt," Matthew said. Now that he had touched the succubus, felt her anguish, he couldn't just leave her here. He had to stick to his plan. He had to try to free them.

"Then why are you here?" Victor asked.

"I've come here to kill you."

Laughter filled the room once more. The room of vampires, the youngest older than a century in age, couldn't take him seriously. He was a rabbit threatening a den of wolves. His irises burned brighter red with anger. Soon they would see he was no rabbit.

"And why is it that you wish to kill me?" Victor said. He didn't make any effort to move. Matthew wondered how fast he was.

"You've hurt some people I care for. I'd like my sword back," he said to the bouncer.

"You won't be getting it…" Victor started to say but trailed off when the bouncer held it out. "Bosco, do not give that to him."

"He doesn't have a choice," Matthew said, drawing the weapon. He could feel the mood in the room begin to change from indifference to curiosity. Soon it would be fear.

"He compelled me," Bosco said, holding his head and backing away from Matthew.

Matthew smiled.

Victor gave a dismissive wave. "That is not possible."

Matthew grabbed the arm of Savass and pulled the female lord into him. He looked into her eyes. "You will obey my every command." She struggled against him. Matthew had to pour power into both his arms to hold her in place while he pushed his will onto her and manipulated her emotions. She was stronger than the lord he compelled in California.

None of the vampires moved to stop him. It was as if they couldn't possibly believe what was happening.

Her will fell. "Kneel before me," Matthew growled at her. She did so.

There it was.

The fear.

It filled the room.

It was Matthew's turn to laugh.

Victor stood and his vampire guise came forward. Bat-like wings unfurled from behind him and his hands turned into long black claws. His fangs were long and wide and his eyes a deep glowing red.

The other vampires changed as well.

"You are the vampire we've been hearing rumors about, the one working for the incubi," Victor said, in a deep rumbling voice.

Matthew nodded.

"I didn't believe the gossip. How could you betray your own kind like that?"

"I did not betray my own kind. I am an incubus." Matthew savored the shocked looks that crossed the faces of many in the room.

Victor studied him. "No vampire can sire an incubus."

Matthew pointed at Savass still kneeling before him. "Just as no vampire can compel another? Just as no child can break away from a feed?" Matthew wrapped an incubus hold around Victor. The old vampire broke from it easily but it was enough to prove what he was.

"Impossible," Victor said. Matthew moved his sword to the ready and took a defensive stance.

Victor moved so quickly that Matthew didn't even see him. The old vampire knocked the sword from his hand and slipped his own hand under

Matthew's jacket and shirt.

Victor pressed on Matthew's stomach and scanned him. "Four pouches…" Victor said as if he doubted his own words. Whispers filled the room as the other vampires watched.

Matthew growled and swiped at Victor's face. Victor caught his wrist and broke it with a snap.

Crying out in pain, Matthew pushed power into healing his broken bone. Victor was faster and more powerful than he was; there was no way he could beat him with sheer strength. Matthew began to run through strategies that didn't rely on overpowering his enemy.

"Leave the service of the incubi. Come fight for us."

Matthew stared blankly at the lord.

"It does not matter what you were before you were turned, you are a vampire now. You belong with us," Victor said.

Ascelina had said the same thing to him. *One of us.* It gave Matthew pause. Unlike the incubi, where he had to fight for their acceptance, the vampires accepted him for what he was. It was so tempting.

Victor put his hand on Matthew's shoulder. "Join us and I'll tell you who your sire is."

Matthew's eyes widened. Could he really know who his sire was? Matthew hungered to stay here with his people and get some answers that he desperately wanted. He'd have to leave Tarrick…his master…someone he was falling for…or rather, had already fallen for. But this was bigger than his feelings for one man.

The succubus groaned on the table. He looked over at her and images of Rosaline chained up in the same manner—naked, bruised, mistreated—flashed through his mind. His eyes settled on the large tattooed vampire that had been violating her when he entered the room and a fierce rage rose within him.

How *dare* he touch her without her permission. Had he done the same to Rosaline? Matthew's choice became clear.

"Kill Victor," Matthew commanded Savass. She lunged herself at the master vampire and Matthew broke away from him.

He scooped up his sword then ran over to the tattooed vampire lord and removed his head from his body with one impossibly quick swing.

One down. Seven to go.

The rest wouldn't fall so easily.

Matthew stopped suppressing his aura of death and pushed power into it, making it as strong as possible. He roared, and many of the vampires fled.

He dove for the duffle bag, ripped it open, and grabbed two of the silver grenades. He stopped breathing as he threw one to each side of him. They hit the back walls and rained silver dust down on the vampires.

The vampires here were so old they only drew breath when they needed to speak, so the dust didn't have quite the effect Matthew had been hoping for, but it still boiled their skin.

A lord flew at him, claws flying wildly.

Matthew pulled out the last two silver grenades and launched them into the lord's chest. They exploded and the lord went down in pain. Matthew chopped off his head before he could recover.

Two down. Six to go.

As Victor busied himself dodging Savass' attacks, a different lord opened a window and yelled out something in a language Matthew couldn't identify.

Matthew lost track of one of the lords and he didn't have time to find him because two others, a male and female dressed similarly in gothic attire, came at him. He grabbed a stake and ran, trying to get himself to a better position—standing in the center of the room was too open. But the two lords kept right on his ass.

Matthew pushed power into his speed and was barely able to dodge their claws. A counter attack was out of the question.

They worked together, herding Matthew towards a corner. Matthew couldn't risk getting pinned there so he sprinted to the door, leaving him open to attack from the male, who sunk his claws deep into Matthew's arm.

Matthew dropped the stake as skin and muscle were torn apart. His left arm would be useless until he could heal it. The lords weren't about to give him a moment to do so.

The female lord surged forward and bit Matthew on the neck, then retreated.

Matthew's vision began to blur and his movements felt heavy. The bitch had injected him with some sort of venom. Keeping the compulsion on Savass was also proving to be near impossible. He'd have to let her go unless he could get away to heal.

He ran from the room but the two lords were relentless. Out of options, Matthew released Savass and focused on pushing power into his speed. He found a flight of stairs leading down, jumped the railing, landed, and sprinted down a hall. Humans and young vampires fled around him.

He passed what looked like a small kitchen (for the humans they kept maybe?) and kept going.

The two lords weren't far behind. Matthew didn't have many choices right now. His vision was getting worse and he was rapidly running out of hall to run down. He wanted to avoid going outside since they could fly and he couldn't.

Matthew. Here.

A deep male voice called to him inside of his mind. He didn't recognize it but it felt familiar.

Out of options, he followed where the voice led him—into a room near the end of the hall. Matthew slammed the door closed and locked it behind him.

He prayed that whoever called to him was friendly because things were not looking good right now.

Thirty-Nine

The room he entered looked like a small church with two rows of pews, candles, and an altar.

On the altar were bowls of blood, and in the center sat a carved sculpture of a skull with horns and long vampire fangs.

"Really?" Matthew said, picking up the skull. "First Ilertha, now you? I don't know what you want from me but I'm getting really fucking sick of this shit."

The door smashed open and the male lord burst through it. Matthew threw the statue as hard as he could at the lord and hit him with such force that his head caved in.

The lord went down. He wasn't dead but he'd be out of the fight until he healed.

Matthew rushed to the door as the female ran in; she paused to look at her partner. Her mistake. Matthew used the distraction to stab her and slice upwards through her skull. She fell to the ground.

He took both their heads off to make sure they'd stay down for good and then stumbled backwards into the wall, the poison making him dizzy.

Four down. Four to go.

Matthew's head spun and he fought the urge to vomit.

The smell of blood—even if it wasn't fresh—on the altar was overpowering. He staggered to it and grabbed a bowl. He downed it in a single gulp. It was disgusting—thick—but it made him feel better.

He pushed healing into his arm and tried his best to clear away the venom. It was slow going. Too slow if he wanted to get back into the fight.

He focused inwards, grabbed both the red strands of his blood energy and the gold strands of stored sexual energy, and entwined them. He used the dual power to push the venom out of his body. It worked. His head cleared.

Reaching out with his senses, he felt many vampires on the floor above him. Most on this level had already fled. Good. He didn't need to kill the young ones who didn't want to fight.

When Matthew pulled his senses back he felt a presence close by, but before he could react, crippling pain spread across his lower back as one of his blood pouches was pierced.

He turned to see what was behind him just in time to watch a female lord pull the dagger out of him and turn into a cloud of fog. The silvery mist floated around him and the lord reappeared and stabbed him again, this time just below his shoulder blade. Then, she once again turned back into fog.

That's a new one. How the fuck was he going to fight something that was essentially a cloud?

At least the vampire was slow moving while she was insubstantial. Slower than him at any rate.

Matthew ran from the room, the wounds on his back bleeding profusely. He poured power into sealing the skin. Healing the pouch would take days—weeks maybe—but at least he wasn't bleeding out. And he still had three pouches left.

Matthew ran past the small kitchen again and had an idea. He skidded to a halt and backtracked into it.

The fog wasn't far behind him.

He pulled the gas line from the wall and waited.

The fog floated in and surrounded him. Matthew didn't know where the lord would appear but he needed a little longer. He dodged around the small space, hoping that if he kept moving it'd make it harder for her to hit him.

The lord appeared and sliced Matthew's lower arm, hitting his bracer, and went back to her fog form.

Matthew kept his power at the ready. The lord began to materialize. Matthew swung his sword hard on the metal stove and sparks flew.

The gas ignited. Matthew pushed what he had into his speed to outrun the explosion. Heat licked his backside and the lower level caught fire.

Fire alarms sounded. He was thankful they weren't anything like the ear-splitting anti-vampire alarms the incubi had.

Once the ball of gas had burned off, Matthew doubled back to make sure the lord was dead. She was. Her crispy body crumbled into a pile of ash.

Five down. Three to go.

Matthew sped up the stairs. Three non-lord vampires were at the top waiting for him. Matthew unzipped his jacket and flung silvered throwing knives into them. They all reeled back in pain. Killing two, Matthew pinned the third against the wall and drank deeply. He forced his senses to stay open while he fed. He couldn't risk being vulnerable.

A scream grabbed his attention.

The succubus.

He broke away and dropped the vampire to the ground.

The second level was filling with smoke and she still had to breathe. Running to her, he found her alone. The vampires had left the poor thing tied up to the table. Matthew wasn't sure where the other three lords were right now. They were suppressing their auras and the chaos of the vampires scattering made it hard for him to figure out who was who.

Fear ran through her and she shrunk away from him as he approached. He didn't have time to calm her. He set down his sword, pulled power into his strength, and ripped apart each of the chains holding her.

Once she was free, he grabbed her and his sword, and ran out of the building, through the back door. He set her down on the edge of a fountain. A couple of younger vampires in the backyard shrunk away when they saw Matthew.

"Are you alright?" he asked as he took off his leather jacket and wrapped it around her naked body.

She just stared at him. Fear pumped through her. Matthew forced his eyes to return to silver and his claws and fangs to recede.

"I work for Lord General Tarrick. You don't need to fear me. What's your name?"

That seemed to help her a little. "Priscilla. Are you really an incubus?"

"I am. And a vampire. Both."

"The High King let you come save us?"

"No. I'll be punished but I accept it. How long have you been here?"

Priscilla bowed her head forward. "Twenty-three years, one hundred and fifty-two days."

Jesus. How could they just leave her here to be used this way? How could Tarrick allow this? Wasn't he their fucking general?

The back of Matthew's neck tingled. Nearby something felt off. He turned.

Crossing the lawn, a tall, winged lord approached; he was the one who had been speaking the strange language earlier. Behind him were eleven gargoyles.

Matthew stepped between them and Priscilla.

"You've made a grave mistake coming to our house tonight," the lord growled at him.

Matthew scoffed. "People keep telling me that I've made all sorts of mistakes tonight but I'm not so sure."

The lord pointed forward and commanded the gargoyles in another language.

Nothing happened.

He repeated the command.

Matthew laughed. "So here's the thing...I asked these gargoyles to show up and I don't think they like you as much as they like me. I'm not really sure what happened to your gargoyles, but I'm going to guess this lot killed them."

The lord's face dropped as he turned to the gargoyles he thought he was commanding. He flapped his wings to take off but the gargoyles were on him before he was even a foot in the air.

Matthew grabbed Priscilla and buried her head in his chest so that she couldn't see them ripping the vampire apart. It was gruesome, even for him.

Six down. Two to go.

When the gargoyles were done, Asper—covered in blood—walked over to them, sat down, and froze in place. The other gargoyles took to the air and began hunting down vampires that were fleeing the burning house. Each terrifying mass of living rock made short work of any vampire unlucky enough to get caught by one. Matthew could feel that they were enjoying themselves. It was scary shit.

"Thanks, I owe you one," Matthew said to Asper. "Can you keep her safe for a bit?"

"Yeeesssss," Asper said with a deep gravelly voice.

Matthew blinked. They could talk?

Well. Okay then.

"Thanks again," Matthew said and then addressed Priscilla, "Stay with Asper, I'm going to get the others and we'll leave."

He wanted to stay and kill Savass and Victor—the only two lords still alive—but it was more important to get her and the others out of here. She was in shock. Twenty-five years was long enough; she didn't need to spend another moment in this place.

Leaving her, Matthew made his way to a plain looking structure farther back. It was only two stories and not raised off the ground. The windows were all boarded from the inside and he could sense four incubi and as many vampires. He gripped his sword tight and smashed open the front door.

He pushed power into his speed and the two vampires that came rushing at him were dead before they even had a chance to swing their own weapons. Running deeper into the building, he came to a closed door, behind it was the incubi and the two lord vampires.

Matthew kicked the door open.

Victor and Savass stood before him. Savass had her clawed hand wrapped around a succubus' neck. The succubus' arms were shackled behind her back. There was also an incubus and two other succubi in small cramped cages. To fit, they had to sit with their knees drawn to their chests and what few clothes they had on were in bad shape. The conditions were terrible.

Matthew growled.

"Drop the sword," Victor demanded.

Savass' claws pressed harder into the succubus' neck

The succubus was Tarrick's daughter, Lena. In her human form, she had the same dirty blond hair and blue eyes as Tarrick. And although she had been captured for over four months, she held herself tall, unwilling to be broken by the vampires.

Matthew was at a disadvantage here and couldn't risk her life. He dropped the sword.

"The throwing knives too."

Matthew threw the sash of throwing knives on the ground.

Victor's red eyes roamed up and down Matthew. "We can fight if we must but my offer for you to join us still stands."

Matthew let out a disbelieving laugh. "I just killed six of your lords, well technically five, but I'm going to count the sixth anyway, and burned your house down and you still want me?"

"I can rebuild a house and I can forgive you for killing my friends because of who you are."

"And who am I?"

Victor smiled. "Join me and find out."

"Even if I wanted to, I can't." Matthew pulled off his bloodied, ripped turtleneck to reveal his bracers and collar. Behind Victor, Lena tried to pull away from Savass but she grabbed her tighter, choking her until she settled.

Victor ignored the scuffle and focused on Matthew. "Those are only a minor setback. Incubi think they have a monopoly on witches but that isn't the case anymore. You have tremendous power within you, that you haven't even begun to tap into yet. Leave these worthless incubi behind. You are destined for greatness. I know you feel it within you. Fight by my side and I'll show you what you are truly capable of. I won't make you kneel before me. I won't put a collar on you."

God, his words were so tempting. He was offering Matthew everything he had ever wanted. Someone to teach him his power, not enslave and use him.

Matthew's eyes drifted to Lena, who seemed confused by the exchange she was watching, then back to Victor.

"And you'll tell me who my sire is?"

"Yes, I will."

"Release the incubi, let them go home," Matthew said.

Victor's face twisted with displeasure. "No. I will not tolerate any loyalty to the incubi, not if we are to fight side by side."

Again, Matthew felt torn. He wanted to be free. He wanted to be with his people—both of his people. But he couldn't have everything he wanted. If he left, he'd be free but he'd be giving up the incubi...Rosaline... Tarrick. For all his convincing that he was using Tarrick, the truth was that he wanted the general and he was unable to ignore the desire that burned within him.

"Alright," he finally agreed. "I'll join you but if this is a trick or you try to enslave me I will kill you."

"This is no trick. I am not an incubus. I give you my word, and that means something among us. Kill her and prove to me your willingness to fight them," Victor said, motioning to Lena.

Matthew's vampire side came forward as he picked up his sword. He grabbed Lena by her arm and drove his sword through her stomach. And kept going, pushing the weapon through Savass' lower abdomen, impaling them both onto the wall.

Lena screamed in pain, and behind her Savass hissed as she tried to free herself from the sword that skewered them both.

"Stay. Don't move," Mathew ordered Savass. It was easier to compel her this time. She fell silent and slumped.

Before he could pull the sword out of the two women, Victor let out a bellowing roar. He moved blindingly fast as he grabbed Matthew by his shoulders and slammed him through the wall. Plaster and wood flew around them.

Victor held tight and kept going, using Matthew's body like a battering ram, smashing through the next room's wall, then the next, and the next, until finally Matthew's body hit the thick exterior wall and the two of them burst out of the house.

Matthew pushed healing into his broken body as Victor tossed him across the lawn. The gargoyles, high above them, paid him no mind.

Victor's wings spread out and he took to the air. He dove down for an attack but Matthew rolled out of the way and sprung to his feet. He pushed power into his speed and ran into the burning main house.

The old vampire lord was right behind him, relentless.

The main floor was beginning to collapse. A hole formed in front of Matthew's feet and he clumsily jumped over it. Victor, with far more grace, bound over the hole but debris from above rained down and he disappeared into the lower level when it hit him.

It was a small break in Matthew's favor, but he didn't think for a moment that this would slow Victor down. Victor was faster, stronger, and far more experienced than Matthew had expected.

He had to find a way to even the playing field.

Matthew ran into the throne room. Heavy smoke clouded the air making it nearly impossible to see anything as he searched for his duffle bag. He shuffled around until he found it and took out the silver chain. He wrapped it around one of his gloved fists, then he took out the crossbow and three bolts and dipped them into the brown liquid before loading one.

Using the thick smoke to his advantage, he stood as silent and still as possible so it would be harder for Victor to sense him. He pulled threads of power into his hearing to pinpoint Victor, who came rushing into the room a fraction of a second later.

He aimed and loosed the bolt. Victor grunted as the bolt hit him. Matthew hoped he hit a blood pouch, where the foxglove would slow his healing, weakening him.

Matthew reloaded and brought the crossbow back up. Before he could fire, Victor appeared out of the smoke and swiped the weapon from his hand. It shattered on the ground.

Matthew punched Victor in the face with his chained fist and followed up by stabbing Victor in the arm with his last remaining bolt.

Victor pulled both bolts from himself and clawed at Matthew, who brought up his arms to defend, receiving deep cuts on them.

The floor below his feet groaned and buckled. Victor jumped upwards and grabbed a beam while Matthew went crashing down a level. The duffle had landed right next to him and spilled the remainder of its contents out as he landed on his back. Hot flames licked his body and he could smell his skin burning. Cries of pain escaped him.

Fuck.

He had to focus, he'd die if he stayed here with the fire burning the damned house down around him.

He grabbed a stake that had rolled next to him and leaped upwards. Victor was gone. The house groaned.

God damn it.

He bound up what was left of the stairs, going up and up until he found a door that exited to the roof. Once outside, he took a moment to try and heal his blistered and blackened skin. He poured his remaining power into healing, he didn't have time to conserve. That was a tactical error on his part.

Victor was behind him and he hadn't even sensed him. The old vampire wrapped a claw around the back of Matthew's neck and leaped into the air. His wings flapped furiously as he gained height, then released Matthew's neck with a push. Matthew's body twisted in the air, but he didn't plummet to the ground like he thought he would, instead Victor grabbed his ankle and continued his ascent.

Before they could achieve a height that Matthew couldn't survive a drop from, he rolled himself up and pushed the stake he was still holding into Victor's heart.

Victor's wings froze as if stuck in place, leaving them gliding for a moment.

The old vampire laughed and pulled the stake from his chest, tossing it away. "You are a young fool," he said and his wings began flapping once more.

Matthew fought the urge to sigh and wished someone had told him that stakes weren't all that effective on ancient vampires. He wasn't sure what he could do here...except die. The older vampire didn't have a scratch on him anymore while Matthew was burned, cut, and running on empty. He struggled in vain as they rose higher and higher.

Desperate, he needed to try something, anything, he unwound the silver chain from his fist. Victor released him and Matthew went plummeting down but not before he managed to toss the chain up with the last of his power.

It warped around Victor's neck and Matthew held tight. When the chain ran out of slack it yanked the lord down with him.

Caught off-guard, Victor went plunging down. He clawed at the chain tightening around his neck but it stayed in place, his wings flapped frantically to slow their descent.

Matthew used the distraction to climb up the chain and swing himself onto Victor's back. With no blood energy left to heal him, Matthew wasn't sure he could survive a fall from hundreds of feet up, but he couldn't let Victor live either. He made his choice. He clawed both of Victor's wings, shredding them.

Victor healed his wings back almost as fast as they were damaged.

Fuck.

Matthew grabbed the base of a wing and pulled. He wasn't strong enough right now to rip it out completely but he managed to dislocate it.

Victor turned his attention away from the chain and back to Matthew. He turned midair and clawed wildly, shredding Matthew's legs to pieces.

Matthew pushed off against him, separating the two of them. Below him, the roof of the second house was fast filling his vision.

Victor was in a tumbling free fall above him.

Matthew wasn't sure of the best way to land; no matter how he hit the building he was going to die or fall unconscious until someone forced blood into him. Assuming she wasn't already dead, Lena would die too, since he was going to lose his hold on Savass.

He was actually amazed he still had control of the lord at all.

Seconds before hitting the roof, he felt solid stone arms wrap around him and his descent turned into a swift glide. The arms released him a few feet above the ground and he went tumbling on the grass.

Behind him a cloud of dust and debris flew into the air as Victor smashed into the house hard.

Matthew couldn't believe it. A gargoyle had grabbed him. It wasn't Asper, she was sitting over with Priscilla. This one was bigger and looked as if it was carved from black stone. Its head had two rows of short horns starting at its forehead and going all the way down to its wings.

Matthew took a deep breath in so he could speak. "Thanks."

The gargoyle's only response was to take off flying back into the air.

"Are you okay?" Priscilla asked leaning over Matthew who was still lying on the grass. He was exhausted and spent.

"Hungry, get away from me." Her smell was unbelievable and her pulse drummed in his ear. His fangs itched to be in her.

"You can take a little from me. I'm used to it," she offered.

"No, I'll find blood somewhere else."

She went down to her knees and held her wrist up to his mouth. "Where? Can you even stand? If you don't kill him, I'll never be free. Just take a little."

Matthew could probably stand but it would take some effort, and there was no way he could fight Victor right now.

He grabbed her wrist and pressed it to his lips. Gently, he eased his fangs in and drank. She stilled for him, and he didn't take much blood, a few pulls, just enough to get him going again. Pushing away the feeling of euphoria, he removed his fangs and licked her wrist.

"Thank you," he said and sat up.

"Please kill him," she pleaded, her voice shaking.

"I will." Matthew pushed himself to his feet and looked around for a weapon. He couldn't find any.

Maybe he could get to those silver daggers inside.

With no other choice, he ran into the building, through the holes in the walls his body had made, to the room with the captured incubi.

Lena was still alive but weak. Her droopy eyes followed Matthew as he grabbed two daggers off the floor. Savass looked dazed, still pinned behind her.

Matthew could sense Victor close. Very close. He opened the door to the room and in the hallway was Victor. Above, the ceiling was gone.

Victor was alive and awake but impaled on a wooden beam. It was long, ten feet or more, and went right through his chest. He was trying to pull himself off it but it seemed stakes did have some effect on older vampires and it was weakening him.

Matthew started laughing. "Of all the things…" he stopped. He couldn't allow himself the feeling of triumph until Victor was dead for good.

Matthew dropped the daggers and went back into the room.

"Sorry," he said to Lena as he pulled the sword out of the two women. "I'll heal you in a moment."

He walked back to Victor and raised the sword above his head.

"Prince—" was the last word Victor said as Matthew brought the sword down on his neck. The ancient vampire's body turned to dust around him. He had never seen a vampire decompose that fast.

Seven down. One to go.

On the ground behind him, Lena groaned. She struggled weakly against her shackles to no avail.

Matthew kneeled beside her and brushed a strand of hair out of her eyes. She tried to speak but blood gurgled up from her throat.

Matthew leaned in and kissed her. She resisted at first. She had been captured long before knowledge that Matthew was an incubus had become public and she had no idea who he was. He pushed energy into her so that she would begin to heal. Her lips responded and she took over, drawing from him what she needed.

She broke away when she had taken everything Matthew had to give. His soavik rippled with pain but he ignored it for now. There were more pressing matters.

"What the pit are you?" she asked, still lying on the ground. The sword wound had healed enough but it was raw and threatened to reopen if she wasn't careful. She'd need to feed again soon.

"I'm an incubus that was turned into a vampire. I belong to House Tarrick, Lady Lena." Matthew couldn't help but smile a little when he thought of Tarrick.

She studied him for a moment. "Dad's fucking you, isn't he?"

"Uh, well—"

"And it's 'Talena' if you are going to use the 'lady' title. Did he actually send you to come get me?"

"Does he name all his children with a 'Ta' at the beginning? And of course not, do you think he would ever disobey an order from the High King?"

"All of us start with T-A, yes. And you disobeyed an order from the High King? Whatever the hell you are, you are in deep shit. I mean, thanks for saving my life, that was a hell of a kiss too, but you are so screwed."

Matthew laughed. She was nothing like Tarrick or Tane. "Believe me, I know. If I unshackle you, are you going to attack me?"

"No. But if you could never stab me again, I'd appreciate it." She motioned to Savass. "I might kill her, though. Did you compel her?"

"Yes. Leave her, I need her blood." Matthew left the room and dug his foot through Victor's ashes. He found a set of keys, returned, and unshackled Lena. Matthew handed the keys to Lena so she could free the other incubi.

"You can compel vampires?" She seemed to want to hear the answer a second time.

"And incubi. And even a hunter that is going to kick my ass when I get back." Thinking of what he had to do to Silva pained him all over again. He hoped that once she knew his reasons she'd be able to forgive him.

"We had one more with us," she said.

"Priscilla is waiting outside with Asper."

"Asper's here?"

Matthew nodded.

Lena mouthed the word 'wow' then began unlocking the cages.

"Wait for me outside. I'll join you in a moment," he told them and they left, led by Lena.

Matthew grabbed Savass and pushed her against the wall. He sunk his fangs into her neck and drank deep. He used the lord's powerful blood to heal his injuries. When he was finished draining her, he was physically healed but mentally exhausted. And he could use more blood but it'd do for now.

Savass was limp in his arms. He removed his fangs and let her drop to the ground.

Eight down. None to go.

Matthew smiled.

He had won.

Forty

Matthew relaxed into the hot shower water as blood and ash and small bits of guts washed off him.

He had already escorted the incubi to the car he acquired earlier. Asper had taken to the sky the moment the group collected Priscilla.

The fire at the main house was still raging, but when they stepped outside of the gates, magic masked it and the fire could not be seen or sensed by outsiders.

Matthew was relieved that Lena knew how to drive seeing as the group couldn't fly—their wings had been clipped. When he grew concerned that they'd never be able to fly again, she assured him that in time they would heal.

They parted ways—Matthew planning to run back. With five incubi, the car was out of space anyway. He gave her the sword in case they ran into any trouble but he didn't sense any vampires nearby anymore.

Lena suggested Matthew wait a bit before heading back. She wanted to talk to her father first and soften him a bit. Matthew was a hundred percent okay with trying anything that might lessen Tarrick's anger. The plan was to wait for an hour and a half before returning.

He used the time to shower in the structure that had housed the incubi. In addition to holding prisoners, there were rooms for servants, guards, and lesser vampires. It was completely empty now. Matthew went through a few rooms until he found one with clothes that would fit him, and he was thrilled to find the water was working.

After the shower, he washed the bottom of his boots off and put on a black shirt that fitted a little tight for him, and jeans sized decently enough. He sat down on the bed and savored a few moments of peace. He had no idea what Tarrick was going to do to him. He had disobeyed. He knew the High King's commands and did it anyway.

'Prince'. That's what Victor had said…what had he meant by that? Was his sire a king? He didn't even know if vampires had kings.

Still hours until sunrise, Matthew stood and stretched. He went to the kitchen and ripped the gas line out of the wall. He wasn't going to leave this place standing.

Grabbing matches, he went to the front door and waited for the house to fill with gas. Then he set it ablaze.

With time to kill, he watched it burn until it was time to leave.

He'd take it a little slower going back this time. It would take him about twenty minutes to return. He had no trouble until he was about three minutes away from the keep.

He was running past a place called Inniswold when a green flash appeared in front of him on an empty side street. He had to brake hard and swerve to the right to avoid hitting the hunter. He tripped and skidded across asphalt landing on his back.

The Argonauts—the team including Prescott and Hiroto—appeared. Silva was with them as well. Before Matthew could tell them that he wasn't going to fight, Silva shot a silver bolt into his stomach piercing a blood pouch and streams of silver chains wrapped around him.

And he had just showered too. Now he looked like crap again with road rash and a bloody abdomen. Not to mention the burning chains.

"Stop," Matthew cried. Another bolt went into him. Pain began to flare through him as his body had trouble keeping up with all the burning silver. "Please, I'm not resisting."

Not that he could if he wanted. They had him pinned by chains he couldn't break and they were rapidly stealing away the little reserves he had right now.

Prescott, in his full armor and horned helm, stood above him. He held his hand out and a syringe full of liquid appeared in it with a flash of green light. He leaned over, injected it into Matthew, and then pulled the bolts from him.

Matthew expected to be knocked out but instead it just dulled his senses and dazed him. He couldn't clear it from his system like he could other poisons.

A van pulled up and they shackled Matthew to the seat. Silver shackles too. They were not giving him any breaks tonight. He wondered if Lena had shown up yet.

The hunters reported that they had him and piled into the van. Matthew watched them sit in silence. They all looked pissed off. Even Hiroto, who normally had smiling eyes, looked displeased.

But it was Silva's eyes that burned into him. Matthew glanced at her and looked away, ashamed.

"Silva, I…" He grunted in pain from all the silver on him.

"Don't speak unless you are asked a question," Prescott told him.

"Silva, I'm sorry," Matthew said, ignoring Prescott's order.

Silva leaned forward and slapped him hard across his face. Then she retrieved a hard leather bit gag from a box under a seat. "Open your mouth, vampire."

Matthew obeyed and she gagged him. The physical pain of the silver and emotional one he was facing now, coupled with the fatigue of the fight, was too much. Tears welled in his eyes.

The rest of the ride passed in painful silence. Once they arrived at Lord Brodeur's keep, they dragged Matthew inside. Incubi, still here from the party, lined the room, leaving the center of the ballroom cleared. Rosaline was standing in the crowd. She looked concerned. Tane was standing next to her, smirking.

Before Matthew were several empty thrones.

Heavy hands pushed Matthew down to both of his knees.

Tarrick, with violet eyes, horns, and claws, emerged from a side room still wearing his tuxedo. Matthew could feel the rage rolling off him.

Brodeur, who had dark hair and matching eyes, trailed behind, looking extremely smug. Tonight Matthew had proven Brodeur was right, having a vampire around incubi was too dangerous—they couldn't be trusted. Or so Brodeur thought. It was clear Lena and the others hadn't arrived yet. Where the fuck were they?

"Whip and foxglove," Tarrick ordered to the hunters.

Tarrick stopped in front of Matthew and loomed above him while Brodeur walked up onto his platform and sat on his throne, settling in for the show.

A bucket of liquid foxglove and a whip was set on the ground beside Tarrick.

If Tarrick started whipping him, Matthew wouldn't be conscious for long, the silver was eating away at him.

Tarrick growled. "I have to say, I'm impressed with how you escaped. It took us a little bit to piece together everything you had done. It was a long play that I did not see coming and I am not an easy man to fool. I'm particularly impressed by the lengths you went through to end up at this party. I didn't think you had the capacity or patience for this level of manipulation."

Matthew wasn't proud he had manipulated Tarrick while they were in bed together. Having Tarrick hold him had felt so good, now it might never happen again.

"But I guess I always underestimate you. I can assure you that will never happen again. We know you went to House Moreau. Why did you come back? Were the vampires not what you expected? Or did they kick you out?"

The questions were rhetorical since Matthew still had the gag in his mouth. Tarrick had already made up his mind about what had happened and the general wasn't bothering to hide any of his emotions right now. Pure anger replaced his normally collected demeanor. In a way, Matthew didn't blame him. From Tarrick's point of view, the vampire he had spent the last year trying to convince the incubi world to accept, had just betrayed him—and it had happened in front of the very people who wanted to see him fail.

"You should not have waited so long to return. Your punishment will be like nothing you've experienced before," Tarrick promised. "Press both your palms on the floor."

Matthew leaned over and put his still-shackled hands on the ground. He whimpered…he didn't want to be whipped. Unwilling to wait on Lena anymore, he let out a muffled cry as he tried to speak.

"Silence. I will remove your tongue if you try to speak again," Tarrick said, standing behind him.

Matthew fell silent.

Tarrick grabbed the whip and dipped it into the brown liquid in the bucket. He flicked the whip forward, it cracked against Matthew's back, ripping his shirt and splitting his skin apart. The foxglove prevented the wound from healing naturally, and Matthew didn't want to push power into it because healing might encourage Tarrick to whip him more.

A second strike hit his skin. And a third. By the fourth, Matthew was crying out each time.

Laughter came from Brodeur as he watched the vampire get tortured. It wasn't just him either. He had plenty of like-minded friends in the crowd that took great pleasure from watching Matthew be whipped.

Matthew's claws came out but he kept his palms on the floor. If he tried to get up, hunters would just push him back down and they'd probably use more silver chains to do it.

There was a commotion in the crowd but Tarrick took no note. He lashed Matthew a fifth time and pulled his arm back to whip him again.

"Devil, Father, did you even bother to ask him why he went to New Orleans? Or did you just dive right into whipping him?"

Everything stopped.

Matthew couldn't see what was happening but he didn't need to. He could feel the different waves of emotions radiating from Tarrick: confusion, shock, disbelief…love for his daughter.

The whip he was holding dropped to the ground and Matthew could hear him running to her. He twisted his head back and saw Lena in Tarrick's arms, who held her tight and kissed her head. Tane rushed over as well and joined in, embracing his sister.

The other four incubi entered the room behind her. Including Priscilla, who was dressed now.

Brodeur stood from his throne and whispered, "Priscilla…you're alive?" Matthew racked his brain to try and recall any information he had on Priscilla but nothing came up.

"Father," Priscilla cried out. Ah, if she was presumed dead Rosaline wouldn't have bothered to tell Matthew about her. Almost all incubi had dead children.

Brodeur's reaction was the same as Tarrick's. He rushed over and grabbed his daughter up in his arms. The other three also had people who knew them in the crowd and were quickly surrounded by friends and family.

Matthew smiled as he felt the joy coming off the incubi in the room. It made him feel as if it was all worth it even though the pain was agonizing right now. He hoped that maybe Tarrick would show some mercy and knock him out, give him blood, or at least take off the silver.

Lena broke away from Tarrick and Tane and walked over to Matthew, who was still hunched over on the floor, burning from the silver shackles and bleeding from his back.

She crouched down in front of him and touched his face. "Sorry we're late, we had to stop for gas. Then we got distracted by a hot attendant."

Of course they had. Fucking incubi.

"How did you get out of House Moreau? How did you get past the lords?" Tarrick asked from behind Matthew.

"You should have let him speak. He is your warrior, isn't he?" Lena asked.

"Lord General. Imperator," a hunter who was wearing what looked to be mobile communication gear around his neck called out. "We're getting confirmed reports that the vampires of New Orleans are fleeing the city in mass."

Shocked whispers filled the room.

Lena slipped Matthew's gag off him and guided him so he was sitting back on his knees.

Matthew chuckled and she joined him.

"What is so funny?" Tarrick asked.

"They're leaving the city because there are no more lords left in New Orleans to protect them," Lena said.

Brodeur stepped forward but didn't release his daughter. "What? Impossible. They've held that location for centuries. They'd never abandon their city."

Matthew used the few strands of power he had left to temporarily take away his pain. He wouldn't be able to do it for long, just long enough to prevent his voice from shaking. "They didn't abandon their city. I killed them all."

Silence fell on the room.

A sharp gasp came from Rosaline. Confusion and relief crossed her face. "They're dead?"

"Yes." Matthew looked up at her. "They touched you without your permission. I took offense and now they never will again."

"You did this for me?" she asked. Her red lips quivered and her green eyes watered.

"Yes. And for Master Tarrick. To bring his daughter back. To bring all the incubi back."

Tarrick walked around Matthew. He said nothing as he studied him through his violet eyes.

"You should have seen it, Dad. Victor offered him his freedom. Offered to tell him who his sire was, offered him power...and Matthew killed him..." Lena stood and straightened herself out. Her body became stiff and formal as she looked at Tarrick. "I'll have my full report to you by tomorrow, sir."

She moved away and took a place next to Tane, who wrapped an arm around his sister.

Tarrick still said nothing. It was as if he was still processing, or trying to come up with a decision on what he should do with Matthew right now.

Behind him, Prescott stepped forward. He still had his helmet on, and Matthew wondered what he looked like under there.

"I'm going to order other teams down. We could kill many while they are running panicked."

Tarrick nodded. Prescott called in the order for all available teams to head to Louisiana and left with the rest of the Argonauts to coordinate the attacks. There were still plenty of other hunters in the room, including Silva, who was stone-faced and unreadable.

Pain from the silver and the whippings returned to Matthew. He couldn't keep it away any longer. He grunted and slumped forward. His chains rattled as he put his hands back on the ground to steady himself.

"Remove the silver shackles and put him in steel," Tarrick commanded.

Hunters pulled Matthew to his feet and swapped out his shackles. He felt a little better but he needed blood. And some sex. But he didn't want to ask for anything right now, not in front of all these incubi who hated him.

Matthew dropped down to his left knee and bowed to Tarrick.

"Look at me."

Matthew did as ordered.

Tarrick reached down and touched his face. Matthew leaned into him and some of his pain lessened. Tarrick's touch always felt so good, especially when he was hungry. His fangs itched as he heard blood rushing below the skin.

Tarrick smiled. "Eight lords, Matthew?"

"Technically seven, Master. Gargoyles got one," Matthew said, his voice tired.

"Whose gargoyles?"

"Yours, Master."

"Asper?" he asked, his head tilted to the side slightly.

Matthew nodded.

"Did you command her?"

"No, Master. I don't think I can do that. I just asked nicely."

"Did Victor really know who your sire was?"

"He seemed to, Master." Matthew didn't want to go into too many details with other incubi around. Everything he said would turn into gossip.

"And you turned that down and came back. Why?" Tarrick wasn't asking for himself, he had already worked out the answer—if he hadn't, Matthew would still be in silver shackles. This was the show.

"Because I'm an incubus. I belong here." Regardless of why Tarrick asked him, the answer was the truth.

It was the first time Matthew truly believed he was an incubus. He was one of them and he would stay here with them. He needed to be part of something and this was that something.

Matthew could hear some whispering in the crowd. He couldn't make out what they were saying because of the drug running through him. He was getting hungrier. This night had been so draining for him. Tears threatened to well but he refused to show any sign of weakness right now. His red eyes drifted to Tarrick's neck and watched the skin move with every pulse. God, it was beautiful.

Tarrick looked over Matthew to the assembly of incubi.

"Lord Brodeur, earlier tonight you were convinced Matthew would be useless to us. That he offered nothing more than what our warriors and hunters can do. Now that you have your daughter in your arms, do you still hold to that?"

"He disobeyed the High King's command..." Brodeur said.

"I'm well aware, that won't go unpunished, but that wasn't my question. He killed eight lords. When was the last time we killed eight lords in a night, other than during an assault or battle with major losses? Not a single incubus died tonight."

"But look at him, he's still a vampire." Lord Brodeur's voice was weak, crumbling.

"He saved me," Priscilla whispered to her father.

"We thought you were dead...if I had known..."

Matthew stopped caring about their conversation. The gentle thud of Tarrick's heart was getting louder each moment Tarrick kept skin contact. Matthew licked his lips. He instinctively reached out with an incubus hold and wrapped it around Tarrick.

Tarrick looked down and smiled at him. "You'll be taken care of soon, Matthew."

Matthew heard Tarrick ask for hawthorn, the drug that could knock a vampire out, followed by a warm feeling spreading through his body.

He passed out a moment later.

Forty-One

Matthew frowned when he awoke inside a jail cell in Tarrick's keep. He had hoped he'd be waking in his own room, or better yet, in Tarrick's. His soavik ached and he needed to feed sexually. Right now he wasn't too picky about who he had sex with, but the prison was empty. There weren't even hunters in the observation room or out in the hallway.

At least he had been given blood at some point. And he was well rested now. He wasn't quite sure but he guessed it had been about eleven days since he was knocked out. Jeez.

Were they having more discussions about him? Eleven days was a long time to be talking about someone.

The shower turned on and Matthew jumped into it. Once he was clean and dry he dressed in the clothes that had been sitting at the edge of the bed. Black shirt, jeans, boots, the usual.

He sat down and waited.

Thoughts of Tarrick bending him over and fucking him hard filled Matthew's mind. He couldn't help it. His hungry body was instinctively trying to force him to seek out food.

He shifted around to readjust the growing erection in his jeans and after a while he stood and began to pace around his cell, trying to get his mind off the hunger. Bored, he reached out with his senses to try and listen in on some conversations to pass the time only to be disappointed when he heard nothing. It seemed Tarrick had added stronger wards around the prison.

Matthew growled.

An hour later Tarrick entered, alone. He was wearing his uniform: the embroidered grey jacket with the white button-up shirt and tight black trousers tucked into his polished riding boots.

Matthew drank him in for a moment until the general shot him a harsh glance. Matthew went to his knee and bowed.

Tarrick said nothing for so long that Matthew thought he was waiting on him to do something. He glanced up and Tarrick scowled at him. Matthew bowed his head back down. His mind kept drifting to thoughts of Tarrick having his way with him.

"Stand," Tarrick finally said.

Matthew did so and adjusted his pants.

Tarrick stood just a few feet away from his cage. He clasped his hands behind his back and stood rigid. "Thank you for saving my daughter," he said, his voice formal, cold.

Something was wrong here. "Thank you for saving mine."

Tarrick nodded. "Regrettably, your actions have had some unforeseen consequences."

"I already know you are going to punish me. I expect it, Master."

"I won't be punishing you."

He wouldn't be?

"That doesn't mean you aren't going to be punished, it's just not going to be by me," Tarrick said.

"Then by who?"

Tarrick didn't answer his question and instead asked one of his own. "Do you know what Victor meant when he said 'prince' to you?"

Matthew had hoped that Lena hadn't heard that, he wanted to keep that to himself. Guess she had. "No idea. Do you know?"

He shook his head. "No."

At least Tarrick was answering his questions. Matthew paced a bit back and forth in the cell, thinking. "Do vampires have kings, Master? Maybe I was sired by one of them."

"In a way. There is one. *She* is queen only because she's the oldest known vampire. She doesn't really rule them per se but she'll act in their interests. If she signs a truce with us, the vampires would respect it. For a time anyway. If you were sired by her, we would know it."

"How would you know?"

"She'd tell us. She and High King Malarath are friendly, depending on the century."

"They are?" The oldest vampire and the incubi ruler got along? That seemed...odd considering the war.

"They are great foes as well. It's complicated. But trust me, if she turned someone we would know. And she would never break the bond with one of her own sired children." Tarrick ran his hand over his jaw, thinking. "There are rumors of ancient vampires, so old they've turned into statues. Victor might call one a king if it woke." Tarrick was lost in thought for a moment then said, "Maybe you are destined to become a Sanguine Dominar..."

"What's that?"

"Death. I think it's unlikely. You show none of the signs." Tarrick didn't look like he was going to elaborate any further.

"You aren't going to feed me, are you, Master?" Matthew asked and put his hands on his lower abs. He found the information about the vampire queen fascinating but he was unable to get his mind off his hunger.

"No. I've been ordered not to." That meant the High King ordered Tarrick. Matthew had come to understand that he was the only one who outranked Tarrick when it came to military matters. And Matthew was a military matter. "You can ask for more blood if you need it," Tarrick added.

"I'm good on blood, unless you're offering yours," Matthew said with a slight smile.

"I'm not."

Matthew's smiled dropped. Tarrick was grim.

"The High King has made a decision about you. An official ruling." Tarrick paused, giving Matthew a moment to prepare for what he was going to say next.

Matthew came as close as he could to Tarrick, standing right in front of the silver plated bars that separated them.

"You are too powerful, too clever, to be allowed to continue with the amount of freedom you have been shown so far."

"What…?" Matthew said. He hardly had any freedoms.

Tarrick continued, ignoring Matthew. "You are being transferred to another facility where you will be kept caged except during training or when ordered to a battle."

"No…" He was going to be caged again. Alone. Anger rose within him.

Tarrick clenched his teeth and continued. "The facility you are being moved to is in the High King's tower. He will be taking over your care personally. You will be calling him 'Master' from now on and I will be addressed as 'Lord General'."

"I came back…"

"I know you did, Matthew."

Matthew balled his hands into fists. "I was offered everything and I came back."

"I know."

"I am loyal."

"Not everyone is convinced that you are."

Matthew looked him in the eyes. "Are you?"

"I think you believe that you are loyal. But loyalty isn't something that can be proven in a year. Give me a decade or two and I might be convinced."

"Please, Master. I don't want to be caged. Torture me for a while and let me come back," he pleaded, knowing it would be useless. Tarrick would never defy the High King.

Tarrick said nothing, standing like a statue.

"Please…don't let them lock me up alone. I'm an incubus. I don't want to be alone again. I need to be with my people."

"You will be moved to New York tomorrow night."

"I want to stay with you. I…" Matthew loved him but the words stuck in his throat. He was too scared.

"You don't love me," Tarrick said it for him.

"I do," Matthew whispered. Conflicting emotions battled inside of him. He was terrified…he had no idea what was going to happen to him and he was losing all control again. The desire to stay with Tarrick, to be close to him, swelled up.

"You don't. It was all manufactured to control you."

Matthew stared at him. "No. That's not true. I know how I feel."

Tarrick's face betrayed nothing. "Incubi are masters of manipulating emotion, you know this, and I have been breaking vampires since I was young. I am exceedingly skilled in doing so. None of it was real."

None? Everything had felt real. Even now, Matthew knew he loved him and wanted to be around him. "I don't believe you. I can feel when you are manipulating me. I can break away from your holds."

Tarrick shook his head. "You could at first, but I adjusted and every time after, I let you think you were breaking from me. It is an old incubus trick. I used your inexperience against you. Given your power, I have no doubt you'll learn to spot when it's happening in the future. Your ability to adapt and learn is truly phenomenal."

Matthew snarled at him. He didn't want his praise right now. Not while his heart was breaking.

"Everything you felt was engineered so that you would feel closer to me," Tarrick said. Cold.

Tears fell down Matthew's face. "Why would you do such a terrible thing?"

"The High King is one of the oldest creatures on this planet. His interaction with life around him is different from the rest of us. I had thought you'd be under my care centuries before he took any real notice of you."

"And your plan was to—what?—have me love you for all that time?"

"Yes."

"And you feel nothing for me?"

"I am not devoid of feelings towards you. You are—" he paused as if looking for the right word and continued when he found it, "—*fascinating* and I'm proud of all your accomplishments here, but I do not love you if that is what you are asking. And you don't love me."

"Stop saying that!" Rage flared in Matthew and his eyes turned red. He did love him. He couldn't believe what Tarrick was saying. He felt so used. Betrayed. "How could you do this to me? How could you be so vicious?"

"Because love is the easiest way to control someone and I needed a way to control you."

Matthew took a step away from Tarrick and scratched at his chest above his heart. It ached. Deep inside of him, it ached. It was worse than any pain he had suffered before. His watery tears turned to blood and his legs trembled. No longer able to stand, he crashed down to his knees and grabbed a cage bar to steady himself. He didn't even notice the pain of the silver. "Why tell me now?"

"You are no longer mine and I think the truth is kinder than letting you long for something that will never be."

Matthew's eyes turned back to silver. Still kneeling on the floor he stopped moving. He felt empty inside. Numb. He didn't want to speak anymore. He didn't want to look at Tarrick anymore. He wanted nothingness to surround him and take away the pain.

"You should know that Lady Rosaline had no knowledge of any of this. I don't think she ever told you, but she belongs to House Malarath. The High King cares for her, which is why she outranks me. She'll be returning to New York in a few days. I believe it's so that she can try to convince the High King to change his mind about having you caged."

Matthew said nothing. Normally he'd be raging by now, trying to break down the cell to kill Tarrick. But he couldn't bring himself to feel anything but emptiness.

Tarrick gazed down at him. As he stood watching Matthew, his face softened as if he actually felt something, as if he might say something kind, but the moment passed and it became unreadable again.

Tarrick turned and marched from the room without saying another word.

Matthew stayed frozen in place all night. Every now and then a tear would escape and roll down his face before dropping to the floor.

Come sunrise he still hadn't moved. His body shut down for the day, still kneeling in front of the cell door, and he was in the same position the next night.

He didn't shower or change.

He stayed kneeling, feeling blank inside.

Around midnight, Silva entered the room trailed by the rest of the Wardens and a second team. They were armed to the teeth and all looked serious.

"Stand and put your arms through the slot," Silva said, shackles in hand.

Matthew didn't move. He didn't even know she was there.

She teleported behind him and jabbed him with a syringe, injecting him with something that dulled his senses, then shackled his hands behind his back.

"Stand up, Matthew," she said loud and firm. It worked to pull him from the trance.

He looked up blankly.

"I won't tell you again."

Matthew made his way to his feet as the cell door opened.

He was pushed from the cage and escorted to a van, where they chained him up.

Silva sat opposite him, and the van headed to Ashwood Academy. Matthew looked out the rear window as they pulled away from Tarrick's keep. It looked so dark and uninviting tonight. He watched until it disappeared as they drove up the twisting road.

Tears welled in his eyes.

He dropped his head and looked at the floor the rest of the trip. He had been such a fool. The incubi had played him. He wasn't one of them and never could be. Victor was right, it didn't matter what he was before he died—he was a vampire now.

He resolved to do everything in his power to undermine the incubi.

Once they arrived at Ashwood he was led to the stone. A handful of hunter cadets he recognized from his months of training saluted Silva as she passed by.

No. Not Silva. They were saluting *him*. It was earning them scowls from the hunters who escorted Matthew, but they continued the salute anyway.

Watching them was bittersweet. He was being dragged away to become nothing more than a weapon. He wished the incubi saw him as these cadets did, as a person, not a soulless machine for them to use.

He nodded to the hunters but couldn't bring himself to smile.

With no pause for ceremony, Silva activated the Ashwood stone, tele-

porting the group to what looked to be an empty floor of an office building, except there were no windows. Matthew was ushered outside. He was
in New York. Even late into the night, the sounds of the city assaulted his
ears. He had trouble adjusting because of the drug flowing through him.

They were on a narrow empty street, behind what looked to be an
abandoned brick building. A van was waiting for them, along with four
other cars—two in front and two behind—all full of hunters. He wondered why they hadn't just teleported directly to the High Kings 'tower',
as Tarrick called it.

Again, he was placed and chained into a van. The Wardens piled in—
four in the back, two up front. There were no windows in the back, but
that was fine with Matthew because he didn't really feel like watching
where they were driving anyway. He returned to looking down at the
floor of the van.

Every moment that passed was one closer to his prison.

Lost in self-pity, he almost didn't sense the vampires approaching until
they were practically on top of them.

Outside the van, an explosion took out the car in front of them. Chaos
erupted. The van crashed forcefully into something.

Matthew jerked so hard against his chains that they cut him deep.
Around him, the unsecured hunters tumbled on top of each other. He
pushed power into healing the best he could while still under the effects
of the drug.

The hunters in the van untangled themselves and readied weapons.

"Keep this van moving," Silva yelled at the driver. As he hit the gas a
vampire lord smashed through the windshield, ripped him from his seat,
and took off into the sky dragging the screaming hunter with him. It happened so fast that the hunter in the passenger seat didn't even have time to
squeeze the trigger of his readied crossbow.

Matthew listened to the hunter's comms. He heard a stream of panicked cries and confused calls.

"Vamps in New York? — This is impossible. — They've never attacked
here before. — They are attacking without wards. — GET VEILS UP,
NOW! — We need backup. — Is Matthew fighting for us? — There're at
least twenty vamps… — …five lords in the field… — Witches! They have
witches with them! — Where the hell is our backup? — Matthew is still
secured. Can we release him? — We need air support. — Backup is two
minutes away and Matthew is not to be released. — Two minutes? We'll
be dead by then. Half my team is down. — Do we have permission to re-

treat? — We need medics. Now!"

The sounds of crashing cars and screams filled the air. One by one Matthew felt the hunters dying around them. The hunter in the passenger seat teleported from the car to help fight but Matthew heard him die with a scream a moment later.

The back doors of Matthew's reinforced mobile vampire prison were ripped off their hinges and tossed aside as if they were nothing.

Standing there was Stolus, the vampire who had been in Tarrick's prison with Matthew, and his vampire lord sire, Ascelina.

Her red lips pulled into a knowing smile. "Hello again, Matthew."

Forty-Two

Bolts flew past Stolus and Ascelina as they rushed into the back of the van. Stolus ripped the hearts out of two hunters with his claws before they could reload.

Ascelina snapped the neck of another hunter, then grabbed Silva by her neck and drove her claw into her lower abdomen, through Silva's teleport rune, preventing her from leaving.

The vampire lord slammed Silva into the wall of the van and Silva's crossbow went flying out of her hand. She tried to draw a stake but Ascelina let go of her neck and swiped the weapon away as if it were only a small annoyance.

With lightning quick speed, Ascelina cut off Silva's sash of throwing daggers and her belt of weapons, letting them fall to the ground. She grabbed both of Silva's hands with her one and pinned them above her head. Silva struggled to get away but she couldn't match the strength of the vampire lord.

The fight going on outside the van seemed to be winding down as hunters who were still left alive retreated to regroup.

"Silva—" Ascelina hissed at her, "—you are going to kill Tarrick for me."

Silva spat at the lord as she struggled against her. The little commander. Fighting until the end.

"No, she's not," Matthew said. Stolus growled at him and Ascelina looked over. Matthew narrowed his eyes. "The honor of killing Tarrick falls to me."

Ascelina nodded at her son. Stolus grabbed keys from a dead hunter and had Matthew unlocked in moments.

Matthew rubbed his arms, still sore from the crash. "Why are you here?"

"I've come to get you as I said I would. The time is right. You are ready to leave them," Ascelina said.

"What…?" Silva gasped, "You're working with her?"

Matthew let his claws come forward. He went over to Silva and grabbed her neck while Ascelina kept her pinned tight. "Did you know what Tarrick was doing to me?"

She looked confused. "Training you?"

"Making me...care for him," Matthew said.

She shook her head.

Matthew believed her. Although, if she had known she wouldn't have told him. She was loyal to the incubi. "I had thought once that we could be friends. I'm sorry I betrayed you. I know now how much that hurts. My intentions were not...I'm sorry...I shouldn't have done it."

"It's a little hard for me to accept your apology when your claws are wrapped around my neck and this bitch is about to compel me to go kill my general."

Matthew smiled. She was facing a terrible fate and she was still tenacious. He removed his hand from her. He wanted to ask her what would happen to Lily when he was gone but there were too many vampires around who could overhear. He didn't want them to know about her.

"Let her go," Matthew said. "Cullip too. Release him from your compulsion."

"Why would you give Tarrick his friend back?" Ascelina asked.

"I'm not doing it for Tarrick. I respect Cullip for the warrior he is. The fate you've left for him is a terrible one. It's dishonorable. If you want him dead, face him and kill him. Otherwise, let him go. And Silva too."

Ascelina took a moment to consider his request.

Matthew put his hand on her shoulder. "Please."

She nodded.

Matthew put his claws away and ran his hand down Silva's face. "Teleport far from here. If I ever see you again, I'll kill you."

Ascelina removed her claws from Silva's teleport rune and the hunter disappeared in a shimmering green flash.

"More hunters approach. Incubi too," Stolus said.

Ascelina exited the van. Matthew followed her and looked around. The side street they were on was empty. The area was lit by a few dim street lamps, fires, and flares. Dead and dying hunters littered the ground. Bystanders who were in the area when the fighting started lay dead as well. Cars were overturned in the street and a building nearby had caught fire. There was a shimmer in the air above him. It looked like a veil, erected to hide what was going on to outsiders.

Matthew didn't see any dead vampires but there were plenty of live ones. Lords were flying in the air. They landed nearby and over twenty vampires collapsed in on them. He grew nervous being close to so many but Ascelina grabbed his shoulder to reassure him. The vampires around him seemed to be just as nervous about Matthew.

Five humans, two males, and three females—*witches*—with wild hair and loose-fitting clothes, took up points around the vampires. They spoke a few words in a language Matthew didn't understand and a warm green flash teleported the group away.

They reappeared in a forest.

The vampires spread out defensively.

The witches weren't quite what he expected. He assumed they would all be women and he had envisioned they would be a little more modern. Instead, they looked as if they lived in the wild with their simple spun clothes and unkempt hair. They each smelled like a different type of tree. He found them attractive and yet felt uneasy around them.

One of the witches came to stand directly in front of Matthew. He resisted the urge to take a few steps away from her.

"Can it be done?" Ascelina asked her.

The witch studied Matthew's collar. He felt magic spark when she touched it.

"We can take the bracers off and remove the tracking spell but the collar will stay. It can only be removed by one of the four names inscribed on here. If I have more time to study it, maybe I can find the loophole."

"Remove what you can. Hurry, they'll be tracking him already."

The witches didn't hesitate. Two worked on his right bracer, two on his left, while the one was on the collar. They began to chant words Matthew didn't understand.

It didn't take them long. The bracers popped off his arms and fell to the forest floor and he felt the collar become lighter around his neck as some of the magic drained away from it.

The vampires fell in again. Matthew wondered if Ascelina was giving orders telepathically.

"I am," she answered his unspoken question and green light once again flashed around the group.

This time they were on a sandy private beach. Above them, on the cliffside, was an impressive modern mansion. The vampires and witches cleared the area, leaving Ascelina and Stolus with Matthew.

"We're in California," Ascelina said, answering a question that had yet to pass his lips.

"Matthew!" a young-sounding voice called to him.

He turned just as Emilia slammed into him. Her arms wrapped around his body. Matthew hugged her back. She looked healthy now, fed and beautiful in a simple blue dress and her hair pinned up.

"I told you we'd help you," she said.

"So you did," Matthew said softly to her.

She didn't let him go as she looked up at him. "Your eyes...the silver suits you...they're gorgeous. And you smell divine now."

He smiled. "Thank you."

"But you aren't staying long are you?" she asked, her big eyes looking up at him. The way she could read him was frightening.

"I..." He looked over at Ascelina. "Thank you for saving me."

Ascelina nodded, then answered another question before he had a chance to voice it. "I do not know who your sire is. I've been asking around without any success."

She really needed to stop doing that. Having his mind read was getting a little eerie.

"Victor Moreau seemed to know who it was," he said.

Stolus, who was standing by Ascelina, scoffed. "Did you kill him because he wouldn't tell you?"

"No." Matthew didn't offer any more details. He didn't owe Stolus an explanation.

"Victor knew many things he did not share with the rest of us." Ascelina breathed in deep and sighed. It looked fake as if she was mimicking something she had forgotten to do a long time ago. "That is how vampires always have been, divided, keeping secrets from each other. It has cost us. Some of us are working to change that. We have a general now and the war is starting to turn for us for the first time in centuries."

"I don't want to fight in your war."

"I know, you are not ready yet and no one here will force you. Stay with us a little while. Allow me to fill in some gaps of your training, and I can go over which territories you'll want to avoid—both incubi and vampire. Many fear you because of your actions in New Orleans."

Matthew glanced at Stolus.

"I don't fear you," Stolus said with a sneer, "I just don't like you."

At least he was honest about it. Matthew didn't feel the same way towards him. He had seen how Stolus sacrificed for his sister during their time locked up. He respected it.

"I will stay a little while—"

Excited, Emilia bounced up and down in his arms. He was certain she was older than him but she reminded him of Lily. She was so happy now that she was away from that damned prison and Tarrick.

"—but I want to try and find out who my sire is. Maybe my actual parents as well. I need answers I think only they can give me."

"You will always be welcome in my home." Ascelina turned and started to walk a long winding path up to the mansion. "Come, children. Matthew needs a little time to himself."

It wasn't long before Matthew was standing alone on the beach. He sat down, removed his shoes and socks, and pushed his feet into the sand. He rubbed his wrists. They felt so light without the bracers.

He ran his fingers along the cool metal of his collar and hoped the witches could find a way to remove it for good, but for now he was satisfied they couldn't use it to track him. Looking out over the water, he watched the waves crashing before him, the moonlight cast a beautiful shimmering glow. Tears of joy escaped his eyes and fell on his chest.

For the first time in what seemed like forever, he was free.

Matthew returns in Sire: Beautiful Monsters Vol. II

Meet the hunters of Ashwood Red in 2017

About the Author

Jex enjoys writing about hidden worlds full of vampire hunters, epic battles, steamy sex, and, of course, beautiful monsters. Find updates for new releases at:
www.JexLane.com